Praise for the Lo̶...

MW00852765

"Douglas brings a light t̶...
two opposites, a grumpy o̶...
companion. Together they̶...

The Daily Mail

"Certain to find a place in the hearts of cosy crime readers everywhere, with its breezy prose, its witty observations and the often hilarious interplay between its two thespian leads – not to mention the cracking mystery at its heart. Stuart Douglas has just delivered the best cosy crime novel since *The Appeal*."

George Mann, author of the Newbury & Hobbes series

"It was a joy to be in the company of these *Dad's Army* detectives. I read the whole book in one sitting. Hugely enjoyable and lots of fun."

Nev Fountain, author of *The Fan Who Knew Too Much*

"Glorious and ingenious! What a lovely start to what I hope will be a long-running series!"

Paul Magrs, author of *Exchange*

"A real tootsy-pop of a mystery thriller, with an irresistible conceit and enough twists and turns to bamboozle the most conscientious of armchair sleuths."

Steve Cole, author of the Young Bond series

"Holmes and Watson by way of Arthur Lowe and John Le Mesurier; a wonderfully mismatched duo who you can't help falling in love with."

Amy Walker, Trans-Scribe

"Lowe and Le Breton are already shaping up to be the next great detective duo. If they don't get their own TV series, it will be a crime."

Kara Dennison

"Edward Lowe and John Le Breton are two of the most unique and disparate crime solvers you could find. Actors as unalike in their dispositions as their methods."

Elizabeth Lefebvre, Strange & Random Happenstance

Also by Stuart Douglas
and available from Titan Books

The Further Adventures of Sherlock Holmes: The Albino's Treasure
The Further Adventures of Sherlock Holmes: The Counterfeit Detective
The Further Adventures of Sherlock Holmes: The Improbable Prisoner
Sherlock Holmes: The Sign of Seven
The Further Adventures of Sherlock Holmes: The Crusader's Curse

Death at the Dress Rehearsal

DEATH AT THE PLAYHOUSES

The second Lowe and Le Breton mystery

STUART DOUGLAS

TITAN BOOKS

Death at the Playhouses: The second Lowe and Le Breton mystery
Print edition ISBN: 9781803368221
E-book edition ISBN: 9781803368238

Published by Titan Books
A division of Titan Publishing Group Ltd
144 Southwark Street, London SE1 0UP
www.titanbooks.com

First edition: March 2025
10 9 8 7 6 5 4 3 2 1

This is a work of fiction. All of the characters, organizations, and events
portrayed in this novel are either products of the author's imagination or
are used fictitiously. Any resemblance to actual persons, living or dead
(except for satirical purposes), is entirely coincidental.

© Stuart Douglas 2025. All Rights Reserved.

Stuart Douglas asserts the moral right to be identified as the author of
this work.

No part of this publication may be reproduced, stored in a retrieval
system, or transmitted, in any form or by any means without the prior
written permission of the publisher, nor be otherwise circulated in any
form of binding or cover other than that in which it is published and
without a similar condition being imposed on the subsequent purchaser.

A CIP catalogue record for this title is available from the British Library.

Printed and bound by CPI Group (UK) Ltd, Croydon, CR0 4YY.

For Julie, always.

PROLOGUE

London, March, 1928

It was all he could do not to scream his rage into the policeman's face. In his mind's eye, he grabbed the fool by the throat and shook him like a puppy that had disgraced itself on the sitting-room floor.

Disgraced.

The word lodged in his head as though it had a physical presence, an actual depth and width and weight, as though it were actually floating behind his eyes, crammed in the space between them and his brain. He blinked to rid himself of it, but while his eyes were closed all he could see was the word, imprinted on the back of his eyelids like a photographic negative. His ribs ached where boots had smashed into them, and he could feel a bruise flowering on his cheek and a tooth loose in his mouth, but that word – that was the only thing that mattered.

"Do you understand what I've told you?" the policeman was asking. "Do you know why you were arrested?"

He ignored the questions. Never tell them anything, that

was the trick. Wait until your lawyer arrives, then let him do all the talking. Give them nothing they can use against you later in a court of law.

A court of law.

Another blink, then another, and he was able to see something other than those terrible, terrible words. He couldn't have that. Of course he couldn't. Not a court, with judges and a jury – and journalists. And outside, photographers and men chasing the taxi, slapping their thick calloused hands on the windows, and women screaming your name like it was a curse.

Of course he couldn't have that.

So not a lawyer, then. A lawyer meant a defence, and a defence logically required an accuser. He would not – could not *– be accused of this thing.*

Not in court. Not where people could see.

In need of an alternative, he looked around the room in which he was sitting.

A wooden table, with a wooden chair on either side. He in one and, in the other, facing him, the uniformed nobody who had wrecked his evening and potentially – only potentially, he reminded himself, fighting off panic – ruined his life.

On the table, his hands, scraped and bloody where he'd held them up to ward off the blows. In front of the policeman, an open notebook. In the policeman's hand, a pencil, poised to write. He longed to reach across and snap that pencil in two.

Definitely not a lawyer, *he thought again. A lawyer meant paperwork. A lawyer meant a record of what had happened.*

There was somebody, though. A friend. Somebody who had told him that he made problems go away. "Nothing's too much trouble for a pal," he'd said. "There's nothing I can't fix for a pal."

Finally, he looked the policeman in the eye. "If it's not too much trouble, could you get a message to someone for me?" he asked.

PART ONE

1

London, October, 1971

So far as Edward Lowe was concerned, a day spent not working was a step closer to the poorhouse. Bills, he was fond of saying, needed paying, whether he was sitting idle or not.

He said as much to his agent as he spooned a third sugar into his tea and reached across the table for a Mr Kipling's French Fancy. "I was up for the voiceover for these, if you remember, Alec." He bit down on the pink fondant icing and chewed moodily. "Didn't get it, of course."

Alec Gent-Browning smiled and shook his head. "I'm sure you'd have been marvellous, Edward," he said, "but you've gone on to bigger and better things, haven't you? The days of worrying about paying the bills are behind you now."

"Are they, though? It certainly doesn't feel that way." Edward was not in the mood to be placated. The second series of *Floggit and Leggit* had finished filming almost a month ago and he'd thought he'd be on to something else by now. But the phone had singularly failed to ring and when he'd dropped in on his agent to mention that fact, he'd immediately suggested they go out for lunch. That was worrying in itself. Agents only offered to pay for lunch when they had either spectacularly good or crushingly bad news to impart.

And Edward wasn't the type to expect spectacularly good news.

All the way through an over-spiced mulligatawny soup and a barely adequate sole and boiled potatoes, he'd been waiting for the hammer to fall, but now, as they moved on to the coffee and petit fours, he wondered if he might have misjudged the situation after all.

"Of course they are," Alec insisted. "You're the star of the most popular comedy on television! How many people recognised you just walking from the car to the restaurant?"

Which was another problem, of course. The great unwashed suddenly seemed to think they were his close personal friends. He couldn't pop to the shops for twenty Craven A and a copy of *The Times* without some scruffy creature in a football shirt and denims pushing their unshaven face into his and saying, "Alright, Eddie! How's about an autograph?" He shuddered at the memory. *Eddie!*

But there was no point in complaining to Alec about that kind of thing. So far as he was concerned, fame was every actor's primary goal, with riches a very close second, and the satisfaction of a solid career of good work a far distant third, if it were mentioned at all.

"Yes, I suppose so," he muttered, and lit a cigarette.

"Denys Fisher are negotiating for a board game, I hear," Alec went on, oblivious to Edward's mood. "And..." He lifted his briefcase out from under the table and flicked back the catches with a flourish. "...there's something here which will put a smile on your face, or I'm a monkey's uncle."

He pulled out a sheet of paper and pushed it across the table. "*Floggit and Leggit* has been nominated for Best TV Programme at the Film and Television Arts Awards, and you and John are both nominated for Best Actor."

Edward grunted and glanced down at the letter. He supposed it was gratifying to be recognised by one's peers, even if it was for this populist rubbish and not for something a little more highbrow. And he wasn't sure how both he and John could be up for Best Actor. Surely there could only be one leading man on the show? Still, if there had to be another actor from the show honoured, he was glad it was John.

In truth, he and Le Breton had become good friends since the real-life drama of the previous year's filming. Almost being murdered by the same lunatic harpy had a real bonding effect on people.

"Well, that is terribly kind of the Film and TV chaps, I must say. One doesn't go looking for awards, of course, but if other people feel they're deserved, well..." His voice trailed off with what he hoped was an appropriate degree of modesty, but then he remembered his earlier complaint. "Though a few offers of paying work would be better still," he concluded, waving for a waitress to top up his coffee.

"Perhaps I can help you there too, Edward," Alec positively beamed. "Mary, my secretary, took a phone call from young Jimmy Rae yesterday. I forgot all about it when the SAFTA letter arrived this morning, but it seems he knows I'm your agent and he was trying to get in touch with you about a bit of work. Theatre, he said. A month in Bolton over Christmas, and the possibility of a tour of Europe in the spring."

Edward frowned. "Not *pantomime*, I hope. I know lots of actors do it at this time of year, but I draw the line at false bosoms."

"No, it's the legitimate stuff, according to Mary. Shakespeare and whatnot." He handed Edward a scrap of paper. "She took his number and said you'd give him a call back to discuss it."

"In which case, perhaps I will. It might be nice to go back on the boards for a bit. A pleasant change from this TV tomfoolery. Jimmy didn't say what the specific role was?"

"Doesn't look like it. But if it's a month, that's perfect timing for the SAFTA thing. The award ceremony is in February, so it's likely to fall between your two runs, assuming that Mary picked Jimmy up right about the European tour."

Edward leaned back to let the girl pour his coffee, then nabbed the final French Fancy. He bit into its yellow icing with a good deal more enthusiasm than he'd shown to the previous one. It had been years since he'd been abroad, and Christmas on the continent had a nice ring to it. Much more the sort of career he should be having, he thought to himself.

He did hope that Jimmy wasn't acting the goat, though. In the eighteen months or so they'd been working together on *Floggit and Leggit* the young actor had shown himself to be talented on screen but prone to practical jokes and tomfoolery off.

Alec was chuntering on about some other client of his, but Edward had stopped listening. A sudden chill had descended on him, a sensation which reminded him strongly of a time when he'd rashly claimed to be able to ride a bicycle to get a part on a TV show. As soon as the words had come out of his mouth at the audition he'd regretted them; he could no more ride a bicycle than he could fly a plane, and that fact was bound to come out sooner or later.

Now he felt the same sick feeling in his stomach when he considered the casual way he'd said it'd be good to get back on the boards. True, unlike bicycling, he'd genuinely spent many years in rep, and had no fears of returning to live theatre per se. But Shakespeare? Had he spent too long in television, where he was able to have another go if anything went wrong, to tackle the world's greatest playwright in front of a live audience? Was he kidding himself? Would this – as when he'd mounted the bike and immediately fallen over in an ungainly heap – end up as a humiliating disaster? Might it not be better to admit that possibility right now, back out while he still could, and stick with what he knew?

He looked down at the slip of paper Alec had given him and pushed it around the table in front of him with one finger. Then, decision made, he picked it up and slipped into his jacket. If he refused this opportunity, he might as well admit he was nothing but a TV hack now and be done with it.

He'd telephone Jimmy as soon as he got home then make arrangements for digs in Bolton.

2

Bolton, Lancashire, November, 1971

Edward was sure that the distance from their digs to the Bolton Playhouse was too far to walk, even if he wanted to – which he didn't – and he was damned if he was paying for a taxi every morning and evening. Which made it all the more galling that theatres – unlike television companies – were unwilling to supply motor cars for the use of their cast.

He poured himself a fresh cup of tea and wondered, not for the first time, whether this entire expedition hadn't been a grave mistake.

The telephone call with Jimmy had been something of a mixed bag, for a start. On the one hand, Alec Gent-Browning had been right; Jimmy had as good as offered him a job in the play he was rehearsing at the Playhouse. On the other, it appeared the director only wanted Edward as part of a duo with John.

"The director's alright for an old geezer," Jimmy had said on the phone. "But he don't really give a monkey's about the art. It's all about the moolah with him, know what I mean?"

Truth be told, Edward wasn't sure that he did. "He's more interested in the box office takings than the performance?" he hazarded, and was pleased to have it confirmed this was indeed the case.

"Exactly! And that's why he wants you *and* John. Add in me, and he can claim he's got half the cast of *Floggit* doing Shakespeare. It'll drag in the punters, he says."

"Is that a prerequisite?" Edward had asked coldly, and, to his surprise, Jimmy hadn't asked what the word meant.

"I reckon it is, Eddie," he'd said. *Eddie again*, Edward grimaced inwardly. "But don't get me wrong; Fagan's no mug. You know how rep usually works – a right royal mix-up of fresh-faced drama-school virgins and drunken old hacks putting on one show at night while they rehearse another during the day, and a new play on every week. It's a good way to learn your craft, I suppose, but it's a bloody killer if you're not used to it. I wouldn't have put your name forward if there wasn't a bit more to this than that.

"Nah, this is much more of a quality undertaking, it really is. Shakespeare only, for one thing. Proper rehearsal time, then a couple of weeks of *King Lear* and the same again of *Hamlet*. The rest of the cast are regulars, some of them have been with the Playhouse for years, but they're all pretty decent. Fagan knows what sells, though, and he thinks for this that's you and John and me on all the posters!" Jimmy coughed. "He actually wanted Joe Riley and Don Roberts and the rest, but they're either already booked up or putting their feet up between series."

"That's probably wise. Neither of them are in what I'd

call the first flush of youth. I must admit I feared for Donald's life when he was hanging off that clock face last year."

Jimmy's laugh from the other end of the line had been long and loud. "Yeah, maybe it's for the best they miss this one," he said. "A month in the provinces might carry them off."

"And there's a European run afterwards, I think my agent mentioned?"

"So they're saying! Amsterdam for a fortnight in the New Year, or maybe it's February. Or March. Anyway, after Christmas."

It had been as bad as speaking to John, Edward thought, remembering Jimmy's vagueness with dates – just as the man himself appeared in the door of the dining room and waved across to him.

* * *

They had arrived at Mrs Galloway's Home for Working Thespians (as it was advertised in *The Stage* magazine), the previous day on a bright, if cold, winter afternoon. After dropping their luggage in their respective rooms, they had decided to take a quick stroll around the neighbourhood before the chilly northern sun set.

It had been more than enough to cement Edward's opinion that walking in the area was akin to strolling through London at the height of the Blitz.

As he settled himself into a seat in Mrs Galloway's dining room the following morning, he elaborated on this point to John.

"Did you see the crowd of ruffians standing about outside that pub last night? And the way that dog bared its teeth at me. Not the dog's fault, of course – a poor master will always lead to a poor dog – but I'd a good mind to take a stick to the brute who was supposed to be holding it. He looked more of a slathering beast than his animal." He shook his head in remembered indignation, and spooned marmalade onto his toast. "We really should have asked the theatre to send a car to pick us up on our first day." He sliced a sausage in half and dipped it into the pool of ketchup at the side of his plate. "I mean, God knows how much a taxi would cost, but it won't be cheap, that's for sure." He chewed disconsolately and stared through the net curtains at the grey skies and steady, apparently unceasing, rainfall outside. "And even if we wanted to walk – which I don't – it's hardly the weather for it."

"No," John agreed, pushing his own half-finished breakfast to one side and lighting a cigarette. "It is pretty grim out there, isn't it?"

"Sorry to intrude," a loud voice cut in from somewhere behind Edward.

He turned and observed a fat man in an ill-fitting jacket at the next table.

"Brian Harvey at your service," said the man. "I travel in brushes. Staying here for the night before I move on to Preston. But I couldn't help overhearing. Am I right in thinking you gents will be making your way to the Playhouse after you've finished Mrs Galloway's fine breakfast?"

Edward nodded carefully, wondering if the man had

recognised them, and whether he would shortly be addressed as Eddie.

It seemed not.

"Because, if you are," the man went on, "there's a bus stop at the end of the street, and the bus from there goes all the way to the Playhouse, or near enough. You could get that and save yourself a fair bit of brass."

A bus? The thought hadn't occurred to Edward – who knew when he'd last been on a bus? – but, actually, why not? He looked across at John, whose face had creased in thought. Probably too working class for him, Edward thought with mean-spirited glee. A bus had been good enough to take his father to the factory every day, and it might be nice to follow in his footsteps. What was acting but a job of work after all?

He made a questioning sort of sound in John's direction, and tilted his head to one side, inviting a response.

"Oh sorry, did you want the rest of this, Edward?" John asked, poking his plate across the table towards Edward. "Do help yourself, my dear chap. I've had enough, but you're quite right – it does seem a shame to let good food go to waste."

"I was simply wondering how you felt about getting the bus to the theatre," Edward responded stiffly.

"Why not?" John laughed. "It's been about twenty years since I was on a real bus, as opposed to one driven by Cliff Richard. It'll be a lark!"

"You'll need to get your skates on, mind," the red-faced diner warned. "They only come once an hour and the next one's due in twenty minutes."

John dabbed his mouth with his napkin and rose to his feet, grinding out his cigarette in the ashtray as he did so. Edward made to follow his example, then, glancing at John's abandoned plate, paused halfway out his chair and sat back down. John was right about good food. If there was one thing that the War – and the terrible news from Biafra – had taught everyone, it was not to waste food. He speared the pair of sausages on John's plate and transferred them to his own.

Twenty minutes was plenty of time to polish these off, and still make the bus on time.

* * *

The bus was only half-full, but everyone on the downstairs deck appeared to be a middle-aged woman with a face like a heap of folded old dishcloths and a shopping bag on her knee. The noise of gossiping Lancashire voices was overpowering. Without a word, Edward followed John upstairs.

The bus pulled away from the stop as he was halfway up the stairs, causing him to fall backwards with a sudden jerk. Only a frantic grab for the railing prevented him from tumbling all the way back to the lower deck, and, even so, he banged the base of his spine painfully against the metal wall of the stairwell.

John, who had already stridden to the top of the stairs, looked back down and offered his hand, but Edward shrugged it off and pushed past him, then headed for the smoking area to the rear. Only when he had a Craven A lit did he speak to his friend.

"He did that on purpose, you know," he moaned, rubbing the small of his back. "They must know they've not left enough time for people to get all the way to the top of the stairs, but they shoot off like Evel Knievel, nonetheless. I've a good mind to write to the company."

John stretched his long legs out under the seat in front and said nothing. Edward couldn't see his face as he turned away to look out the window, but he was sure he heard the sound of suppressed laughter.

"And don't think I can't see you laughing," he snapped.

He was tempted to take further offence, but one of them had to be the bigger man, and given Le Breton's childish sense of humour, it would need to be him. Even if he was, quite literally, the injured party.

"This should be an interesting morning," he said in a conciliatory tone. "I'm very keen to discover what role I'll be playing, for a start." He coughed. "Obviously, one doesn't like to be presumptuous, but, at the same time... well, they've not invited us all the way up to Bolton to play second spear-shaker from the left, have they?"

Secretly, he harboured the hope that Mickey Fagan would have the nerve to cast against type and offer him the part of Lear himself. But, realistically, he'd been in the acting game long enough to know the public was about as likely to accept a five-foot-five, bald King Lear as it was to accept a female one. Still, there was no reason one of the other meatier parts in the play – Gloucester, say, or Kent – couldn't be on the less lanky side. So long as it wasn't the bloody Fool.

John was still saying nothing; in fact, he'd yet to turn away from the window. It couldn't be the view he was admiring – all that could be made out through the incessant rain were rows of identical boxy houses with, now and then, a brief flash of colour as a sad local park, with a single swing perched on top of a grass-free expanse of dirt, shot past. And he surely couldn't be sulking. In fact, now he considered it, they'd barely exchanged a word since they'd left Mrs Galloway's house.

"John?" he said, prodding him in the side. "I was just saying, it'll be interesting to find out what parts they have in mind for us."

"Actually, I already know," John said, finally turning away from the window. "I'm playing the King." His voice was flat and emotionless as he made this unexpected revelation, and Edward was surprised to see that, rather than the simpering half-smile which was as near as John ever came to a triumphant smirk, his face was creased with worry.

So worried did he look, in fact, that Edward even forgot to ask how John knew about the casting, nor did he immediately remember to be annoyed that he'd predictably been overlooked for the part of Lear.

"What on Earth's wrong?" he asked.

In reply, John pulled a sheet of folded, off-white paper from his jacket pocket and handed it over. It was a telegram, apparently from John's agent – Edward recognised the name of a well-known agency in London – which contained only two sentences.

KING LEAR CONFIRMED. STOP. DID YOU
KNOW YOU ARE REPLACING NATE THOMPSON
IN ROLE? STOP.

There was nothing else, and Edward handed it back
with a shrug.

"Nate Thompson, Edward," John said, tapping the name
on the telegram. When Edward continued to look blank, he
went on, "Sir Nathaniel Thompson. That's who we – *I* – am
replacing in this damned show."

Well, that was slightly clearer. Edward knew Sir
Nathaniel Thompson, of course. Or knew *of* him, at least.
A few years older than he and John, Thompson was an
actor of a different stripe altogether, Edward was not
ashamed to admit. A giant of a man, both physically and
professionally, Thompson was a contemporary of John
Gielgud and Ralph Richardson, and cut from the same
cloth. Decorated for outstanding but still secret heroics in
the War, he'd played all the great Shakespearean roles by
the time he was thirty, had been knighted by forty, and had
three marriages and a string of very public affairs behind
him by the time he marked his half-century. If John was
stepping into shoes vacated by the great Sir Nathaniel, no
wonder he looked so glum.

Still, it was hardly a cause for wailing and lamentation.
"In some ways, that's quite a compliment, really, when
you think about it," he offered, in what he felt was a
commendably good-natured and encouraging tone.
"Obviously, Fagan thinks you capable of filling the gap left

by Sir Nathaniel. Unless it's just because you're tall enough to fit the costumes, of course," he added, with a smile (he was only human, after all).

John was plainly unconvinced. He grimaced and shoved the telegram back into his jacket pocket. "I'm afraid you're missing the point, Edward," he said mournfully. "Not your fault, though. The thing is, that telegram was waiting for me after breakfast and, while you were upstairs changing your shoes, I telephoned London for more information." He sighed, but not in his usual way, as though he wished to communicate he was too fatigued to cut the top off his own egg. Instead, it was a sound which seemed to come from the depths of his soul, a long, heavy breath of anxiety and concern which crumpled his face like a discarded paper bag. "Thompson was sacked, you see. Kicked out of the company for continual drunkenness and for missing multiple rehearsals."

"And? I have to say, knight of the realm or not, his feet wouldn't have touched the ground if I'd been running things either."

"Yes, but this is the third time he's been sacked for the same reason and, every other time, he's gone on a spree for a day or two, then come back to the theatre, suitably chastened, and been given his job back."

"Ah, and you're concerned he'll turn up in a day or two and expect the same treatment? Well, I wouldn't worry. We've signed contracts, everything is done and dusted, and, even if he does come to Fagan, cap in hand, he'll have no choice but to send him packing."

"I'm sure you're right, Edward," John said, no happier than before. "But there's bound to be a scene. And I do so hate scenes."

That was hardly news to Edward. Over the previous eighteen months he'd watched his friend avoid confrontation with an almost religious zeal. He had accepted every script change and directorial idiocy without complaint, and gone out of his way to ensure that any potential source of conflict was nipped in the bud before it had a chance to flower. In fact, Edward had remarked to Bobby McMahon, the main writer on *Floggit*, that if Madge Kenyon, the mad killer they'd caught the previous year, hadn't banged him on the head with her gun, John would probably have let her shoot him, just to avoid any unpleasant social awkwardness.

"And there's more to it than that. It could all turn extremely difficult." John twisted in his seat, a look on his face which Edward would have described as anguished if he'd thought the other man capable of so violent an emotion. "We were friends once upon a time, you see. Well, not friends really, more acquaintances who frequented the same pubs and knew the same people."

Which sounded very like a definition of friendship to Edward, but he realised it wouldn't do to say so, and so he remained silent as John rabbited on.

"It was a long time ago. Before the War, almost. We lost touch after that." He frowned. "But even so, it's going to be terribly difficult if he turns up tomorrow, looking for his job back, and he finds me already with my feet under the table."

"You think he might cut up rough? Come at you with his fists flying?" Edward was enjoying John's very obvious discomfiture, he couldn't deny it. It was so out of character.

"Well, no, not that sort of thing." John paused in thought, then grimaced. "Though he did have quite a temper back then, now I come to think on it. And he is built on fairly industrial lines. He's got a good four inches on me, and a couple of stones too, I shouldn't wonder."

Now he fell silent, concentration writ large on his long face. Edward considered whether to enquire further, but John turned away, clearly wishing to be left alone with his thoughts.

Edward lit another cigarette, and left him to it, passing the time by counting the stops to the Playhouse, and hoping they didn't miss it through the filthy bus windows.

3

Seen from the street on which Edward and John stood, the Bolton Playhouse had an air of defiant but elderly grandeur. Rising three storeys high from the square which it dominated, the chipped paint of its frontage was creamy grey in colour, with three separate entrances spaced along the length of the stuccoed facade. A central stone balcony served as a heavy line beneath several tall windows, which allowed plenty of light to fall into the theatre. Solid, if crumbling, Victorian brickwork was decorated with classically inspired columns, cornices and little half-circle windows, which John had a feeling were called architraves (unless that was what they called bishops in the ancient church; he'd been less than attentive in Religious Studies at school, he had to admit). It faced onto a cobbled square, currently empty save for a heavyset man in a donkey jacket who moved away as soon as he realised John was looking at him.

He thought the theatre looked marvellous, for all that each individual element of the building appeared in need of repair of one sort or other.

"The place is falling to bits," Edward complained at his elbow, glaring at the theatre as though it personally offended him. "This is one of the oldest rep theatres in the country, you know," he went on, the affront plain on his face. "Yet the local council have allowed it to fall into this sorry state." He shook his head. "Sometimes I despair, I really do."

"I rather like it," John replied equitably. "It looks lived in. And apparently, there's quite a decent restaurant inside."

"Is there really?" Edward brightened a little and wandered across to peer at the glass-covered noticeboard at the side of the main entrance. "No sign of a menu that I can see, but that's probably all to the good. Keeps the riff-raff out, for one thing." He frowned suddenly and leaned closer to a stone structure at one side, next to a revolving door marked *Box Office*. An empty noticeboard was bolted to its side. "That's odd, wouldn't you say? You can see where there was a poster here..." he tapped the glass, indicating a drawing pin which still held a scrap of paper to the cork board behind it, "...but it's been taken down."

Still frowning, he scurried round John and stepped back into the square, the better to examine the front of the main building.

"And look there, at the marquee," he said, indicating the gigantic poster which was emblazoned across the front of the building, just above the central balcony. "It says *King Lear* clearly enough, but someone's painted over the cast list."

John looked up as requested. Sure enough, a rectangle of white paint covered the lower third of the poster, obscuring the area which would usually have contained the names of the more prominent, or at least most well-known, of the cast. He thought he could make out the top half of the word "Starring" above the level of the paint, but nothing more.

"Obviously the sign they had would have had Nate Thompson's name on it, Edward. They could hardly keep advertising him if he's not going to be in it."

The thought plunged him back into the depression which the sight of the Playhouse had momentarily lifted. What would he say to the man if he turned up at the theatre? He'd been rehearsing opening lines, picturing whole conversations, since he'd spoken to his agent, but still he had no idea how to handle matters if it became necessary.

Edward, however, was still focusing on the defaced marquee.

"Jimmy definitely said that this man Fagan intended to boost sales on the grounds of our involvement. How can he hope to do that if he's not even advertising our presence? He's had plenty of time to put up a new banner." He eyed the building with distaste. "I knew I would come to regret doing this. Corners being cut, evidently."

He hefted his umbrella and pointed towards the central doors of the main building. "Shall we head inside and find someone to speak to?"

John could see no reason not to, and – shrugging off his sense of impending doom – he trotted up the steps and through the door into the theatre. Edward's complaints notwithstanding, it wasn't in his own nature to brood for long. Besides, there was nothing quite like the first day on a new job in a new town.

* * *

The air of faded opulence John had noted from the street continued inside the theatre. Great swatches of purple and white paint covered the walls from floor to high ceiling, but the briefest moment of closer inspection picked out cracks which zigzagged across the plasterwork like forks of lightning. The thick carpet looked from a distance as though it had been expensive once but, like the paint, it had seen better – far earlier – days. Even the gold paint of the banisters which ran down the side of the auditorium was chipped. There was an air of… *tiredness* was the best word he could come up with… all around. Nothing was fresh, and the very air smacked of old triumphs long forgotten.

"It's like something from a second-rate Roman orgy," Edward grumbled at his side, clearly determined not to be jolted from his irritation. "Delusions of grandeur, I call it."

John smiled as the image popped into his head of the portly Edward swaddled in a Roman toga, his little bald head topped with a laurel wreath, directing the participants at an orgy on how to conduct themselves correctly, and lecturing the younger people there on how much better orgies had been when he was a boy. Perhaps he should suggest they do something like that as a dream sequence on *Floggit*. The thought amused him no end until he realised Edward was staring at him and tapping his foot in irritation.

"You would think someone would be here to greet us," he said.

Now he came to think about it, it was surprising there was nobody in the foyer to meet them. Actually, there was nobody around at all. The box office was obviously closed, but they were to meet the rest of the cast on the stage, and he'd rather expected someone to be at the entrance to look after them and show them the way.

Edward cast him one of his long-suffering looks and muttered that he would see if he could find anyone. "Just stay here, and I'll rustle up an ASM or something. But I must say, it's not the most promising start."

He pushed his way through a set of double doors and disappeared into the theatre. John watched him go and returned to imagining him as Nero, playing a fiddle while the Groat Street Market burned.

He really would need to have a word with Bobby about that when they got back to *Floggit*. He'd always rather fancied playing Caesar and, if Donald Roberts wasn't born to play the bumbling Claudius, then nobody was. He was still matching up Roman Emperors to *Floggit* cast members (Jimmy Rae as Caligula, perhaps, or would the elderly Scottish Joe Riley be funnier?) when Edward reappeared through the double doors and beckoned towards him.

"Fagan and the rest of the company are waiting for us on the stage, apparently," he said. "According to the stagehand I spoke to, everyone was here half an hour ago." He tutted and glared around the foyer as though looking for someone to blame for the mix-up. "I did explain that we'd not been told about that, but he didn't seem bothered." He dropped his voice and leaned towards John, holding the door open with his foot. "I popped my head around the door but, so far as I could see, everyone was reading their newspaper and drinking cups of tea, so I don't think we've missed anything important."

He turned on his heel and pushed the door fully open. "It's just through here," he said over his shoulder, letting the door swing shut behind him in his haste to be no later than they already were.

John, still mentally picturing Edward in a toga, followed at a more sedate pace. Plenty of time for being punctual tomorrow – first impressions counted, and he wouldn't want people to get the wrong idea. The last thing he wanted in a new place was for people to think of him as an industrious sort. That wouldn't do at all.

4

In person, Mickey Fagan was nothing like Jimmy Rae had described him. Jimmy had called him a wide boy when describing his plans for the show, and his desire to bring as many *Floggit* cast members together as he could had undoubtedly lent weight to that description, but, in the flesh, he was far from the skinny, flashy tearaway that Edward had expected.

Instead, he was a portly, red-faced man of middle years, with heavy bags under his eyes. What hair he had was parted an inch above his left ear, and combed across in an unconvincing and ill-advised attempt to cover a wide expanse of otherwise bald scalp. Still, he smiled with what appeared to be genuine pleasure when Edward and John entered the auditorium from the lobby.

Fagan was standing on the stage, at the centre of a small group of people. As he made his way down through the stalls, Edward recognised Jimmy, who waved and shouted a greeting, but most of the other faces which turned in his direction were strangers to him. He thought perhaps he recognised one older lady, but her name remained elusively out of reach.

"And here come two instantly recognisable fellows!" Fagan announced grandly as Edward followed John up the stairs to the stage. "Before I introduce our motley crew, I'm sure we'd all like to welcome Edward and John to the team." He started to clap in a slow, exaggerated manner and, a little reluctantly it seemed to Edward, the others followed suit. The effect was more pitiful than welcoming, he thought. He'd half a mind to say something.

But it wouldn't do to appear churlish; he knew how insular established rep companies could be. Besides, first impressions were important, and they would be working together for some time, after all. "Good morning, everyone," he said. "I think I can speak for John when I say how delighted we both are to be here, in this glorious old lady of the theatre."

He realised that, as he'd been speaking, he'd been looking across at the older actress he'd thought he'd recognised, still subconsciously trying to bring her name to mind. She grunted loudly as he finished and glared indignantly back at him. He did hope he hadn't been misheard. "The Bolton Playhouse, I mean, of course, not any of our more... eh... experienced colleagues," he added quickly. But, if anything, the clarification seemed to annoy the old woman even more.

"Since you appear to be directing your words to me, Mr Lowe," she said, her eyes narrowed and cold, "I may as well be the first to introduce myself. Alice Robertson. I play

Goneril, and most of the minor female roles." She smiled and held out a hand in John's direction. "Pleased to meet you, Mr Le Breton," she said, in what Edward felt was a very pointed manner.

"Oh, do call me John, please," John simpered. It was the only word for the way he billed and cooed over the outstretched hand. "And the pleasure is all mine. My mother and father took me to see your Ophelia at the Old Vic in 1915. I shall never forget how wonderful you were in the role. You never do forget your first time seeing a truly great *Hamlet*, do you?"

The old lady positively beamed at John. "How kind of you to say so. And how lovely of you to remember one of my former glories!" She gestured towards the stalls with a wave of her hand. "Though those days lie in my distant past, I fear."

"Not at all, my dear," John began, and would no doubt have gone on to further flights of flattery had Fagan not interrupted him.

"And having met our Goneril, let me introduce our Cordelia." From behind Alice Robertson, a figure which Edward had assumed was an under-sized boy stepped forward. "Judy Faith," Fagan went on, "meet Edward Lowe and John Le Breton."

Judy Faith was petite and blonde, with wide brown eyes and hair cut in what Edward would have called a short back and sides. She was wearing jeans with an enormously wide cuff and a T-shirt with a peace sign embroidered on it. Any wonder he'd thought her a boy. She giggled and wiggled her fingers in Edward and John's direction. "Pleased to make your acquaintance, guys," she said, and giggled again.

Edward wondered what he'd let himself in for. Alice Robertson was plainly too old to be playing Goneril, even if she was the eldest of Lear's three daughters, and this chit of a girl, while at least the right age for Cordelia, appeared to be an actual child.

"How do you do?" he said carefully, considering how best to enquire about her experience – and her age.

But John once again took it upon himself to be ostentatiously charming. "How delightful to meet you, Judy," he said, smiling and waving his cigarette in a languid half-circle. "I must say you're frightfully young to be playing such an important part. You must either be precociously talented, or the world's most youthful-looking twenty-five-year-old."

He chuckled, and the girl laughed. "I'm twenty-one, you cheeky bugger!" she said.

"Judy was a hostess on *Ready Steady Go!* when she was fifteen, and then she did some work for Mary Quant," Jimmy Rae interjected. "She was voted one of the faces of 1971."

Edward knew that *Ready Steady Go!* was a music show of some kind, but the name Mary Quant rang no immediate bells. Perhaps she was one of the new female TV producers? There were a lot more of them nowadays, and it was difficult to keep up with them all.

He nodded in Jimmy's direction as though he knew exactly who she was – it didn't do to look ignorant of the movers and shakers, as he'd heard the new wave of TV types described the other day – but any further discussion of Judy Faith and her career was cut off in any case, as Mickey Fagan called forward another figure from the crowd around him.

"And the last but definitely not least of Lear's children. Our Regan, Monica Gray."

He thought he'd recognised the name when he'd seen it in the cast list, but when Monica Gray walked towards him and shook his hand in what Edward thought was rather a masculine manner, he wasn't sure if they'd ever met after all. Tall for her sex, she towered a good three or four inches over him, so that he risked a crick in his neck as he peered up at her. Her features, even allowing for being seen at such an unflattering angle, were cold and hard, with small, flinty eyes set in a face which appeared to be made entirely of thin skin and sharp bone. Her mouth was equally small and currently pursed tight. She was wearing black flared slacks and a white shirt, open at the collar, which added to Edward's sense that this was not the most feminine of women. Judy Faith had seemed like a boy purely because of her hairstyle and clothes, but Monica Gray exuded an unfeminine strength. He could well imagine her running a servant through with a sword, as Regan did in the play.

When she spoke, though, he realised that not only did he know her, but he had also worked with her before. Where her physical appearance bordered on the manly, her voice was soft and delicate, and he was put in mind of something John had said when describing a woman he'd heard singing in one of his seedy jazz clubs. *A voice like honey poured over sugar*, he'd said, and it fitted Monica Gray perfectly. He knew it at once, and could even – unusually for him – recall exactly where from.

"1963," he said. "An episode of *The Avengers*. You were playing a Chinese assassin, and I was the politician you'd been hired to kill. You crushed me between two giant playing cards in the first act!" he complained, but with a smile, in case she thought he was being serious.

She returned the smile, and the action immediately softened her face. "I-Ching cards, actually," she said.

"You were very striking, even under all that awful yellow make-up," replied Edward gallantly. "I could hardly have forgotten you." He took a step back, in order to see her better, and was struck by just how much a smile changed her face. Where at first he'd thought her features hard and cold, now they seemed warm and friendly. Her eyes twinkled and her fine cheekbones framed her face perfectly.

"And I'm her husband," a harsh voice said from somewhere behind her, as a hand appeared on each of her shoulders and manoeuvred her to one side. The speaker emerged from behind her. He was a broad-shouldered man, taller than Monica, with an extravagant moustache which spread bushily from the usual place on his top lip all the way to his earlobes. *Overcompensating for something*, Edward thought maliciously. "Her agent, too. Michael Gray at your service, Mr Lowe," the other man said, pressing a rectangular business card into his hand.

Edward glanced down at it. *Michael Gray – Theatrical Agent* it said, in a font so florid as to be almost unreadable.

He tucked it into his jacket pocket and shook the man's hand. "Pleased to meet you," he said.

It appeared that the remainder of the crowd gathered on the stage were of minimal importance; at least, Mickey Fagan chose not to introduce them individually. "And you know Jimmy Rae, of course," he said. "He'll be playing Edmund."

Jimmy gave a mock salute and grinned broadly. "At your service as usual, Eddie."

"*Edward*," Edward muttered irritably, but he suspected nobody heard him.

Instead, while John did his usual *hail fellow, well met* act with the Grays, Mickey Fagan stepped back into the light and clapped his hands together. "But, of course, I'm forgetting one other terribly important member of the company. Peter Glancy, who you may remember from a certain well-known detective series in the early years of ITV, is at the dentist this morning, but he'll be back in time for rehearsals, never fear!"

Edward did vaguely remember him, or the series at least, though for the life of him he couldn't remember what it was called. A man's name, he thought, something like *Fabian of the Yard*, but not that. He had the faintest memory of a stocky man with broad shoulders and Brylcreemed hair, and a lot of scenes shot at night with the Thames in the background, but he doubted he could have picked its star out of a lineup, even if everyone else was a midget. *Such is the fleeting nature of fame*, he thought smugly, then felt bad for thinking it.

"I was in an episode of that, you know," John exclaimed, with delight. "I don't think I had any scenes with Peter, but dear Pat Troughton was in it, and we ended up drunk as lords in the Flamingo Club that night, watching Sarah Vaughan singing." He sighed, and said more quietly, apparently for Edward's ears only, "I was supposed to be taking Sally for dinner after filming that day, but Pat convinced me to go for a quick one before I met her, and one thing led to another… No wonder she eventually got fed up of me."

His voice tailed off into an unhappy silence. Edward had heard John speak about his ex-wife Sally several times, but only when they were particularly deep in their cups. Drunk or sober, though, the memory of their married life always left his friend melancholy. Before John could descend further into misery, Edward clapped his hands together in imitation of Fagan a minute earlier. "It's lovely to meet you all," he said loudly and, he hoped, convincingly. "And it sounds as though there are some old friends in the cast, which is always a bonus." He smiled. "John and I can't wait to start working with you all, so if someone could point me to the nearest kettle, I'll make us all a cup of tea and we can kick things off!" Forced jollity never came easily to him, and he felt sure everyone would spot his lack of sincerity, but, if they did, they said nothing; they just joined in and amplified his clap into a round of applause with what he chose to view as genuine enthusiasm.

There was no doubting Mickey Fagan's enthusiasm, at least.

"Well bloody said! Let's get to it!" he cried with a flourish of his hands. "First night is on Sunday coming, so we've only got a week to get Edward and John up to speed."

He looked at his watch. "Let's meet back up here in forty-five minutes and we can start blocking out some scenes."

The various actors and actresses moved off in small groups, one or two of them casting a glance in the direction of the newcomers. Fagan put an arm around Edward's shoulders and guided him towards the back of the stage, where John had already gravitated to speak to a young woman he didn't recognise. He did his best not to stiffen too obviously at Fagan's heavy touch – it did seem quite a liberty to be manhandling him on such a short acquaintance – and maintained his smile, which was starting to make his face ache, until Fagan introduced him to the young woman.

"We won't be starting rehearsals in earnest until ten thirty, but, in the meantime, I thought you might like to meet the most important person in the whole theatre," the red-faced man said with another flourish. "Edward Lowe, meet Alison Jago, my assistant stage manager, without whose constant efforts we'd have ground to a halt a long time ago!"

Up close, Alison Jago seemed more girl than woman. Like Judy, her blue jeans were widely flared out at the bottom and decorated with hand-stitched flowers and butterflies, while her T-shirt had the image of a banana printed on it. Edward doubted she could be more than nineteen or twenty, but she held out her hand confidently enough, and her grip was solid. Besides, he knew that ASM was a good entry point into the theatre for students and the like, so they tended to be on the younger side.

"How do you do?" she said, with a warm smile. She was actually quite striking-looking, Edward decided, with skin the colour of milky coffee, and black hair cut into a sort of pageboy style. Her large, round eyes were brown and blinked slowly as she spoke. She wore no make-up, he was pleased to note.

"Jago? Any relation to Robert Jago, the playwright?"

"My father."

"I've never worked with him, but I saw his *A Stitch in Crime* at the Lyceum, oh, ten years ago, it must have been." Edward turned around. "Do you know him, John?"

John shook his head. "I know *of* him, of course. He's at the BBC now, isn't he? But, no, I've never worked with him."

"Neither have I," Alison said, a little too quickly. "But John was just telling me that you and he first worked together not long after the War." She laughed, exposing small, very white teeth. "That's before I was even born!"

"Alison was kind enough to say that we didn't look old enough," John murmured, evidently pleased by the flattery. Though, had he even recognised it was flattery, Edward wondered?

"Well neither of you do," the girl replied with every sign of sincerity. "Just remember that if you need to know anything about this place – anything at all – come and see me. If I can help, I will."

John gave her a grin. "I believe Edward suggested the first thing we needed was a cup of tea. Perhaps you could lead us to the nearest kitchen and tell us a little more about yourself, and about the Playhouse."

With what was almost a bow, he gestured off stage and then, as Alison Jago started down the stairs, followed in her wake. Edward, with a shrug, told Fagan they would be back shortly, and trotted after the pair of them.

5

John hadn't thought about Sally for months, but all it took was mentioning the time he'd stood her up for dinner for her face to dominate his thinking for a time.

He thought back to what had been a gloriously sunny afternoon in 1936, one of a run of the scorchingly hot summers that were more common before the War. It was shirt-sleeve weather, even in those days when failure to wear a jacket was as good as an admission of criminal intent. Shirt-sleeves and bottles of beer weather, beneath a sun that burned the grass yellow and brown, and made the air shimmer in the heat. Shirt-sleeves, bottles of beer, and a bloody great shed to be shifted from one side of the garden to the other.

It wasn't even his shed. Fred was the name of his shed-owning pal, a one-armed ex-soldier he'd met at the bar of some dance or other. He lived in the upper flat of a four-in-a-block terrace – one of the Homes Fit for Heroes that Lloyd George had promised to the men who'd left bits of themselves in France during the Great War.

"Give me a hand, there's a good chap," Fred had said the night before, holding out his stump and laughing fit to burst. "I seem to have mislaid mine."

"Of course," John had replied, joining in the laughter. "Happy to help."

Which was why he was holding up a filthy shed, half-rotten and stinking of damp wood and rodent droppings, when he first saw Sally. He was none too fragrant himself, the previous night's excesses oozing from his pores like the world's least appealing cologne, but as soon as he saw her in the window of the kitchen at the back of the lower flat, he straightened up and hissed to the other man Fred had roped in to take more of the strain. "Be a pal," he'd grunted as quietly as he could. "I don't want that girl to think I can't shift a shed without sweating like some chap down a coal mine."

She was quite short, he saw, the window exposing her only from the neck up, with fair hair cut in the latest fashion, all waves and curves. Her face was small and round, dominated by large, deep brown eyes, above a button nose and a thin-lipped, delicate mouth.

"Who's that?" he called, *sotto voce*, to Fred, who was sitting in a deckchair, directing proceedings with a croquet mallet.

"Sally, I think her name is. That's her sister's place. She comes down to help with the kids while her sister's husband is at work." He winked in an exaggerated fashion and grinned widely. "She's not stepping out with anyone, I do know that."

John had stopped listening as soon as he'd asked the question. The girl was a good deal younger than he was – he'd turned thirty the year before, and she couldn't be more than twenty – but there was something in the way she was looking across the grass at him that told him that the age difference wouldn't matter.

As though she knew she was being watched, the girl looked up and straight at him. Suddenly she smiled, then turned away, and he had a final glimpse of her back as she dried her hands on a tea towel and dropped it on the counter. Then she disappeared through a door and was gone.

"Any chance you could hold up your end for a bit, chum?"

With a start, John realised he'd forgotten all about the shed, which was only being held off the ground by the red-faced efforts of the other man.

"Sorry about that. I was a little distracted, I'm afraid."

Fred's laughter accompanied him as he shuffled forward with the shed, already planning how to effect an introduction to the young lady in the window.

6

The first morning of rehearsals had gone extremely well. John had been as gracious as a dowager duchess judging a village fête when Fagan had announced him as their new Lear, and Edward had been pleased to be informed he would primarily be playing the Earl of Kent, who spent most of the play disguised as a peasant, which he thought would give him plenty of scope for stretching his acting muscles (a phrase Jimmy Rae had used that morning, and which Edward thought rather good).

The rest of the cast had proven to be quite a bit better – and more friendly – than he'd expected. Jimmy Rae, a nice lad certainly, but one whom he'd have said was far better suited to *Leggit* than *Lear*, had turned out to have an impressive knowledge of Shakespeare and had suggested several interesting little tricks he'd seen in previous performances of the play. Equally pleasingly, Alice Robertson had decided to forgive him for his earlier offence, and quickly showed herself to be a consummately professional actress. She also seemed to have taken young Judy Faith under her wing, showing her where to stand, and – more importantly – where not to. Of the others, Monica Gray continued to confuse Edward slightly, her masculine frame at odds with her soft, feminine voice, but she knew her lines and gave every one of them all she had. He had yet to commit the names of the rest of the cast to memory, but thus far nobody had shown themselves to be incompetent, lazy or – worst of all – inclined to chew the scenery.

He doubted Mickey Fagan would have put up with it if they had. As a director, he was everywhere and in control of everything, one moment positioning Judy just so for Cordelia's opening speech, the next, barrelling over to a stagehand to show him exactly how he would like the set dressing to look at the start of the second act. The sound of his voice seemed to be everywhere, at all times, and Edward quickly found himself warming to the ruddy-faced man. Efficiency and professionalism were qualities to be cherished, he thought to himself as they broke for lunch and he hurried off, trying to recall exactly where the nearest loo was.

* * *

By the time he got back, the only one still on the stage was Mickey Fagan, who took him by the elbow and guided him back through the auditorium and up a flight of stairs to the restaurant John had mentioned that morning.

It was the first time Edward had been inside, and he had to admit that it was quite impressive, apparently in better condition than the rest of the old theatre.

"The restaurant and the bar were both done up three years ago," Fagan said, as though reading Edward's mind. "I think the idea was that people would spend more money on food and drink than they do on tickets." He smiled sadly. "Not enough to save the old place, though."

He followed Mickey up around a bend in the corridor and out into the restaurant's seating area, where the rest of the cast and some of the crew sat round two large plastic tables. Alison Jago waved across and pointed at an empty seat by her side. He waved back and mimed looking at the menu board on the wall, then went across and examined it for real, pleased to see it contained proper food and not just the kind of continental fare which seemed inexplicably to have become popular in London recently. He ordered sausage and chips, and a cup of tea, then carried his tray across to the table. Placing it down, he took the chair between Alison and a man he didn't know and prepared to tuck in.

"Peter Glancy," the new man said, waving a soup spoon in his direction. "I'm just this second in the door, but I was simply ravenous, so I thought lunch first, then back to business with this lot – the usual suspects, as I call them."

Glancy was a well-built man of about fifty, with dark, virtually black hair worn too long for his age, so it hung over the collar of his pale-blue safari suit and swung about around his neck as he gestured round the room. Chunky gold rings on several of his fingers caught the light as his hand took in the entire theatre company, before coming to rest on the figure of John Le Breton.

"And that must be our new Lear. I hear he was in an episode of my show, back in the dim and distant." His face crumpled into a thoughtful pout. "I can't say I remember him. Still," he went on, turning back to Edward with a beaming smile, "you and he have certainly done well for yourselves since then. An award nomination apiece, I hear!"

It seemed to Edward that Peter Glancy heard a great deal. Personally, he disliked gossip, and, with no wish to continue the conversation, he smiled politely and reached over for a bottle of brown sauce, pouring a generous dollop on his plate. Surely the man would take the hint and go back to his own lunch?

Apparently not. "You're a braver man than I," Glancy said, eyeing Edward's plate with distaste. "I spent two years in Italy after *McGregor* finished, and since then I've not been able to so much as pop an English sausage in my mouth." He shuddered extravagantly. "Just tubes of gristle and muck, that's what they are."

Inspector McGregor Investigates, that's what Glancy's show had been called. Week after week of the athletic young inspector driving his little sports car around a curiously deserted London, and bringing very well-spoken burglars and pickpockets to justice. It hadn't been very good, Edward remembered. He ignored the comment about the sausages and popped one in his mouth. It tasted fine to him.

"Your friend's proving awfully popular," Glancy went on, nodding towards John, who was now showing Judy Faith a trick where he blew smoke rings that appeared to chase each other across the table. She laughed and Alice

Robertson joined in. "Though of course he'd have had to be the devil incarnate not to be an improvement on Sir Nathaniel bloody Thompson."

In light of the fears John had expressed on the bus that morning, and even though he'd rather just get on with his lunch, Edward knew this was too good an opening to miss. "Oh, really?" he asked, as though merely making polite conversation. "Was Sir Nathaniel not popular, then?"

"Not popular? That's an understatement. Absolutely bloody loathed, that's what he was. I doubt there's a single person in this room who has a good word to say about him, and not one that'd have him back. I'll give you an idea of how much he was disliked. He's got a bloody big house in the town, not too far from where you're staying, in fact, but a damn sight more expensive. And most of us are in bedsits and digs dotted about the place, with not enough room to swing a cat and barely enough money to keep the electricity meter going.

"Anyway, about six months after he joined the company, so this is a year or so back, he threw a party to celebrate something or other – some honorary award he'd been given, I think – and invited us all along. Free booze and the best of food, and he said everyone could stay the night. And do you know how many people went from here? Three. And one of them was Mickey Fagan, who was obliged really. People would rather eat spam cooked on an iron than spend the evening with him. And that was after only six months, mind. Imagine how much we all hated him after two years."

He leaned across Edward and prodded Alison Jago in the knee. "Isn't that right, Ally darling? Isn't that old swine Thompson utterly *detested*?"

Alison swatted Glancy's hand away and he leaned back again, but not before Edward got a definite whiff of whisky on his breath. It was only twenty past one in the afternoon. Wasn't that a bit early to be drinking, even in the north?

For several seconds, Alison said nothing. Edward wondered if she was disinclined to speak about someone behind their back, or if she was simply trying to find a polite way to disagree with Glancy. In the end, neither turned out to be the case.

"I can't speak for anyone else, but he is, without question, the most unpleasant man I've ever had the misfortune to work with." She spoke slowly, without obvious anger, as though she was testing each word for accuracy before she let it pass her lips. It was clear to Edward that this was simply a statement of fact so far as she was concerned, a conclusion reached after careful consideration, and no more a matter for emotion – or argument, for that matter – than pointing out that today was Monday.

Glancy was delighted by what she'd said. He pulled his chair forward again and drummed his fingers on the table in front of Alison. "Even the public thought so, isn't that right?"

Alison looked at him with obvious displeasure. "I'd rather we just left it there, Peter," she said. "But, since you've brought it up, I suppose it's better I tell the story than leave it to you to come up with a more lurid version."

Glancy grinned, showing two rows of uneven teeth,

stained black by nicotine where they met his gums. "You know I would, darling," he crowed.

Alison looked warily round the room, then spoke in an undertone, just loud enough for Edward to hear. "All it is, is that last month I was here after most people had gone home for the night. I usually am – you know how it is, there's always something needing doing. Anyway, I was looking for somewhere to store a pile of old costumes and I was checking for space in the empty dressing rooms when I heard voices, someone shouting. At first I thought someone was running through lines, but then I realised the sound was coming from Sir Nate's dressing room: whatever was being said, there was far too much swearing for it to be a speech from a play. I still had the costumes in my hand, so I couldn't knock on the door, but luckily it was ajar, so I gave it a shove with my foot and it swung open."

"Go on, tell him what you saw!" Glancy's eyes were bright with excitement (*and possibly drink*, Edward thought sourly) as he interrupted Alison's story, but she didn't even acknowledge him, merely kept on with her story as though he'd never spoken.

"Inside, I saw Sir Nate pressed back against the far wall, and a big man in a dark coat had him by the throat and was choking him. He had his back to me so I couldn't see his face. He must have heard me opening the door, because I only had a second to check all this out before he threw Sir Nate to one side like he weighed nothing, then knocked me flying on his way out the door."

"You didn't see his face at all?"

"Not a glimpse. It all happened so quickly and, like I said, he literally knocked me over. But I knew who he was, all the same."

"You do?"

"God, yeah. Well, sort of. He's a guy that's hung up on Judy Faith; he sends her cards and flowers, waits outside the back door after performances to get her to sign stuff, that kind of thing. I'd seen him hanging around loads of times and Judy's shown me letters he's sent her. He seemed quite sweet, if a tiny bit creepy. That's why it took me so long to realise it was him I'd seen throttling Nate Thompson. It seemed so out of character, you see."

"Do you have a name for this man?"

"Craig Mackay. That's how he signs his letters and cards, anyway."

This was surely the kind of thing the police should be made aware of, Edward thought, recalling the man in the donkey jacket he'd seen loitering outside the theatre when they'd arrived. "What does he look like, this Mackay?" he asked. "A big man, you said?"

"Yeah, he's over six foot, I reckon. Long, dark, curly hair, heavy beard, but scruffy. Like I say, I've seen him about, but I've never really looked at him, know what I mean?"

Edward nodded. "And what did Sir Nate say about the attack?"

"Not a thing. By the time I got back to my feet, he was already up and sitting at the table. He asked if I was OK, but I could tell from his glazed eyes and the smell of booze on his breath that he was dead drunk. I told him I was fine, asked if he was alright, but he just grunted and ignored me until I left."

"And you had no idea why this man might have attacked him?"

"None," Alison said, but Edward had the strongest sensation that she was keeping something back. Before he could press her further, however, Peter Glancy cackled and podded him in the arm.

"He'll have been a cuckolded husband, or I'm a monkey's aunt! Everybody knew Nate was playing around with a married woman, and him not even divorced from his fourth wife, either!"

Alison scowled at Glancy, though again Edward couldn't say for sure if it was because what he'd said was untrue or because she thought it poor form to tell tales. "Like I said, I couldn't say," she repeated. She smiled thinly at Edward and turned away to speak to a young man in overalls sitting to her right, obviously unwilling to engage any further with Peter Glancy.

"You see! What did I tell you? There were too many reasons to hate him, the disgusting old lech!" Glancy clapped his hands together with glee, loudly enough that several people nearby stopped eating and looked across at him, as if expecting him to give a speech. Feeling their eyes upon him, he did exactly that, jumping to his feet and rapping hard on the table with his spoon until everyone was watching him.

"I was just saying to dear Edward here that we are delighted to have him and John swell our ranks at the Playhouse."

There were murmurs of agreement, and one or two nodded heads, though also one or two people whispering to each other. Edward caught the words "drinking already" and "always has to be the centre of attention", but then Glancy spoke again, loudly enough that everyone else was drowned out. "And I was also saying that, while we'd have welcomed them both with open arms regardless, the fact that John is replacing Nate Thompson, an absolute shit of a man, is a wonderful extra bonus."

He sat down again and pulled a hip flash from his pocket, which he held up in a single-handed toast then, perhaps noticing the disapproving glare of Mickey Fagan, returned to his pocket without opening. "Welcome to our cosy little family!" he announced with a grin and a broad wink in John's direction.

7

Even without exchanging a word with the man, John thought he might get on quite well with Peter Glancy. Granted, lunchtime was a little too early to be already three sheets to the wind, but, that said, you couldn't help but admire his lack of shame. *Nil legitimi carborundum*, and all that (good to know that some of the Latin he'd learned at school had stuck, he thought, even if it wasn't the stuff the teachers had shown him).

He acknowledged the raised hip flask with a tip of his teacup, thinking that a swift half and an accompanying short alongside a pub pork pie would be a better way to spend his lunchtime than drinking weak tea and eating a flavourless cod in white sauce. But Alice Robertson was tutting her disapproval at his side, so he turned around in his seat and asked if Glancy was always this way.

"This way?" she repeated slowly. "Drunk and making an exhibition of himself, you mean? Yes, more often than not."

"Is he tipsy? I really hadn't noticed."

"Tipsy as a lord, I imagine." The old woman laid a hand on top of his. "Though it's sweet of you to pretend not to notice. It's the mark of a gentleman. I was taught, as a girl, to ignore the excesses of other people until such point as they need to be addressed."

"And do Peter's need to be addressed?"

"You mean, is his drinking something which impacts the show?" She shook her head. "No, not so far. He's been with the company for three years now, or near enough, and he's never missed a performance yet. Unlike Sir Nathaniel."

It seemed everybody in the building was keen to pass judgement on Thompson now he was *persona non grata*, John thought. "I did hear Nate had been missing performances," he said, half as a question and half as a statement of fact, but mainly as a hint that she should say more. He felt guilty that he hoped for confirmation of what Alison had told them, but if he could tell himself his old friend had been a liability, he'd feel far better about taking his role, even if he did eventually turn up and ask for it back.

"About one a week recently." Alice pushed her plate away untouched and pulled a long, thin cigarette from a little purple purse apparently designed for the purpose. "He didn't used to be so bad, to be fair, but over the past year or so, he became most unreliable. Tight at rehearsals, when he appeared at all, and too drunk to go on when the audience were in." She frowned. "It was the strangest thing, actually. Sometimes I'd bump into him half an hour before the curtain went up and he'd be sober as a judge. Then the five-minute call would go out, and I'd pass his dressing room, and there he'd be, absolutely sozzled, asleep in his chair, and of no use to man nor beast. You'd think he suffered from stage fright, except every other night he was fine, and he obviously loved to be in front of an audience."

She shook her head and slipped her cigarette purse back into her handbag. "Of course, there were other reasons that he wasn't popular, but they're not ones I care to repeat."

John held his lighter out to light her cigarette, wondering if she were the type of woman who liked to gossip, but needed to be encouraged to do so. Did she need to tell herself that whatever information she so gleefully imparted had been forced out of her against her better judgement? "My goodness," he said, playing along, "that does sound mysterious!"

It turned out she was not that type of woman at all. "Not mysterious at all, Mr Le Breton," she sniffed, and John felt the temperature drop by a degree or two. "I'm sure there are any number of people sitting at these tables who will be happy to tell you the whole story. But, as I said, I'm not one of them."

"Of course, of course," he said. "I sympathise completely. I simply meant that he and I were friends many years ago, and he was terribly popular in those days. I'm just surprised to hear that he'd lost the knack, as it were."

It was obviously the right approach to take. What had been a frosty look of disapproval morphed at once into a small smile of understanding. "Oh, I hadn't realised you and Sir Nathaniel were old friends," she said. "Is that perhaps why you were asked to step into his shoes? So much less unpleasant when a friend is involved, I always think."

John thought the opposite was probably true but had no intention of saying so. Instead, he nodded firmly. "We have rather lost touch recently but, once upon a time, we were thick as thieves. Thirty years ago, I doubt there was a week went by when we didn't have dinner together at some point."

"It's such a shame when old friends lose touch. But in this business…"

"Exactly," John agreed. "Though we started out in the same rather horrid little theatres, we all knew, even then, that Nate was destined for better things. And it's terribly difficult to keep a friendship going when you no longer move in the same circles. But he was off in Hollywood, while I laboured on in more humble locations."

Alice threw her hands up in mock admonition, obviously charmed – as he'd hoped she might be – by John's self-effacing modesty. Again, he felt a touch of guilt, this time for manipulating the woman like this. This is what came of spending so much time with Edward, he told himself. Had he become cynical?

"You do yourself an injustice, John," she said, laying her hand back on top of his. "Your career may not have been as stellar as Sir Nathaniel's in every respect, but I believe you too have been in Hollywood, and now look at you – the star of a smash hit on the television." She breathed in sharply. "I don't actually watch situation comedies myself, of course, but I did see a very flattering review in a copy of the *Daily Express* that Monica left lying around."

John waited, hoping she would feel obliged to fill the silence – that was what the police always did in novels, didn't they? But in real life, it turned out that if someone said something to you and you didn't reply, only stared at them like a ghoul, they simply assumed you'd left the conversation and turned their attention elsewhere.

So it proved now.

"Anyway, John, it was lovely to speak to you," Alice said. She reached for the handbag at her feet and stood up. "I like to have a nap after lunch, before we start the afternoon's work, so if you'll excuse me…"

John rose to his feet as she did, and watched her leave the restaurant before sitting back down again. One or two of the others were also leaving, including whoever had been sitting on his other side (a lighting chap of some sort, he thought). Isolated as he now was, an island in an ever-growing sea of empty chairs, he smoked a reflective cigarette and watched Edward eating a custard-covered cake. He too had been cut adrift, though only partially. Peter Glancy was taking his tray to a serving hatch in the wall, but Alison Jago still sat alongside him, her head bowed as she spoke in his ear. For a moment, he considered going across and joining them, but he recalled Alice's talk of a nap, and suddenly that seemed a very good idea. There were a pair of very comfortable old armchairs in the dressing room he now shared with Edward, and one of them seemed to be calling to him, luring him in with its softly upholstered siren song.

He stood and waved a farewell at the few diners still seated, then picked up his cigarettes and lighter.

Yes, he decided, forty winks were just what the doctor ordered.

8

The previous day's rehearsals had gone pretty well in Edward's opinion, all things considered. True, John had disappeared after lunch and missed the first few minutes of the afternoon session, until Alison had thought to look in his – *their* – dressing room and found him fast asleep in a chair, with a copy of the *Racing Post* spread over his face. But Mickey Fagan had chosen to view that as amusing rather than unprofessional, and John had had the good grace to look sheepish when he'd come trotting into the auditorium at Alison's heels.

"Only fitting that we have to wait for the King," Fagan had said, a weak joke which had generated enough laughter for any embarrassment John might have felt to pass unnoticed. Though Edward doubted that John had felt any such thing. For all that he hated confrontation, he was almost impossible to embarrass when it came to his own actions.

It was another way in which they were very different. No doubt a lifetime of nannies at home, fags at school, and a selection of batmen and eager young ladies the rest of the time were the reason John appeared to have no shame. Once, not so long ago, that had annoyed Edward, but nowadays – most of the time – he found it more endearing than irritating.

And he *had* been very good in his first scenes as Lear. Watching him doing a first run through of Lear's "Blow, winds, and crack your cheeks!" monologue, he'd actually felt a shiver go down his spine. Years of sitcom tomfoolery and second-reel movie bad guys had fallen away from him, and he'd become Shakespeare's doomed king.

* * *

Which was why Edward approached the second day of rehearsals with a real sense of optimism and purpose. If John Le Breton could do *Lear*, then so could Edward Lowe.

To his surprise, Mickey Fagan hadn't called on him to do much more than feed lines to John and get measured for costumes on the first day. However, as soon as he and John arrived on day two (by bus again – Edward made a mental note to speak to someone about more suitable transport), he'd leapt into running through his own first scenes, repeating the same lines over and over as he moved around the rehearsal room, checking where he should be standing, and avoiding the tape on the floor which marked out where the various walls and furnishings would be on the stage during an actual performance.

It was all quite exhilarating. Even out of costume, in a rather tatty room in a second-rate northern theatre which had seen better days, there was power in Shakespeare's words. Edward strutted about the room like a man possessed, delivering every line with utter conviction and dazzling the rest of the company with his intuitive grasp of the material. Or at least he hoped so. John's performance had boosted his own confidence, but always at the back of his mind there remained a nagging doubt that he wasn't quite good enough for the Bard.

Still, Fagan seemed pleased with his performance and, by lunchtime, whatever fears Edward still harboured had faded away almost completely, to be replaced by a complacent sense he was born to this role. He said as much to John in the Blue Blazer, the nearest pub to the theatre, where they'd repaired for a lunchtime pint.

"Didn't I say that this would be just the thing we needed to refresh our creative batteries?" he said, as he drained most of his pint in a single, thirsty gulp. "Away from London and stuffy TV studios, and back to real acting in front of real people!"

John also appeared less tense now they'd got their feet under the proverbial table. Edward contemplated asking him about Thompson, but there'd been no sign of the man, so perhaps it was better to let sleeping dogs lie.

The barman – a short, wiry man with slicked-back hair, who wore a white shirt and maroon tie and matching jacket – nodded at their nearly empty glasses and, as Edward reached for his wallet, began pouring two fresh drinks.

"Either Nate Thompson's on a particularly long toot," John said abruptly, as though reading Edward's mind, "or he's decided he's permanently buggered his chances at the Playhouse. I was sure we'd have seen him by this morning, at the latest. He must know that rehearsals for *Lear* have started."

"I think you can relax, John. A chap like that, he'd have shown up throwing his weight around as soon as he knew someone else had taken his place. He wouldn't wait."

"That's not what you said the other day!" John protested mildly. "If he came back at all, you said, it'd be with cap in hand, his tail between his legs." He shuddered. "I did mention he's a hulking big fellow, didn't I?"

Edward knew he had to nip this renewed nervousness in the bud. "Do pay attention, John. He's not coming back, that's what I'm saying. If he had intended to, he'd have come back already, that's what I'm saying."

John nodded but with little conviction, then sipped at his drink and played with his lighter, saying nothing. With nobody to talk to, Edward looked around the pub. The Blue Blazer was a compact little space, with only five tables, each capable of seating four people, and a curved oak bar that took up more than half of the remaining space. A range of gleaming metal pumps were lined up in its centre and, behind them, a large mirror emblazoned with the name of the local brewery reflected down on shelf after shelf of spirits. John and Edward were sitting at the bar, every other table having been full with the lunchtime rush by the time they'd arrived. A fire had been lit and the air smelled of cigarette smoke, spilled beer and furniture polish. Behind them, the chatter of weekday pub voices melted into a single sound, a low rumble, like waves hitting a rocky beach or a car idling at traffic lights. Rain began to fall in heavy drops against the frosted windows and, as John continued to say nothing, staring moodily into his pint glass, Edward felt his eyelids begin to droop.

"Pint of mild and a Scotch to chase it down, mate!" Jimmy Rae's voice was like the booming of a cannon right beside Edward's ear – *or a bullet whizzing past*, he thought, remembering his flirtation with death the previous year. "I thought I was going to miss last orders," Jimmy went on, pointing at the clock above the bar, which showed twenty to two. "Mickey kept me back to discuss some bits and pieces, and I kept checking me watch, but he never took me up on it. In the end, I had to say, 'I really need to shoot off, Mickey', and then run here." He fished in his pocket and pulled out a pound note. "Can I get you boys anything?"

"Just a short for me, Jimmy," Edward said, remembering they had an afternoon of rehearsal ahead and keen to continue the good work he'd done in the morning. John, enlivened by the appearance of the younger man (or simply unwilling to share his concerns with him), quickly finished his drink and waggled the glass in front of the barman. "Same again, please," he said, "And, because my doctor was kind enough to inform me that drinking on an empty stomach is tantamount to a not particularly slow suicide, you'd better shove a couple of packets of crisps our way too. And some pork scratchings, if you have them." He turned to Jimmy, with a grin suddenly full of mischief. "They taste absolutely vile, but somehow they feel more substantial than a packet of cheese and onion."

As the barman went to get their drinks, Edward hoped that John's lifted mood would last and that he was right, and they wouldn't see Nate Thompson at all. He could imagine few things worse than a month of sharing a dressing room with John in this erratic mood.

9

It was beginning to look as though the bloody man wasn't going to stand still long enough to be murdered.

Drunk though he was – drunk though he always was – he somehow managed to keep himself upright as he staggered from the theatre, even as the wind picked up and drove spikes of rain almost horizontally into his face.

The would-be killer who followed a dozen yards behind him turned up his own collar and cursed as his foot splashed down into a puddle of cold, dirty water. It was unlikely there was anyone else around at this ungodly hour to hear him, but still he glanced about nervously. The role of assassin did not come naturally to him, and the Dutch courage he'd taken earlier had already begun to wear off.

The street was deserted, though, and likely to remain that way, and he wondered if perhaps he should just quicken his pace, catch up with the swaying drunkard in front of him, and do the deed there and then, out in the open.

He had just begun to lengthen his stride when his prey

stumbled on a loose paving stone, allowed his right leg to cross almost comically in front of his left, and staggered sideways into the entrance of a tenement block. By the time he caught up, the drunken man was sitting with his back to the stair wall, glaring blearily up and waving one hand in aimless, whisky-sozzled aggression at the dark figure standing over him.

He wondered later if there was something in people, even people drunker than the drunkest of lords, that warned them their end was near. He could think of no other reason why the bundle at his feet surged towards him just as he raised the length of steel pipe above his head. Whatever it was, the unexpected movement was enough for panic to overwhelm him, for chemicals to flood his brain like some caveman hunter surprised by a pouncing sabre-toothed tiger. With no conscious thought at all, he brought the pipe down again and again and again, until the stairway was sprayed with blood in long sweeping arcs and the object at his feet was barely recognisable as a human being.

Quickly, he pulled off his bloodied jacket and shoved what he was already thinking of as the murder weapon into his trouser pocket. Only when he was certain he'd left nothing that could give him away did he get to his feet and step back into the cleansing rain.

10

Next morning dawned muggy and overcast, the sky filled with heavy clouds, dry for the moment but with no likelihood of staying that way. Edward and John hurriedly bolted down their breakfast and were down the street and on the early bus before the skies opened.

On the plus side, this would, hopefully, be their final day of getting the bus. Mrs Galloway had overheard Edward talking with Harvey the travelling salesman the previous morning, and had offered them the use of her late husband's decrepit Ford Anglia. It was currently parked in a friend's garage, but she had arranged for it to be dropped off later that day, for their exclusive use while they were in Bolton.

"I don't drive myself," Mrs Galloway had assured them, "Never saw the need. But it's good to see someone getting the use of the car. And Mr Galloway was such a fan of you both."

Since he had apparently died in 1955, that seemed unlikely to Edward but, still, he was grateful for the loan, and made sure to let Mrs Galloway know it. The thought of being able to drive themselves into work, rather than relying on the dirty, uncomfortable bus service was enough to put him in a very good mood.

John too seemed in fine fettle. When they'd got back from the pub the previous afternoon, he and Jimmy Rae had been huddled together, giggling like schoolgirls and sharing private jokes between themselves as they ran through various scenes. Edward had been pleased to see the improvement in his friend's mood, and it appeared that a night's sleep had not blunted his good humour.

"You know, I do believe that this could turn out to be a lovely little break," John said as they rose to get off the bus. He pressed the bell to alert the driver, then pressed it several times more in a sprightly sort of rhythm. "That's the start of Gene Krupa's drum solo on 'Sing Sing Sing' with Benny Goodman's band, you know," he announced to the other passengers, then pressed the bell again for good luck.

Edward shrugged his shoulders as if to say *what can you do*? and followed John down the stairs, a small smile playing on his lips.

Nothing, he decided, was going to spoil this day.

11

"Sir Nathaniel Thompson is dead."

The speaker was a tall, pale-faced man, clean-shaven but with a dark five o'clock shadow already visible at ten o'clock in the morning. Large circular glasses with brown plastic rims took up much of the top half of his face, above a small, thin-lipped mouth. He spoke from the side of the stage, in the same spot he had occupied since Edward and John had wandered along from the theatre entrance and been invited to join the rest of the company already assembled there.

"My name is Detective Inspector Whyte," he continued. "As I have just explained to your boss here" – he indicated Mickey Fagan with a wave of his hand – "a body has been found, which we believe to be that of your late colleague. In light of this, I would be obliged if each of you would answer some questions about your whereabouts yesterday evening."

Without pausing, he held the same hand up in the air, in the manner of a traffic policeman bringing a line of cars to a halt. "And before you all start shouting out questions of your own, I should warn you all that I am not at liberty at this moment to answer any of them. I can say that we are treating the matter as murder, and that Mr Thompson was the victim of a ferocious attack."

Before anyone else could speak, he gestured again – he waved his arms around more than the most awful am-dram hack, John thought – towards three uniformed officers standing in the orchestra pit. "My colleagues will take seats in the stalls and call you over as and when required. Until your statements are taken, you will all stay where you are, on this stage, and not speak to one another." His smile was perfunctory, and John was reminded again of a bad actor: it was the action of a man fulfilling an allotted role – the public servant, in this case – with not a hint of warmth or sincerity behind it.

Almost before he had finished speaking, the air was filled with the sound of querulous actors voicing their inevitable concerns. It took the intervention of Mickey Fagan, who barked "Will you all shut up, for Christ's sake!" to bring the tumult of noise to a halt. Even that might not have been enough, but one glance at his face – drawn and white, but with eyes rimmed with red – was enough to silence even Monica Gray. "Just do as the man says, please," Mickey concluded weakly, his eyes sliding away from any of the company's that they met.

John looked at Edward, who shrugged. God knows what's going on, he seemed to say. It was obviously serious, though. Of course it was serious, he mentally chided himself. There was a man dead; a man he had known for years.

He wondered at the lack of concern, never mind grief, that he felt. Or rather, didn't feel.

He searched the milling actors for Jimmy Rae, but the younger man was the first name called, and was already making his way down the stairs towards one of the constables.

Thankfully, there were seats arranged on the stage, set up for the morning read-through. Edward and John sat down beside one another, and watched as Judy Faith and Peter Glancy followed Jimmy down the stairs. They were too far away to hear what was being said – deliberately so, John realised – but, whatever it was, it made Judy burst into tears and throw her hands to her face in horror. Jimmy and Glancy were less dramatic, apparently answering the questions calmly and quietly, and nodding now and again in agreement as their interrogators scribbled in the notepads they had balanced on their knees. As they finished, the constables pointed them towards the far end of the stage, where they stood in a small group, still not speaking, but looking over at their colleagues with expressions which John struggled, and failed, to decipher.

Monica and Alice Robertson were called next, and then some of the backstage staff, including Alison Jago, John noticed. She gave him a tight smile as she made her way towards a waiting policeman, and he began to wave, then quickly snatched his hand back as he realised how inappropriate it might look.

Finally, just as he was wondering whether they'd been forgotten, it was Edward and John's turn.

* * *

The officer John spoke to was a heavyset older man, who stared at him as he took a seat. Three stripes on the sleeve of his jacket marked him out as a sergeant. "Good afternoon, sir," he said. "I'm Sergeant Hickey. If we could start with your name…" He stopped and stared at John as though seeing him for the first time. "Actually, I've seen you on the telly, haven't I? You're the posh antiques bloke on that *Floggit* show. John something, isn't it? Something foreign sounding."

"Le Breton. I'm John Le Breton. And, yes, I'm in *Floggit and Leggit.* I play Archie Russell."

The policeman nodded and wrote 'JOHN LE BRETON – ACTOR' at the top of the page. "Don't like it much," he went on, though without animosity. "I only watch the sport myself."

"Well, it's not for everyone," John agreed amicably. He was still unsure how he felt about Thompson's death. What he'd told Edward had been the truth; they had been great pals for a while just before the War. But what he'd missed out was why they'd stopped being pals. Perhaps he should have said, but, even after all these years, it still felt like a private matter, and it was something he'd never discussed with anyone else. He'd be lying, though, if he said he was upset by Thompson's death.

"Now, obviously, the reason we're here talking to you lot is that this bloke's death is being treated as suspicious." Hickey peered at him intently as he spoke, presumably hoping John would blurt out a full confession. In fact, it had only just occurred to him that the death must be suspicious. The police wouldn't have turned up en masse if Nate had simply drunkenly stumbled in front of a car, would they?

"Is there anything you have to say to that?" the sergeant went on after a moment's silence. "Can you think of anyone who might have wanted to harm Mr Thompson?"

"Any number of people, officer. He was not a well-liked man." John laughed, but regretted it at once, as the policeman frowned and shook his head.

"I'm surprised you find this funny, sir," he said. "Would it cause you to change your tune if I were to tell you that Mr Thompson was killed in the early hours, brutally bludgeoned to death not a mile from this theatre?" He leaned forward and lowered his voice. "His skull was smashed in and his brains were halfway up the wall. Hardly a matter for laughter, I would have said."

"No, no, you're quite right. Forgive me, I think I'm still in shock." John tried his best to look like a man in shock then, when the policeman said nothing and the silence became unnerving, blurted out, "I've known Nate Thompson for coming up for forty years, you see."

Hickey pounced on this admission as though he'd only been biding his time, waiting for just such a slip. "So, you were old friends, were you? Or were you one of the people who didn't like him?"

"Neither, to be honest."

"You'd known him for all that time, but you weren't friends? And even though you weren't friends, you still liked him? Is that what you're saying?"

The sudden change in tone seemed like an attack and John felt he needed to defend himself.

"We've not been close for a very long time, but I didn't dislike the man. We just drifted apart." He held out his hands, palms up. "The War, you know. It changed so many things."

"So, you were friends once, but lost touch over the years."

"Exactly that."

"But you were at least in touch enough to know that the deceased…" Hickey looked down at his pad, "…'wasn't a well-liked man' were the words you used. Was this general dislike well-known then, even amongst people like yourself who had hadn't been in touch with him for years?"

Something in the way the policeman said *like yourself* felt a little sinister to John. Sinister, and just a tad accusatory. He felt sweat break out on his forehead and resisted the urge to pat at it with his handkerchief. He knew from earlier in his career, making seventy-minute second features, that nothing made you look more guilty than mopping your brow with a hankie. Why, he wondered plaintively, did he suddenly feel like a suspect? All he'd done was take the man's job, that was all.

He glanced across at Edward, hoping for reassurance, but his back was turned and there was no way of telling how he was getting on. Up on the stage, the rest of the company seemed all to be staring down at him, their eyes accusing him, their very posture enough to make him shrink back in his seat.

The movement caused a drop of sweat to drip into his eye and make it sting, and the tiny, brief discomfort that created was just irritating enough to bring him back to his senses – and to foster a surge of bad-tempered exasperation which was, he liked to think, quite out of character for him.

"This is ridiculous, Sergeant!" he snapped. "It was a byword both in this company and in the business generally that Nate Thompson was a bully, a blowhard and a drunk, and while I hesitate to speak ill of the dead, I personally always found him to be something of a heel! I do not say that I know of anyone who would want to kill him, but I do say that not many people will mourn his passing."

John felt a swell of satisfaction wash over him as he sagged back into his seat, sure that would shut the fat sergeant up, but the effect was rather lost when Judy Faith, standing on the stage next to Jimmy Rae, suddenly gave out an almighty scream and fainted clean away.

12

John was out of his seat well before the policeman, he was pleased to realise. While that overweight worthy struggled in his wake, he positively bounded up the stairs and joined Jimmy Rae at Judy's side.

"What on Earth happened?" he asked as he knelt down next to her. The adrenaline rush he'd felt when running up the stairs had disappeared as quickly as it had arrived, and his knees protested painfully as he creaked downwards to the wooden boards.

"I dunno," Jimmy replied, shaking his head. "I was just saying that getting your brains knocked out for the sake of what was in your wallet was no way to go, and Judy went down like a sack of spuds."

A charming and talented young man, John thought, *but perhaps not always over-endowed with tact.*

Thankfully, Judy was already coming round. Someone handed John a glass of water and he held it up to her mouth. She sipped a little and smiled weakly – and delightfully – up at him.

"Thank you, John," she said. "I'm OK now." She took his arm and pulled herself to her feet. "It was just such a shock, hearing it put like that."

John glared at Jimmy, who shrugged a silent apology, and led Judy to a seat. "Were you very close to Nate?" he asked gently.

At first, he thought she wouldn't reply at all. Her hand was still shaking a little around the glass she held, and she took a moment to drink and steady her nerves before saying anything. "No, not that close. But he was such a help when I first arrived – and I've never actually known anyone who's died before." She looked around for somewhere to put the empty glass. John reached over and took it, enjoying the unusual feeling of not being the one in need of assistance.

"Of course, my dear," he said. "It must have been a terrible shock to you."

"It was just the way Jim put it," she said. "I hadn't thought of it like that."

"Well, you wouldn't, would you?" John said, while Jimmy muttered another apology and offered to rustle up some brandy.

"No thanks, Jim," Judy said. "I'm not much of a drinker, no matter what the papers say – and, besides, I'm starting to feel better now."

Inspector Whyte had been watching without speaking throughout Judy's fall and recovery, but now he stepped forward. "I'm glad to see you're alright, Miss Faith, but I will still need everyone to give their statements to my officers." He frowned and scratched at his jaw. "And, after that, I'll need access to Sir Nathaniel's dressing room. I take it he has his own dressing room, what with being the star of the show and all?"

There was an awkward silence in which nobody seemed willing to correct the policeman. Finally, Mickey Fagan coughed and explained that Sir Nathaniel had recently left the company, but that his old dressing room had been reallocated. "He hadn't come round to collect all of his things, you see, and Judy wanted her own room, so we put his stuff in a bag until he did."

"When did that happen?" asked the inspector. "Leaving the company, I mean? Was he sacked?"

"As it happens, he was let go, yes." Fagan was still white-faced, but his cheeks reddened slightly as he considered the question. "Though I would prefer not to be dwelling on things like that right now. It's not like the reason he left has any bearing on his death." His voice broke and he slumped down heavily on the nearest chair.

Whyte was unperturbed. "I'll be the judge of that, if you don't mind, Mr Fagan." He looked around the assembled actors. "So, which one of you replaced Mr Thompson in the starring role?"

John gave a start at this unexpected turn of events. He hadn't expected to have to speak, and found himself babbling a little as he held up a hand and explained that he was the new King Lear.

"But all of this happened before Sir Nathaniel was killed," he went on quickly. "Edward and I have been here since the weekend."

"Nobody has said yet when Mr Thompson was killed." The inspector's voice held a note of triumph, as though he felt he had scored a valuable point. Before either John or Edward could respond, he held up a hand to forestall any interruption. "I've seen you on the telly, haven't I? Both of you. You're in that show with the old codgers."

Before he could reply, John felt Judy's hand rest on his arm. Beads of sweat dotted her forehead and her top lip, he noticed, and she was still trembling slightly. He pulled over a chair and offered it to her, but she shook her head.

"I think I might go to my dressing room and have a bit of a lie down, actually," she said, looking at Mickey Fagan, who in turn looked across at the inspector. He nodded and assured her that that was fine.

"We'll need to take your statement, miss, but that can wait until tomorrow. And there'll be no more rehearsals today, in case anyone was wondering."

John offered to escort her to her dressing room, but she smiled, shaking her head. "I'll be fine," she said.

John watched her walk across the stage and down the stairs, then disappear through a side door. She seemed quite recovered, but he made a mental note to check in on her later.

Meanwhile, Whyte took off his jacket and laid it across the back of the nearest chair, then rolled up his sleeves. "Right then, while my constables continue taking everyone else's statements, perhaps you could show me this bag of Mr Thompson's possessions, Mr Fagan?"

The two men chatted quietly with their heads close together for a minute or two, then left through the same door as Judy, a uniformed constable following in their wake. What had Whyte meant about the time Nate Thompson had been killed? And what had he been trying to suggest about John taking over his part in the play? He would dearly have liked to speak to Edward about it, but Sergeant Hickey was already walking towards him, notebook open in his hand, and he realised any discussions would have to wait for now.

13

It was an hour later, and the Playhouse had only just begun to calm down.

After everyone's statement had been taken and Inspector Whyte had spent ten minutes nosing around in Nathaniel Thompson's old dressing room, he had announced that he was finished with them for now, and they were free to go about their business.

Once the policemen had left, they had all naturally gravitated back to the stage. To Edward's surprise, the first question anyone asked had been whether this would impact the staging of *Lear*.

"I told him straight," Mickey Fagan had explained glumly, "Nate was sacked over a week ago. Nobody here has seen hide nor hair of him since then and we have a show to put on. People's livelihoods are at stake, I said. *My* bloody livelihood is at stake!"

He looked around the assembled group of actors and backstage workers, and shrugged miserably. "What was I supposed to do, I ask you? I liked Nate about as much as any man ever did, but if he's got himself killed, well… is anyone surprised? The mouth on that man when he was sober could have gotten him kicked from here to Kilkenny, and when he had a few drinks in him…" He trailed off, then muttered, "We can't let the place go dark. Not for something which had bugger all to do with the show. Not when this might be the last show we ever put on here."

"You did the right thing, Michael," Monica Gray rushed to reassure him. "God knows, I wouldn't wish such a fate on anyone, but I've no doubt the police will find he brought it on himself. There's certainly no reason why it should impact us. We've all put too much work into this for it to be derailed because that nasty piece of work finally got his comeuppance."

Edward was surprised to hear the savagery in her soft voice, and to see so many heads nod in agreement. He'd never met the man, of course but, even so, wasn't there a single one of them who would spare a second to mourn his passing?

"It's not as though he were still part of the company," Alice Robertson piped up quietly, then coloured red to the tips of her ears as everyone turned to look at her.

An unusual reaction for a professional actress, Edward thought. But he'd known many actors and actresses who were huge characters when on stage or in front of a camera, but who transformed into timid mice when not performing.

"And the police constable I spoke to did say they believed Sir Nathaniel's death was a robbery of some kind which had escalated in an unexpectedly horrible manner," she continued.

"Yeah," Jimmy Rae agreed. "They told me it was a mugging gone wrong too. Still, you can't help feel sorry for the old sod, can you? It's a bit of a rough end to his illustrious career. Imagine playing Hamlet in the West End and snogging Vivien Leigh in Hollywood, but being remembered for getting your head stoved in up some smelly old alley."

There was a coarseness to Rae which Edward had noticed while filming *Floggit and Leggit*, and earlier, when he'd caused Judy Faith to collapse. He'd remarked on it to John at the time – a preference always to go for the cheap laugh. He'd spent too much time messing around with Clive Briggs last year, engaged in a series of odious practical jokes, and Edward knew he would need to say something next series, as the senior man on set. Still, for the moment, he seemed to be expressing an opinion widely held within the company. Certainly, several heads were nodding again as he finished speaking.

"I'm sure I speak for us all," Monica Gray said piously, "when I say that the best way we can honour Sir Nathaniel's memory is by making this show – a show he helped create, let us not forget – as memorable as we possibly can. Only by producing our very best work can we hope to do justice to the memory of his undoubted genius."

How quickly death can change people's opinion of a man, Edward reflected wryly, as Monica ended by suggesting they spend a minute in quiet reflection – though he doubted anyone had ever been promoted from *nasty piece of work* to *undoubted genius* as hastily as she'd just elevated Nate

Thompson. He wondered if she was even aware of how hypocritical she sounded. Probably not, he decided, and smiled to himself.

He felt John's bony elbow nudge him in the ribs. "You're grinning like the damned Cheshire Cat, Edward," he whispered. "I can guess what you're thinking, but do at least try to look as though you're upset!"

"What I'm thinking?" Edward raised a puzzled eyebrow, but John just shook his head and quickly put a finger to his lips.

"Later," he hissed, which Edward thought rather impressive for a word with no sibilants.

Nobody else seemed to have anything to say. They all stared at the floor, seemingly considering the legacy of the dead man, until Mickey Fagan clapped his hands together. "Well said, Monica," he grunted. "And you'll all be glad to hear that you'll get the opportunity, too. The inspector told me before he left that we were good to get on with things. We'll be closed today out of respect to Nate but, after that, it's business as usual."

There was a general buzz of appreciation at the news, in which Edward joined. He noticed John stayed quiet, though.

"Shall we get out of here?" he asked quietly.

John nodded and, as the others continued to discuss the news, they quickly made their way backstage and from there out into the street.

14

It seemed nobody else had fancied a drink. The Blue Blazer had just opened and, excepting one slumped figure at the end of the bar, who didn't even look up from his drink as they came in, there was nobody else there; hardly surprising at five past eleven on a Wednesday morning, of course.

"Good morning, landlord," John said to the same barman who'd served them the last time they'd been in, and slapped one of the new fifty pence coins down on the bar. "A pint of whatever's most palatable today, please, and…" He looked across at Edward who had taken a seat by the door and was fishing his cigarettes from his pocket. "What will you have, Edward?" he asked.

"A decent whisky, I think. Something from the Islands, if they have it." He frowned and made a face. "You do have proper whisky, I suppose? None of that blended rubbish." The question was addressed to the barman, who looked mildly offended and nodded his agreement. "Make it a double, then, with just a splash of water," Edward added, apparently satisfied.

John pocketed his change, slipping the barman back the cost of another pint as a tip, and carried the drinks over to the table. Once seated, he raised his glass in a toast. "Sir Nathaniel Thompson," he said. "May he rest in peace."

"Sir Nathaniel," Edward repeated and took a sip of the whisky.

For a moment, they sat in silence, and the only sound in the pub was the ticking of the big clock. It was still raining outside, but the barman had already lit the fire and the little room was warm and snug. John drained a significant portion of his pint and sighed heavily. "Seems that everywhere we go," he said, "death follows us around."

"Not just death. Murder."

"Is that worse, would you say? Dead's dead when all's said and done, but an accidental death seems more… I don't know, unfair, somehow."

"Oh, it's much worse," said Edward. "An accident's an accident. Nothing you can do about it. Dreadfully unfair, as you say, but simply blind fate at play, no more, no less. Murder, though… murder requires a murderer. It needs someone to decide to end your life. In my opinion, there's nothing worse than a murderer." Edward shook his head and stared sadly at John, like an old dog slowly blinking, and he realised he was thinking back to last year, when a bullet had nearly taken his ear off. Then suddenly he brightened. "However, if Thompson's death had been an accident, there'd be nothing for us to do now, so there is that."

John had known it was coming, of course. He'd known from the second Inspector Whyte had announced Nate

Thompson's death. Edward had made genuine attempts to downplay what he and John had achieved last year but, as time had passed and the initial horror of nearly being killed had worn off, he had started to mention it more often, and in a much more positive light. He'd always known that Edward had a very strong sense of justice – indeed, that had been the main motivator for them working together – but the success they'd shared had changed something in him.

In most – virtually all – ways, Edward was the same as ever. Still cantankerous, still careful with money, still pompous, obstinate, self-important and impatient – also still courteous, caring and eager to help those in need. He was a good man in so many ways, in John's opinion, that the fact he had become addicted to… well, what had he become addicted to? Not crime, as such, but the *investigation* of crime, certainly.

Years previously, John's ex-wife Sally had briefly taken up skiing, and had insisted John join her on the slopes. This was after he'd come back from the War, and after she'd kicked the drink problem which had nearly ended their marriage. He'd not been keen on the idea, but he had been keen on doing what he could to bring them closer together, so he'd taken a few lessons and agreed to a holiday in the French Alps. The first day there, they'd hired skis and taken a chairlift to the top of the mountain, where Sally had immediately disappeared down the nearest slope. Not wishing to be left behind and desperate to show willing, John had launched himself after her, paying no mind to the sign which pointed out this was a black slope, designated as suitable only for experienced skiers.

The next five minutes had been amongst the most terrifying of his life. But while ninety-nine per cent of his very being had cried out in abject terror as he sped along crumbling snow at literally breakneck speeds, wobbling from side to side on his skis like a drunk man on an icy street, the remaining one per cent had been flooded with adrenaline. It had been utterly exhilarating.

That, he thought, was what Edward had got from their investigations into Madge Kenyon. A rush of something in his blood that made him feel more alive. A chance to kick off the shackles of his workaday life, to stop playing roles written by other people and to inhabit a role given meaning by his own actions.

And now he had fastened on the death of Nate Thompson as a new source of that adrenaline rush. Like a junkie consuming his drug of choice, Edward had found in murder a means of escaping from the world he lived in, and Thompson was simply a new fix.

"You think there's something for us to do?" he asked as casually as he could, disguising his misgivings by turning away and asking the barman for the same again.

"Well, of course I do." Edward's voice was as insistent and filled with excitement as John had feared it would be. "An old friend – albeit one you'd lost touch with, I grant you – has been brutally murdered not a mile from here, and we're in a position to investigate. In such circumstances, I hardly think we can turn the other cheek or pass by on the other side of the road."

"Can't we? I'd have thought that was exactly what we should do." The barman appeared at his elbow with their drinks, and John paid again, waving away any change that he might be due. "Unlike last year, the police seem quite on the ball. That inspector was pretty thorough, you have to agree?"

Edward nodded reluctantly. "He does seem to be more interested in the case than that fool we dealt with before – but, then again, he can hardly deny this is a case of murder." He tilted his glass in John's direction. His smile was one John recognised as signifying a degree of malicious pleasure. "And did I sense that he was a little suspicious of you? All those questions about who took over as Lear, and not knowing for sure when he was killed. Maybe we should begin by investigating you!"

He laughed, to show he wasn't being serious, but the inspector's words had bothered John.

"All very well to laugh," he protested, "but it's not you he was pointing a finger at!"

Edward stopped laughing and gave John a more serious look. "I wouldn't worry, he was obviously just fishing in the dark. No doubt, he was hoping someone would say something incriminating – it'd make things a lot easier for him if it turned out to be one of the company who killed Thompson – and, naturally, that's a possibility we should bear in mind, too. But as soon as he found out we'd just arrived, he must have known that whatever reason Thompson was killed for, it wasn't so that someone could steal his part."

John shrugged, unwilling to acknowledge that Edward was right. "Still, it does make me nervous, answering police questions. And I'm not sure that it's the best idea for you and I to go around sticking our noses into whatever they're up to. You remember last time – they can get a trifle upset about *civilian involvement*."

That was the phrase Inspector Ewing, the policeman leading the enquiry into the deaths caused by Madge Kenyon, had used, and he'd not meant it to be flattering. John doubted that Inspector Whyte would be any happier with their involvement.

"But in any case, what do you think we can do that the police can't? Last time, they made it clear they wouldn't be investigating further, so we did have to step forward. But it's not like that this time, is it? The theatre is positively swarming with policemen."

Edward fussed with his beer mat, squaring it up against the edge of the table, then twisting it around and doing the same thing on the other side. It was obvious to John that he was thinking of how best to phrase what he had to say next.

"What I think," he finally said, still looking down at his beer mat. "What I think is that Nathaniel Thompson was once a good friend of yours. I know that something came between you, and I have no interest in knowing what that was – but I wouldn't like to think you were the kind of man who would allow a spat from thirty years ago stop you from helping catch a murderer now." He cleared his throat and raised his head to look John as straight in the eye as their differing heights (even seated) allowed. "I wouldn't like to think that, and I don't believe it's true. You're not that sort of man, and you never will be."

John knew he was being manipulated – for God's sake, Don Roberts in his near dotage would have known he was being manipulated – but, at the same time, there was a ring of truth in what Edward had said. What Thompson had done had been unforgivable, but there was no forgiveness needed here, just doing what he could to bring a brutal killer to justice. There was that too, now he came to think about it – Sergeant Hickey had said that Thompson had been bludgeoned to death. Surely the sort of person who did that couldn't be trusted to stop at one killing? Perhaps he owed it to the rest of the company to help Edward (who, John was absolutely certain, would investigate on his own, even if John refused to assist him)? And it's not like they would be able to do much, not really.

Decision made – for now – John nodded once, firmly. "Very well, then. If you think there's something we can be doing which might help the police, then I'm willing to come along. But if it turns out the police don't need our help, or there's nothing for us to do, then I want your assurance that you'll let it go, and we won't do anything which might hinder the official enquiry."

Edward looked on the verge of protesting, but then he nodded in return and held out his hand. "It's a deal," he said. He picked up his empty glass and waited for John to drain the dregs from his before heading towards the bar to have them refilled.

John watched his retreating back and shook his head slightly. He really hoped he wouldn't come to regret his decision.

15

The pub closed at two, just as the rain went off. John and Edward stood outside the doors as the barman ushered them out, moving quickly to one side as the drunk who'd been sitting at the bar shoved past them.

"There's a hotel just up the road, lads, if you want to keep drinking," said the barman. "It's licensed all afternoon, even on a Wednesday." Edward shook his head, to John's very slight disappointment.

"Thank you, but we can't waste the entire day drinking. We've got work to do, you see."

The barman shrugged, uninterested, and closed the doors. They heard the sound of a key turning in a lock, and footsteps moving away inside the pub, then everything was quiet and they were standing alone in an empty street.

"So, where to begin?" Edward asked, rubbing his hands together. "I suggest we have a word with Mickey Fagan to start with, see if the police told him anything that he's kept to himself."

John looked sideways at the little man, but, really, there was nothing to be said. He'd told Edward he'd help, so he would. But it already sounded as though they were going to be sticking their noses into areas they were best advised to stay away from.

He remembered awkward interviews they'd carried out before, and wondered how many more he would be suffering through this time around.

* * *

It seemed that, though the police had been keen for the theatre to remain unused that day, they'd not actually seen fit to make much use of it themselves.

There was no tape around the doors, no little piles of white fingerprint powder on exposed surfaces, not even the tell-tale sound of flat feet thumping on the wooden floors as they searched the building.

In fact, the theatre was eerily quiet. *As the grave*, John thought, then regretted the choice of words. He led the way inside, past the box office and Alison Jago's little cubbyhole (both empty), down a corridor to Fagan's office (locked) and then back around and up two flights of stairs (deserted) to the rehearsal space. Mickey Fagan was sat on a folding backed chair, smoking a cigar and flicking the ash into his hand. Hearing the two men enter, he stood up and let the ash fall to the floor, then rubbed his hand on the leg of his trousers.

"Hello,' he said. His voice was flat, and the bags under his eyes seemed, if anything, to have grown in size in the past few hours, so they now hung down like pouches and John had the strangest sensation that, if he pressed them with his finger, he would feel water sloshing about inside. "I didn't expect to see anybody back today."

Edward was already moving across the room, pulling two more chairs from where they were stacked against the wall, and unfolding them beside Mickey's. He took a seat and gestured wordlessly for John to do likewise. Only when all three of them were seated did he explain what they'd come back for.

"We were wondering what the police said after we all left," he said. "John is an old friend of Sir Nathaniel's, and…"

"… the two of you were a big hit last year with the madwoman killing all those girls." Fagan blew air out of his cheeks and pinched the bridge of his nose. "So, no doubt you want to be involved in this one too. That's fine by me, so long as it doesn't impact on the time you need to be here rehearsing. To tell the truth, I don't care what you boys do in your own time, and if you think you can find something the police can't about whoever killed Nate, then more power to your elbow, I say."

Edward was pleased to find Fagan so obliging, though he objected to the characterisation of he and John as ghoulish thrill-seekers. He had thought the man might put up more resistance, but in truth Fagan looked exhausted and beyond caring. Knowing it was best to strike while the iron was hot, he pulled a notebook from his pocket, a new one, and prepared to write. "That's good to hear," he said. "Now then, did the police say anything that we don't already know?"

Fagan scratched his chin, put his cigar to his mouth, then realised it had gone out and lowered his hand. He stared at the unlit cigar for a moment then exhaled loudly again. "The police think it was a mugging that went wrong. That's their words, not mine. Nate's wallet was lying beside his body and all the cash was gone. They think the mugger forced him to hand it over and he fought back." He shuffled around in his seat so he could address both men at once. "If you were friends with Nate, you'll know that does sound like him. He was never the type to give anything up easily – and with a drink in him, he'd be even more likely to put up a fight."

"*Was* he drunk?" Edward asked.

"The police haven't officially said so, but at the time of night they're talking about, so close to his favourite pub, yeah, I'd be astonished if he wasn't. Plus, there's the size of him. Unless this mugger was a giant, he'd struggle to put Nate Thompson down when he was sober enough to defend himself properly."

John could bear witness to that. When they'd had their final falling out, it had almost come to fisticuffs, and he could still remember looking up at Thompson's face and wondering just how hard his massive fists would hit.

Edward, though, had picked up on something else. "Close to his favourite pub, you said? Which one is that? Was he in there that night? Did the police say exactly where – and when – he was killed?"

The flurry of questions seemed to confuse Fagan. He looked from John to Edward and back again, sucked futilely on his unlit cigar, then nodded slowly, as if he were unsure of the answers but willing to have a stab at answering them.

"Some time before five in the morning, they thought, but they couldn't be more exact. And they didn't tell me the exact address, either, but somewhere in Melbourne Street. That's not too far from the Spinning Wheel, a pub Nate drank in a lot, so no huge surprise there. I don't know if he was there that night, but you could ask the barman. It's not like Nate's easy to miss – or forget."

Edward noted down the name of the pub and the address. "Did the police say anything else?" he asked.

Fagan shook his head. "Not much. One thing they did say – this wasn't the inspector, it was one of his sergeants – was not to expect too much. Unless they caught a lucky break, muggers who just take money and leave anything more identifiable behind – rings and chains and the like – they don't often get caught."

"Surely they'll check for fingerprints, though? Appeal for witnesses?"

"They said they might, but the sergeant said that it was late at night in torrential rain, so there wasn't likely to be anybody about. Maybe they'll find something on the wallet, though."

His voice trailed off into silence. "Anyway, I need to be getting on with things, instead of hiding up here, feeling sorry for myself. The show must go on, isn't that right?"

He rose to his feet and walked towards the door. Halfway there he stopped, remembering something. "Oh, I forgot to say. Late start tomorrow, no need for you to show face until after lunch. That inspector asked me to come down to the station to look through some photos they've got of local criminals, see if I recognise any of them, check if they've been hanging around the theatre. God knows how long that'll take, but surely it'll be done by the afternoon."

"That's a point," Edward said. "Do you have any photographs of Sir Nathaniel?"

Fagan laughed. "I imagine there are about a million photographs of Nate in his old dressing room. I know the police have finished in there, so help yourself. One thing Nate was never shy about was handing out signed photos."

He half-heartedly waved goodbye and left Edward and John alone in the empty rehearsal room.

"We need to take a look in Nate's old dressing room," Edward pointed out as soon as the door closed behind Fagan. "We can use the excuse that we're looking for a photo of him, but there might well be something useful in there."

He waited for a minute, then crossed to the door and pulled it open, beckoning for John to follow him.

"Sorry, folks," Mickey Fagan's voice echoed from the bottom of the stairs. "I thought I'd lock everything up since there's just us left here." He met them halfway up the staircase and handed Edward a sheaf of photographs. "And, would you believe it, there was a pile of photos of Nate lying in the box office, so I picked up a few for you."

John wished he had a camera in order to capture the look of disappointment on Edward's face but, in its absence, he settled for ushering Edward out of the room. "That's very kind of you," he said with a smile, "Isn't it, Edward?"

Edward nodded. "Yes it is," he said, through obviously gritted teeth. "Very kind indeed."

Fagan trotted down the stairs ahead of them, but John felt a pull on his sleeve and slowed down so as to keep pace with Edward. "We can check the dressing room another time," the little man whispered. "But tomorrow morning I think we might have other things to do, eh?"

John nodded unhappily. He only hoped they'd visit the pub Nate might have been in before they had to go and examine the place he'd been murdered. He couldn't help thinking he'd need a drink or two.

16

The next morning was cold but dry. Mrs Galloway handed John the keys to her late husband's car with a warning to take good care of it. She also supplied a map of the area around the Playhouse – "The theatre had these printed back in the fifties, so it's a little bit out of date," she apologised – and a warning that the Spinning Wheel had a reputation as one of the rougher pubs in the city.

"I always tell my gentlemen not to go there," she said, looking doubtfully at the two men. "I've never been in myself, of course, but Mr Galloway used to say it was a den of thieves and hooligans."

John promised they would be careful, and with Edward navigating from the passenger seat, they drove off towards the pub.

* * *

To get to the Spinning Wheel, they had to drive past the

theatre. In spite of all that had happened the previous day, there were workmen on ladders at the front of the building, putting into place a large marquee. John pulled to the side of the road so they could see it better. It read:

SHAKESPEARE'S KING LEAR,
WITH THE STARS OF SMASH
BBC COMEDY FLOGGIT AND LEGGIT!

And below that, in only slightly smaller letters, STARRING JOHN LE BRETON & EDWARD LOWE, alongside blown-up images of their faces.

"Much better," Edward announced with satisfaction. "Though I worry Jimmy may have something to say about being billed below you and I."

Looking at him, John wasn't convinced Edward was too worried about that, though. He indicated right and pulled away from the kerb, back into the morning traffic.

* * *

They had some difficulty finding the Spinning Wheel, which John put down to Edward's surprising inability to read a map, and Edward blamed on John's inexplicable failure to follow simple instructions. Only after fifteen minutes of driving around the same half-dozen streets in an increasingly tedious loop did Edward notice a small blackboard at the corner of one building, pointing down an alleyway and directing potential customers to *The Spinning*

Wheel – Hot Food Served Sundays Only. There was no way the car would fit along the alley so John parked up and they walked the rest of the way, down what was little more than a narrow lane lined with metal dustbins and half-open doors from which steam, smoke, and strange and unappealing odours billowed in thin clouds.

The Spinning Wheel was exactly as unprepossessing as Mrs Galloway had suggested. From the outside, it was a perfectly square block of whitewashed cement, with a flat roof, a metal door and a solitary window, which was largely hidden behind a grid-like shutter. A sign sellotaped to the door announced that opening hours during the week were *10.00am to 2.00pm* and *6.00pm to 11.00pm.*

John looked at his watch. Five past ten. He took a step to the left and, with a deep and exaggerated bow, invited Edward to lead the way inside.

The door creaked alarmingly as Edward pushed it open, and then he disappeared into the gloom. For a moment, John stood alone in the alleyway, then a door opened somewhere in the street behind him and, with an alarmed skip which he was glad nobody could see, he quickly followed him inside.

* * *

The interior of the pub did not disappoint. Or rather it did, but only in the entirely expected sense that it was just as much of an eyesore as the exterior. The threadbare carpet was sticky enough to pull at the soles of John's shoes as he crossed the floor to the bar, and what light managed to make its way through the filthy window had a sickly brownish-yellow tinge to it which perfectly matched the nicotine-stained walls and ceiling. Mismatched plastic tables and chairs were dotted randomly about the room, wherever there was space. These provided the only seating, excepting three booths to the right of the door, one of which had a sign taped to its table saying *OUT OF ORDER*, presumably on account of the fire which appeared to have burned away most of one of its fake leather benches.

There were no stools at the bar. Edward was already standing there when John entered, tapping a coin on the counter in an attempt to rouse someone to serve him.

"The place seems deserted," he complained as John joined him. He looked around. "Though that's hardly a shock."

"Maybe we should pop back another time," John suggested. "When they've had a chance to clean up a little."

"This is as clean as it gets, mate."

The voice came from behind them. John turned and found himself face to face with a thick-set, middle-aged man in a short-sleeved shirt and jeans. Tattoos covered both his arms to the wrist. He had the name SANDY inked one letter at time on each finger of his right hand, which was currently held out in greeting. The same name was tattooed on his neck, the letters thin and spindly, like a spider's web.

Over his shoulder, John could see a toilet door swinging shut, which at least explained where he'd come from. For a moment, he'd thought he'd risen from the sticky floor, like some kind of heavily inked ghost.

"I'm Sandy," he said redundantly, exposing a mouth with more gaps than teeth. "I run this place."

Edward stared at him, clearly unsure how to react. John, however, had been thrown out of pubs and clubs across the length and breadth of the country, and in some foreign bars too, and he'd seen much worse than Sandy. He took the man's hand and shook it vigorously.

"Good morning, Sandy. I'm John and this is Edward, and we're after a couple of pints of mild and a quick chat about a pal of ours who used to drink here."

"Two pints it is, then. Take a seat and I'll bring them over."

He lifted a wooden hatch and went to pour their beer, while Edward picked the nearest table, placed a hand on a chair, winced slightly, then gingerly sat down. John, wishing he'd worn an old pair of trousers, followed suit and they sat there in silence until Sandy returned and pulled up a seat beside them.

"Right then, first things first. Are either of you police?"

Edward shook his head and gave the barman a scornful look. "Would we be having an alcoholic drink if we were policemen?"

"You'd be surprised. But if you're not police, what are you? I feel like I know you from somewhere, but we don't get a lot of folk come in the Wheel wearing suits, and I think I'd remember you if I'd seen you in here." Sandy tilted his head to one side, as though a change of angle would reveal their identities to him. No matter how he held it, though, there was no disguising the suspicion on his face. "No, I can't place you at all. You're not local, though, I can tell that much."

"We're actors, actually." Edward had clearly decided not to mess around, for which John was grateful. His seat was sticky and uncomfortable and wobbled this way and that as he moved. He could already feel his back beginning to protest. "We're starring at the Playhouse just now, but you might have seen us on a comedy on the television: *Floggit and Leggit.*"

The transformation in Sandy was instantaneous and complete. Where he'd been scowling before, his face now creased with pleasure and the two men were again given the dubious privilege of seeing his gap-toothed grin close up. "That's it!" he said, snapping his fingers and pointing at Edward. "You're the little fat bloke who runs the second-hand shop, and you're the lanky posh one who helps him out!"

John was happy enough with *lanky* and *posh* – he'd been called far worse by good friends and members of his immediate family – but he could see that Edward objected to *fat* even if he couldn't deny *little*. He visibly sucked his stomach in before replying, but thankfully said nothing in direct response to the description. "That's us," he said. "Edward Lowe and John Le Breton at your service."

Sandy was still grinning like he'd won the football pools. "First time we've had blokes off the telly in here," he said, shaking his head in wonder.

Edward, spotting his moment, pounced. "Actually, that's not quite true. And it's also why we're here. You see, we were told that our dear friend Sir Nathaniel Thompson was a regular in your establishment, and we were wondering when you'd seen him last?"

Sandy's grin was replaced by a look of puzzlement. "Sir Nathaniel? Pull the other one, why don't you – it's got bells on. Nah, we've never had a Sir Anything in here. More than our share of boys pissed as lords, but none of your actual sirs." He began to laugh then suddenly stopped, enlightenment crossing his face so obviously that it was almost comical. "Wait, do you mean big Natty? Massive bloke, must be six-five if he's a foot, talks posh like you." He pointed at John. "Likes a bevvy, got an eye for the girls. Red hair, late sixties maybe?"

The description was unmistakable, John thought. Add in "curses like a navvy" and it was Nate Thompson to the life.

"That's him," he said. "Do you perhaps remember when you last saw him in here?"

Sandy shook his head and grinned, still delighted to discover he'd been serving a knight of the realm. "That's easy enough. It's always hard to forget a night when big Natty's on the sauce. It was two nights ago. He was in here for a bit towards the end of the night, but he seemed like he'd already had a decent drink. He had a couple more and got into a bit of shoving match with one of the other regulars, then stormed off. Said he had other places he could get a drink."

"What time was that at?"

"About ten, or maybe half past – but I couldn't be more exact than that." Sandy was grinning again. "First two stars off the telly, then you tell me Natty's really Sir Natty! That's a hell of a lot for before eleven in the morning."

"And that was the last time you saw him?" Edward was insistent, uninterested in the barman's starstruck delight.

"Yeah. He wasn't in last night, but that's not unusual. He doesn't come in every night." He frowned suddenly, licked his lips nervously. "Why are you asking, though? Is he in trouble? I tell you, he's a boy for getting in trouble. Usually for getting a bit too familiar with other folk's girlfriends – yeah, and their wives – and not caring who knows it."

"Was that what happened the other night?"

"The other night? Oh yeah. No, it wasn't that, not that time. The guy he had a run in with, Cleland Waldie, he's got no girlfriend, never mind a wife." He laughed at the thought. "He's basically just a shaky old alky who comes in here when he's scraped enough together for a drink. He's a perfect match for Natty, though. There was nothing to it, in any case. Cleland spilled some of his pint on Natty and there was a bit of pushing and shoving – the usual stuff when two pissed-up big guys bump heads."

"Did you see which way Sir Nathaniel went when he left the pub?"

"Which way he went? Don't be soft. This place was jumping and there was just me and young Kathleen behind the bar. I didn't even see him leave, never mind see where he went afterwards. That's why I'm saying I can't be exact on the time. I served him about quarter to ten, because I happened to look at the clock, but then when I did the first shout for fifteen minutes to last orders at half ten, he was away. Sorry, I can't tell you more than that."

Edward looked across at John, silently inviting him to ask any questions he might have.

"Did Mr Waldie leave at the same time as Nate?" he asked.

Sandy shrugged. "No idea. Like I said, he comes in when he can afford a drink, but he only usually has enough for one or two. He does the rest of his drinking outside, down alleyways with the other alkies or up at the park. Now, is there anything else I can help you with, because I've got things to be getting on with."

John shook his head quickly. No, there was nothing. Edward shook his head, too, and handed Sandy a pound note for their drinks, which remained untouched on the table in front of them.

While Edward waited for the barman to come back with his change, he whispered fiercely to John. "So, Thompson left here, obviously already quite drunk, at ten twenty-five at the latest. He wasn't killed until sometime in the early morning, your policeman said. What was he doing between times?"

"And what about this Waldie character?" Having no answer, John answered the question with one of his own. "Do you think he could be our man? The barman did say he'd be a match for Nate in a fight."

"Perhaps. It's definitely something for us to look into."

He fell silent as Sandy returned with his change.

"Here you go," the barman said, but John wondered if the minute or so in which he'd been alone at the bar had caused him to rethink what he'd told them. All sign of jollity had gone from his face, and now he stared at them with the same suspicious expression he had shown earlier. "You never did say why you were asking after Natty. Or if he was in any kind of trouble."

Edward ignored the question. He took the handful of coins and walked towards the door without speaking.

John didn't have it in him to be so rude (though he knew Edward wouldn't consider it that way). "He's not in trouble, no. Not now," he explained, keen not to lie, but unconvinced that this sort of verbal gymnastics was any better, morally speaking. "We're just trying to trace his steps the other night."

He had intended to sound reassuring, but realised as he spoke that it sounded more like something the police might say. Seeing the barman's eyes narrow further, he waved a hasty goodbye and all but trotted out the pub door before he could ask any more questions to which he had no good answers.

17

"Well, that was interesting, wouldn't you say?" Edward said as soon as John joined him outside.

He was standing at the entrance to the alleyway, turning Mrs Galloway's fifties map this way and that as he tried to line up the streets it covered with the layout of the area twenty years later. Fortunately, most of the larger streets were unchanged.

"That way, I think," he continued, pointing to the left. He began to walk, knowing John would fall into step alongside him.

"Interesting how?" John asked, obviously preferring to let Edward take the lead, which suited him fine. John was a fine chap in many ways, but nobody would ever describe him as a born leader.

"Waldie, for one," Edward said, counting off each point on his fingers. "The missing time between Thompson leaving the pub and being killed, for two. And did you hear that barman say that Thompson had a reputation for playing about with other men's wives and girlfriends?"

"I did notice that, yes."

"That gives us two new motives for the killing, plus simple robbery." He frowned. "Between you and me, John, I'm not sure that's a wholly helpful development, really. I had hoped this morning would focus our attention, not widen the field. But we do need to find out more about this Waldie. It's possible he followed Thompson out of the pub, or perhaps bumped into him later in the evening, when both of them were even less capable of self-control. People can do the most awful things when they're drunk, and Inspector Whyte did say that it was a ferocious attack."

"I don't think he's going to check the police record on Waldie just because we asked."

"No, but we know a man who will, don't we?"

It took John a moment to realise who Edward meant. "Primrose? You mean Frank Primrose?"

Edward nodded emphatically. "Exactly! He owes us a favour, after all. He'd still be a constable if it wasn't for us! I'm positive he'll be more than happy to provide what assistance he can. I'll call him later."

John looked doubtful, which Edward often thought was his default expression. *Hangdog*, that was the word. As though the world had managed to disappoint him again by asking for something which couldn't possibly be done.

Whatever he was thinking, Edward gave him credit for keeping it to himself. Instead, he asked where they were going next, which showed an unexpected, but admirable, degree of enthusiasm, in Edward's opinion.

"Melbourne Street, of course," he replied, pointing

ahead of them. "It's up there somewhere. Not too far away, if this map is to believed."

* * *

It wasn't *too* far away, but, even so, Edward managed to get them lost twice before they eventually reached the street they sought.

Melbourne Street turned out to be a wide lane off the main road, lined on either side by narrow blocks of maisonettes, each entered via a shared stairwell with two flats per floor and three floors per block. Even from one end of the street, it was easy to tell in which block Nathaniel Thompson had been killed in.

Halfway along, two women stood in front of the entranceway. They had mops in their hands, with which they were scrubbing at the floor. A third woman, hidden from view, shouted something which Edward couldn't make out, then a tide of water sloshed out of the stairwell and into the street. The two mopping women, evidently forewarned, stepped out of the way just in time to avoid a soaking, then stepped forward again and redoubled their efforts. As Edward and John approached on foot, they looked up curiously.

"Good morning, ladies," John began in his most charming voice, but for once it seemed that nobody was buying what he was selling.

Quite literally, as it turned out.

"On your way, the pair of youse," the nearest woman said, waving her mop in their direction, so a few drops of dirty water spun in John's direction and he was forced to make a hasty retreat.

"Aye, be off with you," said the second woman in an Irish accent, glowering in their direction as though they'd accused her of keeping a dirty house. "Can you not see we're busy? We've no time for lads like you two, whatever it is you're selling, no matter how smooth you think you are."

"You can see we've got plenty of mops and buckets already," the first woman added, "and we've got a good church just down the road. So, if you're Jehovahs, you're wasting your time."

Edward wasn't sure which was more offensive – the idea that they might be door-to-door brush salesmen, or the suggestion that they were Jehovah's Witnesses. He hurried to correct the misapprehension. "No, no, we're not here to sell you anything. We're actually looking into the death of a friend of ours. We believe he was killed in this street two nights ago."

The change in the women was instantaneous. What had been hostility changed at once to concern. The unseen third woman appeared from inside, still holding a bucket full of water. She placed it carefully on the ground and joined her friends in the entranceway.

"Sorry for your loss," she said perfunctorily. "It happened right here," she went on with far more animation. "On this very spot!" She tapped the other women on their shoulders and, as one, they stepped out of the way, inviting the two men inside. "Watch your feet there, we've been cleaning the mess, and it's sodden."

Edward edged past the women, but John stood still, staring into the passageway. As Edward followed the line of his gaze, he realised why he hadn't moved.

The floor was as wet as the women had said but, about ten feet in, along the left-hand wall and in a semi-circle on the cement below it, the ground was dyed a deep red. Radiating out from the wide central stain, long, thin threads of red spattered in every direction, like someone had tripped and dashed a tin of paint against the concrete.

The women had done what they could and, other than the ugly red blemish, the stairwell was spotlessly clean. All Edward could smell was bleach, but there was no mistaking the mark for anything but what it was: a good deal more of Nathaniel Thompson's blood than he could afford to have lost.

"Was it one of you ladies who found him?" Edward stepped gingerly around the puddles of pink water until he stood on the far side of the stain.

"It was my Bert," the third woman said with a shudder. "He'd just left for work – he works at the baker's – and he came running back inside, white as a sheet, and said there'd been a slaughter in the stair."

"That was his exact words," the Irish woman agreed. "Maisie came right up to ours, on account of us getting the phone put in last year, and asked us to phone 999 and get the police out. 'There's been a *slaughter*,' she said."

"What time was that at, Mrs…?"

"Winslow," the second woman said. "And I was just up to get Stan's breakfast ready, so it'd have been just after half five."

"But there was nothing there at one, when I put Mr Snookums out," the first woman, who'd been silent since her initial warning, offered out of the blue.

"I'm sorry," Edward said, confused. "Mr Snookums? Is that your husband?"

She laughed and the other women joined in. Edward was reminded of the three witches from *Macbeth*. "Lord, no. I'm not married," she said. "Mr Snookums is my cat. He likes to spend the night out patrolling, so I put him out before I go to bed. And I'd heard the national anthem and then read my book for a bit, so it must have been about one in the morning when I let him into the stair. And there was nothing there then." She pointed behind Edward at the nearest door. "That's my place there, so I'd have seen if anybody had been here."

Edward wasn't sure if she was saying *anybody* or *any body* but he supposed it made no difference. What did matter, though, was that they'd narrowed down the time at which Thompson had been killed. Odd, though, that this new evidence pushed the time of his death later, rather than bringing it forward. After hearing he'd left the pub at half ten, he'd expected that they'd find he'd been killed fairly soon afterwards. He remembered the question he'd asked John in the Spinning Wheel. *What had the dead man done after leaving the pub?*

John, though, had had another thought. With a start, Edward realised he was pointing back down the street and talking in a low voice with Mrs Winslow. With infinite care, he picked his way through the bloodstained water and joined them, looking in the direction John was pointing.

At the far end of the street, the opposite end to the way they'd entered, he could see a wide belt of green. He glanced quickly at the map he still held in his hand: *Lovell Park,* it read. Towering high-rise flats enclosed the far end of the park, but the part nearest them looked quite pleasant, Edward thought.

"So that's all that's up there?" John was saying. "North Street – and that's all shops – and the park?"

"Shops and empty buildings, that's all there is on North Street," Mrs Winslow replied. "And the park, though I wouldn't want to walk through there on my own at that time of night." She sighed and gestured to the other women for support. "It used to be lovely round here, didn't it? But then they built those skyscrapers on the other side of the park and, before you knew it, all sorts were hanging about there. The police come and move them on, now and again, but they just come back as soon as they're gone."

"All sorts?" John asked.

"Gangs of young lads, standing about smoking and drinking. Tramps sleeping on the benches. And much worse than that, Stan says. Grown men getting up to God knows what in the bushes too, he reckons." She shook her head firmly. "You wouldn't get me going up there at night."

Edward pulled at John's elbow and led him to one side. "What are you thinking? There's nothing to be found here. The blood's in the process of being washed away but the police obviously took anything that was lying about in the stair."

John pulled at his earlobe, thoughtfully. "I was just wondering what Nate was doing here. The pub's that way, you see." He turned one-hundred-and-eighty degrees and pointed back the way they'd come. "The theatre's on the other side of that, and you said Peter Glancy mentioned Nate's house being near our digs, so that's even further in that direction. So where was he going when he was attacked halfway along this street, walking *away* from everywhere you'd expect him to be walking *towards*?"

"You think he was going towards the park?"

"In that direction, yes. It might not be the park, necessarily."

Edward glanced at the map, but it didn't even have the high-rises on it, so he doubted it would be much use in pinpointing anywhere Thompson might have been going.

They would have to check for themselves.

18

Melbourne Street joined the much busier North Street at a T-junction at the end of the road. John and Edward crossed at a zebra crossing and soon found themselves walking through the park, with no particular aim in mind, but keeping an eye out for anything unusual.

That covers quite a lot, Edward thought ten minutes later, as what had started out as a promising morning of investigation threatened to turn into merely a nice day out. He told himself that they had achieved a great deal already, regardless of whether John's hunch paid off or not. *A suspect, a better time for the killing and the possibility that Thompson had been going somewhere he shouldn't* – that was more than he could possibly have expected when they'd left their digs a few hours earlier.

The thought of time passing made him look down at his watch. Nearly eleven thirty. They would need to head back to the car soon if they were to be at the theatre for afternoon rehearsals. All they had seen so far in the park were a pair of squirrels (grey, not red, to Edward's disappointment), a large, black patch of burned ground where (if the empty bottles of cider were any indicator) teenagers had been drinking, and a children's playground where more teenagers sat on the swings and sullenly watched them pass.

He was about to suggest that they call it a day when John stopped in his tracks and pointed towards a line of trees. "That's an odd place for houses, don't you think?" he said.

Through the trees, Edward picked out a row of low buildings, seemingly located in the centre of the park. He hesitated for a moment, but decided they could spare five minutes to check them out and, with a nod to John, tramped across the grass towards the trees.

The houses were in fact a row of bungalows, standing alongside a narrow road which ended at the final house but snaked off into the park and, presumably, exited onto the main thoroughfare somewhere nearby. Each house was identical – a small garden to the front and rear, two large bay windows facing the road and a red door set back in a deep porch with a peculiar round entrance, which put Edward in mind of hobbit holes in the Tolkien books.

There was nobody about, and no particular reason to think there was anything for them to see, but the houses were mildly unusual, he supposed, and they were quite… secret wasn't quite the word. Hidden, perhaps, shielded as they were by the line of trees on one side and, to the front, by a small hill which largely obscured the bulk of the high-rise flats on that side of the park.

Slowly, they walked along the road, peering into gardens as surreptitiously as they could manage. At this time of day, everyone was likely to be at work, and Edward felt emboldened to quickly step along one garden path and peer in the windows.

"Just what you'd expect," he told John when he rejoined him on the street. "A three-piece suite, children's toys, some clothes lying about. A typical family home, I'd say."

"Perhaps we shouldn't be spying into people's sitting rooms?" John suggested.

"Hardly spying. More like checking if…"

"Can I help you?"

For the second time that day, Edward found himself being unexpectedly addressed by someone behind him.

The speaker was curly-haired and short, his head barely clearing the top of the hedge from which it had just popped up. John and Edward watched wordlessly as the head bobbed along the hedge until its owner reached the end and stood in the street next to them.

"Howard Dyche," he said, politely enough, though Edward noted he didn't offer his hand. "I live at number two. Can I help you with anything?"

Generally speaking, Edward liked to think of himself as an honest man. He had, to the best of his knowledge, never broken the law. But he was not above a bit of impersonation in a good cause. He was an actor, after all.

"I hope you can, sir," he said, dredging up from his memory the voice he'd used when playing a military policeman in an episode of *Redcap* and hoping that the man didn't recognise either of them. "My colleague and I are detectives working for the National Fraud Squad and we're looking for this man. I wonder if you've seen him around?"

He showed the man the photograph of Thompson they'd taken from his dressing room. It was the least theatrical one they could find – Sir Nathaniel, in a jacket and tie, leaning against some kind of sports car – and Fagan had confirmed it had been taken recently.

Dyche pulled a pair of glasses down from their resting place on top of his head and examined the photograph carefully.

"Why, yes," he said. "That's Mr Thompson. He lives at number six, at the other end of the row." He whistled softly. "I'm not surprised he's in trouble, you know. He's only here one or two nights a week, and I've often seen young women going in and out at odd times – late at night and first thing in the morning. We like to keep ourselves to ourselves here in the Row, but you can't help noticing that kind of thing."

"Are you at home a lot?" Edward asked, wondering just how early Dyche had to get up to notice women leaving first thing.

"Oh, all the time. I'm a writer, you see, so I'm here all day working on my biography of Denton Welch. That takes up all my time... such a fascinating man."

"I'm sure," Edward said hurriedly, before John could speak. He'd been caught before in one of John's interminable discussions about jazz trumpeters and drummers and whatever else, and he wasn't risking another one now. "Number six, you say? I assume Mr Thompson's not at home now?"

Dyche shook his head, as Edward had known he would. "No, I don't think so. I've not seen him for nearly a week, actually."

Edward thanked the man and, with a nod to John, walked down to number six.

It was a house exactly like the others, but the garden had been allowed to run wild. Dandelions covered the lawn like spots of spilled paint, and something had dug under one of the hydrangea bushes, knocking the large plant onto its side and pressing its flowers into the dirt. The windows too, when Edward tried to peer through them, were coated with a thin layer of dirt which blocked much of the view inside. A light in one corner might have been a fish tank, Edward thought, but otherwise it was impossible to make anything out.

John had wandered round the side of the house, but he was soon back.

"There's a metal fence, with a locked gate in it. Must be ten foot high if it's an inch." He gestured down at his trousers. "I wasn't risking ripping my trousers just to examine some chap's back garden." He glanced past Edward, towards the front door. "Hello," he said, "what's this?"

Sticking out of the letterbox was a corner of pale cream paper. John pulled it free and held it out for Edward to see.

"It's a newsletter for a local church," he said, pointing to a handwritten name in the top corner of the mimeographed sheet. "And it's addressed to 'Thompson / Number 6.'"

During the previous year's investigations, there has been one or two memorable occasions when Edward had felt the warm glow which came from a puzzle piece falling into place. Now, as he took the newsletter from John and checked the name, he felt the same elation.

He wasn't sure what it meant yet, but this was definitely something, even if the something it was wasn't at all clear.

"That's the kind of thing that's bound to get Whyte interested," John said, cutting across his thoughts. "It proves he was keeping something secret, at least."

"True enough, as far as it goes." Edward held up a finger and raised an eyebrow. "But is it enough?"

John looked confused. "Not enough how?"

"Well, say we give this to the inspector. What does it actually prove? That someone called Thompson stays at a house in the park. There's nothing to link it to Sir Nathaniel particularly."

"That man Dykes or whatever his name was, he identified Nate from his picture."

"A man he said he barely ever saw, and who he's obviously never spoken to. It's hardly conclusive, is it?"

"I suppose not," John conceded.

"Better to keep it to ourselves for now, until we have more to pass on to the inspector."

Edward couldn't say even to himself why he was so keen to keep information from Whyte. Perhaps it was still the lingering effects of their last investigation, in which the authorities had only hampered them, but for whatever reason he felt sure they needed to keep this discovery to themselves.

They had Thompson's funeral the next day but, once that was out the way and they'd made more concrete progress, perhaps then they could speak to Whyte.

19

Theatrical funerals, in John's experience, could go one of two ways.

Either the deceased was beloved by all who knew him, liked a drink, a lady and a party, and was survived by a crowd of pals who knew exactly how the old bugger would like to be remembered. In which case, the day would be a triumphant celebration, full of singing and tall tales, with a bar bill sufficiently enormous to put a crew of sailors on shore leave to shame.

Or, alternatively, the dead bloke was an unlikeable old sod, who'd pissed off pretty much everyone he'd ever met, with such mourners as he had at his final performance made up of those obliged to attend by the temporary happenstance of a currently shared place of work, plus perhaps an ex-wife or two keen to make sure the coffin lid was screwed on nice and tight. Cue a small plate of limp triangular sandwiches and a cup of weak tea balanced on your knee in a church hall somewhere, while the vicar surreptitiously looked at his watch and wondered when you'd all be on your way.

Sir Nathaniel Thompson's funeral was of the latter sort. The fact the police had released his body so quickly for burial felt like a sign that absolutely everyone was keen to get him in the ground.

It didn't help that it was almost, but not quite, raining. Instead of the honesty of a proper downpour, which would at least have meant that umbrellas could be deployed, moisture seemed to hang in the air, unmoving, like a cloud of tiny hovering insects, each one of which burst upon impact with jacket or trouser leg in a minuscule watery explosion. Standing completely still seemed to be the only way to avoid becoming drenched, but John was sixty-seven next birthday and, though he could remember spending hours at attention in his army days, remember was all he could do now. The spirit was willing enough, but the flesh was attached to creaky bones and tired old muscles, and he was afraid that he visibly wobbled when asked to stand up for too long.

He hitched up the collar of his jacket, wincing as the sodden fabric settled against his neck, and glanced around at the handful of other people stood by the grave.

Edward, as expected, was standing with his hat in his hands and his head bowed. The wet air had coated his exposed scalp with a sheen of moisture which trickled down into his face. As though feeling John's eyes on him, he looked up and peered across the grave through rain-streaked glasses and nodded glumly.

He was, however, one of the few mourners reflecting the solemnity of the occasion, for all that he knew the deceased least well of them all. To be fair, Mickey Fagan – who had known Nate Thompson for almost as long as John had himself – also stood with his head lowered, rubbing the sole of his shoe across the torn grass at the side of the grave. Peter Glancy, on the other hand, kept glancing past the vicar towards the relative warmth of the church. Monica Gray was talking in an undertone to her husband; from the way his hands were drumming on his trouser leg, he was not enjoying what she had to say. Everyone else simply looked bored.

Behind this first row of mourners – and John suddenly realised that none of Thompson's ex-wives had made an appearance – was a thin layer of fans, studded here and there with what could only be journalists, hunched into the collar of their raincoats, scribbling who knew what in damp notebooks, and occasionally wiping the lenses of their cameras for long enough to take a quick snap of the crowd around the grave. *Bloody vulture*s, John thought, and hoped they could see the distaste on his face.

As he scanned the rest of the crowd, he made out the face of Inspector Whyte at the back, standing some distance behind the last of the other mourners, his hat pulled low against the rain but still instantly recognisable. He was looking away from the graveside, but, as he turned back, he caught John's roving eye and nodded. John held up an awkward hand in reply, then let it fall back to his side, realising the action could be misconstrued as waving.

The sound of sudden loud sobbing made him twist his head around. Judy Faith had slumped against the shoulder of Jimmy Rae and let out such a wail of grief and pain that John involuntarily took a step back, his unconscious reminding him that he was not at his best with emotional women. Alice Robertson stepped across and put an arm around Judy, pulling her in close and muffling her sobs in her own tartan tweed coat.

The vicar stopped his droning for a second to ask if Judy was alright, and only when Alice nodded on her behalf did he go on, mercifully bringing the service to a conclusion just as the first drops of actual rain began to fall.

"Finally, Mr Fagan has asked me invite everyone to the Rochester Hotel for food and refreshments," said the vicar. "There's no bus, but I believe there should be enough cars to take everyone who wishes to attend."

He closed his Bible and turned away from the grave. The mourners – Judy, still leaning on Alice Robertson for support, towards the front – followed him in silent procession back to the church (or, more specifically, to the church car park). John fell into step alongside Jimmy Rae, chatting in quiet voices about an upcoming horse race for which Jimmy had a sure-fire tip, and was back on the tarmac of the car park before he noticed Edward hadn't joined them.

He looked back at the grave through the increasingly heavy rain and made out Edward's back trudging in the opposite direction, away from the church. He wondered if he should go after him, but he knew by now that sometimes his friend liked to be alone. Besides, it was unpleasantly wet now, so instead he sheltered in the church doorway with Jimmy and pulled out a cigarette.

He'd barely got it lit when Inspector Whyte joined them.

"Afternoon, gents," he said, lighting a cigarette of his own. "It's always one of the least pleasant parts of my job, going to funerals. And weather like this doesn't help." He waved towards the small crowd of cars now leaving the car park. "To be honest, I'd have expected more people for the funeral of a big star like Sir Nathaniel Thompson."

"It's because it's in Lancashire," Jimmy explained. "He was born near here, I heard, and always said he wanted to be buried nearby. That's why he was at the Playhouse, I reckon. Wanted to be close to home as he got older, or something."

"And the funeral being in Lancashire means that not so many people attend?" The inspector, a Lancashire man through and through if his accent was any indication, sounded offended.

"Too far to travel for a lot of people," said Jimmy. "And he wasn't half as well-known as he used to be. Well, he wouldn't have signed on at the Playhouse if he was still getting offers from Hollywood, now, would he?"

"Have you heard anything, Inspector?" John asked suddenly, knowing Edward would expect him to quiz the policeman while he had the opportunity. "Has any progress been made on the case?"

Whyte eyed him suspiciously. "We've had one or two tests back, yes. But nothing that's likely to be of interest to civilians, though."

Whyte finished his cigarette, and flicked it into the rain,

where it fizzled out in a puddle. "Time I was off," he said. "No rest for the wicked – or for those paid to catch them."

John thought he heard a tiny emphasis on the word "paid", but he took the inspector's outstretched hand and shook it.

"Give my regards to Mr Lowe," Whyte said over his shoulder as he walked towards his car.

"Of course," John replied. The mention of Edward reminded him that he was still somewhere in the grounds, presumably getting soaked.

He considered going to look for him, but Edward knew there was a buffet being put on at the Rochester. He wouldn't want to miss that.

He lit another cigarette and asked Jimmy to tell him more about the wonder horse he'd mentioned.

20

Edward stood beneath a tree on the low hill which pressed up against the wall on the north side of the cemetery. The rain had begun to fall more heavily now, and he was wondering if he should have gone straight to the Rochester, rather than wandering off like this. He wasn't even sure why he'd done so. An irritation at the carry-on at the grave side, perhaps – the young girl Judy wailing like a banshee about someone she barely knew. Or maybe it was a more general annoyance at the lack of respect the rest of the Playhouse company had paid the dead man. He'd not known Thompson at all, but he knew how to conduct himself at a funeral. Whatever it was, he'd suddenly had no desire to be in their company any longer, and remembering the pretty little hill he'd seen on his way in, he'd decided to stretch his legs and clear his head by walking up to it.

Which was a mistake, he now realised.

Heavy raindrops like little water balloons dropped into an ornamental pond at the base of the hill, making the water ripple in a dozen different interconnecting circles. Oddly, the rain, though heavy in terms of individual drops, was not a solid wall of water. In fact, as he looked down the hill towards the car park, the view entirely unimpeded by the downpour, he had the strangest feeling that, if he could only run fast enough and zigzag a little, he could avoid every drop and get to a car without getting wet at all.

"Fat chance of that," he grumbled to himself, the mere thought of running down the hill to the car park enough to give him chest pains.

There were still a few cars parked down there and, at the point at which the tarmac gave way to grass, a figure he was certain was John was standing, peering in his general direction. Just then, a rumble of thunder acted as a prologue to a sudden darkening of the sky and the rain began to fall in earnest. Now there was no chance of reaching a car without being soaked.

As the rainfall increased, visibility decreased in equal measure, until John, the cars, and even the church itself disappeared behind a grey curtain of falling water. Thunder crackled again, and Edward realised with a start that, though there had been no lightning yet, a tree on top of a hill was probably not the ideal place to be during a storm. With a grunt of effort and a grimace of anticipated discomfort, he forced himself to step out from beneath its protection and into the deluge.

As was sometimes the case with thundery weather, the world became eerily quiet as he tramped slowly downhill. Even the sound of the rain hitting the ground was muted by the thick grass carpet on which he walked, but as he took one wet step after another, he began to wonder if he could hear… *something*.

Was that another squelching footstep he'd just heard behind him? He looked quickly over his shoulder, but visibility was as bad up the hill as down, and all he could see was rain. There was no particular reason to fear anyone else up here, of course; they had just as much right to take in the view from the highest spot in the area as he did. So why did he have the strangest feeling deep in his gut, an anxiety he could taste in his mouth as the bitter flavour of soured wine?

"Hello?" he said into the rain, but without breaking stride or even turning his head again. *Best not to risk taking a tumble*, he thought to himself, then wondered why he was so nervous of being slowed down. "Is there anybody there?"

This time he was sure he heard a footstep, slightly out of sync with his own. "Hello?" he said again, more loudly this time, his pace increasing without any conscious decision having been made in his head.

There! A cough, he was sure of it. Muffled, but clear enough in the thundercloud-blanketed air. There was someone behind him, someone who wasn't speaking, someone who was following him.

He realised he was almost running now, felt his chest contract painfully as he tried to drag fast breaths into lungs unused to physical exercise. Behind him, the damp pad of his pursuer kept pace with him. The rain stung his face like hail, soaking his clothes and shoes. His hat fell from his head and he left it behind.

He fumbled in his pocket as he stumbled across the uneven ground, desperate for something to use as a weapon, but there was nothing, just his cigarettes and lighter and some loose change.

The rain came down like sheets of water, and the clouds grumbled above him.

The ornamental pond passed by on his right, and the sight of it gave extra strength to his tiring legs. Not far to the church now. Not far to safety.

And then he stepped into a shallow puddle and, with an agonising gasp, his foot slipped too far forward and he fell, unable to keep his balance on the wet turf. He thrust his hands out instinctively, and prevented himself falling any further than his knees, but, even so, he knew there was no chance he would be able to right himself and get back to his feet before his pursuer was on him.

"Why are you doing this?" he asked, pushing himself around, attempting at least to face in the right direction. "What do you bloody want from me?"

For a moment, Edward thought he made out the shape of a man in the rain, a silhouette only slightly darker than the grey background which framed it, and then a familiar drawl rang out from behind him.

"To get you out of this rain before you catch your death, for a start," John said. "What have you been doing, you silly fool?"

Edward blinked in surprise, and by the time he reopened his eyes the figure, if it had ever been there, was gone. He shuffled round on the grass and took his friend's outstretched hand.

"Don't you think you're getting a trifle long in the tooth for running down hills like Heathcliff on the moors?" John asked with a frown. "You could have done yourself an injury, and all to avoid a bit of rain."

Edward struggled to his feet, as John pointed back the way he'd come. "Jimmy Rae's got the heater on in his car, and there's a pint and a sausage roll waiting for us at the wake." He frowned. "We might need to stop off at Mrs Galloway's and pick up some dry clothes for you. You really are *completely* drenched, old chap."

As Edward peered back up the hill, the lightning finally made an appearance, a single quick camera flash which illuminated the entire area for a moment. In some ways, he would have liked to see a mysterious figure picked out against the skyline, proof that someone had been tracking him through the storm. But there was nobody there, just a second-long flare of white on grey, and the hill and the pond and the tree and nothing else.

Could he have imagined it?

He blinked again and considered the curtain of driving rain, then nodded in agreement. "I've no idea what came over me," he said, unwilling to admit that he'd allowed his imagination to get the better of him. "I thought I saw the cars leaving and didn't want to miss my lift."

John chuckled, but also gave him a strange look, as though not entirely convinced.

Edward shrugged, smiling equally unconvincingly.

"Come along now," he said, taking John by the elbow and guiding him towards the car park. "If we're much later to the wake, all that'll be left of the buffet will be egg and cress sandwiches and some cheese straws."

21

It did Edward's heart good to hear Primrose's voice at the other end of the phone line. For some reason he'd never been able to pin down, he liked the boy, even if only his mother would ever claim the young policeman was anything other than a blithering idiot.

"Hello, Mr Lowe," the thin voice said uncertainly. "What's it like in Bolton? Are you keeping safe? Are there gangs everywhere? I bet there are."

Frank Primrose, the sole policeman for the little town of Ironbridge, had spent his entire life in the corner of Shropshire where he now worked, and had been known to describe a drive to the nearby town of Telford as a "trip to the city". He was not well-travelled, and viewed Edward and John's stint in Bolton as only slightly less cosmopolitan than (and about as hazardous as) a residency in New York. Quite how he had come to this conclusion, Edward had never been able to work out, but a lifetime of reading boys' comics and a fondness for BBC2 documentaries had somehow convinced him that everything north of Shropshire was a battle-scarred hinterland of street toughs and industrial decay.

Edward had intended to phone Primrose the previous evening, when he and John returned from Thompson's wake, but one drink had turned into another, and before they knew it, it was far too late to telephone anyone. Fortunately, he knew that Primrose spent every Saturday afternoon in the police station, catching up with paperwork in a mild panic.

"Not as many as you might think," Edward reassured him on the subject of Lancashire gangs. "Hardly any at all, in fact."

He could hear the doubtful tone in Primrose's voice. "You wouldn't catch me going there." His voice brightened suddenly. "Did you hear that I might be getting a car? It's not decided yet, but since I'm a sergeant, they think I probably shouldn't be on a bike all the time."

Every time Edward remembered Primrose was now a sergeant, he felt a little bit of his faith in mankind slip away.

True, his recent promotion had largely come about due to Edward and John, after Primrose had been fortunate enough to spot John being held at gunpoint in Madge Kenyon's car the previous year. Even so, it beggared belief that the authorities were so blind as to think he would make a good senior officer. This was a man who had, on more than one occasion, managed to lock himself to his own bicycle.

Still, his new eminence meant he would presumably be in a far better position to help them than would otherwise have been the case.

"What it is, is that we – Mr Le Breton and I, that is – were wondering if you could do us a tiny favour?"

"Anything for you, Mr Lowe."

"Right, do you have a pencil there?"

"Uh huh."

"Well then, for reasons which I won't go into here, we need any information you can give us about a Mr Cleland Waldie. He lives in Bolton, but we don't have an address. It might even be that he sleeps rough. Anything you can find out on the man would be very helpful." He paused to allow Primrose to write the name down. "I know it's not much to go on, but he does have an unusual first name, at least, so that should help."

Even across the crackly phone line, Edward could hear the uncertainty in Primrose's voice. "I'll do what I can, but I can't promise anything, Mr Lowe. When they made me up to sergeant they said I wasn't to get carried away, and that... *promotions on the back of letters to the editor were a bloody nonsense.*"

Edward could tell from the pause he'd left, that Primrose was quoting something he'd memorised, a habit he had exhibited before when something had annoyed him. It was a trait they'd used to their advantage at times.

"Is that what they said, was it? Damn cheek, if you ask me. Why, if it wasn't for your eagle-eyed attention to duty, John might have been killed, and me along with him. You're a lifesaver, there's no other word for it. And if that's not cause for a promotion, I don't what is."

The sound Primrose made on the other end of the line

was a cross between a choked cough and an exaggerated gulp. "Golly. A lifesaver. That's very kind of you to say, Mr Lowe."

"I don't say it lightly... eh, Frank. And now you've been given your more-than-justified reward, I'm sure you have access to all sorts of information which might be of use to... well, all sorts of people."

John had suggested once they underestimated Primrose, but Edward had brushed that off as a quite natural instinct to disbelieve anyone could really be as dim as the policeman sometimes appeared. But perhaps there was something in what he said because, instead of offering to get the information on Waldie that Edward had asked for, Primrose made a *hmmm* sound and left the line otherwise silent for a moment.

"What exactly do you need this information for?" he asked, sounding far more like a proper policeman than Edward cared for.

It crossed Edward's mind briefly to lie, to come up with some clever but plausible excuse, but the problem was that he couldn't think of anything to say other than the truth. Lying – as opposed to playing a role – was not something which came easily to him. A good thing, of course, and a sign of a sound moral compass, but inconvenient at times.

"A friend of Mr Le Breton's has been found murdered near the theatre, and we've reason to believe that this Waldie might be involved."

"Oh, why didn't you say that at the beginning?" Primrose asked, any reluctance in his voice gone, to be replaced by the boyish eagerness Edward remembered from their previous investigation. "Leave it with me, Mr Lowe. I'll make some calls" – Edward could picture the delight on the boy's face as he said this – "and be back in touch with whatever I find out."

"I'd be very much obliged if you would. Perhaps you could also see if you can rake up anything on the dead man? Sir Nathaniel Thompson, his name is – *was*, rather. We're away rehearsing during the day, but you can leave a message on this number with our landlady, Mrs Galloway, or telephone in the evening, when we're likely to be in."

Edward read out the telephone number of their digs and waited while Primrose wrote it down and repeated it back. Then, after five minutes of catch-up on events in Ironbridge – mainly revolving around someone tipping cows over in their fields and a mysterious hooligan spray-painting offensive slogans on the police station wall – he hung up, and went to tell John what Primrose had said.

22

Edward had arranged to meet John in the Blue Blazer after speaking to Primrose. When he got there, he was a little annoyed to see Jimmy Rae sitting at the table, too, his jacket over the back of his chair, cigarettes on the table and a pint just started in his hand. Obviously, his was not a flying visit.

"I got chatting to Jimmy in the green room, and he mentioned that Mickey Fagan had told him we were investigating Nate's murder," John explained as soon as Edward came back from the bar. "He's keen to help if he can and, well, we're neither of us as young as we used to be, and I thought maybe we could use a bit of muscle."

He laughed at this description, and at Jimmy, who stood up and struck a series of improbable bodybuilder poses in his shirt-sleeves.

"All muscle, that's me," he said, taking his seat again, blithely ignoring the odd looks he'd received from a couple of the pub's regulars. That was Jimmy to a tee, Edward thought – an exhibitionist and a practical joker, with no conception of the effect his tomfoolery had on those around him, and no concern about how it made him look.

"But seriously," the young man went on, "I'd like to help if I could. I remember the pair of you last year, and I wish I'd offered then. But you know how it was – nobody was really sure what you were up to half the time and, by the time we realised you were onto something, well, it was basically all over."

Edward took a long drink of his beer, buying time while he thought of a polite way to brush Jimmy off. He'd just decided to tell him they were winding things down, that they'd found nothing out and that Inspector Whyte seemed more than capable of carrying out the investigation himself, when Rae leaned forward like a Russian agent in a downmarket spy movie and tapped the side of his nose.

"Don't worry about filling me in, either. John's already told me what you've been up to. The nutter Nate was fighting in the pub, the bungalow in the park, the mysterious ladies in the night… It sounds an absolute gas!"

In spite of himself, Edward glowed with pleasure as Jimmy listed the progress they'd made already (he assumed from context that "gas" was a positive thing). "It's been gratifying how much we've been able to find out already, it's true," he said seriously. "But it is early days, of course."

Jimmy grinned, showing crooked teeth stained by the constant stream of cigarettes he smoked. "And what did Frankie boy have to say?" he laughed.

"Frankie…? Oh, you mean Primrose?" He hesitated for a second, but clearly John had told Jimmy everything, so there was little point in prevarication. "He's promised to check on Mr Waldie and see what he can unearth."

Jimmy nudged Edward in the side with his elbow and winked. "With a bit of luck it'll be another serial killer, eh?"

Edward smiled politely, but already he was regretting bringing Rae into their confidence. He lacked the necessary discretion and had a distinctly coarse sense of humour.

What he said did resonate in one way, though. Obviously – *obviously* – one murder was one death too much, and equally obviously, he'd hate for anyone else to die. But a tiny part of him did think they would do better this time if Thompson's death turned out to be only the first. Last year, they'd caught the killer, but couldn't really say they'd saved anyone. Given the chance again, though…

Edward's musings were interrupted by John's snort of derision. "You're genuinely thinking about it, aren't you? You find the idea appealing, for God's sake! A couple more deaths, just to make it more interesting!"

Edward attempted to defend himself, but it was difficult when he *had* just been considering it. Still, the suggestion that he'd be happy for more people to die was an outrageous one, and when John went on to insist that Thompson had more than likely just been mugged, in the face of all the evidence they had so carefully gathered, he reacted with scorn of his own.

"Don't be ridiculous. You can't seriously believe he was killed where he was, on the way back to his love nest, having been involved in a fight earlier that evening?"

John's face was as flushed with anger as he'd ever seen it. "I'm not saying that's *definitely* what happened, Edward.

I'm saying that you're desperate for it not to be that. You want it to be a murder, and you'd prefer it if it was part of a series of murders. I'm saying you love this… this whole sick thing!"

Out of the blue, Edward remembered something John had said earlier. "When we found out Thompson was dead, you told me you knew what I was thinking and that I should try to look more upset. Is that what you meant? Did you think I was happy someone had died?"

"If the cap fits, Edward. *If the cap fits*. All I know is that we've been warned to keep out of things by the police, and yet we've kept sticking our noses in. We've found things out which the police might find useful, and we've kept them to ourselves because you said that was best. And yes, I do wonder, especially when I see that smug look on your face, whether you get a kick from all the attention."

That was the final straw. With a clatter, Edward pushed back his chair and got to his feet. He nodded to Jimmy, ignoring John, gathered up his cigarettes and matches, and stormed out of the pub.

* * *

The street outside was dark and damp, with a light mist rising from the pavement that caught in the yellow glow of the streetlights. Edward turned up the collar of his coat and began to walk, fury causing his feet to smack on the ground as he stomped off.

It was only after the pub was out of sight that he realised

John had the car keys – and he was damned if he was going to give that arrogant fool the satisfaction of going back and asking for a lift.

He cast about for a taxi, but the street was deserted, empty of both traffic and people. The theatre wasn't far away, though, and Alison had said she often stayed late. He'd get her to telephone him a cab from there.

He felt some of his initial anger leach away as he walked more sedately onwards, to be replaced by a pained disappointment that John should apparently think so little of him. Surely, after all they'd gone through together, he was due more of the benefit of the doubt than he'd been allowed? Surely John knew him better than to think him some kind of bloodthirsty ghoul, excited by the chance to involve himself in murder again? Apart from anything else, he'd nearly been killed the last time.

He'd been walking with his head down against the increasingly insistent wind, but now he looked up and discovered he'd somehow managed to walk down the wrong street and couldn't see the theatre anymore. He came to a halt, the better to get his bearings, and distinctly heard the slap of feet behind him, then a sudden silence.

He'd managed to put the figure in the rain from Thompson's funeral the day before out of his mind but, as he listened for movement behind him, he felt his stomach tighten with fear. He looked across the road at the street sign on the wall; he'd only wandered a single street off course. If he turned left at the next opening, he'd be less than a hundred yards from the theatre entrance.

Without looking behind him, he crossed the road and headed towards the junction. Immediately, the sound of footsteps echoed behind him, bouncing off the houses on either side of the narrow street. The wind, funnelled along by the same tight layout of buildings, was stronger here, and the mist he'd encountered outside the pub had cleared. He risked a glance over his shoulder and saw a tall man in a long coat walking purposefully towards him. He had long hair, tied back in a ponytail that caught in the wind and whipped over his shoulder and across his face, which was covered to the eyes by a thick scarf.

As Edward turned away and quickened his pace, he thought he heard his name being called. He had no intention of stopping, however.

He reached the junction and turned left, thankful that the connecting street on which he found himself was short and well-lit. Not quite running yet, but definitely considering it, he rounded the corner into the little square in front of the theatre and was relieved to see people standing at the entrance.

Again, he heard his name called out behind him. He ignored the shout and hurried across the cobbled square. Only when he was in the theatre doorway, with Alison Jago asking why he was so out of breath, did he feel safe to peer back the way he'd come.

Standing at the corner of the junction he'd just left, the man who had been following him was lit up by a streetlight. His face was in shadow, but Edward had the impression of dark skin and a brooding look peering out from under heavy eyebrows. His glasses were spotted with rain, which made it difficult for him to make out any further detail, so he took them off and quickly wiped them on the hem of his jumper. When he put them back on, the man had gone and the square was empty except for himself and Alison.

That was twice he'd been followed now. He would need to speak to John. With a sinking feeling, he remembered their row. That avenue was closed to him for now.

Alison looked at him with a question in her eyes, but he just shook his head. "It's nothing," he said quietly. "I just got myself mixed up a little in the mist." He pointed to the door. "Shall we go inside? I'd like to order a taxi to take me home."

As she held the door open, he glanced one last time into the square. It was wet and misty and turned a cold yellow by the streetlights which lined its edges, but the only things that moved were a pair of crows eating spilled crisps over by a bin, warily watching him back, ready to fly, if need be.

He knew how they felt.

23

Furious anger wasn't an emotion that John had experienced much. It had always struck him as rather fatiguing, and a terrible waste of energy.

But Edward's insistence that, no matter the consequences, and no matter that they'd been warned off by the police, they – or rather he – would continue to stick his nose where it wasn't wanted was enough to make any man angry.

Even so, he already regretted his harsh words. *If the cap fits*, indeed. Could he have sounded any more pompous? He glanced across at Jimmy, but he was still studiously reading the plastic price list behind the bar and wouldn't meet his eye. Only when John picked up his glass and asked if he fancied another, did the younger man turn around.

"I think I'll pass, John, if you don't mind," he said. "I'm a bit tired and could do with an early night." He grinned, but it was half-hearted at best. "Too many late nights are bad for me skin, apparently." He drained his pint and wiped the white froth from his moustache with the back of his hand.

John watched him leave and raised a hand to wave goodbye when he reached the door, only to find himself unable to move as Jimmy stepped back and held it open for a woman to enter. His breath caught in his throat as the woman glanced round the pub, saw John and walked towards him.

"Mind if I sit here?" his ex-wife Sally said, her cheeks dimpling as she beamed down at him with the full force of her lovely smile.

* * *

It was the strangest thing. He thought about Sally a good deal, of course, but he'd been thinking of her even more than usual since he'd arrived in Bolton. And then, like a genie appearing from inside a bottle, there she was, slipping into the seat opposite him, flicking a finger off Jimmy Rae's discarded beer glass and asking what she had to do to get a lemonade around here. It was like she'd never left.

He'd jumped to his feet, banging the table with his knee, and mumbled a soft, strained "hello". She'd handed him the empty glasses, he'd taken them to the bar and ordered a lemonade for Sally and a G and T for himself, and now here he was, watching her in the mirror behind the barman, as she pulled out a compact and made minute adjustments to her make-up.

He hadn't seen her for, what… six or seven years, but he'd always known she would age well. It helped, of course, that she was so much his junior – she was in her mid-fifties, but looked a good ten years younger than that. Her hair was still short and blonde, cut in a softer style than when they were married, with longer feathers of hair brushing her neck as she angled her face to check her lipstick in the pub's artificial light. She was wearing a green dress which fell just below the knee, with puffy sleeves and a low neckline. Not as fashionable as when she was young, but wonderfully elegant.

The barman was speaking to John, holding his hand out, and so he dropped a handful of coins into it and told him to keep the change. He walked back across to the table, his brain working at full capacity, as he tried to think of something intelligent to say when he sat down.

"No lemon," he said as he placed the drinks in front of her.

She stared at him in confusion until he pointed to her glass. "They had no fresh lemon for your drink," he explained.

Sally laughed, and it was John's turn to feel confused. He should logically despise his ex-wife. She'd run off with the insurance man, after all. But he knew he'd never stopped loving her, and her unexpected presence was stirring feelings which he probably shouldn't encourage.

"I'll live with a lemon-free lemonade," she smiled. She ran her finger around the rim of the glass, looking him up and down as she did so. "You're looking well – if a bit surprised to see me. I heard you were in town and thought, *why don't I look him up?* The lady I spoke to at the theatre – Alison, is it? – was very helpful. She said you'd be in here."

John wondered if it would be too rude to just stand up and go to the toilet. *Hide in the toilet*, to be more accurate. This was too confusing a situation, and he needed time to think. But it *would* be too rude and, besides, Sally was still speaking.

"It's been a while, hasn't it?" she asked, but he could tell it was a rhetorical question, just filler before she got to the important bit. She'd always been that way, always liked to work up to revealing any big news. And more than a decade of marriage had taught him to recognise when she had big news to impart. Some things you never forgot. "And I thought, better to speak to you in person rather than write you a letter. You see, we need to talk."

He nodded, waiting for her to speak, but she remained silent, staring at him with an unusual intensity. "I didn't know you were in Bolton now," he said, to fill the silence.

"Not quite Bolton. A bit more upmarket than that. Cheadle Hulme, to be precise. But, yes, it's coming up for a year since I moved there. Ever since Martin and I split up."

There it was. Tacked onto the end like an afterthought. He remembered Martin – of course he did – the insurance man with the chiselled chin and the sparkling smile who'd been standing in his hallway one day with Sally's clothes in a suitcase in one hand and Sally in the other. And now they'd split up.

"Oh, have you split up?" he asked, face as deadpan as he could make it.

"For good this time," she replied. She shook her head and John thought he saw tears forming in her eyes. He hesitated, then reached across the table and squeezed her hand. "We've split up before – well, you know we have, I turned up on your door often enough – but not like this. We'd both just had enough. So, earlier this year, he packed his bags and moved out. I couldn't afford that big place on my own, so we sold up and I headed north. It's a lot cheaper than London."

Now she'd started talking, it seemed Sally was unable to stop. For several minutes she went on with barely a breath, describing her house in Cheadle Hulme (such a funny name, he thought, like a character from *Round the Horne*), telling John about the boys' new boarding school, describing her life as it was now. Through it all, John waited for the inevitable new man to appear. Sally was incapable of a solitary life: her need for company at all times had been one of her defining qualities. But, as she came to the end of her story, no such man had warranted a mention, and suddenly John had the wildest, and best, thought. *Was she here to get him back?*

She hadn't pulled her hand away when he held it, and now he added his other one, gently lying it on top of hers and slipping his fingers amongst hers. "You do sound like you've had quite a time of it," he said, resisting the urge to add "my darling". *Not too fast*, he thought to himself. "Maybe I could take you out for dinner one night, and we could talk more? I don't know how Bolton – or Cheadle Hulme, for that matter – does for jazz clubs, but there's bound to be somewhere we could go onto for drinks and dancing?"

As soon as the words were out of his mouth, he could tell it was the wrong thing to have said. Instantly, she pulled her hand away and sat further back in her chair. She picked up her glass – to prevent him holding her hand, John thought.

"I don't think that's wise, John," she said, and smiled to take the sting out of the rejection. "We do need to talk, but I was hoping we could do it here, now."

"Of course." He had gone too fast – or perhaps simply misunderstood – but it wasn't in John's nature to be unkind or to hold a grudge. If all Sally wanted to do was talk, then that was fine. If she needed help, he'd always be there for her.

"What it is, is that I need you to start paying maintenance money again. Obviously, when I was with Martin, he supported me and the boys financially, and so I was happy for you to cancel your payments, but now I'm on my own again, there are school fees to pay and rent to find, and I'm afraid I can't make ends meet." She sipped her drink and caught an ice cube in her mouth. John watched its shape pressing against the inside of her cheek as she continued to speak. "You know I wouldn't ask if I didn't have to, but… well, it's the boys I'm thinking of mainly. They'd hate to have to leave their school."

"Of course, of course. Don't worry about it. I was never keen on stopping those payments in the first place, if you recall, but he… Martin… insisted. I'll speak to the bank in the morning. We can't have the boys leaving their pals, can we?"

He could hear the false note in his voice, but hoped she could not. The money meant nothing – *Floggit and Leggit* was hugely popular, and the success of the first series, and his own role in it, had led to a substantial pay rise for the second one. But what Sally had said had brought a few matters to the front of his mind. He wondered why she'd waited a year to tell him, and what had caused the final break, and he groaned inwardly as he realised that he'd not seen his boys in far too long. He wondered too about mentioning that Nate Thompson was dead, but decided in the end, that some things were better left unsaid. She obviously had enough on her plate.

"I knew you'd understand," Sally said, placing her now-empty glass back on the table. "I can't tell you what a weight this has taken off my mind." She rose to her feet and John did the same. "Thank you," she said, and kissed him on the cheek. For a moment, John inhaled the familiar scent of Chanel No 5 and honeysuckle soap, and then she was gone, and he was alone in the pub again.

He put his hand to his face, certain that the spot where she'd kissed him would be warm to the touch, then pulled it sharply away, knowing he was too old in the tooth for such foolish romantic notions. He glanced around the bar, embarrassed, but nobody was looking at him.

Feeling more alone than was healthy, he sat back down and lit a cigarette. There was an inch of beer left in the bottom of his glass. He finished it and looked across at the whiskies behind the bar. Unexpectedly, the evening had become one for hard spirits and lots of them.

24

London, 1936

In the end, John had taken an uncharacteristically direct approach to meeting the girl in the kitchen window. He'd waited until later that evening, gone to her sister's door and asked to speak to Sally. From somewhere inside the house, he'd heard voices talking in whispers and giggles, then Sally had appeared, drying her hands on a towel.

"Good evening," she said, and her voice was delightfully soft and somehow golden. "Can I help you?"

Mentally steeling himself, John smiled and asked if she was hungry.

"A little," Sally had said. "We're having supper in about an hour." She'd smiled in return, exposing small, even, perfectly white teeth and creating a tiny dimple in one cheek. "Why do you ask? If you're a friend of Fred's, I imagine you're about to invite yourself to join us."

John's experience of women at that point had been quite extensive in terms of number, but unfortunately narrow in terms of duration and, indeed, nationality. Put plainly, it consisted of kissing one of cook's assistants at school, a handful of brief flings with older female co-stars, and rather a lot of one-night dalliances with ladies of easy and quite reasonably priced virtue in Cairo during the War.

Romancing had never been on the menu. Still, years in the theatre had taught him to take full advantage of such a perfect feed line.

"Quite the opposite, in fact," he said, standing up a little straighter. "I've actually come to ask if you'd care to join me for a bite at the Carlton this evening? Dress entirely informal."

She'd coloured very prettily, he recalled. "Well, aren't you the forward one?" she said, mock offended. "I'll need to check with my sister. And you'll need to present your credentials to my father before then, of course."

"Including a detailed breakdown of my intentions towards you, I assume," he'd asked.

Silly, harmless stuff, but she'd laughed at that, the first time he'd heard her laugh, the first time he'd heard a sound which would fill him with joy every time he heard it in future.

"Pick me up at seven?" she'd said.

He'd nodded and she'd closed the door. No more than a minute of conversation all told, but it was a start.

He'd made to leave, had in fact been halfway down the driveway, already whistling a happy tune to himself, if memory served, when he heard the door reopen behind him. With a sinking feeling which he could still bring to mind three decades later, he turned back, expecting to see her sister standing there – or worse, her father. Instead, it had been Sally herself, beckoning to him with a crooked finger and awfully sweet half-smile.

"One tiny detail to be cleared up," she'd said, the half-smile widening to a full one. "You apparently know my name, but you never mentioned your own."

"John," he'd said. "John Le Breton."

She'd already begun closing the door, and her reply reached his ears via a soft puff of air as it closed completely. "In which case, I'll see you at seven, Mr Le Breton."

Actually, he thought he might have skipped back down the road.

25

Years previously – decades previously, in fact – Edward had had his first ever first night. It had been at a theatre long since torn down and turned into flats, a theatre so long gone that he couldn't even remember its name, but the sensation he'd felt then was the exact same as the one he felt now.

He stood on stage and waited for the curtain to go up, his stomach churning and the sharp stab of indigestion just painful enough that he worried he was having a heart attack. He glanced right and left but the others seemed calm as could be. Peter Glancy was staring blankly into space, poised to say the play's opening line, and Jimmy Rae had his eyes closed and seemed to be doing some kind of deep breathing exercise.

True, John, standing in the wings, was muttering *Attend the lords of France and Burgundy, Gloucester* over and over again, and his voice was loud enough that Mickey Fagan had to walk over and tap him on the shoulder. But otherwise, everywhere was still.

The only sounds came from the other side of the curtain. Edward could hear the audience chatting and moving about, seats banging down and voices calling out the names of their friends, and then the lights must have dimmed because even those sounds died down and, for a long moment, the entire theatre was silent.

The curtain began to rise and Edward had one last quick glance at the position of the other actors on the stage. Then the sick feeling in his stomach suddenly disappeared as he waited for his cue.

* * *

"What a triumph!"

Mickey Fagan slapped John Le Breton on the back and beamed at the assembled company where they sat around the larger rehearsal room.

"If there's been a better *Lear* in a regional theatre in the past fifty years, I'm damned if I've ever heard of it. I won't single anyone out, mind you – I don't believe in it. This is a team we've put together here, and it's as a team we succeed or fail. And tonight has been a success, a rip-roaring success! The reviews will be worth a read, you mark my words."

It was almost midnight, and a boy had been sent to pick up early copies of the local newspaper. The cast had had a chance to get changed and – for those so inclined – risk the chance of a freezing deluge in one of the temperamental theatre showers. Now they sat where they could find space and, in the manner of actors everywhere, dissected and examined the entrails of their performances.

Edward was delighted with his own evening's work. He'd been worried that too long in television might have eradicated his ability to project his voice into a large auditorium, but, from his very first speech, he'd been confident that everyone could hear him. After that, he'd been able to concentrate on his performance. Alice Robertson came up and congratulated him – *so real, Mr Lowe, so much feeling* – and Jimmy Rae handed him a whisky in a plastic cup and made an "O" sign with his fingers, which Edward knew was intended as praise of some kind.

Out of the corner of his eye, he glimpsed John with Alison Jago, admiring a sumptuous bouquet of flowers which had been left at the back door for Judy Faith. Their friendship had been strained since the argument in the Blue Blazer the previous night – indeed, they'd barely exchanged a word away from rehearsals since then. Edward regretted that they'd fallen out, but he had no intention of apologising. The accusation that he revelled in other people's untimely deaths had wounded him, and he was damned if he would be the one to come begging for forgiveness. Still, he wished it had never happened, and had already decided that he would be magnanimous should John choose to say sorry.

Without realising it, he'd been staring at John as he thought about their disagreement. Their eyes met and John smiled his half-smile, held up his own plastic cup in a toast, and then began to make his way across the room. Edward, recalling his intention to be the bigger man, did the same, and they met in the middle of the room.

John was the first to speak. "Congratulations on tonight," he said, a little stiffly, Edward thought, but not insincerely. "You were splendid, I thought."

It was kind of him to say. Suddenly, Edward's insistence on making John apologise felt foolish and childish. "I could say the same about you, John. As good a Lear as I've seen."

"Oh, that's so good of you to say. I did wonder how it would be. If I was still able to perform live, as it were."

Edward laughed. "I had the exact same worry. I kept thinking how embarrassing it would be if I opened my mouth to speak my first lines, and nobody in the audience could make out a word I was saying."

John's laugh was loud enough for several people to turn in his direction. "Just imagine! Everyone cupping their hands to their ears and shouting 'speak up, for God's sake'." He looked down at Edward, his laughter dying away. "Look, Edward, I want to say how sorry I am for the things I said in the pub yesterday. I wasn't in the best of moods, and I took it out on you. Quite inexcusable, I know, but I'm desperately hoping you can excuse it, nonetheless."

"Nothing to apologise for, nothing at all."

"Well, thank you for that, even so."

John held out his hand. "Friends?" he said.

Edward thought the gesture unnecessary but well meant, and shook the offered hand.

"The papers are in!"

Mickey Fagan's shout interrupted the two men's reunion as they, like everyone else in the room, flocked across to the door, where the boy who had been sent for the early newspapers stood with a thick pile in his hands.

Edward grabbed one and quickly flicked to the theatre reviews, with John standing over his shoulder.

"*A Shakespearean masterclass!*" Edward read out loud, causing a ripple of cheers and applause to spread across the room, where it met similar waves of sound as other members of the company relayed the review to those around them. He continued to read. "*Television's John Le Breton is superb as the tragic King Lear, more than capably supported by his sitcom colleagues Edward Lowe and James Rae.* Oh, that's very good. *Those wondering whether the tragic loss of Sir Nathaniel Thompson would adversely affect this production can rest easy – these stars of the small screen look as comfortable alongside Playhouse regulars like Peter Glancy and Alice Robertson as one could hope.*"

There was more but, since it didn't mention either himself or John, Edward read it to himself then passed the newspaper to John. He felt a delicious warmth inside as he contemplated his performance and the flattering review. He downed the warm whisky he was holding, then, feeling too hot and hemmed in by the crowd around him, pushed his way past congratulatory back slaps and out into the corridor.

It had always been this way, he remembered, dredging up a memory from his days in rep. After first-night nerves came first-night performance, then first-night reviews. And regardless of whether the reviews were positive or not, he needed to clear his head afterwards. He walked a little way down the corridor, so that the noise from the rehearsal room was muted and stood by an open window breathing in the night air. He realised John had followed him out.

"I just had a thought," the other man said, looking behind himself, checking he wasn't being overheard. "Everybody is in there celebrating. Wouldn't this be a good time to take a look in Nate's old dressing room? I know Judy's had it for a while now, but there might be something there that's been overlooked."

It was a good idea, Edward had to admit. He knew from Fagan that the police had searched Thompson's main residence and found nothing untoward, and they'd had a quick poke around the theatre too, but it was almost a cliché in the profession that an actor's real home was his dressing room – it was possible something had been missed. He might well have left a spare key there, for instance.

And they still had to consider the possibility he'd been killed by one of his colleagues. John was right, better nobody else knew what they were up to.

Without another word, the two men headed for the dressing room.

26

Empty theatre dressing rooms could be desolate places at the best of times, Edward thought, but when a recent occupant has been beaten to death in an alleyway, they become positively unnerving.

He flicked on the light switch and shivered at the cold air trapped inside the windowless room. A fireplace opposite; a make-up table on the right, covered in half-used sticks and compacts; a battered wooden table in the middle, scarred by years of use, beside a chair with a stained back; a pile of cardboard boxes stacked to the left – the room contained all the paraphernalia of an actor's life.

Almost all the dressing rooms in the theatre were identical, Fagan had told him, and this one looked very like others he'd been in. Crucially, in so cramped a space, there was not a lot of places in which even something as small as a key could be hidden.

He moved to the make-up table, aware of John behind him shifting the boxes about. As expected, there was a single long drawer in the middle of the table, with two smaller drawers on either side. He opened each one and tipped the contents onto a space he cleared on the tabletop. There was nothing there. Pens and pencils, discarded make-up, a cigarette packet with one cigarette in it, scraps of cloth and fragments of script – all the usual actor's detritus. He half-remembered a spy film and reached into the space where the drawers had been, feeling for a lever or a switch or, failing that, something taped to the wood. Again, there was nothing.

From the corner of his eye, he saw John knock a cardboard box of costumes over. It tumbled from the top of the pile on which it rested, bounced off the table in the middle of the room and spilled its contents across the floor. "Buggeration," John muttered to himself, as Edward painfully knelt down, a touch of arthritis in his knee flaring up, to help gather the clothes up.

Some of the slippery satin costumes had slid under the make-up table; Edward had to lie down to fit his arm into the gap. He was just about able to grasp the furthest one, a particularly slick green jerkin, teasing it back towards himself with the tips of his fingers, but it caught on something. Try as he might, he couldn't get enough purchase to pull it out. John, watching him, was impatient to be done.

"Just leave it, Edward, for goodness' sake. There's nothing here for us, and Judy could appear at any second. It's only one costume, she'll never notice it."

Edward shook his head as he used the edge of the make-up table to get back to his feet. "Nonsense," he snapped, angry at something he couldn't quite specify. "You don't make a mess and then just leave it. Didn't they teach you that at your public school?"

He knew he was being unfair, but his arm ached where he'd over-stretched it, and John's laziness always rubbed him up the wrong way. "Sorry," he said. "I didn't mean that the way it came out." He rubbed at his arm. "But I can't reach to get that last jerkin or whatever it is out."

Fortunately for their continuing friendship, John knew when Edward needed to be humoured. He dismissed Edward's apology with a wave, and examined the back of the make-up table, where it was jammed up against the wall. Fitting his fingers into the moulding behind the mirror, he gave the table a heave and shifted it six inches forward.

"There you go," he said, reaching for the trapped piece of fabric. "That's it… wait a minute, what's this?"

There was excitement in his voice. Edward rushed across and peered down at the wall as John explored the space further.

"There's something sticking out: the jerkin's caught on it." He gave a pull and, with a tearing sound, the satin jerkin came away from the wall. He handed it to Edward and wriggled back down behind the little table. "It's a nail, I think, but it's loose… ah!"

With a hard shove, he pushed the table forward again and stepped back so Edward could see what he'd exposed. In his hand he held a square of plywood, with a nail hammered through one edge. Crouching down, Edward could see a hole in the wall which the plywood square had been covering. He reached inside and pulled out a wooden box.

It was the size of a shoebox, made of dark wood, with carvings of a maypole and dancers parading around on its lid. Edward carried it across to the large table in the middle of the room and laid it down. He glanced across at John, who nodded, and then carefully lifted open the lid.

A Yale key lay inside, but otherwise it was empty. He took the key out and laid it on the table, then felt inside the box for any hidden compartments. There were none, but as he levered the lid back and forward on its wings, a scrap of paper which had been trapped in the mechanism fell out and fluttered to the floor.

John bent over and picked it up. It was shiny, glossy even, and mainly plain white, with just a flash of colour constrained by a thin black line at the ragged edge. "From a magazine?" John offered, handing the paper to Edward.

"Or a book, perhaps. Something upmarket."

"Either way, what happened to the rest?"

Edward had no answer. He tucked the scrap of paper in his wallet and handed the box back to John. "I'll hold onto it, if you want to stick the box back where we found it. No point in advertising what we've been up to. There's no point in involving the police either, I'd say. Not yet."

John gave him a querulous look and seemed on the verge of protesting. Edward braced himself for an argument. He knew what John was thinking, they should give the key and the scrap of paper to Inspector Whyte, but what would the police do with either piece of evidence? Complain that they'd not spoken up sooner, probably – or do the bare minimum and then close the case, insisting it was merely a mugging gone wrong. He couldn't allow that to happen, not when they were making such good progress.

"Someone's been following me," he blurted out suddenly, unaware that he intended to speak until the words were already tumbling from his mouth. He'd known he had to say something to stop John insisting they go to the police, but he already suspected he'd said exactly the wrong thing. A mysterious figure stalking him through the fog was hardly the kind of news designed to convince anyone they should continue to investigate alone.

"What?" Whatever John had been about to say, that at least was plainly forgotten. "How do you mean, *followed*?"

"Just what I say. I actually first thought it at Nate Thompson's funeral – you remember when I slipped coming back down the hill in the rain and you helped me up? Well, the reason I was running wasn't because I feared missing the buffet, it was because I thought there was someone chasing me. I couldn't be sure it wasn't my imagination, though. But the other night, after we rowed in the pub, there was definitely someone following me in the fog. He even called my name."

"My God. What did he want? Did you speak to him?"

"No, I got to the theatre before he could catch up to me, and Alison Jago was standing at the door so he hung back. But I saw him clear as day that time, across the square."

John shook his head, and stared over Edward's head, obviously deep in thought. Finally, he nodded. "Well, we don't know if he meant you any harm, do we? It could be he wanted to tell you something important, something useful for the case. You didn't recognise him? He couldn't have been someone from the theatre?"

Edward shook his head. He could be wrong, but he had the distinct impression John was trying to convince himself there was nothing to worry about. "It was too far away to be sure who it was. But I must admit, I hadn't thought of that. Perhaps I should have spoken to the man," he said carefully.

John toyed with the box in his hand, opening and closing the lid. "Perhaps, but I do think what you said before was right," he said, closing the lid for the final time. "If the killer is someone in the company, then the last thing we want is to let them know we're looking into what might have been happening at the theatre. And if the chap following you has something to tell you, then involving the police more than they're already involved could scare him off."

The look he gave Edward was a strange one, a mix of firm agreement and… was it… *worry*? Certainly withholding evidence from the police could get them in trouble, but it wouldn't be the first time they'd done it.

He waited to see if John would say anything else, but instead he crouched down to replace the box, so Edward turned away to put the last of the spilled costumes back into their box and return it to its position at the far end of the room. As he turned back, his eye fell for a second on the fireplace and his breath caught in this throat.

"The fires in the changing rooms aren't used anymore, that's what Mickey Fagan said, isn't it?" he said, already moving round the table to the fire. As John stood up, Edward knelt on the hard floor and lifted a handful of ashes from the grate. "Then what's this, then?"

He held out the ashes in the palm of his hand. They were, for the most part dark, grey or black, with brittle lines of lighter shading across the top which crumbled to dust as he touched them with a finger. But here and there amongst the ashes, tiny fragments of paper could be seen. Edward pinched one of them between his nails and held it up to the light.

It was too small for any words to be made out, but Edward fancied it was writing paper, rather than the glossy magazine paper they'd found in the wooden box. He picked out more of the tiny scraps, but there was nothing more concrete to be made of any of them.

"A letter?" John asked.

"Perhaps. Or a list." Again, he slipped the fragments of paper in his wallet. "Whatever it is, we'll hold on to it for now."

John said nothing, just manoeuvred the make-up table back into place and stood by the light switch, ready to turn it off and plunge the room back into darkness.

He had something on his mind, Edward was sure of it, but for now he would settle for the fact they were talking again. If there was something troubling him, perhaps he was just feeling the death of his former friend more than he was admitting? Edward would wait and let John tell him in his own time.

He returned his wallet to his jacket pocket and gestured to the door, and towards the noise still coming from the rehearsal room. "Time we were getting back."

One thing he'd learned over the last eighteen months: John Le Breton would tell you his secrets when he wanted to, and not before.

27

When John had seen Edward looking across at him during the after-show shindig, he'd felt an enormous sense of relief. Ever since he'd spoken to Sally, he'd been unable to get her out of his mind – the few hours when he'd been on stage had, in fact, been the first time all day when he'd not been obsessing about her.

Why had she come to the pub? For all her protests, she could have written to him just as easily to ask him to restart maintenance payments. Why had she waited until he was alone, and what had she meant by kissing him? True, it was only on the cheek, and she had refused the offer of dinner – and hadn't so much as given him her address – but surely a kiss meant something, even nowadays?

He'd been pleased to discover he was able to put thoughts of her to one side while he was performing. The second the curtain came down for the final time, however, all he could think about was her face, even while he was making Alison and Judy laugh with a rather risqué story about a trip he'd taken with Peter Sellers and Terry-Thomas.

Small wonder he'd welcomed Edward's olive branch. In a curious sense – a terribly curious sense – investigating Nate Thompson's death was a much-needed alternative to thinking about Sally.

That his suggestion of checking Nate's dressing room had proven a fruitful one was a further distraction. Usually, he was the one hectoring Edward to tell the police whatever they'd found out, but, at the moment, he was happy to go along with the little man's unwillingness to share information. Between their visits to the Spinning Wheel and Nate's dressing room, they'd amassed a fair amount of new evidence. Hopefully by concentrating on that for the next few days, he could return Sally to the back of his mind, where she'd existed perfectly happily for years.

He did feel guilty about so lightly dismissing the man who'd been following Edward, though. Still, maybe he was right and the man, whoever he was, did want to share important information. Surely someone with ill intent on his mind wouldn't have shouted out his target's name, as this one apparently had?

He followed Edward back into the rehearsal room, conscious that he'd not spoken since they'd left Nate Thompson's dressing room. With some effort, he shifted the expression on his face from pensive and concerned to delighted and excited.

He *had* just received glowing reviews for his Lear, after all.

28

Now that they were performing *Lear,* and rehearsals for *Hamlet* hadn't yet begun, John and Edward had most of the day to themselves, and only had to report to the theatre in the late afternoon.

Which, Edward told John as they parked in Melbourne Road again, was handy, given they now had a house to break into.

* * *

The Yale key fitted the lock of number six perfectly. Edward twisted it and pushed open the door in one movement, keen not to be seen loitering outside.

He felt a twinge of disappointment when he saw there were no letters on the floor just inside the door. It would have been useful to be able to prove that the house belonged to Thompson, over and above the fact that the key to the place had been hidden in his dressing room. He consoled himself that there was bound to be something inside which would serve just as well.

"Any chance I could come in too?" John asked plaintively behind him. He realised he was blocking the doorway and stepped aside to let the other man pass. The gentle *snick* as John carefully closed the door behind himself was a reassurance they would not be disturbed.

The front door was solid wood, and there were no windows in the hallway, so he felt safe enough switching on the main light, illuminating the hall and revealing four doors, two in the left-hand wall, one in the right, and the final one at the end of the passageway opposite the front entrance.

"Left first?" John whispered.

Edward nodded and pushed open the first door, revealing a dim room, lit only by a streetlight that shone through the large bay window to his left. Quickly, he moved across and flipped the blinds shut. That done, he switched on the wall light.

The room thus revealed stretched most of the length of the house. The flooring was mainly polished wood, with colourful woven rugs carefully arranged here and there to give the impression they'd been casually tossed into place. A modern gas fire, with a tall copper flue and a pine surround, faced a pair of uncomfortable-looking chairs with, between them, a small smoked-glass table. Other than that, there was no furniture at all in the near end of the room.

The far end, on the other hand, was crowded by a large, heavy dining room table, with seating for eight people.

"That's a lovely bit of oak," said John, running his palm across its surface. "Lovely bookcases too," he went on, moving over to the matching shelving which took up the entirety of one wall. "No books, though."

"None at all?"

"Not one." John flicked on a small lamp. "There's a space in the dust, though. It looks like there was something here at one point."

Edward peered down at the smooth rectangular break in the thin layer of dust which coated the bookshelves. There was no telling what had been there but, whatever it was, it had been removed quite recently. The dust hadn't yet had time to cover up the gap.

There was nothing else in the room, except for another door at its far end, beyond the dining table.

Edward pushed it open and stepped through into a reasonably sized kitchen. Again, other than the usual appliances, there were no signs of habitation. They opened each cupboard and drawer, but all they found were pots and pans, all of which looked brand new. Even the bin was empty.

It was as if nobody had ever lived there.

* * *

The other rooms were almost the same. A bathroom devoid of soap, toothpaste or washcloth; a large bedroom that contained only a neatly made bed and a wardrobe in which no clothes hung; and a smaller spare room, converted to an office by the look of the furniture (a desk with a typewriter on it, a high-backed chair, a filing cabinet). Everything was empty except for the bottom drawer of the filing cabinet, from where John straightened up in triumph, brandishing a handful of books like Chamberlain waving his useless piece of paper.

"Well, here's something," he said simply, laying the books out on the desk. They were mainly the sort of books he'd have expected an older theatrical gentleman to be interested in: books on fine art and gardening, a biography of Ellen Terry, and a guide to basic carpentry. A thin paperback with a rather lurid cover on which a buxom young woman appeared to be having trouble keeping her dress fastened was unexpected, it was true, but perhaps *Lord Vladimir's Intended* was not what it seemed?

Edward flicked the book open and the first words his eyes fell on were *her naked heaving bosom*. Swiftly, he flipped it shut, as though he feared contamination.

"A bit fruity, is it?" John asked with a smile.

"Basically pornography," Edward replied, his face burning. "Frankly, I can't imagine what use Sir Nathaniel would have for such filth."

"He *was* a single man. I'm sure he had the same urges as the rest of us," John reminded him, but his smile wavered then disappeared altogether.

Edward was glad to see that the man had some sense of decorum. Thompson wasn't yet cold in his grave, after all.

He prodded the paperback to one side and opened the Terry biography at a random page, reading, with no interest, about her first husband. He was about to close the book when he had a thought.

He took out his wallet and prised out the fragment of glossy paper they'd found in Thompson's dressing room. Annoyingly, it wasn't a match for the paper stock in the Terry book, the gardening one nor the carpentry guide. He knew he'd struck gold as soon as he flipped open the fine art book, though. The paper inside was the exact same as the scrap he held in his hand and, as he lined up one against the other, it was clear that even the margins matched perfectly.

"Look at this," he called to John, who had moved across the room to check behind the filing cabinet. He flicked through the pages of the book, looking for a torn corner but, to his disappointment, there was none to be found.

"It has to be from here," he insisted as John joined him and took the book from his hands.

"I rather think it might be," John said a moment later, spreading the book wide and using two of the other books to weight down its edges so that it stayed open. He ran a finger down the middle of the book and cast an inquisitive look at Edward. "You see?" he said. "Some pages have been cut out completely."

Eagerly, Edward examined the book. John was right – a razor or something equally sharp had been used to slice a group of pages from the book. He took a mental note of the page number immediately before the missing pages and turned to the index.

"The High Renaissance," he read aloud, frowning as he realised the entire chapter had been excised.

"That covers quite a lot of ground, I should think?" John asked mildly. "Not that I know much about old paintings."

"I imagine so. But I can't think of a single reason why anyone would cut a section from a book like that."

John shrugged. "Perhaps he wanted to keep that section when he handed the book back?" He lifted the cover of the book on Ellen Terry and tapped the first page inside. A rectangular sheet of white paper had been pasted there, with a folded slot at the bottom in which a cardboard slip might comfortably have sat.

"It seems they're all library books," he added, as though the discovery was unimportant. "I would think that means we can take them back and confirm that Nate lived here."

Not for the first time, Edward despaired of the other man's attitude. It was all very well sighing your way through life as an actor, where there was usually some obliging runner or ambitious extra willing to pander to your every whim and indulge your every delusional notion (or so he'd been told – in Edward's experience, a public-school accent helped no end in that respect). But away from that world, in this one where murders occurred and evidence must be gathered, a little more enthusiasm and vim wouldn't go amiss. He glared at John, who had picked up *Lord Vladimir's Intended* and was flicking through its pages with as little energy as he did everything else.

"I'm surprised they stock this kind of thing in a library, you know," he said, looking up and giving Edward a half-smile, ignoring – or not noticing – the baleful look he received back.

"Indeed," Edward snapped and snatched the paperback from John's hands. He added it to the pile of larger books and picked the whole lot up, regretting he'd not thought to bring a carrier bag with him. "There doesn't seem much point staying here. Someone's cleaned up. Or perhaps Sir Nathaniel reserved this place for just one thing." He felt his cheeks redden again, but plunged on, determined not to be distracted from his point. "Either way, there's nothing for us here. I suggest we take these books with us and visit the library at the earliest opportunity. As you say, presumably the library will have Sir Nathaniel's name on record, which at least should prove this house was his."

John nodded and reached over to the books in Edward's hands, plucking *Lord Vladimir's Intended* from the top of the pile. "I'll hold on to this one, if you don't mind," he said with a smile. "I was just saying to Jimmy Rae that I could use a little night-time reading."

29

The first time had been calculated, for all that it had gone wrong at the end, but this time, it was as though a beast had taken him over, sliding under his skin like a medieval demon, digging its invisible claws into his organs and hooking on, inhabiting him completely for the briefest of spells... and then departing, its terrible work done, leaving him alone in the dark, sobbing by the body of the girl.

How could this have happened, he thought? How could he have let it happen?

It seemed so long ago, the first time that he'd seen her, nervous but excited, like a puppy newly taken from its mother. She'd moved – glided – across the stage, and he'd thought at once: 'This is the one. There can be no other.'

From that moment on, he'd plotted how to make her his own.

But time had passed and she'd remained out of reach, always out of reach, refusing to catch his eye, not hearing her name when he called it. But there was no accounting for the perfidy of women, and he never doubted she would be his, forever.

And then, tonight…

He'd watched her from the street outside – risky, he knew, but the impulse to see her was too strong – and seen her laughing with the others, then stop, her perfect face wrinkling in concern. A word or two of explanation, and they went on while she turned and went back inside the theatre.

He'd followed her to her dressing room, keeping far enough behind that even if she should look around, he would still have time to slide into the shadows. It would have ruined everything if she'd seen him too early. She'd have screamed, for one thing; someone might still have heard, someone might have come running.

It would all have been over, and everything would have been for nothing.

But if she'd suspected his presence, she'd given no sign, and he'd followed her inside, along the dimly lit corridor and then, as she'd gone into her dressing room, he'd been able to step in behind her and close the door without her realising. He'd got his hand over her mouth before she'd even registered he was there, and when he'd spun her around and her eyes had widened so very, very much, he'd moved in close to her, eager to hold her, eager to explain why – and how – they could and should be together.

But it had all gone wrong. Everything from that moment on was sketchy and incomplete, his memory fragmentary and blurred, like lines from a book read by a crying man. He remembered her teeth biting his hand and her nails scratching his face. He remembered striking out in panic and pain, but after that he remembered nothing until he had come back to himself, in the dark room, with her corpse staring up at him, accusing him.

For an instant, he had considered running, simply running, back down the corridor and out into the streets, and from there... but there would be nowhere safe to run to if he'd given into panic. He could see that now, and luckily he'd seen it then. Seen it in her eyes, staring up at him not in accusation, nor in regret, but in sorrow and warning.

So, he'd taken a length of cord from one of the boxes stacked in the corner, a belt for a tunic, a remnant of some dusty play or other. He'd clambered up and tied one end around a pipe, the other around her neck and then carefully let her dangle. He had no note – it would be so much better with a note – but it would have to do.

He could only hope it was enough – in every sense.

30

London, 1940

John and Sally married in February 1940, on a cold but sunny day, with the first snowdrops of the year already appearing and wild daffodils sprouting in the ground around the church wall. Food rationing had been introduced the previous month, but had yet to make any significant inroads into people's eating habits, so their wedding lunch had been almost as splendid as it would have been pre-war. The bride wore a dress designed by Edward Molyneux, the groom wore a top hat, tails and a white bow tie, and everyone agreed they made a delightful couple.

It was an idyllic time, in spite of the declaration of war a few months earlier. Even if Chamberlain had been wrong when he assured everyone that Herr Hitler was a man to be trusted, nothing much happened for the longest time, as Europe basked in what was later tagged the Phoney War. Soldiers massed in training camps across the country but came home on weekend passes, the RAF bombed Germany with pamphlets rather than bombs, and "blitz" was yet to become the most hated word in the English language. London, where they'd bought a tiny flat, was so peaceful it was hard at times to believe there was a war on at all.

And then John's call-up papers arrived. Present yourself at such and such a place, at such and such a time. Bring all necessary underclothing (what an odd way of putting it, he'd thought) and don't expect to be home any time soon.

They'd been married for less than a year when he threw a suitcase in the back of their battered old Riley and left for war.

31

The theatre was cold and dark, and Edward was reluctant even to turn on a light, for fear someone would come to investigate. Luckily, John knew Alison Jago kept a torch in her little cubbyhole. He switched it on and aimed it at their feet as they made their way cautiously backstage.

"Are you sure this is absolutely necessary?" John asked for the third time, as he barked his shin on the base of a clothes rail propped in the shadows against a wall. "Couldn't we just drop the thing in Mickey Fagan's office and let him find it in the morning?"

"And have Inspector Whyte ask how nobody had noticed it before, and why it was there at all? Talk sense, John."

"I suppose that could be rather awkward," John admitted. "Back in the box it is, then."

The idea to return the park house key to the box in Nate Thompson's old dressing room had been Edward's, of course. Left up to John, they'd have put it in an envelope and posted it to the police station, or dropped it down a sewer. But Edward had insisted – rightly, John admitted grudgingly – that the police needed the key, and that posting it would merely raise awkward questions about who'd sent it.

He shone the torch beam onto the nearest door. A sheet of paper with the name JUDY FAITH written on it in black marker had been pinned to it. "Here we are."

He turned the handle and gently pushed the door, which creaked like something from a Universal horror movie. "It's pitch black in there," he complained, arrowing the thin beam of light towards the make-up table, seeking the board behind which the box was hidden. The dressing room was so dark, however, that it was almost a solid block, an absence of colour through which no light could penetrate. There was a coldness in the air, too, and he suddenly shivered. He hesitated on the threshold, reluctant to enter.

Edward had no patience for such qualms. "That's because there are no windows on this side of the building. But all we need do is pop the key back in the box and leave. Surely that's not beyond our abilities?" He pushed past John, keen to be done with their errand and back at the hotel. "Best not put the lights on, but shine the torch down here, please. If I remember right, it was just to the side of— oh, hell! What on Earth?"

From the darkness, John heard a thump and a loud scrape, followed by Edward cursing under his breath.

"I banged my damn hip on something – the table, if I'm not mistaken. And there's something else too, something hang… Oh my God."

"What is it? What can you see?" John flashed the torch towards Edward, and then followed his outstretched finger in the direction of the far wall. At first, he couldn't decide exactly what he was looking at; a pair of shoes, was it? Quite plain, but with a small kitten heel, and above them shapely, stocking-clad legs.

Was someone standing in the dark, watching them?

It was only as his gaze moved upwards to take in the bottom of a slip peeping out from beneath an A-line skirt that he realised the shoes were at least a foot off the ground, suspended in mid-air. He twitched his wrist with a groan and the beam of light angled upwards, to land upon the protruding eyes and swollen tongue of Judy Faith, and the rope tightly encircling her neck.

32

There was no doubting Judy was dead.

John quickly slapped on the main dressing room light and hurried across, hoping they might be in time to save her, but the increased visibility only made the horror clearer. The rope had cut a red line into her throat and stretched from there to the water pipe which ran along the ceiling in all the dressing rooms. Judy's lifeless eyes stared at him as he climbed on a chair and used his penknife to saw through the heavy material that held her aloft. He braced himself to take what he sickly realised was literally her dead weight, and lowered her body onto Edward's shoulders. Only once he'd clambered down and helped lay the body on the floor was he able to close her eyes and fall back against the make-up table behind him. His head spun and spots danced before his eyes. Bile burned in the back of his throat and he thought he might vomit.

"Why...?" Edward's voice trailed off into silence. He was looking down at Judy's body, the rope she had used still held between his fingers. "Why would she do this?" he asked, offering it to John, as though it held the answer to his question.

John had no answers, only questions of his own, which he forced out through the layer of numb horror which enclosed him. "Should we take it off her, do you think? She looks so… undignified like that."

Edward shook his head and rubbed his palms across his eyes, his manner suddenly business-like. All an act, of course, but John knew of old that this was the way his friend reacted to terrible events. Always do now what needs to be done now, and grieve later. "I think we best leave things as they are," he said briskly. "The police won't thank us for interfering with a crime scene. They'll want things left as undisturbed as possible." He lifted Judy's right hand and indicated the first two fingers. "A couple of her nails are broken, though, so perhaps she changed her mind at the last moment and tried to remove the rope?" He sighed and gently tilted her head to one side. "And I think that's maybe a bruise coming up on her cheek there. I wonder if she could have banged herself on something as she… well, thrashed about at the end."

John felt tears stinging his eyes and a lump grow in his throat until he was unable to swallow. The idea that this beautiful young woman, someone who had only that afternoon laughed and called him a gorgeous old fox… the idea that she had died in such despair was almost too much to bear. "Well, we can cover her at least," he said angrily, though he knew Edward was right. He pulled off his jacket and knelt to drape it over Judy's body. For a moment he wondered if he ought to cover her face, just as they did in the movies, but it seemed somehow wrong, as though she would be unable to breathe. Besides, the coat was too short to cover both face and body, so he settled for shielding her from her knees to her chin. He rested a hand against her cold cheek. Edward nodded in understanding as he got back to his feet.

Only now did either man think to look about them. Edward pointed towards a chair tipped over on the floor. "That's what I fell over in the dark, then I banged into the table. Yes, look..." he indicated the dust on the floor, which had been disturbed at one end by the movement of the table from its usual place. "She must have been standing on it. The chair, I mean."

John glanced down at the upturned chair and nodded, still numb but with a desperate desire to be busy, to be doing something. "I don't see any note. Do you?" The table, scarred by cigarette burns, took up most of the available floor space. A half-drunk cup of tea and an ashtray – the product, it seemed, of the Guinness brewery – sat at one end. But other than a sheaf of paper which John recognised as the *Lear* script, lying fanned out on its surface, there was nothing on which Judy might have written an explanation for her actions. "I've always understood that people who take their own lives tend to leave a note, explaining why they've done what they've done," he said. In truth, there was one obvious explanation which occurred to John, and he didn't care, at that moment, to consider it more fully.

Edward had no such reservations. "Do you think this is something to do with Thompson's death? Could she have been involved?"

"I have absolutely no idea," John snapped, angry again, his fury burning away the emotional blanket which had enclosed him. "Perhaps we should leave that kind of thought to the police too?"

"Of course, of course," Edward agreed quickly. He shuffled his feet, looking down at them, avoiding John's eye. "Well, I think that's all we can do for now. Do you want to wait here, while I go back to the office and telephone Inspector Whyte?" A loop from the cut end of the rope protruded from under John's jacket and Edward rubbed it between his fingers again. "I'm sure I've seen this before, you know," he muttered as he left the room.

John listened as his footsteps disappeared down the corridor. He had no wish to touch the rope again, but he peered down at it nonetheless. It was thicker than he'd thought when he was cutting through it; not a single strand, but dozens of thinner strings twisted around one another like the braids he'd been forced to put in his sister's hair as a boy. Where he'd sawn through it, individual strings had sprung apart, so it had frayed and splayed out at the end. It reminded him of something too, but he couldn't put his finger on quite what. He looked around the room, keen to focus his attention anywhere other than on Judy Faith's face. The thought occurred to him that, if Judy had left her note on the table, perhaps Edward had knocked it off when he had blundered into the room.

He crouched down and peered beneath it, but the weak light from the naked bulb in the ceiling served only to create a room full of shadows and he could make nothing out. There was a switch on every make-up table in the theatre that turned on an arc of small, bright lights arranged around the mirror behind it, however. He turned these on, then stepped across to the doorway and stood there, staring into the noticeably brighter room, searching for a flash of white paper against the dark floor.

To the right, the make-up table took pride of place, with Judy's body on the floor between it and the cold fire grate. Straight ahead, a long wall covered in crooked and torn posters advertising justly forgotten shows ran from the table to an untidy pile of old chairs stacked in three unsteady columns in the far corner. Another shorter wall, this one largely obscured by the piles of boxes he'd poked amongst a few days earlier (which he now saw were cryptically marked with phrases like *Tempest, Summer '51* and *Disaster Panto*) joined up with the other long wall which led back to the open door in which John stood. But though he strained his eyes peering into corners, and his muscles lifting chairs and boxes to check behind them, there was no sign of anything which might be a suicide note.

It was all depressingly grubby, to John's mind. Not the place for anyone to die, far less someone as full of energy as Judy Faith. He found his mind wandering, as it had done all his life when he felt stressed. Presumably Judy Faith wasn't her real name, he thought, and wondered if Fagan knew what it was. Probably not. But he would have her manager's details, though, and he was bound to know. He probably gave her the name, come to think of it. Her family would need to be told, of course; he shuddered at the notion of having that particular task. How do you tell a mother her daughter is dead, far less that she had reached so low a point that suicide was the only escape?

The only escape… unbidden, the one question he'd been trying to avoid asking himself forced its way to the front of his mind. What *had* Judy escaped by killing herself? The obvious answer was the one Edward had hinted at – some connection to Nate Thompson's murder. But why would she have been involved in that? *How*, for that matter, could she have been involved? Thompson had been well over six foot tall and a good eighteen stone; Judy had been five foot two at most, and he doubted she'd have tipped the scales at eight stone, not even if she were wringing wet, as his nanny used to say. She could no more have beaten Thompson to death than she could have learned to fly.

But what else could it be?

The thought was still bubbling away in his head when Edward reappeared in the doorway and announced that the police were on their way.

33

Inspector Whyte was surprisingly phlegmatic, considering he was investigating a second death linked to the theatre in a matter of days. In fact, he had seemed more irritated than concerned when he appeared at the stage entrance and followed Edward and John to Judy's dressing room.

"Don't they have heating in this place?" he complained, rubbing his hands together then loudly blowing into them as he stood in the doorway and looked inside. "Still, it should make the doctor's job a bit easier. Cold air stops the body from decomposing, makes it easier to establish an accurate time of death." He stepped inside before anyone could reply, then leaned back into the corridor to shout at a uniformed constable standing there. "Houliston! Get yourself back to the entrance and wait there for Doctor Jenner. I doubt he's been back here before, and we don't want him getting lost."

"Right then," he went on without a pause, "you say you found the young lady's body hanging from the ceiling half an hour ago?"

"Thirty-four minutes, to be precise," Edward agreed. "I looked at my watch as soon as we got poor Judy down." He smiled. "I knew that was the kind of information you'd want to know."

"Did you now?" There was no corresponding warmth in Whyte's voice and, not for the first time, Edward wondered what they'd done to upset him. A moment later, as though reading his mind, the inspector provided an answer. "It's very good of you to think of us, but I want to make one thing crystal clear. I thought when we came here earlier that I'd heard your names before, but I assumed it was just from the telly. When you phoned the station again just now, though, I remembered where I'd seen them. You two were involved with that woman who killed those kids last year, weren't you? The one whose dad was shot by the Jerries?"

Edward nodded and smiled. "I did hope you'd remember that…" he began to say, but Whyte hadn't finished speaking. "You made a right mug of the inspector in charge of that case, that's what I remember. Delivered a killer on a plate by two old coots, and left looking like an idiot who couldn't find his arse with his hands. Well, be in no doubt, I won't be the next officer left with egg on his face because of you two. This is a police investigation, and doesn't need any assistance from a pair of nosy old geezers, even if you did get lucky once. The only role either of you have in this case is as witnesses. And if I find you've stepped out of those roles, the next ones you'll be playing will be as prisoners in the cells, charged with interfering with the course of justice, impersonating a police officer and any other bloody thing I can think of." He stopped and glared at each man in turn. "Do I make myself clear?"

Edward didn't trust himself to speak but John, who always hated an awkward silence, nodded and murmured "crystal clear, Inspector," in a placating tone. For a moment, it looked as though the policeman had something more to say to them, but instead he talked across Edward's head to one of a pair of constables standing by the door, waiting for instructions.

"Get the drawers of that dressing table emptied, see if you can find anything useful in there. And you," he went on, indicating the other officer, "get your torch out and see if these two managed to knock a suicide note onto the floor while they were busy trampling all over a potential crime scene. It may look like a suicide, but you never know, do you?"

As the men busied themselves at their tasks, he turned back to John and Edward, whose face had turned a dangerous colour of deep red. "We'll be viewing this one with a pretty open mind, I reckon. Two suspicious deaths in the space of a week in the same vicinity is the kind of thing that makes me suspicious. But Mr Fagan is on his way, so I think I'm done with you pair for now." He waved a hand in the air, obviously dismissing them. "We'll need to take your statement and fingerprints later, so don't go too far. Though since you also conveniently managed to handle the body, I expect they're all over the bloody place."

"Conveniently!" Edward exploded as the inspector turned away. "Just what are you implying...?" he sputtered. But just then the third constable appeared, slightly in front of a stout man in a long mackintosh and battered felt hat – presumably the police doctor – who entered the room and placed the bag he was carrying on the table. The inspector took him by the elbow and led him to the body. Before Edward could cause an unpleasant scene, John pulled on his arm in turn and guided him away.

"Come along, old chap," he said soothingly. "I can see you're getting yourself worked up, but shouting will only send your blood pressure racing." He glanced around quickly; nobody was watching them. Quietly, he dropped the key to the house in the park onto the floor and kicked it one side. "Besides, it'll get us nowhere. Let's head down to the kitchen and see about a cup of tea." He tried to smile but, as he did so, he caught sight of the doctor pulling his jacket from Judy's body, and the attempt came to nothing. Instead, he grimaced, feeling the lump return to his throat, and wordlessly led Edward down the corridor.

34

If the clock on the kitchen wall was to believed, they were kept waiting for less than an hour, but for John the period between leaving Judy's dressing room and a young constable arriving in the kitchen to take their statements was an interminable and insufferable one. When the tranquilising effects of shock began to wear off, the sheer horror of the situation flooded over him, and it was all he could do not to burst into tears.

This was nothing like the death of Nate Thompson, a man who – though, strictly speaking, a friend – he'd not set eyes on in decades, nor even like the deaths of the previous year, horrible though those had been in their own way. At least then, each of the girls had been strangers to him, their deaths tragic in a largely abstract sense. But he had been fond of Judy, for all their relatively brief acquaintance; she had made him laugh and had seemed so full of life. The loss he felt now was a personal one.

He glanced across at Edward, but his friend was lost in his own thoughts, his earlier anger seemingly forgotten.

Only when the police officer politely coughed from the doorway did he raise his eyes from the now cold cup of tea he held in his hands.

"Sorry to intrude, but the inspector wants me to take your statements." The policeman was young and wiry looking, with neatly trimmed dark hair and a prominent Adam's apple. He glanced around the tatty kitchen. "Showbusiness isn't as glamorous as they make it look on the telly, eh?" he laughed, but neither Edward nor John joined in. "Anyway," he went on awkwardly, "if I could start with you, Mr Lowe. Could tell me what you saw when you arrived in the lady's dressing room?"

It only took five minutes for Edward to explain what had happened, and no time at all for John to announce he had nothing to add. The young constable seemed satisfied. He closed his notebook and, picking up his helmet from the table, prepared to leave. At the last second, though, he turned back to Edward, with a frown creasing his forehead. "Actually, Mr Lowe, I do have one more question. Why were you both in the theatre at this time of night in the first place?"

John waited to see what Edward would say. Given the events of the evening, he could see no reason to keep the existence of Thompson's little bolthole a secret any longer. Still, might the fact they had failed to alert the police about it at the beginning look a tad suspicious? After all, Thompson had died soon after they arrived – soon after he'd taken the man's job, he realised with a sickening lurch in his stomach – and now they'd discovered poor Judy's dead body in a place they had no real right to be. Admitting to having withheld evidence could place them in… well, an invidious light, to say the least.

"I had left my script in my dressing room and needed it for the morning," said Edward. "Mr Le Breton was kind enough to accompany me to the theatre to collect it, and we passed Miss Faith's room on the way to my own and saw the poor girl hanging there."

Edward gave no indication that anything he'd said was other than the absolute truth, and the policeman seemed entirely satisfied. He made a final note and tucked his notebook in his jacket pocket. "That's all we need from you just now," he said. "You're free to go, but if we need to speak to you again, we can contact you here, is that right?"

Edward nodded and muttered "of course", which was lucky, as John was sure his own mouth was still hanging open at the brazenness of his friend's easy lies. He watched the policeman until he had disappeared back along the corridor, then turned his attention to Edward once more.

"What on Earth are you thinking of? You can't just lie to the police, you know," he said, making a conscious effort not to raise his voice. The last thing he wanted was to bring the constable back again.

Edward was sanguine. "Come now, John, you heard that pompous fool of an inspector. *The next role you play will be as prisoners*, indeed! And as for the disgraceful imputation that we *conveniently* disturbed a crime scene! Allowing that poor girl a shred of dignity was all we did, and to suggest we had some underhand motive for doing so… frankly, that told me all I needed to know about the character of Inspector Whyte. A man cursed with an unpleasant, duplicitous nature, who naturally thinks that everyone else is as untrustworthy as he. I simply wasn't having it – and I certainly had no intention of assisting his enquiries." He placed the teacup which he still held in his hands onto the table, and gave a small, cold laugh. "Didn't he say that he didn't need our assistance? *Nosy old geezers* was the phrase he used, if I recall correctly. Well, so be it. If the inspector wishes to know about Sir Nathaniel's love nest, then he will need to find out about it the hard way."

John stared at the little man, who had crossed his arms and squared his shoulders exactly like the character he played in *Floggit and Leggit*. He knew that Edward had formed a real contempt for the police force during their investigations the previous year, but he hadn't realised until this moment just how deeply that contempt ran.

"And if they should find out we haven't told them about it? Or the papers we found in the fireplace?" he asked. "I don't know about you, but I can't help but feel that I'm rather too old and delicate for a spell of hard labour."

"You're hardly fine china, John," Edward chided, but with a slightly warmer smile. "But I doubt it's a prison matter in any case. If need be, we can simply tell them at a later date and plead our failing geriatric memories."

"That's not really the point though, is it, Edward? *Someone* murdered Nate Thompson, and the things we found in that box have something to do with it, I'm sure. And we still don't know why poor dear Judy did what she did. Perhaps she was involved in some way after all. Either way, we're withholding potentially vital evidence."

"Do you really believe that little Judy Faith would be able to beat a grown man like Sir Nathaniel Thompson to death? My God, man, she didn't have the *reach*, far less the strength to do so. I know I wasn't as close to the girl as you were, but, no, I think I can safely say she had nothing to do with that."

"Well, yes, I did have the same thought." Satisfied for the moment, John rubbed his hands across his eyes, and contemplated the cracked linoleum floor beneath his feet. Without warning, he felt dog-tired. Perhaps the after-effects of shock still lingered, because the grief and pain he'd felt earlier, and which he knew he would feel again in the very near future, had temporarily receded and, in their place, they'd left an emptiness and an overwhelming desire to sleep.

"Come on, Edward. You heard the man. We're free to go. They don't want us here, and I don't want to be here. What say we head back to the hotel and sleep on it? Things are bound to seem clearer in the morning."

Edward sighed. "Yes, you're right, of course. They certainly couldn't appear any more confused than they do just now." Groaning, he levered himself to his feet. He took their cups to the sink and ran water into each one. "I assume the theatre won't be open tomorrow. Fagan will let everyone know, I suppose." He too seemed exhausted by the evening's events. He let the tap wash away the dregs of tea from the cups. John fancied he saw him slump for a few moments, then the little man squared his shoulders and, shaking himself like a wet terrier, turned on his heel and headed out of the door, only glancing backwards to call "are you coming, then?" as an apparent afterthought.

John heaved himself up with a groan and followed in his wake, already dreaming of bed and the blessed relief of unconsciousness.

35

In the darkness, John sat bolt upright in bed, jerked awake by a sudden realisation.

A sea anemone!

That's what the end of the rope had reminded him of. He'd seen lots of them once, scuba diving off the coast of South Africa during a rest day from filming some movie or other. Sally had been with him: she'd said how pretty they looked, swaying against the rocks. Their guide had been rather a grumpy chap, though, and he'd taken great delight in telling her they used their colourful fronds to lure unsuspecting fish into range before stinging them to death.

Upon returning to Mrs Galloway's, he'd said goodnight to Edward and stumbled to bed with a final glass of whisky. But desperate as he was to escape into sleep, the memory of Judy's dead body had obstinately lingered, and he'd struggled to drop off. He'd discarded *Lord Vladimir's Intended* and tried to read the copy of *The Virgin Soldiers* which lay by his bedside – a gift from Jimmy Rae, who'd played a small role in the film version the previous year. But though reading usually worked, it had taken a second glass of whisky before he had eventually slipped into an uneasy slumber.

Only to be rudely awakened by the memory of a colourful sea anemone, and the miserable thought which had lodged in his head and refused to be shaken free.

Was it *certain* that Judy had taken her own life?

Obviously, it *looked* that way, there was no denying it. But perhaps there was a good reason there was no note?

He felt his breath catch in his throat as the thought took root and would not be discarded. Could it have all been a set-up, a scene created to suggest suicide, but in fact hiding murder? Inspector Whyte had suggested as much, after all.

Switching on the bedside lamp, he thought back to Edward showing him Judy's lifeless hand. *A couple of her nails are broken*, he'd said, and, yes, the nails on her index and middle finger had been ragged where they'd snapped off. But wouldn't *all* her fingernails be in a similar condition if she'd been trying to force them between the tightening rope and her neck? Why would you only use a couple of fingers to try to save yourself?

And as for the bruise on her cheek…

He struggled to picture the dressing room as they'd found it. The rope had been attached to the pipe which ran along the ceiling, but that pipe was close to the wall. Even if Judy had changed her mind at the last second, too late to stop the terrible act she'd put into motion, even if she had struggled and kicked… even then, what could she possibly have hit her face against? There was nothing jutting from the wall more solid than a tattered poster, and even if she'd somehow twisted in the air and struck the wall itself, her forehead or her shoulder would have been far more likely to have taken the brunt of any blow than her cheek. Considered like that, he wasn't sure it was even possible for her to have struck her cheek against anything substantial enough to leave a bruise.

Almost without the awareness that he was doing it, John swung his long legs out of bed and reached for his trousers.

* * *

"I've never heard such a ridiculous idea!"

Edward's voice was petulant as he stared up at John from his bed. "I know this evening's events have left you shaken – I'd be lying if I didn't admit that I'm also still processing what's happened – but even if I had any desire to return... there... at..." He lifted the alarm clock and peered at it short-sightedly. "...four in the morning, I very much doubt Inspector Whyte would be happy to see us. No," he'd said, replacing the clock on the bedside table, "I won't be a party to such foolishness, especially on such a flimsy rationale."

He'd paused then, sniffed and, not unkindly, went on, "But if you're sure it's so important, I suppose we could get a few hours' sleep and then nip across in the morning at, say, seven, before anyone else arrives? That is, if the whole theatre isn't locked up tight and covered in police tape by now."

With that, he'd reached over to his beside lamp and pointedly sat with his hand on its switch. "But I *would* appreciate those few hours of rest, so if you don't mind..."

John took the hint and beat a hasty retreat.

36

True to his word, Edward had presented himself at seven sharp and, after a short drive through the deserted streets, they had found themselves slipping inside the stage door of the theatre, which was singularly unburdened by police banner and tapes, much to Edward's expressed disgust.

He pushed through the outer door, still complaining. "Though since I still fail to see why this... what did you call it again?... *anemone* makes you think Miss Faith was murdered, I suppose the police can be forgiven for treating the matter as a simple suicide."

John wasn't completely sure why he now thought differently, but the certainty he'd felt when he'd sat up in bed had not left him. "They didn't say they were definitely treating it as suicide," he reminded Edward. "And I told you, it's not the anemone itself, it's what it does. It pretends to be one thing, when in fact it's quite another. And the other thing it is, is quite deadly."

"Thank you for that, John. That clears everything up."

The sarcasm in Edward's voice was unmissable, but he hadn't had much sleep, so John was willing to make some allowances. "Don't mistake me. I applaud your keenness, of course I do, and I remain convinced that you and I are as likely to provide useful information to Inspector Whyte's enquiry as any of his own men. But I do wonder what you hope to find in the poor girl's dressing room?"

In response, John switched on the torch and shone it around the room, desperate for a clue to jump out from the dust and the dirt.

And then, to one side of the make-up table, the light picked out a section of dust which had been swept in a wide arc. Behind it, almost hidden in the shadows, there was a single large boot print. Beyond it, the dirt had been swept towards the wall, but around the boot print, the grime was undisturbed.

"There." John pointed across to the disturbed dirt. "There's a footprint over there."

"Is there?" Edward peered myopically downwards, but the look on his face made it clear he failed to grasp the significance of John's find.

"Yes. A fresh footprint. And it's too large to be yours and too wide to be mine – and there's no reason why the police would have been stomping about over there. Don't you see? Someone's been in this room recently. Perhaps Judy didn't kill herself." His voice fell to a whisper. "Perhaps she was murdered!"

"Yes indeed." Inspector Whyte's voice was loud in the little room. "Perhaps she was."

John and Edward spun around as though on the same piece of string and found themselves standing toe to toe with the burly policeman.

"Perhaps she was murdered, and perhaps she committed suicide. Perhaps that footprint – which, for your information, one of my constables spotted about two seconds after entering the room last night – was made by someone bracing themselves to haul a young woman up by her neck. One foot planted for leverage…" The inspector stamped hard on the ground with his right foot in demonstration. "The other sliding backwards as it loses traction on the floor." Again, his actions reflected his words, his left foot sliding back until it bumped against the wall behind him. He mimed pulling on a rope, his face twisted with the mock effort. "But the struggles soon cease, and our mysterious man ties the rope off and makes his escape, leaving his victim dangling, all set for two busybodies with nothing better to do to come along and find it."

Edward opened his mouth to speak, but Whyte was obviously expecting that. "Be quiet!" he barked, and Edward – to John's surprise – meekly closed this mouth.

"Or perhaps the young woman had done something terrible, or feared something even worse might happen, or had just had enough of her life. And she tied off a rope from a pipe in her dressing room, stood on a chair and kicked it away. And, later, a couple of old fools manhandle her corpse and plant their big bloody feet all over the place." He stopped and looked from one man to the other, as though daring them to speak. "And maybe *that* was an accident, and maybe it wasn't."

"I can assure you…" Edward began, but Whyte held up a hand, and his voice trailed off into nothing.

"You can assure me of nothing, Mr Lowe. Your assurances *mean* nothing to me. In fact, I only want to hear one thing from either of you. What were you doing here last night? Why were you in the theatre in the middle of the night, finding dead bodies? And don't give me any guff about forgetting your script. Mr Fagan told me you've had your first performance; he said none of you need your scripts anymore."

John glanced at Edward, trying to gauge what they should say. Surely now was the time to come clean? At worst, they would have to admit they'd kept back some evidence. Was that a serious thing? He wasn't certain, but he rather thought it was. Could they go to jail if they told Whyte about the key and the house in the park it belonged to? It was all a horribly confusing situation, and he had no idea what to do for best. He desperately wished Edward would say something.

"I'm not as good as I used to be at remembering my lines, Inspector," Edward said stiffly, every inch the offended old thespian, forced to admit his secret frailty.

It was all John could do not to clap but, at the same time, he wasn't sure this was the right approach to take. They'd lied to the police before, but never quite so boldly and never quite so directly.

Whyte *hmmm*ed, making no attempt to hide his disbelief. "And you agree with that, Mr Le Breton? You also say that you stumbled across Miss Faith's body by chance, while you were on an errand of mercy, keeping your friend company in case he was scared in the big, dark theatre?"

The sarcasm was as plain as Whyte obviously intended, but John chose to ignore it and instead respond only to the part of the question he felt comfortable answering. "I do agree, Inspector. Edward is quite right when he says we found Judy's body by sheer chance." He felt tears, real ones, prick the corner of his eyes. "I only wish he hadn't."

Whyte stared at him for an uncomfortably long time, then gave a single, sharp nod. "Very well, if that's what you choose to claim, far be it from me to doubt you. But perhaps you can illuminate me on why you're both back here at this early hour?"

Now John felt on more secure ground. Before Edward could say anything, he explained about the anemone.

Whyte listened in silence. When John finished, he said "an anenome" in the same tone one might use when reading from a menu in a strange language, pronouncing each syllable individually, hesitant and doubtful.

He held out an arm, fingers extended, pointing at the open doorway. "Probably best if you gentlemen left now. I'll have one of my men come around and put some tape up, just in case you manage to forget this is a crime scene." He smiled coldly. "After all, you did say your memory isn't what it once was, and I'd hate to have to take you down to the station if I ever find you in this room again."

Without another word, Edward and John left the room, John at least feeling like a schoolboy dismissed by the headmaster, glad not to have been punished quite as badly as he'd feared.

"I suppose you intend to ignore everything the inspector said?" John asked as they walked back to the car. "And there's no point in my trying to persuade you otherwise?"

On anyone other than Edward, the look he shot John in reply would have been described as impish. "Actually, I was just wondering what time that library opened. We've probably got time to stop somewhere for a spot of breakfast before we take those books back."

37

John pulled their borrowed car into a parking space directly in front of the library.

It was a squat, concrete building, whitewashed and utilitarian. A revolving door opened onto a scuffed linoleum-covered floor, and a smell of disinfectant and paper that reminded John of school visits when the boys were very young, and he'd still had a family to go home to. He pushed through an interior door into the library proper, which at least had a carpet, though it smelled just as unappealing.

Metal shelves were arrayed along each side of the wide room, bolted at right angles to the wall on either side, with more criss-crossing them towards the rear. A couple of large wooden tables had been placed in the centre, with discarded books on them. Around these sat a handful of older people, reading newspapers and sheltering from the cold outside. A wide desk, with a lady librarian sitting behind it, was just inside the door on the right-hand side. A large sign on the desk, white with black capitals printed across it, read *SILENCE IS GOLDEN*.

John made his way across to the librarian, with Edward close behind, puffing slightly as he hurried to shoulder his way in front, brandishing a carrier bag filled with the books they'd taken from Thompson's love nest.

The librarian looked up at Edward without much interest as he dumped the bag on the desk and, with a groan, asked if she could help him with an enquiry.

"Of course. That's what I'm here for." The librarian had grey hair tied in a bun, with thin lips, well-plucked eyebrows and small, beady eyes, which peered out from behind wing-tipped glasses. She had barely any accent, Edward was delighted to hear. There were times when he found broad Lancashire speakers quite tricky to understand.

"Ah, quite," Edward breathed heavily as he tipped the books out of the bag and stacked them neatly on the desk. "We've come to return these library books. I'm afraid that we're doing so on behalf of a friend who is currently incapacitated, though, and we're afraid they might have more books still out." He laughed unconvincingly. "We don't want him to end up owing a fortune in fines, do we!"

"These books are late," the librarian frowned. "A fine is therefore already due. And presumably any others will be equally late?"

"More so," John piped up, and smiled what he liked to think of as his most charming smile. "Even with your stalwart assistance in identifying them, we'll need to toddle back to our friend's house and find the other books."

It was hard to tell if the smile had any effect. The librarian – Linda Hardy, according to a small name badge pinned to her cardigan – continued to peer up at the two men without speaking, then flipped open the first book and ran a finger down the stamped dates on the inside cover sheet.

"The third of November," she said to herself, then spun around in her chair, and reached for a wooden box on a shelf behind her. Once she'd placed it on the desktop, John could see it contained thirty-one stiff black plastic dividers, between which sat columns of miniature orange wallets, each one holding a tan-coloured sliver of card. Linda flipped to the plastic divider marked "3", and pulled out a single orange wallet. Her eyes narrowed as she glanced down at the writing on the front of the wallet.

"You said that your friend was incapacitated?" she asked. "So, you didn't want *him* to be stuck with a heavy fine?"

John heard the emphasis she placed on *him*, but he had no chance to speak before Edward agreed that yes, that was exactly the case.

"We've no idea when he'll be back on his feet," he said, nodding his head, and reaching for the square of orange card.

"That's funny," responded the librarian, snatching the card back. "We don't get many gentlemen customers who call themselves *Mrs*. None at all, in my experience, actually."

Edward was commendably unruffled. "It must have been his wife who took the books out," he said calmly, his hand still outstretched, as though the whole silly mix-up would be sorted in a second.

"Then why didn't she give you all the books he had out, then? For that matter, why didn't she bring them down here herself?"

"She's incapacitated too. Their car... went off a bridge." The words were out of John's mouth before he could snatch them back and, even as he spoke, he could feel Edward's eyes glaring balefully in his direction.

"They were lucky to survive, then," the librarian said, now turning to him, the card still gripped in her hand.

"It was a very low bridge. Over a very shallow stream."

"But high enough to incapacitate them both? Maybe they weren't so lucky, after all."

John could feel sweat trickling from his hair across his forehead. "The car landed rather badly," he said, blinking the stinging sweat from his eyes.

Linda the librarian made a huffing sound which made it clear what she thought of John's story. "I have to applaud their priorities, in that case. After a terrible car crash like that, their first thought was to get two of their friends to take their library books back."

"They're very civic-minded people," John said weakly, wishing he were anywhere but here, caught in the sharp-eyed glare of the world's most suspicious librarian.

"What are their names, then?" she asked, settling back a little in her chair and crossing her legs, as though she already knew they'd have no answer.

"I've had enough of this nonsense!" Edward snapped at John's side and, with a burst of speed of which he wouldn't have thought himself capable, reached forward, snatched the library card from the librarian's hand and made for the exit door.

Fortunately, given the two men's limited ability to sprint, the loss of the card seemed to have left the librarian in shock. Rather than follow, she simply sat, her mouth moving soundlessly as if obeying the sign on her desk. The two men were in their car before she even got as far as the door. As they pulled away, Edward caught a brief glimpse of her in the rear-view mirror, shaking her fist like a comedy villain.

Edward handed the square of orange card to John as he turned the car around the corner and accelerated along the road. "So, what does it say? That is a name and address written on the front, I assume?"

John peered down at the scribble on the card. The address was one he didn't recognise, though logically speaking it must be somewhere reasonably close by the library. But the name was a different matter altogether.

MRS SALLY SIMPSON it said, in thick, handwritten capitals.

That was a name he knew all too well. The day that Sally had married Martin Simpson had been one of the worst of his life.

38

Rather than go back to the theatre, they drove back to Mrs Galloway's, where Jimmy Rae had agreed to meet them. They went up to John's room and took seats on either side of the bed. Edward showed Jimmy the library card he'd stolen. It was only as he did so that he realised he'd just committed a crime, and he felt his stomach sink into his boots.

His dismay must have shown on his face. "I don't think Linda the librarian recognised either of us," John reassured him as he poured each of them a large gin and tonic from the bottles he kept in his bedside cabinet. "And it's not like the police are likely to be interested in a stolen bit of tatty cardboard."

Which was true, as far it went. But – leaving aside a vague and illogical feeling of annoyance that he hadn't been recognised – it wasn't really the point. The reason good people didn't break the law wasn't because they were afraid of being caught and punished. It was because it was the right thing to do. Laws existed for a reason, and it was incumbent on people to obey them. That was one of the cornerstones of civilised life.

And yet, at the first hint of an obstacle in their way, he'd turned into a thief, without so much as a second thought. He'd grabbed something which didn't belong to him and *done a runner*, as he'd seen it described on *Dixon of Dock Green* the other night.

"But why did you pinch it?" Jimmy was smoking one of his vile foreign cigarettes – French, Edward thought, or possibly Turkish – and the smoke was already filling the room in clouds of noxious fumes. He made some time in which to consider his reply to the question by going across and pulling open the bedroom window, allowing some of the smoke to make its way outside.

"I had no choice," he said finally. "John had embarked on an extremely implausible tale of crashed cars and miniature bridges, and it was obvious that the bloody woman had no intention of helping us further."

"But couldn't you just have taken the card off this librarian bird, read it, and handed it back? Rather than pinching it, you know?"

He had a point. But Edward no more liked to think of himself as a man who panicked than he liked to think himself a thief, so he brushed the suggestion off with a grunt and a dismissive wave of his hand. No, he decided, he'd been decisive and taken the necessary action. Anything else would have been sheer folly.

John, who'd been quiet since their flight from the library, spoke up before Jimmy could say anything further. "It may just be me, but I can't help thinking that would actually have been ruder than taking the thing and running. Rather like not taking the dear woman seriously." His tone was as mild as ever, and he accompanied the remark with a tiny, self-deprecating movement of his mouth and shoulders, but Jimmy evidently thought it answer enough and didn't raise the question again.

"Fair enough," he said with a grin. "I keep forgetting you two were brought up during the Napoleonic Wars. Things were probably a lot different back then." His grin widened, and John laughed. Even Edward had to smile at the cheek of the younger man. He'd been called Napoleon in his time – he'd heard more than one of the crew on *Floggit* whisper it behind his back, in fact – but this was the first time anyone had suggested he'd actually been around during the little Frenchman's heyday.

"Very good, Jimmy," he said, letting his smile indicate no offence had been taken. "But, all joking aside, now we've removed it from the library, we need to make use of the information it contains." He pointed to the writing on the card. "Do you recognise the name?"

Immediately, Jimmy shook his head. "I've been racking my brains for the last few minutes, but I can't think of any Mrs Simpsons – except for the American bird who married that King who buggered off. And I don't suppose it's her!"

"No, I don't suppose it is," Edward agreed more sombrely.

"You've got an address for her, though." Jimmy ran his finger along the bottom two lines on the card. "King's Drive in Cheadle Hulme."

"As it happens, Mrs Galloway has a collection of maps which belonged to her husband and which she was kind enough to lend us, so I'm sure we can find it."

"Cool! We should take a hike down there tomorrow."

Ever since that unfortunate argument with John in the pub, Jimmy had been entangled in their investigation. Edward had initially not been keen on involving him, but he was still concerned that someone was following them, and a younger man's physical strength could well come in handy. Not that he couldn't look after himself – hadn't he faced down a gun-wielding extra just last year? – but even so…

"I take it you heard about the hidey-hole the police found in Judy's dressing room?"

At first, Edward had no idea what he was talking about. He stared at Jimmy and at John's stricken face behind him for a long moment before he realised that he meant the space under the make-up table which they'd ransacked.

"A hidey-hole?" he managed to say before the delay became suspicious. "What kind of hidey-hole?"

"A hole in the wall, Mickey reckons. Hidden behind a cupboard or something. That inspector bloke was pretty excited about it earlier on. Came rushing in like he had Lester Piggott on his back, shoving folk out the way and demanding to know if Judy had asked if she could have Nate Thompson's dressing room after he was killed."

"And had she?" It was a question which would never have occurred to Edward, and he silently, but still grudgingly, tipped his hat to the inspector.

"Seems so. At least, Mickey said she'd wanted it for a

while and, after Nate kicked the bucket, he said she could have it."

"That's hardly surprising, is it?" John's mild voice interjected with a note of caution. "Half the company are stuck two to a room, and not everyone's as much of a delight to share with as Edward." He smiled his usual lopsided smile, but there was something about the way he looked across the bed which left Edward sure something was bothering him. What could it be? He raised an eyebrow in a way he hoped communicated concern, but John avoided his eye and stared down at the floor.

"True," Jimmy said, oblivious to the sudden tension which Edward had felt flare up between himself and John. "There are nights when I'm at my digs, lying in bed reading, and all I can hear through the wall is Pete Glancy snoring like a lumberjack taking a chainsaw to a massive bloody tree. Maybe she just wanted away from whoever she was stuck with."

"Alice Robertson," John supplied the name, and Edward marvelled again at his friend's ability to ingratiate himself in any situation. Personally, he could barely remember everybody's name, but John knew their dressing room arrangements, and probably what they'd had for breakfast too.

"Was there anything in this hidey-hole the police found?" John asked. Edward kicked himself for losing focus on the most important topic under discussion. Of course, they knew exactly what the police would have found: a wooden box with nothing in it. The question now was how to return the key without altering Inspector Whyte to the fact they'd had it in the first place.

Jimmy shook his head. "Not so far as I know. A box and some bits of paper in the fireplace, I think. But Mickey said that Whyte's now thinking that whatever was in the box is what got both of them killed. And whoever killed Judy took whatever it was."

Jimmy rose to his feet, downed his drink and placed the glass on the bedside cabinet. "Time to hit the town," he said, lighting another cigarette. He smoothed down the front of his shirt, ran a finger along his moustache and rearranged the medallion which hung from his neck. Edward wondered, not for the first time, at the modern craze for jewellery on men. It was all a little *feminine*, he thought, twisting the signet ring on his little finger.

"If you two fancy a trip to see Mrs Simpson tomorrow, give me a shout," Jimmy offered from the doorway through a thick cloud of smoke. "Trouble seems to follow you around, and you aren't as young as you used to be, are you?"

He laughed, gave a cheery wave and was out the door before either man could reply.

Edward was glad he'd gone. Jimmy was a nice boy, no doubt of that, and a very decent actor, in spite of his unorthodox background, but he and John had things to discuss about which Jimmy knew nothing, and he'd rather keep it that way for now. He glanced over at John, who was staring into space, the glass in his hand seemingly forgotten and in danger of spilling onto the floor. He reached across and pushed it back upright. John's smile was vague and unfocused.

"Before we do anything else," Edward said, "I think it best we consider how to let Inspector Whyte know about Thompson's secret love nest." He held up a hand to pre-empt any objections from John, but to his surprise the other man said nothing and just sipped at his drink. "I know you dropped the key in the dressing room, but there's no guarantee they'll find it, and I'm sure you agree that Whyte needs to be made aware of its existence." He looked across the bed, but John's attention seemed entirely taken up by his glass, which he twirled in his long fingers. "And, besides, we have a new avenue of attack. This Mrs Simpson was presumably the married lover that Peter Glancy mentioned. A chat with her is bound to be interesting."

As soon as Edward mentioned Mrs Simpson, John looked up. It was as though a switch had been turned on in him. "Surely *that* won't be our avenue to explore once we tell the inspector about Nate Thompson's house in the park?" he said. "We can hardly drip-feed him information as and when we see fit, after all." He shook his head. "No, if we tell him about the second house, then I rather think we'll also need to tell him about the library books and Mrs Simpson, and take an immediate step back ourselves."

Edward was aware he had a tendency to consider the police as a necessary – and often not so necessary – evil at times. The previous year, he had been baulked and ignored by the authorities to such a degree that, in his mind, it had led to at least one young woman dying who might have been saved. Inspector Whyte admittedly appeared to be cut from a different cloth but, even so, he wasn't quite ready to trust him yet.

"Yes, I see what you mean," he said to John. "Better we speak to Mrs Simpson and then present the whole thing to the inspector as a package."

"That's the spirit," John said, tipping his glass in salute.

Edward had the queerest sense that John sounded like *him*. Usually, it was his job to chivvy John along, to raise his spirits, encourage him to be more energetic, convince him that the police need not be involved in their investigations.

Yet, here was John filling that role, even down to suggesting that they press on without informing the authorities about some fairly major developments. It was most peculiar, he decided, but not without its benefits.

He tilted his own glass in John's direction. Yes, there were definitely some benefits to this new John Le Breton.

39

If Nate Thompson's funeral had been a frigid, rain-drenched affair, devoid of warmth in every respect, Judy Faith's was the exact opposite.

After an eternity of grey Lancashire skies and what felt at times like unceasing rain, the weather in Judy's hometown of Brighton was bright, sunny and unseasonably warm. Some of the men in the crowd waiting outside the crematorium for the funeral cars to arrive had loosened their ties and undone the top buttons of their shirts, and certain of the older ladies fanned themselves and angled their hats to keep the sun out of their eyes. "You'd never know it was November," a young woman in an outrageously pink dress remarked to John as he stood at the door and shielded his eyes with his hand.

"It is rather hot, isn't it?" he said politely, but the girl had already switched her attentions to a young man on her other side, and John wondered if she'd actually been talking to him at all.

Beside him, he felt Edward stiffen and tut under his breath. "What's the matter, Edward?" he asked. "Too hot for you?"

"Not at all. I mean, it *is* hot, but not too hot for everyone to forego suitable funeral attire." Not wishing to draw attention to himself, he nodded at various of the younger mourners who, John now realised, were all wearing bright colours in fashionable styles, rather than the more traditional and more sombre dark clothing he, Edward and the other older people had chosen. Even Jimmy Rae had forgone a black tie in favour of an open collar and a blue-and-white cravat knotted high up his neck.

"Is this some kind of new thing?" Edward asked Jimmy irritably, flicking the bottom of the cravat with his finger. "Something to do with the hippies?"

Jimmy only laughed. "It's what Judy wanted. She said loads of times that when she died, she wanted everyone to wear bright colours. She wanted her funeral to be a celebration of her life." His smile faded as quickly as it had appeared. "She didn't expect it to be so soon, though."

"No, I don't suppose she did."

There were many more people at this funeral than there had been at Nate Thompson's. All the way from the main gate and along the short drive to the main chapel, a crowd had gathered which spilled here and there into the road. They were mostly young people, fans of Judy's work, with a leavening of older journalists, easily identified by their scruffy suits and ever-present notepads, and, here and there, a photographer. Nearer the chapel, separated from them by a red rope, colleagues of Judy's – actors, musicians and writers mainly – stood and smoked in small groups. John recognised a saxophonist he'd seen play wonderfully well at Ronnie Scott's amongst the musicians, but it was as though the different creative sorts had been subconsciously separated by profession, and the musicians and actors didn't overlap enough for him to introduce himself.

A small car park to one side of the driveway was similarly crowded, with vehicles parked in every possible space. Idly, John wondered how easy it would be to get away afterwards – it looked as though their bulky Ford Anglia was blocked in by a gleaming American-style motorbike. He turned to point out the potential problem out to Edward, but the little man was staring past him, so he turned again, though for the life of him he couldn't see what had caught his attention.

"Over there," Edward said quietly. "To the left of the car park, on that grassy mound."

All John could see on the little patch of grass was a tall man in a donkey jacket, standing by himself with tears rolling unashamedly down his face. It was tricky to make out details at such a distance, but he was almost as wide as he was tall, with a large, square head and thick black hair and beard. Unlike the other mourners, nobody appeared to be with him, and nobody went over to offer him comfort, even though the sound of his sobbing was audible across the noisy chatter of the crowd.

"Doesn't that look like Alison Jago's description of Judy Faith's admirer? The chap who had Nate Thompson by the throat? Craig Mackay, was it?"

As though Edward had called him by name, the big man's head whipped up. He dragged a hand over his eyes and stared at the two men for an instant, then turned and walked away, quickly merging into the mass of mourners. He was taller than almost everyone around him, so John was able to follow his progress until he reached the end of the driveway and disappeared into the street outside.

In his place, two funeral cars entered through the crematorium gates.

Long and black and brightly polished, the cars moved at walking pace along the drive, with a tall, thin man in a black frock coat and top hat measuring the pace in front. As they moved past the crowd of mourners, John was pleased to see everyone wearing a hat remove it, and everyone – save for one photographer, who continued to take snaps of the passing procession – bow their heads.

The cars came to a halt in front of the chapel, only yards from John. He could see a wooden coffin inside the lead car, and felt his stomach turn over, exactly as it had done when he and Edward had found Judy's body. At his side, he heard Jimmy Rae mutter what sounded like a prayer, then someone appeared in the chapel doorway and invited them all to enter. Edward hesitated for a second, still looking at the spot where Judy's admirer had disappeared, then led the way inside.

The interior of the chapel was cool and bright, with marble walls and tall windows through which sunlight streamed. Rows of chairs were arranged on either side of a central aisle – just like a wedding, John thought, then grimaced. He followed Edward and the rest of the theatre company down the aisle to a seat half a dozen rows from the front and waited for the chapel to fill up. He twisted his head around and counted the chairs. Eight seats on each side of the aisle, say twenty rows deep. So, room for one hundred and sixty mourners, he decided. Barely enough for those on this side of the red rope, never mind the fans who'd stood on the other side.

There was the family too, of course. A middle-aged couple, presumably Judy's parents, walked down to the front and sat in the two seats nearest the aisle, he in his best suit with his hair slicked down across his balding scalp, and she in a dark coat and hat, a handkerchief pressed to her face, barely muffling her sobs. Two younger men – Judy's brothers, perhaps – took the next two seats. One reached over and put an arm around the crying woman, and she leaned her head on his shoulder, still sobbing.

"Did you see Inspector Whyte?" Edward hissed quietly in his ear. "Sitting at the back, across the way." He put a warning hand on John's arm. "Don't look! I wonder if he spotted Mackay?" He frowned. "Presumably he does know about him – we should check that. Though he might be here to keep an eye on the other members of the company, hoping to catch one of them acting strangely, looking for evidence of disharmony in the ranks. We should be on the lookout for that too, of course."

John found it hard to care about the inspector. Throughout his life, he'd taken care to keep his serious attachments to a minimum. Not in the way Edward did, by erecting a barrier through which people rarely passed, but rather by limiting such attachments so that he was only especially close to a small number of people at any one time. Even at school, he'd had one or two special chums amidst a plethora of more casual acquaintances. The same pattern had continued in the army, in rep, and then in television and movies. His was essentially a sedentary personality, he knew that. He preferred not to be inconvenienced, he liked other people to care for him, but not too much. He hated to be hurt.

So – for all that women undoubtedly liked him a great deal – he had never been a ladies' man. In a profession where monogamy was often seen as a peculiar concept even in the abstract, he had never cheated on any of the women he'd let into his life, no matter how seemingly minor the dalliance.

But he had been very fond of Judy, even in the short period he'd known her. He'd never had a daughter, only sons, but he'd thought more than once that had he had one, he would have been delighted if she'd turned out like Judy.

And then there was Sally, back in his life like a tiny blonde tornado, able to wreak havoc with the slightest of touches.

Sally, who somehow was linked to Nate Thompson.

Sally, who might even have been Thompson's lover.

Again.

40

London, 1945

It had been a lonely time for Sally. How could it not be, after her new husband went off to war for five years?

He'd not been back in all that time. He'd been stuck in Egypt for the duration, at no risk after the first few months, but too far away for it to be worthwhile coming home. He'd had letters, of course, filled at first with stories of the improvements she intended to do to the flat in his absence, and tales of nights out with friends and of evenings spent huddled underground, hiding from Nazi bombs. After their first year apart, her letters had stopped for a while. John had put that down to U-boats sinking mail ships, but still he was relieved when he received a small pile of letters one afternoon. There was much more talk of the Nazis in these letters, and much less of good times with friends. John had the sense that Sally now lived in constant fear, convinced the Germans would invade at any second.

He wrote to his best friend in the world, Nate Thompson, and asked him to look in on Sally. *Keep an eye on her for me, old boy*, he'd written. *Sally's not built for living under siege. She needs bright lights and dancing, bottles of champagne and dishes of oysters. See what you can rustle up, there's a good chap*! He and Nate had met during the run of a play, and bonded over a shared love of Tommy Dorsey and fine whisky. He was based in London during the war, doing something terribly secret with counter-intelligence in Richmond, and had been a regular visitor to their flat after they'd married. Sally had always liked him.

John had gone back to his none-too-onerous war duties with an easy mind, certain Nate would sort things out.

* * *

In due course, the war finally ended and Captain John Le Breton was shipped home. As he stood at the rail of the ship every night of the two-week journey, sailing north through the Mediterranean, he thought of Sally, and wondered if she'd have changed much in his absence. Even though Egypt had been safely in Allied hands for three years, he'd not had a letter from her in six months, or from Nate.

He'd written to her to let her know when he was due back in England and couldn't help but be disappointed when there was nobody to meet him at the docks. Still, it was only an hour's drive to the flat, and he'd soon rustled up a lift.

It was strange – and cold – being back in London. The paved streets and the electric streetlights looked wrong, somehow, and the wind cut straight though him and chilled him to the bone. As a result, when he jumped out of the car that had brought him from the ship, he paused for only a second to wave his thanks to the driver before bounding up the stairs to the main entrance of the building, keen to get out of the wind and to be reunited with Sally.

He didn't have a key – God knows where that had ended up – but the flat door was unlocked and he positively burst through it, shouting Sally's name as he shouldered open the sitting room door.

He would remember the sight of Sally, half undressed, wrapped in Nate Thompson's arms for the rest of his life. It was just about all he could clearly remember of the next few minutes. Ineffectual punches were thrown, then his arms were pinned to his side by Thompson, who was babbling some kind of explanation. Sally was crying and shouting his name, everything was blurred and indistinct, except the sharp smell of spilled whisky and Sally's face, caught for an instant in his mind like a photograph, red-faced and swollen, with mascara running down her cheeks like two train tracks.

The next thing he knew, he was outside the flat again, waving down a taxi and telling the driver to take him to the nearest decent hotel. It would be six months before he and Sally next shared a roof.

41

John rose late the day after Judy's funeral. It went without saying that the show was over. There would be no further performances of *King Lear* at the Bolton Playhouse, though Mickey Fagan had hinted that the European trip might still be on. As though anybody cared about that.

He washed, shaved and downed two aspirin with a glass of water from the bathroom sink. His head ached abominably from drinking after the funeral, and his eyeballs felt like they had a heartbeat all of their own. He had hazy memories of Peter Glancy singing "Danny Boy" and Jimmy Rae doing some ridiculous new dance with Alison Jago, but, other than that, it was a bit of a daze.

He wished he was back in Ironbridge, filming *Floggit and Leggit* and being looked after by one of the lovely ladies in the crew.

He pushed open the hotel dining room door and walked in, wincing at the sunlight that shone through the window in the front wall and the view of the sea beyond it, which looked almost white in the bright light.

The only consolation was that presumably everyone else felt just as bad as he did.

Most of the theatre company had booked into the hotel, but only a handful were still eating breakfast by the time he made an appearance. Pleasingly, however, every one of them was bent over as though any sudden movement might kill them, and the only sound which could be heard was a faint groaning from Peter Glancy, who sat with his head flat on his table and his eyes tightly closed.

More by habit than any desire for conversation, or even company, he made his way through the tables and took a seat across from Edward.

"Frank Primrose telephoned this morning," he said, then, 'Oh, and good morning, John."

Annoyingly, now that he was closer to him, Edward looked relatively sprightly. Certainly, he looked a good deal better than John felt.

"Morning," he muttered. "What did he have to say for himself?"

"He's actually in London, attending a course at Hendon, but he finishes at lunchtime today, so he's going to get the train down and visit. He said he had quite a lot to tell us."

John groaned, loud enough for Peter Glancy to briefly lift his head up and look around before settling it back on the table. "I really don't think I can cope with Frank's incessant babbling today, Edward, I really don't. I feel absolutely wretched as it is, and Frank Primrose's *Report from Ironbridge* is not likely to make me feel any better."

Edward nodded and pulled a bowl full of sugar cubes towards himself. "It's a buffet-style breakfast," he said unexpectedly, apparently having moved on from the topic of Primrose's visit. "You can have cornflakes, if that's all you want, or you can take a plate from the sideboard – there's reasonable bacon and sausages under those silver lids, and eggs as well, but I wouldn't recommend them. Like rubber." He sniffed. "I can't say I care for the arrangement. It's just a way of getting you to serve yourself, and the food's not up to much when you do." He stirred his tea. "But it's all that's on offer, and there are kippers, which I wish I'd had in retrospect. Why not get some food inside you and see how you feel? Primrose isn't due until half one, and our train back to Bolton isn't until six, so we've plenty of time to speak to him."

John had struggled to his feet and taken a step towards the sideboard which held the breakfast plates when the meaning of Edward's words percolated through his alcohol-befuddled brain. "Back to Bolton?" he said, turning towards the table and, not trusting his legs to hold him for long, sliding back into his seat. "What do you mean, back to Bolton? Surely the show's cancelled now, Edward. Nate had already left when he was killed, but poor Judy…" His voice trailed off miserably. "I was thinking I'd just head home to London and have them send my clothes on later. Bolton – and Amsterdam, for that matter – are both firmly off the menu."

"You'd leave both murders unsolved?"

"That's what the police are for, Edward."

"At the very least, we need to go back to Bolton to tell Inspector Whyte what we've found out – about the house in the park and the library books, and Cleland Waldie and Mrs Simpson. Primrose might even have more information. We can't just go home and forget all about it."

In his hungover state, John had forgotten that Sally was Mrs Simpson and that, once Whyte knew about the library books and the house they'd been found in, it wouldn't take him long to push her to the front of those people he wished to talk to. And – he realised with a sickening lurch – if they discovered who she was, they would also discover she was his ex-wife. Hadn't Whyte hinted he was a suspect right at the beginning? Only a joke, they'd thought at the time, the idea that the title role in a provincial production of *King Lear* was worth killing over. But that John might have murdered a man who'd had an affair with his wife and who'd now taken up with him again? That sounded far more plausible, even to him.

Edward was right. They did need to go back to Bolton. Whether Edward decided to speak to Inspector Whyte or not, it was imperative that John was there, to steer the investigation away from Sally and himself, if he possibly could.

"And besides, if you'd been down in time this morning, you'd have heard Mickey Fagan saying that, though there was no way we could go on with *Lear*, there was nothing to stop us shifting to *Hamlet* a week early instead. He suspected the Amsterdam trip might need to be cancelled, but he said we had a duty to the Bolton Playhouse to keep going there,"

That clinched it. He couldn't go back to London, even if he wanted to. He shuffled slowly across to the breakfast buffet and dropped two sausages onto a plate. One bounced straight off and onto the floor and the other rolled alarmingly in sympathy with his shaking hand before it too slid over the edge and disappeared from sight.

He sighed and poured two cups of coffee, both for himself. It was going to be a long day.

* * *

It had been said of Frank Primrose that he'd have made a much better Jack Russell than a policeman. Faithful, none too bright but filled with a frantic energy when roused, he had been the constable in Ironbridge when *Floggit and Leggit* arrived in town and, following a crucial yet largely serendipitous intervention which ended up saving John's life, had been promoted to sergeant by a chief constable grateful that no television stars had been shot in the head on his patch.

In no way giving the lie to the idea of his doglike devotion, he positively bounded up to Edward and John when he saw them sitting in the corner of a pub around the corner from the hotel that afternoon. John was gingerly nursing a half pint of beer, taking occasional sips and wincing every time he moved his head, and Edward was drinking a pot of tea. Neither man looked in the mood for Primrose, but Edward at least made an attempt to rally in the face of such obvious enthusiasm. John simply groaned and took a gulp of his beer, which he immediately regretted.

"Hello, Mr Lowe," Primrose took a seat opposite the two men and gave them a look which seemed to John to be one of great concern. "Hello, Mr Le Breton. Golly, you don't half look sick. Have you been not well?"

Edward smiled and John felt his mood lighten. There was something about Primrose, often annoying though he could be, which made you feel a little better about yourself. "Entirely self-inflicted," he said, finishing off his drink and deciding he'd no desire for more.

Primrose smiled in return. "You were at a funeral, Mr Lowe said. How can you get drunk at a funeral?"

"You can get drunk anywhere, if you try hard enough, Frank."

"I've never been to a funeral. I've never been invited."

"Well, you're missing nothing. They're surprisingly grim affairs, between you and me."

Edward had been following this exchange with obvious and mounting irritation, and now he took the chance to interrupt. "Yes, we were at a funeral," he said. "That's one of the reasons we got in touch. Remember, I asked you to find out about two people, Cleland Waldie and Nathaniel Thompson?"

Primrose nodded and pulled his police notebook from his pocket. "I did what you asked and made some enquiries, and I found quite a bit out." He smoothed a page in the notebook out on the table in front of him and began to read. Recalling his inept notetaking when they'd first met, John was impressed by the improvement in his abilities.

"First one was the easiest one, this Waldie bloke. He's got a record and a funny name, so he wasn't hard to find – he's been arrested for public intoxication, resisting arrest, breach of the peace and one count of resetting stolen goods. He did six months in jail for that last one, but the rest he got let off with a slapped wrist by the JP. I couldn't get an up-to-date address for him, but he's not been in trouble with the police for nearly ten years. One report did say he'd been diagnosed with something called Parkinson's Disease a few years back, and that was probably why he hadn't been in trouble for a while."

John felt a twinge of disappointment mixed with a greater sense of relief. As soon as they'd found Judy, he'd known that Waldie couldn't be their man – why would he attack an actress he couldn't possibly have known? There was something else too, something someone had said to him earlier which he could sense at the very edges of his thoughts but which he couldn't quite pin down.

Edward, he saw, was shaking his head. "I did wonder whether Waldie was likely to be our man for both deaths," he said. "But he doesn't sound the type, does he? It would have been nice if the man had a long record for violence, but if he's kept his nose clean for ten years, it seems implausible that he's suddenly gone on a murderous rampage."

John saw Primrose's ear prick up at the mention of two deaths. But, before the policeman could ask any questions, he asked one of his own. "And what about Nate Thompson, Frank? Were you able to find out anything about him?"

"Oh plenty, but none of it what you might call official." He closed his notebook and returned it to his pocket. "I didn't write this down, because it's not really the sort of thing we're supposed to talk about." He scowled. "They'd have my guts for garters if they knew I was telling you. But I don't mind, not if it'll help find who killed your friend."

"It's really very kind of you, Frank," John assured him, though he felt rotten for letting him think Thompson was a friend.

"Yeah, well, it's like this, you see. This Nathaniel Thompson hasn't got a criminal record, but he has been arrested a few times and let off with a warning. Mainly for stuff to do with drink – driving under the influence twice, drunk and disorderly once, a couple of domestic callouts – but there was one funny one. It was from *ages* ago, though, so I don't know if you'll be interested?"

"Anything you have, Frank. You never know what could be useful."

"Right, well, it seems like Mr Thompson was in trouble with the law back before the War. The report's gone missing – probably got burned by those Nazi bombers – but there's a memo which talks about it and it says he was arrested for *public morals*, whatever that means, and then let go without charge the next day. The bloke who wrote the memo wasn't happy, I can tell you. He called the chief inspector who let him go some pretty rude names."

Edward shifted uncomfortably in his seat. John had noticed before that he had almost a sixth sense for what he'd been known to call "matters of the flesh" and that whenever they came up, he squirmed with embarrassment. "Public morals, eh? That sounds pretty serious."

"Sounds pretty mucky to me," John grinned. "I wonder if old Nate was caught in flagrante behind some bushes?"

"In where?" Primrose asked, writing the phrase down in his notebook.

"Just outside Dungeness, Frank, but it's not important." It was uncharitable and unchristian and probably the sign of his own dubious morality, but the thought of Nate Thompson being caught with some London doxy and his trousers around his ankles had worked a kind of magic on John. The last vestiges of his hangover had miraculously dissipated and suddenly he felt that all was all right with the world. "Does anyone fancy another drink?" he asked, ignoring Edward's furious glare.

"This is hardly the time for hilarity, John," he snapped brusquely. "There was no indication at all what this breach of public morals entailed?" he asked Primrose, who shook his head mournfully.

"Nothing, Mr Lowe. Just that memo complaining about his release."

"Was there a date?" John asked as he rose to his feet and headed for the bar.

Primrose flicked through his notebook. "Fourteenth of March, 1928," he said. "At least that was the date on the memo."

So, before he'd known the man, John was pleased to discover. Whatever nasty behaviour he might have got up to, it hadn't involved Sally. He left Edward quizzing Primrose further and headed across to the bar. By the time he came back, laden with drinks and crisps, Edward had given up that particular avenue as fruitless and was instead listening to Primrose listing various breaches of public morality he'd come across. He'd obviously thought of several, as he'd managed to count every finger on his left hand. "...

and there's doing your business outside," he concluded, his voice dropping to a whisper. "But you can't really arrest someone for being caught short, can you?"

Edward nodded, a dazed look on his face. "I don't suppose so, no," he said, reaching for the glass John handed him and taking a large gulp of the gin and tonic it contained. "Anyway," he went on, "that's all very useful information. You've been extremely helpful, I must say."

Primrose smiled shyly and bobbed his head. He drained his lemonade in one go then stood up. "I need to go and catch my train," he said.

John and Edward shook his hand and watched him leave, then returned to their seats.

Edward leaned forward conspiratorially. "I didn't want to say in front of young Primrose, but I thought I saw something in your face earlier on. Do you know anything about this public morality business?"

"No, nothing to do with that. It was just... there was something he said which reminded me of something else, but I can't quite remember what exactly." He grimaced, tugged at his ear thoughtfully and considered the whisky in his glass. "No, it's not coming to me. But it might, if I stop concentrating on it. Maybe another drink will help, actually."

And if that didn't help, perhaps the addition of a few more might do the trick. He drained his glass and slid it across the table to Edward. "Your shout, I believe," he said, with a soft smile. They did have three hours before they needed to leave for the train back to Bolton, after all.

42

For the first time since Edward and John had arrived in Lancashire, the sun was really shining. The trip back from Brighton had been a miserable one, with the dank, grey weather of the passing countryside matching everyone's melancholy mood, but, as they'd come though Crewe, bright winter sunlight had broken through the clouds and pierced the gloom on the train.

John and Edward had shared a taxi from the station to the theatre with Mickey Fagan and Alison Jago, half-listening as the other two had discussed what was needed to bring *Hamlet* to the stage with only a few days' rehearsal. Edward was to play Polonius and the ghost of Hamlet's father, it seemed, and would be needed as soon as they got back to run through lines with Monica Gray, who was playing an implausibly elderly Ophelia. John, as Hamlet's stepfather Claudius, would need to block out scenes with Jimmy Rae as the Prince, but not until the following day.

As Alison and Mickey bent over a sheet of paper on

which they'd scribbled some sort of set layout, John leaned closer to Edward and whispered in his ear.

"I wonder if it might not be a good idea for me to pay the mysterious Mrs Simpson a visit tomorrow while everyone else is busy coaching Monica?"

He hoped it wasn't too obvious that he wanted to make the visit without Edward. In fact, he'd rather nobody spoke to Sally at all, and wished they could allow her involvement with Nate Thompson to be swept under the carpet.

But they couldn't do that, he knew that much. Not with Judy dead. This was the only way he could think of to confront Sally without Edward becoming aware of who she was – and, her possible involvement in murder aside, he had things he needed to say to her that he didn't want to say in front of his friend.

The fact that Sally might have got herself entangled with Thompson again had bothered him far more than he would have expected, he had to admit. It was foolish; they were divorced after all. But the memory of the earlier betrayal was one which had stuck with him. He wasn't by nature a jealous or possessive man, but to have his trust trampled on by two people he was so fond of had wounded him terribly. The idea that Sally had returned to Thompson's arms – even decades later – was enough to make his blood boil.

Edward was looking at him curiously, his head cocked to one side like a chubby little robin redbreast. "We certainly need to speak to her sooner rather than later," he admitted cautiously, "but I'm not sure it's safe for you to go there on your own. She may be alone, but, at the same time, we've no way of knowing what accomplices she might have. If Thompson was as large as I've been told, I struggle to imagine a single woman killing him in quite so violent a manner. No," he concluded firmly, "I don't think it's wise at all for you to beard her in her den on your own." He smiled thinly. "After all, the last time you were alone with a woman during an investigation, she tied you to a chair and threatened to shoot you in the head."

What he said made perfect sense; John couldn't deny it, but nor could he tell Edward that he had good reason to believe the woman in question *would* be alone, and that he knew for a fact that he would not end up in the same situation as he had with Madge Kenyon.

"You and Jimmy are supposed to be working on lines together, aren't you?" Edward asked unexpectedly. "He's keen to help out, so could you convince him to go along with you? I'd feel happier knowing you had a younger man with you, to provide some backup, if needed."

It wasn't ideal, but John could see no way around it. "A bit of muscle, eh?" he said, and shrugged. "Well, if you think it necessary, I'll speak to Jimmy. I'm sure he'll be over the moon to get involved."

"I'd feel better if you did." Edward's face twisted into a scowl. "It's quite annoying that I can't come along, but I suppose it makes sense. And this way I can speak to people here and move things along faster." He glanced at his watch. "Let's go and collect the car. We've missed dinner, but perhaps we can convince Mrs Galloway to rustle us up a sandwich."

* * *

The change in the weather continued into the next day, which was breezy but bright.

"If you can drop me off in front of the theatre, I need to report to the rehearsal room for line readings with Monica," Edward said as he lowered himself into the car. "Once I've finished that, I'll have a nose around, I think, see if I can't speak to one or two people."

John was pleased to see Edward had a new urgency about him since they'd left Brighton. Speaking to Primrose and more or less ruling out one suspect had obviously put a spring in his step, but he thought the real reason for this new energy was that his friend was concentrating on finding Judy's killer rather than dwelling on her death.

He knew many people thought the little man prickly, pompous and bad-tempered, and he was all of those things. But they also assumed someone like that must also be unfeeling and selfish, which was far from the case. In reality, John thought that a lifetime of suppressing his feelings, removing from him the safety valve of public displays of emotion and causing him to bottle everything inside, had made Edward care *too much*. John had recognised the previous year that Edward coped with horrific things by figuring out why they had happened and that, by doing so, he took back control of situations which might otherwise have left him bereft. The fact that he was happy to split their forces meant he was feeling positive, which could only be a good thing.

He pulled the car away from the kerb and headed towards the theatre. He hoped that Edward's positivity would extend to understanding why John had kept Sally's involvement a secret, should his visit to her flat mean he needed to be told.

43

By the time Edward had finished running through lines, John was still not back from investigating the address they'd been given by the library. His earlier enthusiasm had been worn down by Monica's constant complaints about her husband, and he'd initially intended to head back to the hotel for a snack and a sleep, but the nagging sense that to do so would somehow equate to shirking his duty led him instead to satisfy himself with an underwhelming egg and cress sandwich from the canteen and a quick nap on a chair in his dressing room. Not much refreshed, and more than a little grumpy, he stirred himself to go and speak to the rest of the cast about Judy, beginning at the top, with Mickey Fagan.

* * *

"And I'm telling you, with a maniac on the loose, preying on young women, Monica's nerves are shredded. It was all I could do to get her out of bed this morning. If it wasn't that she's always wanted to play Ophelia, I doubt I could have convinced her to show face."

Edward came to a halt, his hand grasping the handle of Fagan's office door. The voice was Michael Gray's, raised in pitch to something not quite a shout, but not far off it. He leaned in closer.

"Obviously, I'm sorry to hear that Monica's finding things difficult." The other voice was quieter, but even so, Edward recognised it as belonging to Mickey Fagan. "We all have to pitch in just now, though. It's either that or cancel the run completely, and we decided to press on, if we could."

"Not everyone is pitching in the same amount, though, are they? Now that we've switched to *Hamlet* a week early, and with Monica playing Ophelia, she's got a lot more stage time and a lot more lines to learn. She's taken the extra work on without complaint, while some others seem to be getting away with doing nothing."

"You did just say that it was the thought of playing Ophelia which got Monica out of bed, though. It is a promotion, after all, and Monica did originally read for the role."

"And was stopped getting it because Nate Thompson wanted Judy as Ophelia, just like he wanted her to play Cordelia, no matter how much of a better actress Monica is."

"They are both now dead, Michael," Fagan pointed out, and even through the door, Edward could hear the warning tone in his voice. "Perhaps you might bear that in mind?"

"I am aware! But it's hardly germane, is it? Except in the sense that it's because they're dead that all this increased responsibility has been heaped on poor Monica's shoulders!

Like I said, it's playing havoc with her health, which is something else which you need to be taking into account."

Edward wondered if he should come back later, but he'd told John to be on the lookout for disharmony amongst the company, and this sounded exactly the sort of thing he'd meant. He shuffled forward as quietly as he could and pressed his ear to the painted wooden door.

"And you think that this should be reflected in her pay?" Fagan was saying, his voice rising in volume as he did so. "Have I got that right? You think that because Monica has been given a handful more lines after the brutal murders of one of my oldest friends and a poor girl at the very start of her career – and with Judy's body barely in the ground too – the first thing we should be sorting out is a few more quid for your bloody wife? Have I got that right?"

The door suddenly shivered in its frame in response to a loud crash from within the room. Alarmed, Edward jerked forward, his hand inadvertently pushing down on the door handle, and – as the means of keeping the door closed was removed – tumbled inside before he could stop himself.

He had a second to take in the situation before anyone spoke – Fagan standing behind his desk, his face even redder than usual, Gray in front of it with his back to the door and, at his feet, the smashed remains of a large glass sculpture which Edward had previously seen sitting on the filing cabinet in which Fagan kept scripts, contracts and the other paperwork required to run a busy theatre.

"Now see what you made me do!" Fagan was saying as Edward managed to come to a stop just short of barrelling into

Michael Gray. "I've had that award— well, hello, Edward!"

Gray turned around as Fagan called out the greeting. For a moment, Edward caught a glimpse of a thin, calculating smile. Gray seemed pleased with the damage he'd done. Edward was reminded of Inspector Whyte's description of Nate Thompson's death – a ferocious attack, he'd said. Michael Gray clearly had difficulty controlling his temper… Then the smile was gone, any sign of emotion smoothed away. "Mr Lowe," he said stiffly, then turned back to Fagan. "Well, I've said my piece, and told you where we stand. Think on it and let me know what you come up with." He poked at the broken glass with the toe of his shoe. "You better get that cleaned up before someone cuts themself," he said and slipped past Edward and out the door without another word.

Fagan waited until the door had closed behind him, then shrugged in Edward's direction. "Sorry about all this." He gestured down at the broken glass. "I'm sorry about things generally, really. This hasn't ended up the nice little working holiday you probably expected, has it?"

Edward could hardly deny that. Two murders were hardly normal, even in theatrical circles. Though, given that Judy was the second dead young woman he'd personally discovered in the past two years, perhaps it would be fair to say it was becoming distressingly normal for him. He shook his head anyway.

"Not really, no," he said, pleased that Fagan hadn't asked him how he'd come to be hanging around outside his office door. "But the show must go on, eh?" He was aware how trite he sounded even as he spoke, but it seemed to satisfy Fagan.

"Were you looking for me?" he asked, and again Edward shook his head.

"No, not at all. I was just passing and heard a crash." He coughed diplomatically. "I thought perhaps there had been an accident."

"Oh, just me being clumsy, I'm afraid, throwing my arms about when I'm explaining something. I was giving some directions to Michael and the back of my hand caught the top of the award I got from the German Tourist Board for putting on a series of Brecht plays in Dusseldorf in '51."

Edward allowed the obvious lie to pass unremarked. "Michael is his wife's agent, isn't he?" he asked instead.

"Yes, he is." Fagan smiled sheepishly, perhaps aware that his deceit had fooled nobody. "I take it you heard a little of what we were talking about? Michael wants a pay rise for Monica since she's now playing a bigger part in the play. But even if I had the money to give her more – and I don't – she's been desperate to play Ophelia since I put this cast together, and has never tried to hide it. Between you and me, I had to have words with her at one point, after one of the cast approached me about her undermining Judy."

As he spoke, he came out from behind his desk and crossed to a cupboard door set into the wall. He opened the door and took out a small brush and pan, which he laid on the desk. "I'll sweep all the glass up later," he explained. "But what was I saying? Oh yes, Monica tried to make Judy look bad from the start. You know the sort of thing: standing just off her mark so that Judy had to twist around to speak to her, deliberately stealing her light, that sort of thing. But she was better behaved after I spoke to her."

"You say one of the cast approached you about it?"

"Yes. Nate Thompson, actually." He laughed, but it was a sad sound, Edward thought. "I know he had a reputation for being… well, not as pleasant as he might have been, but he always looked out for Judy. He even said it would be better if I spoke to Monica, rather than him doing it, because he was the leader of the actors and he didn't want anyone to think he was playing favourites. Which was quite thoughtful of him."

Edward nodded. "I must say, I approve. As the leader of my own little team on *Floggit*, I spend a fair amount of time just keeping the peace. Actors can be terribly self-absorbed, I find."

"You don't need to tell me that, Edward. But, actually, Nate wasn't being entirely even-handed and impartial. He made it plain as soon as Monica came on board that he didn't rate her. Put it this way – Monica Gray would never have played Ophelia if Nate was still around."

"Really?" That was interesting. Was it mere coincidence that the two people who had stood between Monica Gray and the role she coveted were both now dead? He needed to find out more about the Grays, he decided.

He made his excuses to Fagan, and left him on his knees, sweeping up the broken glass. The little ASM, Alison, had seemed both knowledgeable and reasonably discreet – plus he had the feeling she was keen to be of assistance. He thought it might be a good idea to pick her brains a little more.

As he made his way to the stairs, he wondered how John and Jimmy were getting on.

44

As a conversationalist, Jimmy Rae was very different to Edward Lowe but, to John's disappointment, he had the same inability to read a map. He'd been fine during the half hour drive along the A6 from Bolton, but as soon as they'd got to the outskirts of Manchester, he'd got them completely lost.

John turned the car down what he was positive was a street they'd already visited twice in the past five minutes and glanced quickly across at the other seat. Jimmy sat with the map spread out on his knees and a frown of concentration on his face. Cigarette ash fell from his mouth to the map. He brushed it off with the side of his hand and sighed heavily.

"I reckon it's because I never did National Service," he said. "Never got shown how to read a map, you see."

"Don't be too hard on yourself, my dear chap. During the War, I was barred from map reading after I got my little squad lost in Egypt for two days. It wouldn't have been so bad, but we were in the centre of Cairo at the time."

He smiled, hoping Jimmy would realise he was joking. Edward could sometimes miss his jokes, so he was pleased to see Jimmy laugh.

"I think I know where we went wrong," he said, running a nicotine-stained finger along a line on the map. "This line here is King's Road, and I think we should have gone left from there onto King's Drive, but there was a speck of fag ash covering it up. If you do a three-point turn then head back along and take a right, this Simpson bird's place should be at one end of the road."

* * *

The turning in the road no longer existed. The two men stood on the pavement beside a set of black metal bollards and stared down the street in front of them.

"No wonder we couldn't find it," Jimmy said, holding the map up in front of his face with one hand and pointing at the street sign on the wall with the other. "This is King's Drive, and, according to the map, you can drive along it. Looks like the council have blocked this end off since the map was printed."

John nodded. "We'll just need to walk down, then," he sighed, but without moving from his position at the end of the road. Obviously, he needed to speak to Sally and hopefully what she had to say would exonerate her from involvement in recent events, but, as he stood there, mere minutes from speaking to her, he would have given a great deal of money to be somewhere – *anywhere* – else.

Luckily, Jimmy had no such compunctions. He stuffed the map in his jacket pocket, blew a ring of smoke into the air and slipped between the bollards. With no choice but to follow, John locked the car door and reluctantly entered King's Drive behind him.

* * *

The street was made up of attractive red-brick houses, pressed up close to one another, with patches of garden to the front and dirt paths to the side leading, presumably, to larger spaces at the back. The first two houses they passed had cars parked outside raised up on bricks, as though the closure of the street had marooned them there, unable to escape. John felt a similar sense of panicked enclosure as his unwilling footsteps took him closer to Sally.

The address they'd got from the library card was for number ten, at the other end of the street from the point at which they'd entered, and a long bend in the road meant the lower numbers were obscured until they reached the apex of the bend. Jimmy was still walking slightly ahead and, as he rounded it, he turned back and gave a shout to John, who was lagging behind.

"Hey, I think there's a taxi parked outside number ten. There's some blonde talking to the driver."

John hesitated for a second, harbouring the faint hope that Sally might be gone before they could speak to her, then broke into an unconvincing jog. He caught up with Jimmy at the start of the straight section of the road, just in time to see Sally look up as she opened the taxi door and catch his eye.

For several slow heartbeats, she stared at him, then she stepped inside the taxi and slammed the door shut behind her. Jimmy ran forward, shouting for the taxi to stop but, with a puff of exhaust fumes, it – and she – was gone.

He came to a halt, hands on hips, wheezing as he tried to catch his breath, and John wondered if now would be a good moment to suggest he cut back on the cigarettes. It was a ludicrous thought, he knew, but the relief he felt was like a shot of whisky entering his bloodstream, making him feel dizzy and warm at the same time. He might have to confront Sally at some point in the not-too-distant future, but it wouldn't be today, and that was the main thing.

That, and the fact he didn't have to tell Edward yet that he'd been keeping Sally's involvement a secret from him.

* * *

"She knew you," Jimmy said as they walked back to the car. "I could tell from the look she gave you." He half-closed one eye in the exaggerated pose of a detective on television thinking. "She's more than just a pal, isn't she? I know birds, and the look she gave you – pure smut, that was."

John doubted very much that Jimmy really "knew birds", as he put it. He had at least thirty years' more experience with women than the younger man, and he wouldn't dream of making such a claim. But he felt a warm glow in his chest at the thought that Sally still carried a torch for him, no matter how dim the heat it gave off or how long it had been since he'd seen it lit in earnest. He hoped Jimmy was right about that at least, though perhaps with a slightly more romantic air than "pure smut", which he thought rather a vile phrase.

In any case, there was no point denying it. "Yes, I know her," he admitted, but carefully, ready to backtrack if he felt it necessary. "She and I were married, once upon a time."

Jimmy whistled through his teeth. "So that's the famous Sally, is it? Her that ran off with the milkman?"

"The insurance man," John corrected him. "She ran off with the insurance man. He was lodging at the house and I was away a lot," he explained, then felt a faint disgust with himself for feeling the need to explain at all.

They'd reached the end of the street by now. Jimmy stopped and leaned back against one of the bollards that closed it off to traffic. "Wait a minute now, though. Didn't Eddie say this was the bird shacked up with Nate Thompson in the park? But that means…"

John could see the exact moment Jimmy added two and two together.

"So your ex-wife was having it away with your ex-mate, and she was shacked up with him when he got bumped off. Bloody hell!" He grinned widely and John thought for a moment he was about to clap, but instead he tapped a cigarette out and lit up. For the best part of a minute, he smoked in silence, blowing smoke in circles in the frosty winter air and occasionally casting a sidelong glance at John. Finally, he stubbed out the cigarette and faced John with a more serious look. "Why did he have a secret pad in the park, though? Why not just move your ex-missus into his actual house?"

It was a good question. Neither Edward nor John had considered the *why*, only the *what* and the *how*. He shrugged, feeling more miserable by the minute. There were so many questions Sally needed to answer, and this was just one more. "I have no idea, Jimmy," he admitted unhappily. "I was hoping Sally would be able to tell us."

"Fair enough. But I'm betting Eddie doesn't know any of this, does he?" Jimmy said, grinning again.

John shook his head, not meeting his eye. Ideally, he'd prefer it if Edward didn't find out until he'd had a chance to speak to Sally privately, but he could think of no good reason why Jimmy shouldn't tell him.

"Well, it's none of my business," Jimmy said. "I reckon if you wanted Eddie to know, you'd have told him already. And I also reckon that, if you'd spoken to her today, you'd have told Eddie when we got back. So, if you were to come back first thing tomorrow, say, and have a word with her then, you could tell Eddie and nobody'd be any the wiser about any delay, would they?"

It took a moment for John to let this sink in. Then he clapped Jimmy on the shoulder and gabbled his thanks, too relieved to care that he was probably acting like a fool.

Jimmy brushed it all off. "It's no big deal," he said. "I'm sure you've got your reasons."

John felt he owed the other man an explanation. He'd been so understanding, and without John even having to ask. He lit a cigarette of his own and told Jimmy the story of meeting Sally and marrying her, and eventually her leaving him (missing out the affair with Thompson, which for reasons he couldn't satisfactorily explain even to himself, he still thought of as a private matter). Then he told the story of her appearing in the pub in Bolton ("I just missed her!" Jimmy exclaimed) and discovering she had taken out the library books.

"She's involved in this somehow, obviously," he said at the end, dropping the cigarette stub on the ground and grinding it under his shoe. "But I don't know how exactly. I just can't believe that she'd be up to anything underhand."

He sounded pitiful even to himself, his voice a whine of self-justification and willing ignorance. He didn't *want* to know how she was involved. He knew his main emotion when he'd seen her get in the taxi and drive away had been relief, a sense of freedom from immediate worry, a joyful realisation that the inevitable could be put off until another day.

"Like I said, fair enough. But you can't keep her a secret forever, John," Jimmy's warning voice broke into his thoughts. "I'm sure she's not up to anything, but you need to tell Eddie some time. Speak to her tomorrow if you can. If not, it might be time to speak to him anyway – and maybe to the police too."

There was nothing more to be said.

45

As he walked down the corridor from Fagan's office to Alison's cubbyhole, Edward had to pass through the foyer, where Inspector Whyte was standing speaking to Peter Glancy.

With John and Jimmy off looking for Mrs Simpson, he realised this wasn't the best time to become involved in a chat with the police. He pushed open a side door, resigned to speaking to Alison later, but the creak of the unoiled hinges was enough to make Whyte look up and catch his eye.

"Just the man," the inspector called over, waving for Edward to join him. "If you've got a second, Mr Lowe, I need to check something with you."

Edward made one last attempt to avoid the inspector. "I'm actually rather busy. I'm looking for Miss Jago."

"That's as may be, Mr Lowe, but, with respect, in light of recent events, I think I take precedence over your social life."

Edward bridled at the insinuation, but knew he had no choice. He would just have to hope that whatever Whyte wanted, it would not involve any direct questions about the areas he and John had been investigating. He liked to think he'd acquired many useful traits as an investigator, but lying well was not one of them.

By the time he'd crossed the foyer, Glancy was making his excuses and leaving, though not before casting a worried glance in Edward's direction. Inspector Whyte underlined something in his notebook and watched him go. Only when they were alone did he speak again.

"Mr Glancy was just telling me something quite interesting," he said without preamble. "He was telling me that there's been a…" He looked down at his notebook. "*A great hulking brute of a man* lurking about the stage door since Judy Faith joined the theatre. He said Judy told him about this man, and that he even sent her presents and cards, and the like. I wondered if you might be able to shed any light on him?"

Obviously, he meant Craig Mackay. Edward paused, wondering whether to mention seeing him at Judy's funeral, but decided discretion was the better part of valour in this instance. "I know who you mean, yes. I've not seen him myself, but I believe his name is Craig Mackay."

"Is that right?" The inspector scrawled the name in his notebook, then looked back up at Edward, holding his eye. "Anything else you can tell me about him?"

Edward shook his head. "Not really, Inspector. As I say, I've never seen the man personally."

Whyte said nothing, only continued to stare at him. Edward felt a trickle of sweat form at the back of his neck and attempted a small laugh. "But he's well enough known around the company as an admirer of Miss Faith's that even John and I have heard about him, so I'm sure someone will be able to help you."

"Speaking of Mr Le Breton, you haven't seen him, have you? He and Mr Rae are the only other members of the cast I need to speak to, but nobody's seen them all day."

"Really? No, I'm afraid I haven't seen either of them. I do know they were intending to go over their scenes together for the new play. Perhaps they've gone somewhere quiet to do so?"

The inspector nodded. "Well, if you see them, let them know I'd like a word. I'm heading back to the station now, but I can be reached on this number." He scribbled a telephone number in his notebook and ripped out the page, then handed it to Edward. "I'll be there until six or so tonight, and then back again tomorrow morning at eight. I doubt Mr Le Breton can help if you can't, but Mr Rae's been with the theatre a bit longer, I believe?"

Without waiting for a reply, he tucked the notebook into his jacket pocket and turned towards the front entrance. "And Miss Jago is sitting on the stage. Or at least she was five minutes ago," he said over his shoulder as he pushed one of the heavy doors open and walked through it. The door swung closed behind him and Edward found himself alone again.

He heaved a small sigh of relief and headed down to the main auditorium.

46

Alison was sitting on the edge of the stage, drinking tea from a mug so big that it dwarfed her face when she brought it to her mouth. Edward walked along the front of the stalls until he stood directly in front of her feet and coughed meaningfully.

She brought the mug down from her face and placed it on the stage. "Mr Lowe," she said cheerfully. "What can I do for you?"

"Call me Edward, please," he replied, surprised at himself for doing so.

"What can I do for you, *Edward*, then?" she replied with a smile, pleased – and perhaps flattered – by the informality, he thought.

"Hopefully, you can supply me with some information," he said.

She placed her hands flat at either side of her legs and used them to push herself down off the stage, landing with a thump beside Edward.

"Anything I can help you with, I'll be happy to. Why don't we take a seat and you can tell me what you're after?"

Edward sat down in the front row of the stalls, and Alison sat beside him. He had a quick look around, but there was nobody else to be seen. With everyone busy rehearsing *Hamlet*, there was no reason for anyone to be near the stage.

"As you know," he began, "John and I have been looking into Nathaniel Thompson's death." He swallowed, experiencing another of the jolts of grief which had come over him now and then since he and John had found Judy's body. "And we were the ones who found Miss Faith in her dressing room."

Alison said nothing, but she blinked and nodded.

"And the thing is," Edward went on, "it seems very unlikely to us that the two deaths aren't linked. What are the chances of there being two different killers hanging around this one little theatre? So, while John is off… er, following up another line of enquiry, I've been asking about, and Monica Gray's name came up as someone who had been…" Again, he paused as he sought the right words. "…well, less than friendly towards Judy Faith. And I've also been told that Nate Thompson had reason to complain about her, and that possibly he blocked her advancement into more important roles. Would all of that be fair to say?"

Alison didn't answer immediately. Edward appreciated that. Too often people were inclined to begin speaking the first second they had a chance, barely taking the time to think before they blurted out whatever came into their heads. It was good to see Alison take a moment to consider her answer.

"Yes," she said finally. "I'd say that was a pretty fair summary. Don't get me wrong, I'd be gobsmacked if Monica had anything to do with any of this, but she did dislike Sir Nate and she did go out of her way at first to make Judy look bad. But it was just petty professional stuff – the sort of thing you see in the theatre every year. You must know what it's like? John said you both came up through rep?"

Edward grunted his agreement. He'd not heard the phrase *gobsmacked* before, but he could guess its meaning. Professional squabbles were almost the lifeblood of regional theatre, the source of much of the energy which propelled exhausted, often bored, actors to give their best, spouting the same clumsily written lines for the fifth, tenth, fifteenth time that week.

"And that's all it was, do you think? Just the usual theatre politics?"

"I think so. Monica's been around for long enough to know how it works. Sir Nate obviously wasn't too keen on her and he made it obvious he preferred Judy. But I reckon she also knew that Judy really was a better fit for Cordelia, even if she wouldn't admit it. I mean, she's about twenty years too old for that part – you might as well cast Alice!"

Edward laughed at the comical thought of the elderly Alice Robertson as the headstrong and determined teenager Cordelia and, after a moment, Alison joined him.

"What about her husband, then? Did Michael feel the same way?" he asked, recalling the smashed trophy in Mickey Fagan's office.

Alison stopped laughing as though struck. Her face crunched into a scowl and her mouth twisted in contempt. "That ignorant pig? I wouldn't put anything past him."

The change in her tone was remarkable. Edward kept quiet, knowing from experience that she would say more unprompted than if he interrupted.

So it proved. "He's a nasty piece of work. He calls himself an actor's agent, but he's married to his only client and all he cares about is how much money he can make off her." Her tone was furious and bitter, with a level of anger which Edward thought seemed personal.

"You don't like him?" he said quietly.

"He called me a dusky maiden the first time he met me and tried to kiss me, and said I'd only got the ASM job here because of my dad when I told him to bugger off. Even if he were the world's greatest agent – and he's definitely not – I'd still say he was a worm of a man."

"He tried to kiss you?"

Alison laughed. "I suppose it's sweet that you think that's the worst part of what he did." She held out her hands, palms towards herself, pointing towards her face. "My mum's Sri Lankan; she met my dad during the War and I came along just as they were starting to give up any hope of having kids. The colour of my skin's been enough to hold me back more than once, and the fact my dad's successful just means he thinks I should be doing something more important with my life than running about after Mickey Fagan at the Playhouse."

Edward didn't really know how to react to any of that.

He knew he had little experience of women, but he thought *dusky maiden* sounded rather complimentary. He made a mental note that this was not the case.

"Of course," he said. "But do you think Michael Gray is capable of violence?"

Alison frowned, considering the question. "Of the sort of violence you're talking about? I really don't know. A casual backhander across some lippy woman's face, definitely, but actual murder? Perhaps, if he thought there was enough in it for him and was sure he'd get away with it." She pulled a pen from her pocket and chewed on the end of it thoughtfully. "I'm trying to give up cigarettes, and this helps me think," she explained. "But, no, not really. I don't think that he'd have killed Sir Nate and Judy just to get Monica a better role. Especially since even he must have realised the play would be cancelled when Judy was killed."

Edward thought back to Gray's conversation with Mickey Fagan. He'd known Monica would have bigger roles in future with Judy out of the way, and hadn't delayed in asking for more money on the back of that.

Two years ago, Edward wouldn't have thought that enough of a motive for murder, but, after seeing Madge Kenyon kill four strangers for something which had nothing to do with them at all, he now wasn't so sure. People were capable of the most terrible, pointless evil.

"I'll tell you who I could believe it of, though," Alison piped up unexpectedly.

Edward had only been half-listening, but his ears pricked up. "Hmm, yes? You have someone in mind?"

"Maybe. You remember I told you about the man who attacked Sir Nate in his dressing room that time?"

Edward recalled something John had once said to him about conversations tending to come around to whatever you wanted to talk about if you waited long enough. He'd scoffed at the time, but perhaps there was something in it after all. "Craig Mackay?" he said.

"Exactly. Well, what I didn't tell you at the time was that Nate Thompson did say something after Mackay attacked him. I didn't mention it when I was telling you the story before because I didn't want to give Peter Glancy any more gossip to feed on, but if you're looking for someone who might turn violent…" Alison bit her lip, evidently carefully considering her next words. "I'm not saying this means anything – it might mean nothing at all – but, like I said, Nate was drunk as a skunk, and I don't think he even knew I was still there. He was sat in his chair mumbling to himself, and I definitely heard him say 'he'll find it harder to kill me than he thinks.' Something like that anyway."

"And you think he meant this man Mackay?" Edward frowned. If Mackay adored Judy Faith so much that he saw himself as her Sir Galahad, physically defending her against Nate Thompson, why on Earth would he harm her?

Alison obviously saw the doubt on his face. "Like I said, it might mean nothing. Nate was very drunk and he'd just been roughed up a bit. He probably had no idea what he was saying."

"Perhaps not. But it could be he meant Mackay was capable of killing Judy, if he couldn't have her for himself.

The man's obviously unhinged, hanging about the theatre, pestering the actresses, and it's not as though crimes of passion are the exclusive domain of the French."

Now it was Alison's turn to look doubtful. "I did mention Craig Mackay to the police when I was interviewed on that first day. In fact, I was sitting where you are now, and the policeman I was speaking to was sitting here." She made a face, the corners of her mouth turning down in thought. "Actually, I mentioned it just as Judy screamed and fainted, and everyone rushed over to her. Perhaps he never wrote it down in all the furore? He might not even have heard me."

That would explain why Whyte hadn't made the connection, Edward thought. Chaotic scenes had followed Judy Faith's collapse. She'd been so shaken that she'd had to have a lie down and, by the time that had been sorted, Whyte and Mickey Fagan had gone off to examine Thompson's dressing room. In the confusion, it was easy to imagine Alison's story being overlooked.

He remembered John's words about not drip-feeding information to the police, but he thought this was an area which required resources only the authorities could supply.

"I think perhaps we need to telephone Inspector Whyte," he said.

47

Inspector Whyte had just reached the police station when they telephoned. As soon as Edward told him what Alison had seen, he arranged for a police car to come to the theatre and pick them up. Half an hour later, they were seated opposite him in his office.

"I'm aware that you have in the past expressed some reservations about the force, Mr Lowe, and having now looked at the case notes for the Kenyon murders, I will admit – to some extent – that, last year, perhaps not everything was done as well from a police point of view as it might have been."

His tone was unexpectedly conciliatory, if a little hesitant, and Edward felt himself sit up a little straighter in his seat as he went on to praise their earlier investigation.

"You did some good work then and it may be I was... precipitous, shall we say, in warning you off this time." He smiled across the table, a tiny gesture which caused his mouth briefly to turn up at the corners then just as quickly return to the horizontal. Though his tone was friendly, the smile suggested he was speaking if not unwillingly, at least without pleasure. "What I'm trying to say is that I'm grateful to you and Miss Jago for coming in, and particularly pleased you were able to bring to my attention a matter which, for one reason or another, had been allowed to slip through the cracks."

He smiled again, just as unconvincingly. Edward wondered if someone had told him to play more nicely, or if this was just the way he was when forced to admit to an error. Either way, it was clear that nobody had previously reported Alison's information about the man who'd attacked Thompson in his dressing room.

"In that spirit," the inspector continued, "I am now in a position to tell you that we took a man into custody earlier today who we believe to be the person seen hanging about the theatre and pestering Judy Faith." He spoke slowly and oddly formally, as if reading from a report. Edward was certain now that he was not enjoying this conversation.

"Craig Mackay is the man's name, as you presumably have guessed. I can tell you that his shoe size is a match for the one we found in Miss Faith's dressing room. He's downstairs in the cells, but I've asked for him to be brought to an interview room, where I hope you will be able to confirm whether or not he's the same man you saw assault Mr Thompson in his dressing room."

He closed the folder in front of him and tapped it on the desk. As he rose to his feet and ushered them towards the door, Edward thought he heard him mutter something under his breath. He thought it might have been "Let's bloody hope so."

* * *

Craig Mackay had a head, in Edward's opinion, which resembled that of a bear far more than was natural. It was as wide as it was long, a huge, square expanse enclosed by long, dark hair that fell to his shoulders and a thick beard which spread up his cheeks to a point only an inch below his small brown eyes. When he opened his mouth to reveal little white teeth and prominent incisors, Edward began to wonder if it were possible that the man could have a grizzly somewhere back on his family tree.

He had a body to match, oversized and heavy, with hands like shovels and fingers like fat sausages. Only his nose, which was long and tapered to a sharp point, belied the impression of... Edward's thoughts stumbled to a halt as he tried and failed to recall the word for being like a bear. *Orsine*, was it? Something like that, anyway.

Regardless, he was definitely the man they'd seen at Judy Faith's funeral, even down to the donkey jacket slung over the back of the chair on which he sat.

What he definitely wasn't, though, was the man who'd followed him through the fog – he'd been big but, even allowing for the fact he'd never seen him clearly, and only at a distance, he'd not been as big as Mackay.

Still, he was glad that the bear-like man was safely on the other side of the two-way mirror. He glanced across at Alison Jago, who was similarly observing Mackay, while Inspector Whyte impatiently tapped his foot and asked for the third time if this was the man she had seen with Judy.

"Yes," Alison said, nodding emphatically. "That's the man."

Whyte gestured to a constable by the door, who slipped away, only to reappear a moment later on the other side of the glass, reapplying Mackay's handcuffs behind his back and leading him from the room. As he walked towards the door, he turned to stare in their direction, and Edward saw that one of his eyes was bruised and swollen. "I'm surprised given the size of the man, that it took you so long to identify him, to be honest, but I suppose it's good that you took the time to be sure." Inspector Whyte laughed, a hollow thing, with no pleasure in it. "You'd be surprised how cunning lawyers can be. Always ready to claim that the police have led witnesses on or fed them the answers they want to hear."

Alison shook her head. "No, it wasn't that. I knew that was the man I saw around Judy as soon as I saw him through that window. The reason I took so long was that I wasn't quite so sure he was the one I saw arguing with Sir Nathaniel in his dressing room." She shrugged. "I only saw him from behind, you see, and one big guy looks much like another from the back. But when he reached up to scratch his beard just now, I saw that little tattooed triangle on the back of his hand, and I remembered seeing the same thing on the man fighting with Sir Nathaniel."

Whyte had listened to this little speech in silence, as though making sure he had it word-perfect for the benefit of judge and jury at a later date, but as soon as Alison fell silent, he said, in a far quieter voice than usual, "For the avoidance of any doubt, Miss Jago, can I just confirm that you're saying that Craig Mackay is not only the man who has been stalking Judy Faith, but he is also the person you saw engaged in a violent confrontation with Sir Nathaniel Thompson shortly before his death?"

Alison nodded. "That's right. Check his right hand. There's a little blue triangle tattooed there. That's how I can be sure."

Edward felt a warm glow of satisfaction as Whyte repeated, "A small blue triangle."

"That's very good work," he said, beginning to slap Alison on the shoulder in congratulation, then stopping with his hand already in the air, before changing the gesture to an awkward tap on her arm. It wouldn't do to be over-familiar, he decided. "Rather more than you expected, eh Inspector?" he remarked with what he hoped was not too obviously a note of sheer glee. "Quite drops the solution to both murders into your lap, wouldn't you say?"

For a moment, Whyte said nothing, and merely stared at Edward. Then, as though sparking back to life, he gave his thin smile again and shook his head. "Not really, Mr Lowe, no. It's certainly interesting, and obviously Mr Mackay is now a person of real interest to this investigation – to *both* investigations, I should say – but, as things stand, this proves nothing, and is as likely to be wholly coincidental as it is to be genuinely linked."

Which was damned ungracious, in Edward's opinion, especially given all he'd said earlier in his office. He opened his mouth to speak, prepared to unleash the full force of his anger – but, at that precise moment, the constable who had taken Mackay away popped his head round the door and let Whyte know he was needed elsewhere.

"Sorry, duty calls," the inspector apologised, without sincerity, Edward suspected. "But I'll need you to put what you've just told me down in a formal statement, Miss Jago, if you wouldn't mind speaking to Constable McCracken before you leave."

As the policeman walked towards the door, their meeting clearly over, he came to a halt and turned back to Edward, with a look on his face that he couldn't quite place. "Thank you for bringing Miss Jago in, Mr Lowe," he said, with a cough. "Without her, we probably wouldn't have linked Mackay to Mr Thompson quite as quickly, and her statement will come in handy if we get him inside a courtroom." He continued in the same half-abashed, half-grudging tone. "I believe in paying my debts, though, So, if you're interested, I'll let you know what we find out when we speak to Mackay, if I can."

He nodded once, briskly, and left the room before anyone could reply. Edward and Alison exchanged a look.

Edward cleared his throat and fished his cigarettes out of his jacket pocket. "It seems the inspector has finally begun to show sense," he said. "Not before time, I'm sure you'll agree. If only we could be sure he'll share all the evidence he gets from Mackay." He peered through the two-way glass at the empty room on the other side. "Do you know, I think we might finally be making some progress," he muttered to himself with satisfaction.

48

John and Jimmy returned from their abortive visit to Sally's house with nothing to report. The mysterious Mrs Simpson had not been at home, but John had apparently posted a note through her letterbox to say he'd be paying a visit the following day, if she could be in.

Edward would normally have been disappointed at this failure to progress matters, but with Alison's revelations about the assault in Thompson's dressing room and the confirmation it was the same man who'd been stalking Judy Faith, he had too much to tell the others for any temporary delay to bother him too much.

"And Whyte assured me he'd keep us up to date with proceedings," he concluded with undisguised satisfaction. "He said he was in our debt, in fact."

"Jolly good show," said John. "Well done, both of you."

The three men and Alison had taken over the tiny back room they'd discovered to the rear of the Blue Blazer. It was a space just big enough for a table and four chairs – and, unusually, a stuffed gorilla which stood in one corner and glowered glassily down at the drinkers.

Edward had thought John would be more effusive – it was quite an advance in the case after all – but he seemed distracted. He'd not been himself for a while, truth be told. They'd need to have a talk at some point, he decided, to find out what was troubling him.

Jimmy also appeared to have something on his mind, but, whatever it was, he put it to one side to slap Edward on the back and congratulate him on a job well done. He leaned in and gave Alison a quick peck on the cheek – and she appeared to welcome the attention, he noted with a smile.

"I believe that Whyte and his men are intending to search Mackay's flat in the morning," he explained, watching John, hoping to engage his attention, but he was staring into his glass, a pensive look on his face.

It was all rather underwhelming and, when John announced he was tired and was going back to Mrs Galloway's, Edward didn't object. He just hoped that he'd have got over whatever was troubling him by the morning.

* * *

When Edward got up the following day, he found a note from John pushed under his bedroom door.

I thought I'd go and visit that Mrs Simpson early, when she's sure to be in. I've taken the car. Can you get yourself to the theatre, and I'll meet you there?

Well, Edward thought grumpily, he didn't have much choice, did he? If John had the car, he'd have to get the bus into town and hell mend him. He washed and shaved, got dressed and went downstairs for breakfast in a disgruntled mood, a mood made worse by the absence of kippers and the presence of a pot of – at best – lukewarm tea.

The trip on the bus, sitting alone upstairs while a crowd of children pestered him for cigarettes and called him *granddad*, only served to add fuel to his burgeoning bad temper. By the time he barked his shin on one of a collection of boxes and crates which were partially blocking the entrance to the Playhouse, he was about ready to bite somebody's head clean off. He leaned over and peered inside the offending crates, but all they contained was set dressing and costumes, presumably for storage or for shipping to Amsterdam for the European performances in the new year – if that even happened. With nothing else on which to take out his irritation, he kicked angrily at a wooden frame designed to hold one of the pictures which adorned the walls of Lear's castle and grabbed a pile of servants' jerkins in his hand, before allowing them to drop again, suddenly recognising how foolishly he was behaving.

"Good morning, dear Edward," Peter Glancy said from behind him. "What can those poor costumes have done to annoy you? And what have you been up to? That dreadful inspector chap is looking for you and young Alison. Have you been doing things you shouldn't have with the help, you naughty boy?"

He cackled and Edward would have told him exactly what he thought of him and his ridiculous mannerisms, had it not been for the mention of Inspector Whyte. He glanced up at the clock above the box office. Ten to ten. Could the police have already been around to Mackay's flat?

"Where is he?" he asked Glancy brusquely, refusing to be drawn into the other man's idiotic games. "The inspector, I mean."

"He's in that little cupboard Alison calls her office. He's had her in there for about ten minutes. Dirty old bugger that he is!" He laughed again, but Edward was already walking away.

The door to Alison's cubbyhole was closed and he stood outside it for a long moment, wondering whether this would be the end of their investigation. If Whyte had found something incriminating in Mackay's flat, perhaps he'd be able to link both deaths to him, and that would be that. Part of him was pleased to think he might have assisted in catching another killer, but an equal part thought it all seemed too easy, all a little too pat for real life.

He knocked firmly on the door and went inside.

Alison was sitting on a desk with her feet dangling in mid-air, directly across from the only chair in the room. Inspector Whyte sat in this, speaking on the telephone which, Edward suspected, had been the sole purpose of the space when it had been built.

"Yes," he was saying, "that's right. Nothing we can do about it. But give him the usual warning first. Yes, exactly that. OK, I'll be back later and we can take a look then."

He replaced the receiver in its cradle and nodded a greeting to Edward as he said hello and took up the only available free position, leaning against the wall just inside the door. It was lucky that none of them were claustrophobic, he thought idly.

"That was the station I was speaking to," Whyte explained. "I've already told Miss Jago, but now I'll tell you, like I said I would. We've let Craig Mackay go."

He held up a hand to forestall Edward from speaking. "Now, before you start, I should tell you I'm not happy about it either, but we searched his room and, besides a couple of scrapbooks filled with clippings about Miss Faith taken from the newspapers, there was nothing suspicious there. Certainly, there was nothing to suggest a link to Sir Nathaniel, or to put Mackay in the frame for either murder." He paused, a troubled look on his face, and Edward wondered if he'd said something he shouldn't have.

"Actually, I suppose it'll come as no surprise to you both we are now officially treating Miss Faith's death as murder too. The forensics lads came back with their report, and something about the state of a bone in her neck means she was already dead when she was hoisted up on that rope. Probably strangled, in fact."

Edward shuddered at the cold way in which Whyte had described Judy's death. He hoped he never became so hard-hearted. "But you don't think Mackay had anything to do with either of them?"

"I didn't say that. Personally, I think that bugger still had some questions to answer about his relationship with Thompson and Miss Faith. However, he has a solid alibi for the time of Thompson's death at least, and his solicitor thinks that's enough to warrant his release. My boss agrees too. For now."

"But you did ask him about what Alison saw, though? Surely you did that at least?"

Edward was aware he was allowing his bad mood to affect the way he spoke to the inspector, but releasing Mackay felt like one disappointment too many on what had already been a pretty poor day.

Whyte looked at him sharply, then nodded his head. "Of course we did. He said he did go for Thompson in his dressing room, but only because Thompson was always so nasty to Judy – his words – and because he claims he saw Thompson strike Miss Faith when he was waiting at the stage door one evening."

"You believed him?"

"Again, I didn't say that. But he was very insistent that it happened, and it doesn't seem entirely out of character for Sir Nathaniel. The police were called out twice to his flat in London a few years back by his then-wife. Claimed he'd knocked her about a bit. According to the reports, both parties were drunk and it looked like the wife had given as good as she'd got, so the responding officers put it down as a domestic dispute and didn't get involved." He sniffed. "Still, where's there's smoke…"

"Why would he hit Judy Faith, though?" Alison had sat quietly so far, but now she spoke up. "He was the one who brought her into the Playhouse. I always thought he was very fond of her. I'd have said she was the only member of the company he *wasn't* a total shit towards."

Whyte grunted with irritation. "I've no idea, miss. But the investigation is still ongoing, and Mackay's statement has opened up several new avenues of enquiry." He stood up, their chat obviously at an end. "Now, I think that I've more than satisfied my end of the bargain. The police force thanks you for your assistance up to this point, Mr Lowe, Miss Jago, but I'd be obliged if that was the end of your involvement in the case. If I need to speak to you again, I know where you are."

He squeezed past Edward and left without another word. Alison looked over and sighed. "That's us told."

"It would seem so." Edward felt deflated; he was sure Alison could hear it in his voice. Mackay looked like being another dead end, they were no closer to discovering the identity of the woman who lived in the park house and he still had no idea who'd been following him. All the positivity he'd felt the previous evening had dissipated.

He only hoped that John was having more luck.

49

Try as he might, John was finding it hard to shake off the feeling he was betraying both Edward and Judy Faith by keeping Sally's presence in the city – and in Nate Thompson's life – a secret. As he parked the car by the bollards in the weak morning sunshine, he thought back over the last few weeks and, as usual, could construct no version of events in which Sally emerged with any credit.

Obviously, she was the married woman that Peter Glancy had mentioned. The library books from the house in the park proved that. But she'd never mentioned Thompson when she'd dropped in on him at the pub. In fact, she'd let him assume she was alone in the north. She must have had a reason for hiding that detail, that much was clear.

What wasn't as clear, though, was whether she had any involvement in his death. John was sure not, but how much of that was wishful thinking on his part? He been besotted with Sally since the first time he'd clapped eyes on her, and he knew he was never impartial when it came to her. He locked the car door and began the slow walk along King's Drive.

There was no taxi outside number ten this time, and a light shone through curtains which hadn't been opened to welcome the day yet. It was the weekend, to be fair. He'd still be in bed too, for preference.

He rapped with his knuckles on the front door.

Almost at once, he heard footsteps approaching the door, then it opened a little, caught on a golden chain. The side of Sally's face, one eye and part of her nose and mouth, appeared in the gap and peered out. She blinked once and gave a little start of surprise, then tried to close the door.

John rammed his foot in the quickly closing space and let out a gasp as the heavy wood banged hard against the side of his shoe. "I'm not going anywhere until you and I have had a little chat," he said, in his most forceful tone. He heard her swear under her breath through the door and then the pressure on his foot lessened as she slipped off the chain and pulled the door open.

"Well, don't just stand on the step like a bailiff," she said. "Come inside, and I'll put the kettle on."

* * *

The house was cosy and warm, with music playing somewhere and the smell of cooking bacon in the air. Sally pointed through a door to the left. "Make yourself comfy, and I'll put the tea on. I'd offer you a bacon sarnie, but I've only got a couple of rashers." John waved away the offer and went through into what was evidently the sitting room.

The music was coming from a little stereo unit in the corner – *Tapestry* by Carole King, according to the cover of the record that lay next to it. Quite pleasant in an obvious kind of way, he supposed, though not his sort of thing at all – or hers, back when they'd been a couple. He wondered if that was the influence of Nate Thompson or Martin the bloody insurance man? He opened the curtains and took a seat in one of the overstuffed armchairs which had been placed on either side of a little gas fire, then looked around the room.

Nothing was new, he saw. Nor was there much he would have identified as belonging to Sally, or even showing what he knew to be her taste. Presumably, the place had come furnished. Cheaper than getting your own place, which was sensible if she was short of money, but he also had the sense this wasn't a house that had been lived in much. A television in the corner was angled in such a way that it faced none of the chairs and, except for Sally's collection of records piled up on the floor by the record player, there was nothing which John would have thought of as a distraction from simply staring into space. No books and no magazines: the only newspaper he could see was the previous day's *Telegraph* which was open to the crossword (almost completed, he noted). Unlike the house in the park, this room was in good need of a dust and a run-around with a Hoover, but there was the same sense of emptiness, of a lack of human occupancy. He picked up the newspaper and a pen that lay beside it and filled in one of the missing crossword answers, then gave a guilty jump as Sally spoke from the doorway.

"You never could leave me to finish a crossword by myself, could you, Johnny?" she said with a smile, pushing an ashtray to one side to make space for the tea tray she carried. She poured two cups and handed one to John, then took the armchair opposite him. "It's a bit of a dump, I know, but it'll do for now," she said, sweeping her hand around to encompass the room and, by extension, the whole house beyond it.

"Did you have to move here after Nate died?" John asked suddenly, hating himself for springing the question on her, but determined to stick with the plan he'd come up with while walking from the car. *Get in quick with a big question and keep her guessing what you know.*

"After Nate died?" Sally forced a puzzled look onto her face, but John had seen her lie before, and he wasn't fooled. From nowhere, an uncomfortable tension had entered the room.

"Yes, I assume when he died, you had to move out of that nice house in the park," he said, pressing his advantage and feeling awful about it.

"Nice house in the park?"

To his surprise, this time she seemed genuinely to have no idea what he was talking about now.

"Number six," he said. "A lovely little bungalow. Don't tell me you've forgotten it already?"

"John, you've completely lost me. What bungalow? I've been renting this place for about a year now. I've never stayed in any bungalow, never mind one in a park." She stood up and left the room. When she came back, she had a letter in her hand. "Here," she said, handing it to him.

It was a gas bill, addressed to *Sally Simpson, 10 King's Drive, Cheadle Hulme,* and dated June.

"So, you were never..." He hesitated; Jimmy had described it as "shacking up" but it seemed rather an unpleasant term to John. "...living in sin with Nate Thompson, then?" *My God*, he thought and nearly laughed, *I could be somebody's maiden aunt.*

Sally did laugh, and the sound acted like a lever, releasing some of the tension in the room. He laughed along with her until she gasped out "living in sin" and collapsed in another fit of the giggles. Only when she'd regained her composure was she able to answer.

"Not in a park, no," she said, wiping her eyes. Suddenly, her face was deadly serious, all trace of hilarity gone. "I'm so sorry, Johnny, I never wanted you to find out at all and, if you had to, I didn't want it to be like this."

"You were in a relationship, then?" John felt unexpectedly cold and detached, very unlike his usual self. "You and Nate Thompson?"

"Almost since I came to Cheshire. But I had my place here and he had his big house in Bolton. We spent most of our time at his. I'd never even heard of this bungalow in the park until you mentioned it just now."

"When did you see him last?"

"Last? About two weeks ago. A couple of days before he was killed."

"You know he's dead, then? I don't want to be unkind, but really, you don't seem overly upset."

Sally's forehead crinkled into a frown. "We'd been drifting apart for a while. His drinking had got worse. He was an unhappy man in a lot of ways. I thought I could change him, make him more like he was before, during..."

She stopped, blushed and lifted her teacup to her lips.

"During the War," John finished the thought for her. "The other time you and he were an item."

Sally nodded, red to the tips of her ears. "I'm sorry about that, too, you know that. But I'd left Martin and moved here, I went along to the theatre one night and our paths crossed and... well, there you go, I'm sure you can guess the rest."

John stood and crossed to the window. It was easier to discuss Sally and Nate without looking at her.

"So, were you a couple when he was killed?"

"We'd rowed." He heard her take a deep breath behind him. "He told me to get out. We were at his place, we rowed and he kicked me out. And that was the last time I saw him."

"You came back here?"

"Yes. I had nowhere else to go. And, to be honest, I felt like it was time."

John racked his brain, trying to think what else he should be asking. He could see Sally's reflection in the window; she'd stood up and was staring at him. In an ideal world, he'd have turned around and taken her in his arms. But this wasn't an ideal world.

"What did you row about, if you don't mind me asking?" he said instead.

"Oh, this and that. His drinking, mainly." In the window, he saw her turn her head away from him as she spoke. She was hiding something.

"I'd heard he was drinking a lot," he said cautiously.

"More and more. He was drunk more often than not towards the end. He…" She hesitated and he heard the break in her voice. "He became abusive."

"Physically?"

"Yes, that. And mentally too. He said cruel things."

She was still not looking at him and, for all the shaking in her voice, her face seemed composed enough. He had the strongest feeling she was lying. But why she would blacken Thompson's name like this, he had no idea. Surely not because she knew he hated the man? Was she playing with him?

He felt heat rising from his neck to his face at the thought. Without turning around, he asked "Did he cut off your money?"

Her head snapped round in the window. "Why do you ask? Isn't the fact he hit me enough for me to leave?"

"Nate died on Tuesday night. By the Saturday, you'd arranged to meet me in the Blue Blazer and asked me to restart your maintenance payments. I just wondered if those events were connected."

"I hadn't worked since I met Nate. He didn't like the idea of me working, and I wasn't about to argue. I was in his will, though – no doubt you find that suspicious too." Her reply was angry, but John noticed she didn't answer his question.

"I'm sorry to have to ask these questions," he said more gently. The anger he felt rising and falling as he spoke to

Sally wasn't something he was used to, and he was finding this interrogation – for that was what it was, he admitted to himself – exhausting. "Edward and I are just trying to figure out how Nate was killed, and if the death of a young woman at the theatre is related to his murder."

"The death of a young…" Now John heard real emotion in Sally's voice. He turned away from the window and for a moment caught her look of horror before she quickly composed herself and frowned in confusion. "Has someone else died?"

"An actress at the Playhouse was found dead in her dressing room. The police think she killed herself."

"How terrible. The poor girl. Do they know why she did it?"

He shook his head, tired as he'd ever been, and desperate for this to be finished. He never thought he'd ever want to get away from Sally but, at that moment, he would have happily been anywhere else. Though he couldn't put his finger on any specific lie, he couldn't shake the feeling that almost nothing she'd said had been completely true.

"No, they haven't said," he said then, with a sudden fierce burst, "If you never set foot in Nate's bungalow, how did a pile of your library books end up there?"

"Library books? Oh, those weren't mine. Well, one was – a romantic thing, *Lord Somebody's Betrothal* or something like that. But the rest were Nate's. He didn't have a library card and couldn't be bothered getting one, so I got any books out he wanted on my card." She smiled sadly. "I've spent my life with men who need looking after, haven't I? It seems to be my type."

"It does seem that way. Poor you." He smiled back, his anger leaching away again. It was so hard to stay angry with Sally.

"You do know that you'll need to speak to the police, don't you?"

He thought she might protest, but instead she nodded. "I know. But not today."

"And I'll need to tell Edward about you, and about your relationship with Nate."

"He doesn't already know?"

"No, not yet. It was only me who knew who Mrs Simpson was when we took the library books back, and I was rather hoping I could keep you out of it altogether." He shrugged. "I'm afraid that was rather a forlorn hope, but I'm sure once you tell everyone what happened between the two of you, you'll be free to go on your way."

Sally didn't look convinced. "I wish I were as confident."

A gentle bong from the clock on the mantelpiece reminded him it was nine o'clock. He needed to get to the theatre before anyone noticed he was missing, and he needed to speak to Edward.

"It'll be fine," he said, giving the words all the force he could muster. "You'll see." There was nothing else he could think of to convince her, so he picked up his hat from the table he'd tossed it on. "I need to get back but, if you'd like, I can come back later with Edward, and we can go and speak to the police together?"

Was it his imagination, or did she seem happier at that thought? He hoped so. He'd never spoken to her so harshly before, but he knew the police would press her harder still, and he'd like to protect her from that as much as he could.

He turned to go and then impulsively leaned forward and kissed her on the cheek. He regretted it immediately, and waited for her to pull away, but instead she brought one hand up to his face and held it there for a second before stepping back.

"Thank you for being so understanding, Johnny," she said, and he thought he saw sadness in her face again. Then she was all business, chivvying him to the door and promising she would stay in all day, waiting for him to return with Edward.

He walked back to the car in a mixture of emotions. On the one hand, he'd believed Sally when she said she'd never set foot in the house in the park. Which begged the question of who'd cleaned the place up after Nate Thompson's death? But she was definitely holding something back, probably related to money, not a topic either he or Sally had ever been comfortable with.

He reached the car and stood for a second, finishing his cigarette. He suspected his upcoming conversation with Edward was likely to prove an equally uncomfortable one.

50

John parked the car in the square in front of the theatre and hunched into his coat as a sudden winter shower started from nowhere. Even in the drizzle, he was in no particular hurry, and he dragged his feet as he got closer to the entrance, hesitating on the steps up to the doors, and finally stopping under the awning to smoke a cigarette.

What was he going to say to Edward? The truth? That he'd met Sally in the pub across from the theatre and told nobody? That he'd realised days ago she was involved with Thompson? That he'd been to see her and she'd denied having anything to do with the house in the park?

Yes, that was the place to start, he decided, pulling calming clouds of cigarette smoke into his lungs and holding them there until the tips of his fingers began to tingle. Start at the point which makes her look least guilty, that was definitely the way to go.

He flicked the cigarette butt into the rain and went inside.

* * *

Twenty minutes later, he felt absolutely wretched.

He'd found Edward easily enough, enjoying a second breakfast of sausages and potatoes in the theatre restaurant. "No kippers at Mrs Galloway's," he'd explained through a mouthful of mash, pointing with his knife at the chair next to him. "Pull up a pew and I'll tell you what Inspector Whyte had to say for himself."

It was that which left him feeling wretched. As soon as Edward had information pertinent to their investigation, he shared it with John, regardless of how it made him look. Good news or bad, Edward kept nothing back, harboured no secrets. He discovered something, he told John. Which was how it should be.

John, on the other hand...

He listened while Edward described his meeting with Alison and Whyte, and felt the other man's grave disappointment that Craig Mackay had been released. When Edward told him about Thompson's possible attack on Judy Faith, and his previous heavy-handed relationships with women, he winced out loud as he remembered Judy's similar accusations.

"Something troubling you, John?" Edward asked, peering at him with concern in his eyes. "I've noticed you've not been yourself the last day or two. You've seemed... distracted. As though there's something on your mind."

Now was the moment, he knew. The pressure of keeping so many secrets from his friend had been causing him physical discomfort, and this was his chance to relieve that pressure.

In a babble of words which struggled to come close to an actual narrative, he recounted his various meetings with Sally over the past few days. He left out nothing, even covering her wartime fling with Thompson, though it pained him to admit it. He finished off with Sally's promise to go to the police with them, then sat back, mentally steeling himself for the tongue lashing which he knew must follow. And well-deserved it'll be too, he told himself.

Edward, however, simply sat in silence for a moment then shovelled the last of his sausage and mash onto a fork, and from there into his mouth. Once he'd finished chewing, he pushed his plate away and lit a cigarette before speaking.

"As you know, John, I've never married. I came close once, but that was a long, long time ago, in another country."

"And, besides, the wench is dead," John said, nerves getting the better of him. The instant he saw the look on Edward's face – a look which said that his little joke was both in poor taste and factually correct – he wished he could take the words back.

Edward continued as though he had, in fact, never spoken. "I never married, and I've never been what anyone would call a ladies' man. The minds of the fairer sex are, to me, largely a closed book. So, I suspect that the ties which bind a man and his wife – or his ex-wife – are ones that I don't understand. I can't deny that I wish you'd told me all this earlier, but I can see that perhaps you felt a greater loyalty to someone who, I know, meant a great deal to you for a number of years."

There was something sad and distant about Edward as he spoke, John thought. He was not a man to share his feelings easily, and John was aware that he knew very little about his past, other than those areas which related to his work. This was as close as he'd ever come to talking about his romantic life. He held his breath as Edward stopped speaking and looked over his head, deep into the past.

Then, with a shake of his shoulders and a cough of embarrassment, Edward was back in the room. He took off his glasses and polished them as he spoke.

"And I don't think that any real harm has been done, either. Sally has said she'll go to the police and I'm sure Inspector Whyte will be keen to speak to her. She may have fallen out with Sir Nathaniel some days before his death – indeed, now I think about it, I wonder if the row they had was the pretext for the drinking bout which led to him being dismissed from the Playhouse – but she may inadvertently know of some interaction he had while they were still together which could shed light on his final movements." He frowned and resettled his glasses on his nose. "We also still have no idea why I've been followed twice recently, nor by whom, but it would be a strange thing indeed if that was unconnected to our investigations."

"Did you mention being followed to Whyte?" John asked.

Edward shook his head. "I didn't. I can't be sure that anyone *was* actually following me, and we've only a few days more before we're finished in Bolton. It seemed like something which would only complicate matters and perhaps take the inspector's eye off more important things."

John wasn't sure how much of that was true, but realised he was in no position to insist on other people revealing everything they knew. "Fair enough," he said. "There's still something nagging away at me, something somebody said that was important, though we didn't recognise it at the time. I just can't seem to dislodge it." He shook his head, annoyed with his faulty memory, and looked up at the clock. "Never mind. I'm due to do some bits and pieces with Alice just now, but we could take the car to Sally's at, say, one this afternoon?"

"I think perhaps if we take Inspector Whyte along with us, it might be best? Save Sally having to go into a police station?"

It was just like Edward to be so thoughtful, John thought in an excess of affection. "That's a splendid idea," he said. "We can telephone first and pick him up on the way, assuming he's free."

"And, of course, if we can bring Whyte yet more information, I do think he'll be more likely to keep us in the loop about any other developments."

In light of Edward's understanding attitude about Sally, John decided to let him off with this rather cynical sentiment. He waited until Edward had returned his plate to the counter, then led the way downstairs to telephone Inspector Whyte.

51

He took some convincing, but Inspector Whyte eventually proved amenable to the idea of going to visit Sally in Mrs Galloway's Ford Anglia rather than in a police car.

Edward sat in the back seat alongside Jimmy Rae, with John driving and Whyte in the passenger seat. *The guest of honour*, he thought sourly, staring at the back of the man's head. They'd been kept waiting for the best part of an hour while the girl they'd spoken to at the police station tracked Whyte down, and then another half-hour while he was driven over to the theatre. It was coming up for half past two before they finally started off for King's Drive.

There was no chatter in the car, but Edward wasn't surprised. Though they'd convinced Whyte to take an unmarked car to see Sally, that had come only after a long discussion in which the inspector had questioned just why he was only now hearing of John's wife, a lecture on the potential criminal offences related to the withholding of evidence, and an argument about the problems well-meaning but unreliable civilians caused police investigations. John had come as close as Edward had ever seen to hitting someone when Whyte referred to Sally as "the woman Simpson", and Whyte had threatened to have all of them arrested for obstructing an officer in the course of his duties when John had then refused to give Sally's address until Whyte guaranteed she would not be taken into custody.

The atmosphere in the car was, therefore, strained to say the least. Only Jimmy seemed unaffected. He'd rolled down the window to blow out his Turkish cigarette smoke and was whistling what sounded to Edward like the first two lines of "A Maiden Fair To See" from *HMS Pinafore*. It was an irritating sound and he was considering asking him to stop, when he realised that total silence would be even worse. He stared out the window and wondered how much longer they would be.

As it turned out, they would only be another couple of minutes. Just as Jimmy flicked his latest cigarette butt out of the car window, he muttered "It's just down here," to nobody in particular, and John turned the car down a side road and pulled to a halt in front of a row of black metal bollards.

"We need to walk from here," John announced. He got out of the car and waited for the others to emerge. He raised his eyebrows towards Edward and inclined his head slightly in the direction of Inspector Whyte. "Bloody idiot," he mouthed silently.

Edward smiled but said nothing. They did need the inspector to see things their – or more precisely, John's –

way, or Sally could yet find herself doing her talking down at the station. He waved a hand towards the bollards instead, inviting his friend to lead the way.

Having heard the full story of John's two visits to Sally's house, Edward was relieved to round the bend on the road and discover there was no taxi parked outside the door. He quickened his pace as John, in anticipation of seeing Sally, opened up his long legs and strode down the road. Within a minute, they were all standing in the little garden in front of Sally's house and John was rapping on the door.

Nobody answered.

John tried again, knocking more loudly this time, then switched to a black metal knocker and gave that a frantic thump or two. Jimmy meanwhile cupped his hands against the glass and peered through the front window. "Doesn't seem to be anyone in," he called across, just as Inspector Whyte moved John out of the way and gave the door a series of mighty kicks.

"You can't kick in the door," Edward complained loudly, watching as John took an unsteady step to the side and sat down on a rusty metal bench partly concealed by an overgrown hedge.

"I'm not kicking the door in," Whyte snarled, his face red with effort. "I'm trying to get the lady's attention. If that should also happen to damage the door such that it opens, well, I'll be sure to apologise once I'm inside."

He kicked the door again and, with surprisingly little drama, it flew open and rebounded against a rubber stopper before it could crash into the hallway wall. Whyte caught the door as it bounced back and held it open.

"Hello," he called inside. "Is there anyone home?" He paused for a second. "Is there someone hurt inside, or in need of assistance?"

There was no reply. "It looks as though someone might be hurt inside and unable to call for help," the policeman said with a grim smile. "Consequently, I am within my rights as a police officer to enter and ascertain whether assistance can be rendered."

He stepped inside. Edward glanced at John, who was still sitting on the bench, his face ashen, and followed the inspector, with Jimmy close on his heels.

There was nobody in the house. Whyte thundered up the stairs and Edward heard the sound of doors banging open and shut. A few minutes later, the inspector reappeared in the sitting room in which he and Jimmy were waiting. In his hand he held a white envelope.

"This was lying on a bed upstairs," he said, holding it out to Edward. The name *JOHN* was written on the front in an elegant copperplate script. "She's bloody gone, though." He kicked at the base of one of the armchairs by the fire, lifting it briefly off its feet. "And that's on your bloody pal."

There was no missing the anger on his face. "Get in here, Mr Le Breton," he shouted through the open sitting room door. "Your wife's done a runner, but she's left you something behind."

John shuffled in, his long face as pale as the envelope Whyte held out to him. "She's gone, then?" he asked hollowly.

Edward nodded. He watched as John tore open the envelope and pulled out a single sheet of paper. John read it slowly, then handed it to Edward.

Dear John, it began. *I'm sorry I had to leave but I had no choice, really. I had a think after you left, you see, and I realised that I have far less faith in the authorities than you do. Perhaps it's because I'm not famous like you, but I think that once they find out my links to Nate, I'll be the centre of their investigation. And I couldn't bear that. I know that you'll have to tell them all you know, and that probably means that Nate's will won't be settled any time soon, but that's the price I'll have to pay for now. Hopefully, in time, they'll find who did kill Nate and I can come back, but in the meantime, please do believe how fond I remain of you, and please do understand how sorry I am to place you in this unfortunate position. Please keep an eye on the boys for me. All my love, Sally.*

Edward passed the letter to Whyte, who quickly skimmed it, then tossed it on the table in front of him.

"This is your fault, Mr Le Breton," he said with a cold, almost clinical, fury. "You knew that your ex-wife was involved romantically with Sir Nathaniel, and you knew she was a beneficiary in his will. You also knew that she and he had fallen out recently over money, that she had no other source of income but him, and that they were separated at the time of his death. You knew, in short, that she had a motive for killing him, and yet you said nothing." He held up his hand as John, seeming to shake off his trance-like state in the face of Whyte's attack, began to protest. "I know you think that she didn't have the means to kill him – what was it Mr Lowe said to me earlier? Oh yes, John thinks Sally's far too small and weak a woman to bludgeon a big man to death – but that's hardly a problem when the small, weak woman knows when the big man is going to be dead drunk, is it? And being a small, weak woman is no impediment at all to murdering another small, weak woman and then trying to make it look like suicide!"

Edward had his eyes on John, willing him to defend himself, but, as Whyte finished speaking, he spun round and gaped at the inspector.

"What do you mean, another small, weak woman?" he asked, though he was sure – sickeningly so – that he knew exactly what was meant.

"We have reason to believe that Miss Faith and Sir Nathaniel were engaged in a sexual relationship up until his death. Mrs Simpson was not his only lover."

"How…?" The change in John was impossible to miss. His head snapped up and he fixed his eyes on the inspector. "How could you possibly know that?" Even his voice, usually so languid and soft, sounded different; cold and hard as flint.

Whyte chuckled, seemingly determined to get a rise out of John. With a sick feeling in his stomach, Edward realised he was doing it deliberately, baiting the tall actor in the hope he would say something that he shouldn't. Edward had no idea if John even *knew* anything he shouldn't, but he could see the uncharacteristic rage in his friend's eyes and realised he was likely to say something he would regret, one way or another.

"Yes, Inspector, I'd be interested to know that too," he said quickly.

Whyte considered for a moment. "Yes, OK, I suppose there's no harm in telling you that." The look he gave John was a dangerous one, though, and Edward wondered just what he was holding back. There was certainly something; he could see it in Whyte's face, in the way he leaned forward, in the fingers tapping on his knee as though impatient to be released.

Whatever it was, John was oblivious. "Tell us, then," he growled, and again Edward marvelled at the change which had come over him.

"There was a key, of all things," Whyte said, smiling now. Edward was reminded of the snake in the *Jungle Book* cartoon from a few years back. "Just lying on the floor in Miss Faith's dressing room – Mr Thompson *and* Miss Faith's dressing room, I suppose I should say. Funny thing, it was lying plain as you like in the middle of the floor. Strange nobody had noticed it earlier. Maybe I need to have words with my lads, make sure they pay more attention to what's at their feet. Because none of them spotted it until after you two left. *Right* after you two left, actually."

He chuckled again, but Edward could see it was all an act, a prelude to the trap about to be sprung. "Odd thing about that key. It was a door key, a brand new one too. Not the kind of key they use in the old houses around here. It even had a little number stamped on it, in case the owner lost it and needed another one made. It's amazing what they think up nowadays, don't you think? Anyway, I had one of the lads go round every estate agent in the city, asking if they recognised the key – and, would you believe it, he got a result at the first place he went to! A name and address and everything!"

He reached into his jacket and pulled something small out of his pocket. With a sharp snap, he put the key onto the table between himself and John. "Recognise it, Mr Le Breton?"

John shook his head, his eyes never leaving those of the inspector.

"No? Now, that is strange, because we went round to the address, a nice little place in Lovell Park, and you'll never guess what we found. Your fingerprints on the *inside* of the front door."

He pushed the key across the table until it sat directly in front of John. Edward swallowed hard as he heard the trap clatter shut. "Are you sure you don't recognise this key?" the inspector asked John again.

52

The sound of the door key snapping onto the table was one which would haunt John for years. Like the report of an assassin's shot, it made his heart race and his mouth dry up whenever he thought about it.

When Whyte had pressed him for the second time about it, he'd stared stupidly down at the table and said nothing. The previous five minutes had been a blur and the snap of the key had struck him like a physical assault, as though someone had slapped him across the face and woken him up from a deep sleep.

There was nothing he could say, though. The anguished look on Edward's face and the quickly stifled gasp from Jimmy Rae told him that. If he admitted they'd been in the park house, who knew what the inspector might make of it. Hadn't he already suggested that John might be involved in Nate Thompson's death? He'd starred in enough cheap melodramas to know that the police could connect any number of innocent elements and somehow conjure up a guilty verdict.

He'd been angry, furiously so. Initially at Sally for running off when she'd promised she'd stay. He couldn't take the time right now to think through what that meant about her guilt or innocence, but he knew he'd have to face that question at some point. And then he'd been angry at Inspector Whyte for suggesting that Judy had been involved with Nate too. The very idea was repellent, a sweet young girl like Judy and a revolting old roué like Thompson.

Now, as he calmed down and his hot anger turned first to a cold fury and now a terrible fear, he sat in silence and waited for Whyte to speak again.

"Cat got your tongue, Mr Le Breton?" he said after a full minute had passed. "Well, it doesn't really matter, as it happens. We've got no interest in how you came to be inside a house belonging to Nate Thompson. We've made enquiries and we know enough about you and Mr Lowe's movements to rule you both out of our enquiries. Besides, perhaps you visited him there? You did say you were old friends."

Whyte was toying with him, he could feel it, but all he could do was sit and take it, and wait for an opportunity to defend Sally.

"You said this house was somehow linked to Judy Faith? You said she and Sir Nathaniel were a couple?" Edward asked.

"Thank you for reminding me, Mr Lowe," Whyte said, once again playing the conscientious public official. "Yes, that's another odd thing. The house was spotlessly clean, like someone had taken a bucket of bleach to it. But we did find a few fingerprints, here and there. I wonder if you can guess whose they were?" He paused for barely a second. "No? Well, it's probably not necessary to list them all, and I've already told you one of the names. But we also found Judy Faith's fingerprints on a bedside lamp."

"And on that flimsy basis you've decided she was Thompson's lover?"

John had lost track of the point Edward was trying to make. Was he defending Judy or Sally? Not that it mattered; there was more to come from Whyte. He could see it in the man's face.

"Of course not! That would be ridiculous," the inspector said, reaching again for something in his jacket pocket. John thought he resembled some cheap working men's club magician, but the thought brought him no pleasure.

The object Whyte held now was another envelope, smaller than the one from Sally and more feminine. Even across the table, John could tell it was perfumed. Whyte slid a fingernail under the flap in the back and pulled out a thin handful of sheets of matching paper.

"What we have here is a love letter one my lads found wedged under the make-up table in Miss Faith's dressing room, written by her and addressed to Mr Thompson. It's pretty racy stuff. Made the young constable who discovered it blush, so it did.

"We think it possibly came from the wooden box we found behind the make-up table. Which means it likely was removed after Sir Nathaniel was murdered. We think whoever took the rest of the contents of that box dropped it and didn't notice."

Edward exchanged a quick glance with John, remembering the fragments of writing paper they'd taken from the fire grate. "And what do you conclude from all of that?" he said.

Whyte grinned broadly. "I thought we'd never get here! You're all bright men, I'm sure you can figure it out for yourself, but just in case you need it spelled out… what we suspect – *suspect*, not *conclude*, Mr Lowe, it's a crucial difference in the world of law enforcement – what we suspect is that Mrs Simpson, having fallen out with her rich sugar daddy over his relationship with Miss Faith, and knowing she was in his will, bumped off Mr Thompson while he was in an advanced state of intoxication.

"We further suspect that Miss Faith feared Mrs Simpson also intended her harm. You'll recall her reaction when given the news of Thompson's death and then the carry-on at his funeral? Well, what you don't know is that Mrs Simpson was also at the funeral. I was standing further away from the graveside than anyone else or I'd have missed her, but she was there, I can assure you, standing behind a tree, watching what was going on. Of course, I didn't know who she was at the time. But I think Miss Faith did and that's why she collapsed so dramatically." The inspector slipped the letter back into its envelope and laid it on the table. "Now we can't say for certain at the moment, but conceivably Miss Faith knew something which implicated Mrs Simpson in Thompson's murder. Or perhaps she acted in a jealous rage. Either way, we think Mrs Simpson killed Miss Faith. And having successfully – or so she thought –

covered up one murder, she attempted to do the same again by disguising this death as a suicide. Then, when that ruse failed, and knowing – thanks to her ex-husband – that the net was closing in on her, she absconded to places unknown." The grin disappeared from his face, to be replaced by an expression of cold authority. "How does that strike you as a theory, Mr Lowe?" he asked.

John waited for Edward to say something to refute the inspector's wild claims. But instead, the little man turned away from the policeman.

"My God, John," he said, "You've let a possible double killer go free. You let your feelings for your ex-wife blind you to the truth and then gave her enough warning that she was able to slip away before the authorities could catch her."

Edward had always been one for obeying the rules, John knew that. He'd told him so often enough. But, even so, he couldn't believe his friend would turn so quickly on him just because the police had a theory. Hadn't they had all sorts of theories last year, and each of them proven wrong in the end? Hadn't they just arrested Craig Mackay and then had to let him go? What was Edward thinking of, accusing Sally – accusing himself! – of something so incredible?

He felt the anger he'd suppressed before bubble back to the surface. "What on Earth are you talking about, Edward? A double killer? Why, because this idiot claims it?" He saw the inspector bridle out the corner of his eye, but ignored him, all of his attention focused on the man he thought was his friend. "A pompous fool, you called him! But now you're ready to take his word for whatever bloody nonsense he spews out."

He was spitting as he spoke, and he could feel his face burning red. He must look a sight, he knew, but he was beyond caring. He felt rather than saw Jimmy Rae put a hand on his arm, but he shook it off angrily. "I thought you were a man of integrity and sense, Edward. Vain and self-important, yes, and far too fond of your own voice – but still someone I could trust to act in the right way. But now I see the truth. You're nothing more than you've always been. The jumped-up son of a shopkeeper, deluding himself he's as good as his betters, but never more than a harsh word away from bending the knee to any fool in uniform!"

Now Edward too was bright red. John stared at him, breathing hard, and waited for him to respond. He'd heard him eviscerate enough directors over the past couple of years to know exactly how vicious Edward could be when roused. A small part of him knew he was being unfair, but he needed to vent his anger.

"Is there anything else you need me for just now?" Edward asked Inspector Whyte stiffly. "If not, if you'll excuse me, I think I'll walk to the end of the road and pick up a taxi."

John took a deep breath and prepared to tell Edward to wait. Before he could speak, though, the little man turned to Whyte. "The best of luck in finding Mrs Simpson. I can only apologise that we allowed her to escape justice."

The words died in John's throat. Wordlessly, he watched Edward leave and heard the front door close with a careful *click*. Jimmy Rae, standing to one side, looked embarrassed by the situation, but Inspector Whyte's face was unreadable.

"I think that's probably all I need any of you for, if I'm honest. I've no reason at the moment to think you deliberately warned your ex-wife to flee, but if new evidence comes to light which shows you did, you can expect a further, much less pleasant, visit."

He swept the key and the two envelopes into his hand and rose to his feet. "I'll need to keep hold of Mrs Simpson's letter to you. If you come down to the station at some point, you'll be able to collect a receipt. I have your contact details, so, if I need to get in touch, I know how to." He nodded to Jimmy as he pushed past and headed out the door.

John sat with his head in his hands and wondered what had just happened.

An hour ago, he'd been on the way to see a woman he still loved, in the company of his best friend.

Now, he had neither woman nor friend, and no prospect of regaining either.

INTERMISSION

53

**The Film and Television Arts Awards Ceremony,
London, February, 1972**

"Aren't you going to go over and speak to him?"

David Birt, producer and co-creator of *Floggit and
Leggit,* tapped Edward on the arm, and pointed across at
John Le Breton, who was standing at the bar, laughing at
some joke the barman had just told. They were in a private
suite at a hotel around the corner from the Royal Albert
Hall, beginning what everyone hope would be a successful
evening with a few sociable drinks and some relaxing chat
with colleagues.

Or at least that was how David had described it on the
invite which had landed on Edward's doormat soon after he
got back from Bolton. The reality was somewhat different.

Everyone knew that he and John had had a falling out
– he assumed Jimmy had told them, but he didn't blame the
boy for blabbing – and, as a result, it felt from the first that
the rest of the cast were tiptoeing round the subject as though
walking on eggshells. That would have been annoying

enough, but while Edward squirmed with awkward embarrassment every time somebody mentioned his former friend, or when their eyes inadvertently met across the room, John appeared to be having the time of his life, constantly crowing with laughter with one group or other and even, at one point, demonstrating some sort of soft-shoe shuffle on the carpeted floor for the benefit of a pretty young make-up girl. He was far too old for that kind of thing, Edward thought sourly, but it went to show the character of the man, and the obviously low value he placed on their own friendship.

"No, I am not," he said to David, and sipped his whisky, glowering across the room.

David audibly winced and walked away, and, for a moment, Edward felt bad. He knew the producer was keen that his two stars be reconciled before the award ceremony, but, really, he was the wronged party – he wasn't the one who'd hidden valuable evidence and allowed a key witness, now a strong suspect, to escape. He'd been good enough to accept John's apology before, when he'd suggested Edward was drawn to murder for his own gratification, but this time, no, he would not be going over to speak to him.

He drained his whisky and stood there with his empty glass in his hand, unwilling to go up to the bar while John was still standing there. He felt a tap on his arm and looked around to find Joe Riley at his side, holding two glasses.

"The whisky in here is dreadful watery stuff," the old Scotsman said in his broadest brogue, "but when you're as deep as we are in Sassenach territory, you take whitever you can get."

He handed one of the glasses to Edward and tipped the other forward before taking a sip. "Your good health, Edward."

"And yours, Joe. Thank you."

Riley smiled just as he did on the show, a thin, avaricious half-grin, like an undertaker who'd stumbled on a particularly wealthy corpse in need of burying. "Aye, weel, it's a free bar, is it not? I'm always happy to stand my hand at a free bar." He laughed, an infectious sound which quickly pulled Edward part way out of his foul mood.

"You're still not talking to that lanky drink of water Le Breton, then?" the Scotsman asked conversationally. "That's for you to decide, of course, but I hear it was over that baukle Natty Thompson?" He shook his head and sucked air through his teeth. "He was always a troublemaker, that one, even when he was a young man. I wouldnae be losing a friend over him if I could help it."

"You knew Thompson?" Edward had been inclined to change the subject – the last thing he needed was a lecture on the joys of friendship from the world's grumpiest Scotsman – but if there was something to be learned about Thompson, it might still be useful. It looked as though the police were confident they had their man (or rather woman), but, over the past few weeks since he'd returned from Bolton, he'd realised he still had some reservations. He'd realised, too, that he'd been too quick to accept Inspector Whyte's theory.

"Aye, I did, back in the days when I was working with Hitchcock and the like. Your man Thompson was just starting out then, but he'd already been marked by all the directors. A boy tae watch, you know? And didn't he know it! Ach, I should have had a splash of water in this muck," he complained, swallowing a mouthful of whisky with a grimace. "But, aye, Natty Thompson fair loved himself. You'll have seen the like yourself – a wee bit of praise and the young lads get it into their heids that they're big men, and they start running about with a bad crowd. That was young Thompson. Away up the West End with some real flash lads, dancing at the clubs wae floozies and daft wee bits of girls with nae morals about them at all. He nearly got himself sacked from the film we were making, the terrible state of him in the morning."

He drained his glass and placed it down with a thump. "I heard a wee rumour he had to be bailed oot the cells mair than once and then jump in a taxi to the studio, his hair no' even brushed and him still wearing his clothes from the night before." He laughed and beckoned a passing waiter across. "Another of they whiskies, son, with a wee splash of water in it," he said. "Whit I'm saying is that you dinnae want to be falling out with John over an eejit like Thompson. Especially when he's deed as a doornail now. Good friends are hard tae find at oor age. I thought even an auld fool like yourself would know that."

He gave another smile and wandered off after the waiter. Edward finished his own drink and looked again at the bar. John was still there, standing alone for once, gazing around the room with what Edward thought was a melancholy look on his face. Perhaps Joe Riley was right. Sally was John's ex-wife after all, and he'd never hidden the fact that he continued to carry a torch for the woman. It was hardly surprising that he should try to shield her if he could. An unfortunate ending, of course, but John could hardly be blamed for that. He'd obviously expected her to stay in town, and he'd been as shocked as anyone to find her gone.

Yes, he decided, perhaps he'd been too harsh. Would he have acted any differently? He'd never been married, of course, but there had been women in his life at times. He brought the face of one in particular to mind and considered how he'd have acted in the same situation. Would he have done his utmost to protect her? Yes, he would. He'd have done whatever it took.

Still, there was that line about Edward being the jumped-up son of a shopkeeper, and how he'd been bowing and scraping to Inspector Whyte. Protecting Sally didn't explain that. Far from it. He felt the anger bubble back up the surface.

A loud dinging sound interrupted his thoughts and brought the level of chatter in the room to a soft mutter. David Birt climbed on a chair, the knife he'd just tapped on his glass still in his hand. "That's the cars arrived," he announced. "You all know who you're with, so if you could make your way outside, that'd be smashing."

In a commotion of scraping chairs and querulous voices, everyone got to their feet and pulled on their coats, and, for a few moments, the room was a bustle of cast and crew and their partners pushing and shoving their way to the door. Like a bobbing cork, Edward found himself buffeted along in their wake until, with a grunt of annoyance, he forced his way into a clear space by the bar, right next to John.

There is no such thing as an accident. A line from a TV play in which he'd played Sigmund Freud popped into his head as John caught his eye, and he wondered how he'd managed to end up standing beside the one man in the room to whom he had nothing to say. *People will swallow any old nonsense if you say it in a foreign accent*, he thought balefully and prepared to turn away.

"I'm supposed to be sharing a car with David and his wife and Joe Riley," John said suddenly. "But I think it makes more sense for the two cast members up for Best Actor to step out of the car together, don't you? It'll make for a better picture for the newspapers." He coughed again and looked down at Edward, an uncertain smile on his lips. "Do you think there's space in yours for a rather foolish, oversized actor?"

For a moment it was on Edward's lips to refuse the request, but John did have a point about the two of them stepping out the car together. That would certainly be the professional way to arrive.

"I'm sure we can squeeze you in, John," he said, though without returning the smile.

* * *

The BBC were obviously hopeful that *Floggit and Leggit* would do well, because they'd loosened the purse strings enough to book a pair of Daimler limousines to ferry the cast to the London Palladium, where the ceremony was to be held. Each car held six people, but as soon as John told

David Birt he intended to travel with Edward, the producer announced that the two stars of the show would have one of the cars to themselves.

Edward could still hear Donald Roberts gently assuring Joe Riley there was plenty of room for them all in the second car as he slid into one of the seats facing John and closed the door behind himself.

The car started up with an almost inaudible purr and pulled into the road. Neither man spoke. John picked up a sheet of stiff card from the seat beside him and studied it closely, unwilling, it seemed, to meet Edward's eye.

"Prawn cocktail to start," he said, unexpectedly. "Followed by steak Diane with new potatoes and peas, and Black Forest gâteau for pudding. Someone's left the menu for dinner this evening," he explained, handing the card across to Edward.

Before he could examine it – no soup course? he wondered – John spoke again, his tone far from its usual unhurried indolence. "I wanted to say, Edward…" he stopped, seemingly unsure of how to proceed. "I wanted to say," he repeated, "how sorry I am for the way I spoke to you. Back in Bolton, I mean. I make no excuses and I have no defence. I allowed my feelings for Sally to cloud my judgement, and I took my anger at her out on you, who had done nothing at all to deserve it. I behaved like an absolute swine, I won't – *can't* – deny it, and I can only hope you can find it in your heart to forgive me. I meant nothing of what I said, I hope you know that."

He fell silent, his long face set in as miserable a pose as Edward had ever seen.

"Well, I… that's…" Edward wasn't sure how to react. He'd wanted an apology, of course, but now he had one, he realised he didn't care to see his friend so crushed. He remembered Joe Riley's words, and also some harsh ones of his own, cruel things he'd said in the heat of arguments. "Let's say no more about it," he said finally, and it felt as though a great weight had been lifted from his shoulders. "We all say things we regret when we're angry." His smile was tentative – he was relieved to forgive John, but he wondered how long it would take to forget what he'd said – but John's smile lit up his whole face.

"Thank you for that, Edward," he said simply, sitting up straighter in his seat and holding out his hand. "And, while I remember, may the best man win."

Edward knew he was trying to smooth things over, and so pretended not to understand for comic effect – and just long enough to suggest a lack of concern over mere awards – then took John's hand in his own and said, "Oh, you mean the Best Actor thing. Yes, quite right – may the best man win."

"So long as it's not John bloody Alderton."

Edward laughed, the last of the tension between them ebbing away. "Exactly. The man's a damn show-off."

* * *

In the end, it was Frank Finlay who won the Best Television Actor, but by then Edward and John were quite tipsy, and neither of them were really in any state to cross the floor to the podium at which David Frost stood waiting to hand out the award.

Floggit and Leggit lost out too, much to David Birt's annoyance. "I may be reading too much into things, but there's an awful lot of ITV shows winning tonight," he declared drunkenly, while his wife pulled at his arm and told him to be quiet.

Most of the rest of the cast had dispersed to other tables by that point or left for after-show parties elsewhere in the city. Edward caught sight of Jimmy Rae leaving with Wendy Richard and Marty Feldman, and wondered if it would be acceptable to make his own exit soon.

"Fancy a last one in the bar?" John asked, slurring his words a little. They'd not spoken yet about Sally's disappearance, but Edward had told him what Joe Riley had said, and their friendship seemed once again to be back on an even keel.

"Why not?" he said, holding onto the table carefully as he levered himself to his unsteady feet and pondered whether another drink was really a wise move. "Did you get a letter about the Amsterdam run of *Hamlet*, by the way?" he asked, taking a second to gain his balance before he risked crossing the room to the hallway which led to the bar.

"I certainly did," John confirmed, still sitting. "It seems it's not cancelled after all. Leaving in two weeks' time. Sounds like we're in the centre of town, quite a nice hotel, too, by all accounts."

"Let's hope so. Mrs Galloway's lodgings were perfectly satisfactory for what they were, but I do think I'm getting too old for staying in digs."

John suddenly looked serious. "But what about Nate Thompson and Judy? I know I dropped the ball with Sally, but we did uncover quite a bit, and I'd hate if it was all for nothing." He reached over to the empty table to his right and picked up a half-full bottle of red wine someone had left behind. There were several unused wine glasses at his elbow, and he emptied the bottle into two of them. "I'm not feeling any great desire to stand up just yet," he declared, pushing one of the glasses towards Edward. "Why don't you sit back down and bring me up to date. Have you heard anything more from that inspector, for instance?"

"Not a massive amount, in truth," Edward said, resuming his seat. "You remember that he said he'd let me know if there was any progress with that chap Mackay?"

"Yes, last I heard was that he'd seen Nate Thompson manhandling Judy Faith, but that there was nothing to link him to either of them other than that."

"That's right. Well, he's disappeared, seemingly. Alison Jago telephoned last week to say the police had been on to her, to ask if he'd been seen around the theatre. Apparently, he was supposed to go into the station for something and he never turned up. They went round to his place, but his landlady said he was gone. He'd left most of his stuff with her for safekeeping but he'd definitely moved out. Alison said the police didn't seem too bothered."

Edward shifted in his seat and looked awkward. "They've issued a warrant for Sally, you know. Wanted for questioning."

John nodded. "I'd heard."

"I've not spoken to anyone else from the theatre except for Alison. Have you? I must admit I'm a little unsure about this Amsterdam trip. I was looking forward to it, but now it feels… cursed, I suppose."

John shrugged unsteadily and rocked in his seat. "Peter Glancy called shortly after the last Bolton performance, but only to ask if I could put him in touch with my agent. Seems his has died of old age and he needs a new one. Other than that, I've seen Alison a couple of times when she's been down visiting Jimmy and I happened to bump into them in town, but nobody else."

So, Jimmy and Alison Jago were a couple now. Edward filed that piece of information away for later. "I imagine it'll be fine," he said uncertainly. "And it'll be nice to see Amsterdam. I've not been there since the end of the War."

Any reply John might have made to that was lost as a waiter came up and politely asked if they were finished. Edward gazed blearily around the room; they were the last guests. Waiters with their collars undone and waistcoats unbuttoned were moving among the empty tables, moving plates and glasses onto trays and sweeping rubbish into large plastic sacks.

"Yes, yes, we're all done," Edward said. He swallowed the dregs of wine in his glass and wondered where he'd put his coat. John had closed his eyes and begun to snore gently. He shook him by the shoulder and, with a certain amount of comical stumbling, the two old friends headed out into the London night.

PART TWO

54

The Amsterdam Playhouse – De Stadsschouwburg, their Dutch guide informed them – was a big step up from the one in Bolton. Like many of the buildings in Bolton, it was mainly constructed from dull red brick, but that was where the similarities ended.

"Built in the Neo-Renaissance style and completed in 1894, following the destruction by fire of the original building, this fine example…" The guide's voice faded away as Edward stopped listening and concentrated instead on memorising the journey from the theatre, where they were scheduled to put on a first continental showing of *Hamlet* two nights hence, and the hotel, where they'd dumped their bags an hour earlier. Mickey Fagan had insisted that everyone come on the guided tour of the Playhouse he'd arranged, but Edward suspected he wasn't the only one who'd rather have had a bath at the hotel, and then dinner and an early night. The journey from London had been a long, dull one, necessitating a train to Harwich, a ferry from there to Rotterdam, then a three-and-a-half-hour coach ride to Amsterdam. Edward had barely had time to wash and change his shirt before Fagan was chivvying them all out the hotel and into a set of taxis.

"…moved to its current location in Leidseplein on the thirteenth of September 1789. The first performance in the new building was…"

Edward cast a sidelong glance at John. Their reconciliation before the awards ceremony had come as a much greater relief than he'd expected, but he was painfully aware they hadn't resolved the source of their disagreement. He'd hoped they'd speak during the journey over, but every time he thought an opportunity might present itself, one of the other members of the company had joined them. He had at least managed to secure them bedrooms next door to one another, so, if the worst came to the worst, they could speak that night.

In a more general sense, he wasn't convinced this Dutch run of shows was a very good idea. He'd called it cursed when speaking to John in London and, looking at his colleagues as the tour guide pointed out another exquisitely decorated gilt cornice, he thought it likely they'd agree with him. Everyone looked tired and despondent. If Fagan's intention with this tour was to raise spirits, he was going to be disappointed. Peter Glancy was the only one even pretending to show an interest; the rest shuffled along behind him like children forced on a dull school trip.

"Lovely building, isn't it?" Alison Jago caught up with him and slipped her arm inside his.

"Charming. Full of colonnades and cornices and whatnot."

She laughed quietly, putting a hand over her mouth so the guide wouldn't hear. "Yes, I've got no idea what he's on about either."

He laughed, too, a little too loudly, earning him a stern look from Mickey Fagan.

"How have you been?" he asked.

"Fine, I suppose. The Playhouse has been under a cloud since *Hamlet* finished. And, by then, it was coming up to the Christmas season, so we did the usual. It was all OK, but you could tell nobody's heart was in any of it." She shuddered. "It's like the theatre's haunted. Nobody likes being there on their own after dark anymore, not even me. It feels… chilly, I suppose. Cold and unwelcoming."

She looked genuinely upset, Edward thought, remembering how lovingly she'd once spoken of her place of work.

"…formerly the home of the National Ballet and Opera…"

The tour guide droned on, but they were nearing the end now. Edward could see the door through which they'd arrived on the other side of the nearest archway and, sure enough, they were steered in that direction. They came to an untidy halt by the door, and the guide gave a little bow and taught them how to say "goodbye and good luck" in Dutch. Edward smiled politely, but he'd forgotten it by the time they were back out on the street.

"Well, that was dull as a wet Sunday in Grimsby," John said, coming up behind Edward and Alison. "I think most of the cast are heading back to the hotel. It's a quarter of an hour walk, apparently, or we can see if we can rustle up a taxi."

Edward had intended to get a taxi, but it was a pleasant evening and he'd just remembered an errand he had to complete. "I'd quite like to walk back, if either of you fancy joining me?" he said. "I've actually got a cousin who moved over here in the fifties. He lives close to a tram stop, apparently, so I wouldn't mind checking the timetable and the route if we pass a terminus."

Alison was going for dinner with Jimmy; he came up and threw his arms around her waist, then took her away with a cheery wave to John and Edward.

John, however, was happy to walk. Edward briefly considered bringing up Sally as they made their way to the nearest tram stop, but they were both tired. Instead, he told John about Amsterdam after the War, and John regaled him with tales of his service in Egypt and the numerous mishaps he seemed to have been involved in.

Half an hour later, they arrived back at the hotel, but by then they were both yawning and ready for bed. Edward decided any chat about Sally could wait. They were here for a week and, besides, the trail had gone stone cold.

There was plenty to time to have that discussion later, he thought, as he made his way up the stairs to his room.

55

The hotel they were staying at in Amsterdam was what a holiday salesman would undoubtedly describe as *rustic* or *quaint*, which was to say it was small, packed to the gunnels with mismatched knick-knacks and in grave need of a good dusting.

Edward had started complaining about it in an undertone as soon as he'd discovered that a continental breakfast largely consisted of fresh fruit and yoghurt, and had continued to do so, in an ever-increasing volume, through his shock at the duvets on the beds ("what's wrong with a sheet and a proper blanket?"), the presence of showers rather than baths ("how can you possibly get really clean when the water only spends a second on your skin?") and the fact he'd been offered mayonnaise rather than tomato ketchup with his steak and chips ("Why are these chips so thin? And why are they called French fries? The English invented chips – everybody knows that!").

John had found the constant moaning a little tiresome,

but felt it was too early in their reconciliation to say anything negative. He'd been relieved the previous evening, therefore, when Edward announced he had a cousin who lived in the city who he was intent on visiting. The first performance of *Hamlet* was scheduled for the next night, which left him the day to himself.

He'd just found a cosy spot on a couch in the hotel lounge, with a pot of tea and a plate of lemon-flavoured biscuits on a little table by his side, and a day-old copy of *The Times* in his hand, when Sally popped her head around the door and asked if he was at home to visitors.

* * *

He'd choked so hard that the tea had gone down completely the wrong way and Sally had to rush in and provide several hearty thwacks on his back before he'd regained his composure enough to ask where she'd been, why she'd run off from Cheadle Hulme, and what the hell she wanted with him now.

"I think you probably meant to ask those questions in a different order, Johnny," she smiled, taking one of the lemon biscuits and dipping it in his tea. She chewed it slowly while he coughed and swallowed until his throat felt less painfully constricted and he was able to speak more coherently.

"Very possibly. But don't think you can avoid answering them by being delightfully charming." He narrowed his eyes in what he thought of as an inquisitorial fashion. She seemed tired, her skin pale, and her hair brittle and untidy, but he knew he had to get answers, no matter that it felt him feeling like a heel. "Let's start with why you ran off and take it from there, shall we?"

Later, when he looked back on this conversation, he realised he'd not really been all that shocked to find Sally in Amsterdam. Or not in Amsterdam as such, but wherever he'd gone next. He was old enough, if not wise enough, to know he'd probably been kidding himself in Bolton when he'd wondered if he and Sally might have a future together, but, at the same time, he'd had the most vivid sense that whatever she was up to, he and she were not done with one another yet. He sat back, his throat still too sore for a cigarette and his teacup in Sally's hands, then crossed his arms and waited for her to speak.

"I had no choice, really," she said. "You said yourself that, if I'd stayed, the police would view me as a suspect in Nate's murder, and I couldn't bear that. Far better just to slip away and avoid any unpleasantness." She put down the cup and put a hand on his knee, staring into his eyes as though willing him to believe her. "*I* know I didn't kill Nate, and *you* know I didn't kill Nate, so what was to be gained by having the police paw through my life?"

He found he couldn't disagree. In his own mind, he was satisfied that Sally had nothing to do with Nate's death, and perhaps it had been better to escape any unnecessary unpleasantness. Hadn't he based most of his life on that very premise?

He shifted his leg a little and she pulled her hand back. He might agree with her reasoning, but he didn't care for the feeling that she was manipulating him. "And what have you been doing since then?" he asked. "How did you end up in Amsterdam?"

"I need to give you a bit more background first, then I'll tell you everything I've been up to." She twisted the sleeve of her blouse in her hands, seeming nervous for the first time (for the first time in about twenty years, John thought). "I think I told you that Nate made me the sole beneficiary of his will."

She fell silent, leaving a space for John to consider this reminder of the best motive she might have had for killing her lover.

"You said when we spoke in Bolton that you'd rowed before he was sacked from the theatre," John said slowly, catching her eye and holding it, but wishing he was doing something else entirely. "You said it was about money, but you never answered my question about whether that was why you came to see me."

Part of him dreaded hearing her answer and another smaller part congratulated himself for remembering to ask the question again. There had been a time, not so long ago, when he wouldn't have pressed the matter. The role of inquisitor was not one with which he was comfortable, but he thought he was getting better at it.

"It was just to tide me over until the police let the lawyers release the will. I'd no idea how long that would take but, even when I met you in that pub, I was already thinking it'd be good if I was out of the country until that happened." She shrugged, and John thought he saw a spark of anger flare up in her eyes. "That bastard Martin took all my savings, and a girl – and our sons – needs to eat."

"You do know that makes you look more guilty, don't you?" It pained him to say it, but it was the truth. "Nate stopped supporting you, you rowed over it, he walked out on you – and two days later he's found murdered and you get everything in the will." It was a cruel way to put it, he knew, but the police would be just as harsh. Better she was prepared for that.

It would have been easy for her to cry then, to tug at his heartstrings. He'd known any number of women for whom that would have been their first reaction. But Sally had never been one to play the weak woman card. Quite the opposite in fact.

"You said Nate was beaten to death," she said. "Can you really see me managing that?"

That was her trump card, of course. No matter what Whyte had said, it was a physical impossibility for Sally to have overpowered Thompson, no matter how drunk he might have been; and the idea of her trailing him from the Spinning Wheel then bludgeoning him to death in a doorway was ludicrous. But he already knew the police saw things differently.

"No, I can't. But the police force isn't as awfully fond of you as I am, or as willing to give you the benefit of the doubt. You can't keep running, though." A thought occurred to him. "You still haven't got the money from Nate's will yet, have you?" Suddenly he felt as tired and sad as Sally looked. "Have you come to see me to ask for money again?"

He thought he saw the ghost of some emotion flit across her face then, but it was so fleeting he couldn't be sure exactly which it was. Guilt, he would have assumed, but instead he had the strongest feeling she was still angry, though oddly the anger wasn't directed at him. "I'll come back another time," she said. "When you're in a better mood."

She rose to her feet – even standing up, she was barely taller than he was seated – picked up another lemon biscuit from the plate and walked out the room. John watched her head pass in front of the lounge window as she walked down the street, and he suddenly wondered what she was doing in Amsterdam.

56

London, 1961

They'd got over Sally's infidelity, of course. How could they not when he loved her as much as he did? But, after that, there'd always been something wrong.

Fractured was how John thought of their marriage when he was drunk, as though it had been bent out of shape and then forced back, leaving a tiny hairline where the injury had occurred; a hairline that time and constant attrition had widened into a gaping abyss through which their love tumbled and was lost.

When he was sober, he just looked at her and saw her in *his* arms, then he behaved like a shit towards her and went out and got drunk. She soon got sick of apologising, and gradually they stopped talking altogether. He started to sleep in another room, eating out, staying late at Ronnie Scott's or the new Establishment Club. As his career took off, he was away shooting more and more, and she went back to drinking alone.

They'd limped on for years like that, neither of them willing to admit the marriage was over. The arrival of Alan and Michael, their two boys, had each promised a new start, but it had never been quite enough.

Then one day she'd announced she was going to advertise for a lodger. Someone to keep her company in the evenings, she'd said. He'd been on his way out the door, suitcase in hand, taxi at the kerb waiting to take him to the airport, then on to Rome and two weeks filming with George Cole and Una Stubbs.

"Do whatever you want," he said and slammed the door behind him.

He never even met Martin Simpson, the insurance salesman who rented the spare room, until nearly a month later.

57

Mickey Fagan had taken the decision to present only *Hamlet* in Holland, so there was almost nothing for the company to do during the day except sightsee, eat and drink. John spent the day in his room, brooding about Sally, but Edward returned late in the day from his cousin's house, boasting of the proper roast beef and potatoes he'd had for dinner.

"He has it shipped in from England, you know. He's friends with a local butcher, who arranges it. Lovely bit of roast beef and all the trimmings. Quite reminded me of home."

It was on the tip of John's tongue to remind Edward that they'd been away from London for less than two days, but the little man seemed so happy, he decided it would be churlish to burst his bubble so cruelly. Instead, he made noises designed to indicate his jealousy, all the while thinking that beef shipped from the UK on a ferry then cremated in some ex-pat's oven sounded absolutely hellish. He'd had battered white fish in a piquant sauce for dinner and rather thought he'd got the best of that particular bargain.

They were sitting in front of the fire in the hotel, finishing their coffee, when Jimmy Rae came in and suggested a walk. "I've been stuck in here all day going over my lines, and I could do with clearing my head and maybe stopping in a bar somewhere for a quick half?"

"A capital idea," Edward declared, pushing himself to his feet and casting about for his coat and hat. "I was just telling John here about the roast beef I had at my cousin's, and I have to admit a walk might be just the thing to help me digest it."

John watched the two men bustling about and wondered if he could make his excuses and have an early night with *Lord Vladimir's Intended*, which he'd found stuffed inside his travelling bag, left there since they'd been in Bolton. But if he stayed in by himself, he doubted the book would be any real distraction, and he'd just brood about Sally and what she was doing in the city. And he'd been doing that all afternoon as it was.

He also wondered whether he should mention Sally's reappearance to Edward. He'd intended to do so as soon as the little man got back, but he'd immediately begun recounting every moment of the meal he'd just had and, by the time he'd got to the pudding of spotted dick and custard, John hadn't the heart to upset him. But now, with Jimmy there too, it might be a good time to give him the news. He couldn't risk another falling out like the one they'd had last time he'd kept something secret regarding Sally.

"Wait for me!" he called through to the hallway.

* * *

A clock somewhere in the city chimed seven o'clock as the three men walked down the street, keeping up a brisk pace against the cold, which threatened to force its way through their jackets and leave them shivering.

Jimmy had spotted a little back-street bar about half a mile away and they followed him in that direction, talking about the upcoming first performance of *Hamlet* and the fact that they would soon be back at Ironbridge, filming for *Floggit*.

"I heard from Joe Riley on the phone yesterday," Jimmy said, a cigarette hanging from the side of his mouth as he spoke. "He said he's got to have an operation, poor old bugger. He wouldn't say what kind of op, but I reckon it must be to do with his waterworks." He shook his head. "He's always had trouble down there, he told me a while back."

"He isn't as young as he once was," John protested mildly. "That sort of thing will come to us all in the end."

He was finding it difficult to turn the conversation in a direction from which he might mention Sally and was, consequently, happy to talk about anything, in the hope that – as so often happened – it came to such a point naturally.

"He says he's been hoping to pop over and see us," Jimmy went on, unperturbed, "but the op's put paid to that."

It wasn't the best opening he could have hoped for, but it would have do, John decided. "Talking about people coming to visit, I've got some news which might be of interest," he said awkwardly.

As soon as he spoke, Edward came to a sharp stop and Jimmy had to step quickly to one side to avoid running into the back of him. Edward peered up at John and narrowed his eyes.

"Someone's been to see you?" he asked.

"Sally," John replied.

Jimmy flicked the remains of his cigarette over a nearby wall and into the dark canal on the other side. While he lit another, Edward indicated a nearby bench. "Perhaps we should take a seat?" he suggested quietly.

They sat, each of them taking a moment to light up, then John began to speak. He explained how Sally had appeared at the hotel and told them what she'd said. He also told them how she'd stormed out, and how he had no definite idea why she'd turned up at all. It pained him to admit it, but it was probably just because she needed money.

When he finished, he looked across at Edward. The little man had been listening intently, barely breathing, and now he nodded once, as though confirming something to himself. "I didn't think we'd see her again," he said finally. "You remember what we said at the awards thing: better to leave this to the police before one of us gets hurt. But if she's back on the scene, it must be for a good reason – and I don't think the chance of tapping you up for a few pounds is a good enough one. You're paying her maintenance now, I think you said?"

"The first of every month. Enough for herself and to pay for the boys' school fees and whatnot."

"So why come to you for more money? And why come to Amsterdam at all? She presumably knows this is a short run and you'll be back in London soon enough."

"I wondered that myself," John replied defensively. "But I couldn't think of a reason."

Jimmy stood up so that he could address both men at once. "Perhaps she had another reason for being here and just took the opportunity to see you? You know, a 'ships passing in the night' sort of thing."

"Then why not say so?"

"Now there you've got me. But presumably you'll find out when she gets back in touch like she said she would."

The three men considered this in silence as they finished their cigarettes. Then Jimmy pointed down the road. "It's getting a bit bloody nippy. How about we continue this conflab over a beer?"

There being no objection from either Edward or John, they repaired to the bar.

58

Next morning dawned bright and sunny. It still wasn't warm by any stretch of the imagination, but, as John looked through the suitcase he'd thrown in one corner of his hotel room, he decided he could risk a light cotton jacket over a short-sleeved shirt rather than the heavy overcoat which had been his constant companion in England for the past few months. He slipped on cream trousers and matching deck shoes to complete his outfit, and made his way downstairs for breakfast. So much of his time was spent in hotel and B&B dining rooms, he considered idly as he tucked a linen napkin into his shirt and made a start on a boiled egg.

As they'd walked from the bar the previous evening, Edward had complained of a sore head and there was no sign of him now. Jimmy Rae, however, was standing in the doorway and, seeing John, came across to join him.

"I just bumped into the manager bloke. He says Eddie's having breakfast in bed today. Feels a bit under the weather, apparently."

John carefully cut a slice of toast into strips and dipped the first one into his egg. "It's the first show tonight. I hope he'll be well enough for that."

"Should be. Just a bit of a sore head and a stiff neck, the manager said. I expect he'll be down later on."

John grunted, not really paying attention. He would go up and check on Edward later if he hadn't made an appearance, but, at the moment, he was finding it difficult to get his mind off Sally and her visit the day before.

He began to tell Jimmy his latest theory – that Sally had decided that she wanted him back and couldn't pluck up the courage to tell him so – when the other man pointed to something over his shoulder. John twisted his neck and found himself peering at the hotel manager who was walking towards them.

"Mr Le Breton," he said, pronouncing John's name in a way he found quite delightful. "I have just received a message for you from a Madame Simpson. She says can you meet her outside the Rijksmuseum at ten o'clock this morning?"

"That's a turn-up for the books, eh?" Jimmy said to John once the manager had left them to continue their breakfast. "Maybe you are irresistible after all."

"Perhaps. The way she keeps popping up is rather disconcerting, though."

He looked at the clock and realised it was already nine. He shoved the last piece of toast in his mouth and climbed to his feet with a heavy sigh. "I suppose I'd better get a move on if I want to be wherever that place is by ten. You know, there was once a time I could eat a meal without any drama at all. I'm sure all this running about plays havoc with my digestion."

* * *

The Rijksmuseum, when he got there, was the sort of building it would have been hard to miss. More like the Houses of Parliament or a palace for a minor European royal than what John thought of as a museum, it dominated the street on which it stood, stretching for a distance in both directions in red brick with dozens of high, arched windows and peaked, turreted roofs of grey slate.

Only as he reached the main entrance did it occur to him that Sally hadn't said where she'd meet him specifically and, in such a large building, it would be easy for them to miss one another. He walked the length of the exterior, but there was no sign of her, so he bought a ticket and went inside.

The interior was more like a British museum. High, curving, white ceilings rose above plainly utilitarian walls and floors, each room separated by wide, doorless arches and lit by the high windows he'd seen from the street. Everywhere people milled about or stood behind the red-roped barriers which protected the many exhibits from curious, potentially damaging fingers. John rather liked a bit of art, and he'd have happily spent the morning pottering about inside, but he was keen to speak to Sally, so he ignored the mass of paintings and sculpture, and wandered from room to room, eyes peeled for his ex-wife.

Eventually, he found himself in a long room with painted red walls and a gorgeously decorated golden ceiling. There was nobody else about – the exhibits were less interesting than the decoration, John thought, peering at the coins and scraps of material lying in the handful of glass cases dotted about the room – but he was tired from his walk across the city and frustrated at his failure to find Sally. He lowered himself gratefully onto one of the brown benches which were to be found throughout the building and reached for his cigarettes.

His lighter had been playing up for a few days and it chose that moment to stop working completely. He patted his jacket and turned out his pockets in a fruitless search for matches, and was just about to put the cigarette in his mouth back in the packet, when two men walked into the room and stood reading the sign in Dutch beside the doorway. A third man pushed past them and walked over to examine the exhibit closest to John. It seemed the perfect opportunity to ask for a light.

"Excuse me, my dear chap," he said, hoping the usual rule on foreigners speaking English applied, "but I wonder if I could touch you up for a light?" He held up the cigarette and shook it in a hopeful manner. "My lighter's on the fritz, you see."

The man – a swarthy European type with a prominent mole on his right cheek and his hair tied back in a dark ponytail – smiled and nodded.

He reached into his jacket pocket and pulled out a revolver.

"If could just stay where you are, Mr Le Breton," he said in English only slightly marred by an accent John couldn't quite place. *Eastern European*, he thought, then realised it probably didn't really matter.

"Of course, my dear fellow. Happy to oblige." He smiled his most disarming smile. "My feet are killing me after walking halfway across this lovely city, in any case."

Out of the corner of his eye he saw the other men manhandle two golden posts and a length of red rope across the doorway to the room. Then each of them turned his back on the room and took up a position facing into the museum.

"This is an old part of the museum," the mole man said. "It is not often visited, and my men have put up tape saying it is under renovation. We will not be disturbed, you will be pleased to hear."

In truth, John would really rather have heard the exact opposite. He was already *quite* disturbed, but he'd have welcomed yet more disturbance quite happily.

"You may be wondering why we wish to speak to you?" said mole man, the gun never wavering in his hand.

"If it wouldn't be too much trouble, that would be kind of you."

"We have been following you and your friend Mr Lowe for some time, hoping to put a proposition to you. Unfortunately, on every occasion when we have come close to speaking to you in England, you have evaded our men and the opportunity has been lost."

"It was you following Edward after Nate's funeral! And on the way back to the theatre!"

"Quite so. My… employer…" He said the word as though unsure if it was correct, or perhaps knowing it was not, but doing the best he could in a language not his own. "…was hopeful that we could come to an arrangement amicably – and that is still his intention – but time is running out, and it has become imperative we speak to one of you today to explain the job we wish you to do for us."

Until this point, John had been wondering if he was about to be killed and, as a more minor concern, *why* he was about to be killed, but Mole Man's words indicated that this wasn't to be his last day on Earth, and he allowed himself to relax slightly.

"Wait there, what have you done with Sally?" he asked, as his more relaxed mind suddenly found itself with the capacity to think of something other than his own imminent demise.

"Sally?" Mole Man looked confused.

"Don't play games with me!" John pushed his hands down on the bench, preparing to launch himself at his captor, but a wave of the pistol towards his head and a soft *tut* was enough to dissuade him. He slumped down, but only a little, and stared up at Mole Man. "My ex-wife Sally. Short girl, not quite five foot two, pretty little face, if perhaps a little rounder than most. Blonde hair, brown eyes, can have a bit of a temper when she doesn't get her own way. Sally!" he concluded, more in irritation than concern, he told himself. If they weren't going to shoot him and they wanted to come to some sort of deal – though he couldn't for the life of him imagine what kind of deal that might be – then they were hardly likely to have bumped off his ex-wife.

"I have no idea what you're talking about, Mr Le Breton, and no time to waste on foolishness. If you would stand up please and hold your hands out, I will restrain you, and then we will walk out of this room and leave the museum via one of the staff exits."

It was the queerest thing. He stood up, fully intending to do whatever Mole Man said, far more concerned about Sally stumbling into this frankly bizarre kidnapping than any risk he might himself be in. He actually got to his feet and held out his hands towards Mole Man, who lowered his gun to fish some plastic ties from his pocket.

Just for a second, while the gun dipped and the man's attention was briefly elsewhere, he remembered Madge Kenyon's gun pointed at his head in Ironbridge and the way he'd rugby-tackled her while still tied to a chair. It was no more than an instant, but, in that moment, he tensed his leg muscles as he had then, and prepared to rush his captor.

It might have amounted to nothing – he might have come to his senses in time, realised that even if he knocked Mole Man over, he had two, presumably equally well armed, confederates at the door – had Jimmy Rae not suddenly appeared around the edge of that door, swinging what seemed to be a gold metal barrier post in a wide arc towards the first of those men.

It connected with a thud like a chef's mallet hitting a slab of pork and the man buckled at the waist. Reversing the post in his hands so he held it like a short golden lance, Jimmy charged at the second man while bellowing at the top of his voice. John thought Jimmy might have shouted

"Banzai!" but his attention was otherwise engaged at that moment by the roundhouse punch he'd launched at Mole Man. As his fist swung in a mighty arc through the air, he was dimly aware that the second guard had caught Jimmy's lance and wrenched it from his hands, and that the young actor was now on the ground with blood pouring from a wound on his forehead. He felt his own fist connect with the side of Mole Man's neck, knocking him off balance and, with quite the loudest sound John had heard since the war, pulling the trigger on the gun he still held in his hand.

John rocked back, pain shooting up his arm where he'd hit the man, and his ears ringing from the discharge of the gun. He stumbled into the low bench and tripped over it, falling backwards in what felt like slow motion, with just enough time to see Mole Man running towards the door before the back of his head struck the grey tiled floor and everything turned an all-encompassing shade of black.

59

When he came to, all he could see was the plump face of Edward Lowe peering down at him with concern. "He's coming round!" he said and pulled away, allowing John to take in a little more of his surroundings.

He was lying in bed in his hotel room, with pillows propped up under his neck and head, and a light cover over his body. Edward, Alison Jago and Mickey Fagan were crammed around the bedside, each of them looking exactly as if they hoped one of the others would give him the bad news.

In the end, it was Fagan who spoke. "You've had a crack on the back of your head where you fell over that bench," he said. "The doctor's been out to see you and he said we need to keep an eye out for concussion, but otherwise you're in reasonably good nick for a man of nearly seventy who knocked himself out on a museum floor."

That wasn't it, John thought. If he was fine, then that wasn't the reason for the long faces leaning over him. "Where's Jimmy?" he asked, remembering him lying on the ground with a thug towering over him, and terrified to hear the answer.

"He's in a bad way. In the hospital."

"My God," John struggled to sit up and felt a wave of nausea flood over him. "Will he be alright?"

"He should be." Fagan's combed-over hair flapped in front of his eyes as he shook his head, and he quickly scooped it up and smoothed it back across his scalp. "It's a terrible thing when two pals can't go sightseeing without being mugged." He caught John's eye and held it, obviously not convinced that was what had happened.

"Is that what they were, muggers?" John asked, keen to give nothing away until he'd spoken to Edward. "I can't remember anything at all after going into the museum."

"It's what the police think," Edward piped up from behind Fagan. The little man had been uncharacteristically quiet since John had woken up, but now he stepped in front of the others and laid a hand on John's shoulder. "They think Jimmy fought back against a gang of pickpockets – it seems they're quite common round the tourist areas – and in the struggle the gun they were using to hold him up went off. You were lucky really, the Dutch police said. If it hadn't gone off, Lord alone knows what might have happened. People have been killed in these kinds of robberies before now."

With his back to Mickey and Alison, Edward silently mouthed *we need to talk*.

"As it turned out," he continued in a louder voice, "the robbers fled without getting anything, but Jimmy took a nasty blow to the head, and you fell and knocked yourself out. The police took Jimmy to the hospital and he's got a bit of concussion and needs stitches in his forehead and across his scalp. They're keeping him in for a day or two. They initially wanted to keep you in too, but you insisted you were fine to come back here, and then you passed out again when we got back. We were just discussing calling the doctor when you woke up." Edward winked and stepped back from the bed. "We should probably let John get some rest," he said. "I know we're not to let him sleep just yet, so I'm happy to sit and chat with him for a bit."

John groaned loudly, decided that was a little too theatrical, and fell back onto his pillows with a more restrained sigh. "If you wouldn't mind, I am a bit fagged out." A thought occurred to him. "But what about the show tonight?"

"Cancelled," Fagan replied with heavy sigh of his own. "The run's cancelled. You can't have *Hamlet* without the Prince and Jimmy's in no state to go on stage for three hours, even if he weren't in a hospital bed." He laughed, a mirthless, tired sound. "Bad enough that we were stuck with Monica playing Ophelia but, with the best will in the world, we can't also have Edward or Peter playing Hamlet in their sixties. We'll be here for another couple of days while I speak to the owners of the Stadsschouwburg, but then we'll be off home." He gave himself a shake, clapped his hands together and gestured towards Alison, who had stood silently throughout their conversation. "Come on, my dear. Time we left these two to discuss whatever it is they're not telling us." He laughed again, and John thought he heard a more genuine note to it this time. "They think we're idiots and don't know what they're up to."

Alison bent down and quickly pecked John on the cheek. "You take it easy, you hear?" she said.

She and Fagan left the room, and Edward pulled up a chair. "So, what actually happened?" he asked.

John's head was still muddled and heavy, and he had an overwhelming desire to close his eyes. He fought the urge, though, and was rewarded by a thought bubbling its way to the front of his brain. "Have you heard from Sally?" he asked, cursing the head knock that had driven this most important of questions temporarily from his mind.

"Not a word," Edward assured him. "She was there when you were attacked?"

"No, but I was there to meet her. She never turned up, though, at least not before we were cornered by Mole Man and his thugs."

"Mole Man?"

John explained about the man with the mole on his face and the "arrangement" he had spoken of. He was about to describe Jimmy's attempted intervention when he realised that Edward had gone as pale as he felt.

"What's the matter, old chap?" he asked, twisting his head around to make sure nobody was unexpectedly standing behind him.

"Dark complexion and dark hair tied in a ponytail, you said?"

John nodded.

"Tall? Six foot at least?"

"Yes, I should say so. Why do you ask? Do you know him?"

Edward sat down on the side of the bed. "I think he was the man who followed me back in Bolton. You remember, the night we argued in the pub and I stormed out?"

"Of course. He shouted your name in the fog."

"He was a tall man too, with long, dark hair."

"The same man, do you think?"

"It has to be."

"And this time poor Jimmy took the brunt of it."

Thinking of his name reminded John of another question which would have occurred to him before, had he been feeling completely himself. "What was Jimmy doing there anyway? Was he following me?"

The look on Edward's face was a mix of embarrassment and stubborn determination. "Jimmy came to see me as soon as you left to meet Sally. I was feeling a little under the weather, or I'd have gone myself, but he volunteered to go after you and make sure you didn't come to any mischief." He gave John a long look. "I know you're sure Sally is entirely innocent of any wrongdoing, but I can't pretend I don't still have my suspicions about her. And it looks as though I was right to do so."

"This was nothing to do with Sally," John explained carefully, but without rancour. In Bolton, he'd allowed his own worries about Sally to affect him badly, and he'd taken them out on Edward, almost losing his friendship in the process. He was determined not to fall into that trap again. Whatever Edward said or believed, he knew he did so out of a genuine concern for his friend and for the investigation. "Mole Man hadn't even heard her name before. I think they'd been following me since the hotel, and it was pure coincidence that I happened to wander into a quieter area of the museum, where they could get me on my own."

Edward grunted, clearly not convinced but willing to be mollified for now. "Very well, let's proceed on that basis. What exactly did this Mole Man say he wanted us to do? It must be important if they've been trying to contact us since Bolton."

"And it must be pretty damn dodgy if they weren't able to simply pop into Mrs Galloway's or knock on our front doors when we went back home."

Edward nodded. "That's a very fair point. I think, between that and their willingness to pull a gun on you, we can assume that whatever it is, it's likely to be illegal. This has become an altogether too dangerous situation. We need to go home and put this all behind us for good."

Bless Edward, John thought with a flush of affection. Of course it was going to be illegal. And he was right about the best thing they could do. Go back to England, forget all about Mickey Fagan's theatre company and get on with making *Floggit and Leggit*. But Sally was in Amsterdam by herself and she'd come to him for help. There was no way he was willing to go home without her.

"I can't leave without Sally," he said firmly. He wondered if Edward would argue, but instead he inclined his head and stared thoughtfully at the floor.

"Of course. Apart from anything else, we need her to come back with us." He held up a hand. "As I said, you believe she's innocent, and she may well be. But until she returns to England and speaks to the police, she'll never be free from suspicion. Surely you don't want a life like that for her, constantly on the run, unable to go home?"

What he said make sense. That was no way to live. John swung his legs out from under the covers and held out a hand to Edward. "Give me a hand up, then. We'll not find Sally lying here in bed."

60

In the end, even after several hours of sitting in the hotel lounge drinking hot tea, John was still too unsteady on his feet to venture outside.

Instead, he telephoned the hospital. The nurse who answered said Jimmy was awake and responsive, which sounded promising. He heard her giggle and say something which sounded very much like "You are a terrible man, Mr Rae," which sounded more promising still. *Even multiple stitches and a possible concussion weren't slowing the lad down*, he thought with a smile. He only hoped Alison didn't choose an inopportune moment to visit.

More worryingly, there had been no word from Sally at the hotel reception. Edward had asked him to go over exactly what she'd said when she'd come to see him and the precise wording of the message she'd sent via the hotel manager.

"'Meet me at the Rijksmuseum at ten' was all she said. Nothing more than that, no location inside the museum or anything like that. That's why I was wandering about."

"And you definitely didn't see her?"

"Not a hair of her."

Edward made a face. "We'll just have to wait for her to get back in touch, then. But, in the meantime, what do we do about this Mole Man fellow and his gang? I suspect you'll disagree, but on the surface at least, it does seem as though Sally led you into a trap."

Now John frowned. The problem was, he couldn't deny that Edward had a point. It felt like a coincidence too far that Sally should turn up in Amsterdam, arrange to meet him and then he should be jumped by a gang who knew about him and Edward, and who wanted a job of some description done for them. "Perhaps," he said finally. "I do find it hard to believe, but, at the same time, it does increasingly fly in the face of probability that Sally's not involved." The headache which had bedevilled him since he'd woken up was finally starting to clear, but it was too late to go out looking for Sally now, even if they had an idea where she might be. "Hopefully, she'll get back in touch tomorrow."

"If she doesn't, it does point to her guilt, you know. If she knew nothing about these gangster types, then she's no reason to think you've been hurt and will just assume you weren't able to make your rendezvous at such short notice."

That made sense. John sat back in his chair and stared out the window at the dark street. Surely Sally would contact him tomorrow.

* * *

By the following morning, John was feeling entirely recovered. He bounded down the stairs for breakfast in an unexpectedly good mood, refreshed from a full night's sleep and convinced, in the slightly chilly light of morning, that he would hear from Sally before the day was out.

Edward was already seated when he entered the dining room, but he was just finishing up. He pulled the napkin from his collar as John walked up and lit a cigarette. John grabbed a coffee and a croissant from the sideboard and took a seat opposite him.

"I tried one of those," Edward complained sourly, indicating the croissant. "It's like someone made a morning roll out of crêpe paper. Damn thing fell to pieces when I tried to cut it in half to put the jam in."

John carefully cut a short incision in the middle of the pastry and spread a thin layer of butter inside. "I had them in Paris a few years back. They're wonderfully light and fluffy, I always think."

"Hmm." Edward grunted and turned his attention back to the newspaper which John saw he'd laid out on the table in front of him. "There's a little bit about Nate Thompson in the announcements section," he said, spinning the paper around and tapping one part of the page. "It says his will has been read but, due to an ongoing police investigation, no money has been released to the beneficiaries yet."

John felt his good humour take a lurch downwards. He checked the date of the newspaper – two days previous. Could Sally have known that the will was stuck when she'd come to see him yesterday? She hadn't said, and he wasn't sure if it would be better or worse if she had known. Worse in the sense that she was alone in Amsterdam without any money or even the promise of any, but better in that at least she had come to him. Money wasn't something he thought about much, but he was reasonably sure he had quite a lot of it. He'd be more than happy to give some to Sally.

Suddenly he had no desire to sit around drinking coffee. He wanted to be out looking for Sally, to be reassuring her that he could look after her financially until Thompson's bequest was released.

"How do you feel about a walk along to the Rijksmuseum?" he said, that being the first possible destination which popped into his head. Sally was hardly likely to be waiting there for him, but it was a starting point.

"I suppose we could take a walk along there," Edward agreed reluctantly. He went through to the hallway and returned with John's coat and hat, as well as a walking stick he'd evidently picked up from the hatstand at the door. "Just in case you get dizzy on the way," he explained.

John was rather touched by his friend's solicitude. It had only been a few weeks since they'd made up, and Edward made no secret of the fact that he was not entirely convinced of Sally's innocence, but the way he fussed about, making sure John was wrapped up and secure before they set out, was really quite touching.

So, it was all the more unfortunate, then, that they'd barely turned the corner from the hotel when two men walked up behind them, pulled black sacks over their heads and threw them into a van.

61

"Finally, we meet."

The speaker was plainly a dangerous man – later, that was the first word which came to mind whenever John was asked to describe him. But in every other respect he was completely nondescript. A little older than himself, John thought, around seventy at a guess. Medium height, his hair receding but once brown, clean-shaven but with neat sideburns running the length of his ears, conservatively dressed but not old-fashioned, he wouldn't have stood out in any crowd.

Except for the danger, which shone from his grey eyes like a beacon promising terrible things to anyone who crossed him.

Even in the crisp March air, he wore no jacket, only an open-necked shirt. As he approached them, passing through a crowd of equally dangerous-looking men who parted respectfully to let him through, he turned a chunky gold ring on his finger and smiled thinly.

They were sitting on two hard wooden chairs in what John had tentatively identified as the back room of a florist. It was cold and functional, grey flooring, grey painted walls and with a ceiling of untouched rough concrete. The scent of flowers in bloom was overpowering.

"Mr Lowe. Mr Le Breton." The man addressed each of them in turn, his accent difficult to pin down, but definitely English, well spoken but unemotional. "My name is Buchanan, but it's probably best that you don't try to remember that fact." He chuckled, and the men nearest him joined in. "You've led my colleagues a merry dance, here and in England, I've got to admit. To be honest, I wondered if somehow you knew what we were after, you seemed so keen to avoid us. First, at Sir Nathaniel's funeral – such a pity he had to die…" The man's voice dipped as he quickly crossed himself. "And then again when Diego here tried to speak to you as you walked from the pub to the theatre. I thought our chance had gone when I heard the Amsterdam shows had been cancelled. So, imagine my delight when I discovered it was back on, and I was able to turn you into a captive audience at the Rijksmuseum yesterday." He shook his head and sighed. "May I say how much I personally regret the injury caused to Mr Rae. Please pass on my apologies, but he was foolish to attack my men – and, once attacked, they had no choice but to defend themselves. It *is* regrettable, all the same. Far better if we could have put our proposition to you without the need for violence."

The man stopped speaking and cocked an eyebrow in their direction. "This is where one of you is supposed to say

'What proposition?' or something like that, and I explain the little job I want you to do for us." He stepped closer and took Edward's face in his hand. John noticed the ring he'd been turning was loose on his finger, as though it had been made for a bigger man. He gave himself a mental shake. This was not the time to be noticing unimportant details. A vision of Jimmy Rae, blood pouring from his scalp, came to mind, and he shuddered.

"This one is barely conscious," Buchanan growled, straightening up and glaring at the men around him. "Stevie, you were in charge of this. How did Mr Lowe come to be hit so hard?"

One man, presumably Stevie, ran a hand through his hair and said "He fell in the van. He must have banged his head."

Buchanan's eyes narrowed. "That was sloppy work, Stevie. Next time, be more careful. I will be unhappy if Mr Lowe is injured. *Very* unhappy. Pierre, where are you?" He snapped his fingers and another man came forward. He carried a black Gladstone bag, looking for all the world like an English doctor from a forties stage play. He knelt beside Edward and lifted up his eyelids.

"He is only dazed," he said, reaching inside his bag and pulling out a small brown bottle. He unscrewed the cap and held it under Edward's nose. The little man spluttered and coughed and opened his eyes. He tried to sit up, only to find a meaty hand pushing him back down. He began to say something, then snapped his mouth shut and glared at the men around him. John admired the level of contempt he managed to put into that single look.

"Good to have you back with us, Mr Lowe. For your benefit, I'll repeat what I just said to your friend here. Well done for avoiding my men back in England, but had you spoken to them rather than running from them, you would have discovered they simply wished to put a proposition to you."

"What sort of proposition?" Edward asked fiercely, as Buchanan let out a loud guffaw.

"That's more like it," he said when he had stopped laughing. "Mr Le Breton was disappointingly unwilling to join in my little game." Again, he twisted the ring round his finger. "You ask a very good question, Mr Lowe, and one with a very simple answer. I wish you and Mr Le Breton to transport certain items for me, that is all."

"Certain items?" Edward's voice was weak, and John twisted his head to check he was alright. His face was redder than usual, but other than that and the fact that his glasses were slightly askew, he seemed much the same as usual.

"Two paintings, to be exact," Buchanan said, and snapped his fingers again.

Yet another man emerged from the crowd around them, this one carrying a black briefcase, which he held open so Buchanan could extract two sheets of paper. He held these in front of Edward and John, one in each hand, and invited the men to examine them.

Each of the sheets of paper held the image of a painting in a frame, photographed propped against a whitewashed wall and, John assumed, somehow blown up to fit the page. The first painting was of a pale-skinned man with long brown hair reaching down onto his chest and a black beret perched on the back of his head. He wore a brown fur wrap over one shoulder and, in the top right-hand corner of the frame, a window showed the countryside beyond him.

The second painting was smaller and less distinct, but appeared to show a blue-clad figure in a broad-brimmed yellow hat walking along a leaf-strewn path with fields and trees in the background. Even John, who thought of himself as a Philistine when it came to art, recognised the style of Vincent van Gogh.

"*Portrait of a Young Man* by Raphael, painted in 1513, and *The Painter on the Road to Tarascon* by Van Gogh from 1888." Buchanan folded the sheets of paper up and returned them to the briefcase. "Missing since the end of the War: believed destroyed during the Allied bombing of Magdeburg in 1945. As I am sure you have realised by now, they are neither missing nor destroyed, but instead have come into my possession. I have sold them to a collector in England, and all I need now is a way of getting them over the North Sea and through English customs undetected." He smiled, but only with his mouth. His eyes remained focused on the two men before him. "I need hardly add that the ownership of these two priceless pieces of art is... disputed, shall we say?"

"Is this why you killed Nate Thompson?" Edward asked. "Did he discover what you were up to?"

"Killed Nate? Why, we didn't kill Nate. It would've made everything a damn sight more straightforward if he was still alive. Kill Nate, indeed!" He chuckled again and shook his head in wonderment at the foolishness of the suggestion.

But John had remembered something which Edward had obviously forgotten. "He was your original choice for this job, wasn't he?" he said. "You remember the library book with the missing pages, Edward? 'High Renaissance', you said they were. Don't you see? Nate was looking up the Raphael painting he'd be smuggling into England. He was to be the original courier!"

"Well done, Mr Le Breton." Buchanan lightly clapped his hands together in John's face. "Though I'd thought you'd have figured that out already. Maybe I've been giving you too much credit. But you're right, of course. Poor old Nate was supposed to be doing this job for us, before his untimely demise. He owed me a favour and, when I discovered he was in the perfect position to repay that favour, well, how could he refuse?"

Edward had been waiting for a chance to speak throughout this exchange, and as John took a moment to consider this obviously rhetorical question, he took the opportunity to pose one of his own. "If you don't mind me asking, if you didn't kill him, then who did?"

Buchanan shrugged, uninterested it seemed. "I've got no idea. Why should I care? I'm a realist, Mr Lowe. If I have a job for a man and that man is killed, I accept the fact and seek a new man. I don't waste time looking for whoever did the killing. Now, enough questions," he went on with sudden intensity. "I'm going to explain to you how you'll bring my paintings through customs and you're going to listen."

Edward opened his mouth to speak again and, as casually as if he were swatting a fly with a rolled-up newspaper, Buchanan leaned forward and slapped him hard across the face.

Edward's chair tipped over and he fell backward on to the floor, crashing against the concrete with a sickening thud. John gave out an involuntary cry which he immediately bit off, as Buchanan wiped his hand with his handkerchief, his face betraying no emotion at all. "Pierre," he said, and the doctor hurried forward and crouched down beside Edward.

"He's fine," he announced as two other men manhandled the chair back upright, with Edward in it. He had a cut on his lip but otherwise seemed unhurt. From somewhere behind John, he heard a grunt of satisfaction, then a hand appeared over his shoulder and positioned Edward's glasses back on his nose.

"Like I said," Buchanan sighed, "that's enough questions for now. I'll explain what'll happen and then – perhaps – I'll answer questions afterwards. Once I've finished and I'm confident you understand your task, you'll be released and left to make your way to your hotel."

Buchanan gave a groan and rubbed at the small of his back with a grimace. One of the men behind him scuttled off and returned with a chair, which he sank into with a grateful sigh. "My back's in pieces," he complained. "I'm getting too old to be standing around in the draughty back rooms of shops. Now where was I? Oh yes – in two days' time, when you leave Amsterdam for the coast, you'll have my paintings with you, packed into the frames of a couple of set paintings. Who's going to bother examining those at customs, I ask you? All you need to do is unscrew the back of the frame, slip one of my paintings in behind the one that's already in there, then screw it back up again. You're the stars of the show, nobody will blink an eyelid if they see you around the props and whatnot – and I hear you've got some experience in poking about places you shouldn't be." His grin invited them to join in.

Edward glared at him, but John smiled back weakly.

"Later, back in England, one of my associates will break into the theatre in Bolton and remove the paintings. He'll be very careful to leave no trace he's been there and, since nothing will actually have gone missing as far as the theatre's concerned, there's no reason to think anyone will notice a thing. But by then, you'll have done your bit, shepherding the paintings over the border, and dealing with any unexpected snags that might have come up. Our relationship will be over, and you'll be free to continue making your little television show."

He looked first at Edward then at John, and waited until each man had nodded his understanding.

For the next few minutes, he talked the two men through the details of his plan to smuggle the two Nazi-looted paintings across the North Sea. It was, John was forced to admit to himself, simple enough that even he and Edward couldn't mess it up. Unscrew a couple of frames, hide a couple of paintings, make sure nobody opens the frames before they got back to England.

When Buchanan had finished speaking, there was a

moment of silence, and then he said, with a smile, "Now then, any questions?"

"Why should we help you?"

Buchanan looked down at Edward, still smiling. "See, now's the time to be asking questions. Although, strictly speaking, I meant questions about the plan. But you were polite enough to listen to me without interrupting and it's a good question. One I think perhaps I should answer, if our arrangement is to be an amicable one."

He raised his hands in front of himself and, theatrically, clapped them together. Behind him, the crowd of men parted to form a corridor, along which two figures walked towards Edward and John.

The smaller of the two figures was a man with slicked-back, jet-black hair and a pencil-thin moustache. His skin was an olive colour, and John mentally marked him down as an Italian. The other, taller man was clean-shaven, blond-haired and blue-eyed, with what John thought of as a Swedish look about him.

"You haven't met these two colleagues of mine," Buchanan said. "That's a lucky break for you, because they're not the sort of men I send when I want a word with someone. They're not the type to put a proposition to two elderly English actors." He held out his hand and the Italian placed what appeared to be a Polaroid photograph in it. "No, they're not that type at all. When you meet either of these two, it tends to be the last time you meet anyone at all." He picked up the photo between his thumb and forefinger and held it in front of Edward and John.

Edward gasped as he recognised Alison Jago. The picture was of her leaving their hotel in Amsterdam, wearing the jeans and T-shirt she'd had on the previous day.

"You take my meaning, gentlemen? If you don't help us, I might have to send one of these boys to visit your friend." He shrugged. "They're foreigners, too. They don't have the same... tenderness... when it comes to the ladies." He paused for a second to let his meaning sink in, then leaned forward and tucked a slip of paper in Edward's pocket. "If you need to, you can contact us on this number."

John nodded. There was nothing else to do. As someone came up behind him and replaced the black bag over his head, he heard the man's voice.

"Otherwise, we'll be in touch soon," it said.

62

"Bloody hell, that's a turn-up for the books!"

Jimmy Rae's easy laugh was muffled by the bruising which still coloured his jaw a deep purple, but it was enough to break the tension in the room.

They had convened in Jimmy's hospital room. John and Edward were sitting on a pair of hard wooden chairs, and Alison was perched on the edge of the windowsill. Edward was still unhappy that she'd come with them, but since she'd seen them at the hotel, being pushed out of a van with hoods over their heads, they were in no position to refuse her assistance.

Edward had just finished telling the others about their meeting with Buchanan and his criminal gang.

"So those buggers that duffed me up, they were just wanting to talk to you two?" Jimmy laughed again.

Edward was astonished at his attitude. There was a devil-may-care side to Jimmy which he simply didn't understand. The younger man seemed to positively revel in dangerous situations. Perhaps, he conjectured, watching the way Alison was looking at him, it was something to do with impressing the ladies. For himself, he was still shaken by the encounter. He prodded his tongue at the cut inside his lip and shuddered.

"That's about the long and the short of it," John confirmed, poking at the bump on the back of his head with one of his long fingers. "Ironically, if Edward had stopped to chat with the fellow who was following him in the rain after Nate Thompson's funeral, we'd have had a lot less trouble."

"So, Nate was their first choice for this little smuggling job then?"

"It looks that way. Buchanan said that everything would be much simpler if he was still alive. They had him lined up to smuggle the paintings, but then he got himself killed, and we were the replacements."

"I wonder what hold they had over him? You'll do it because they threatened your Sally, but what leverage did they use with him?"

Edward winced inwardly and risked a quick glance at John. The other man was poker-faced, giving nothing away. They'd decided between themselves it was best not to worry Alison or Jimmy by telling them the truth about who Buchanan had threatened. Better to let them think it was Sally for now. However, he had his own theory about the gang's hold over Thompson.

"I think it's connected to whatever was in those letters we found burned in the fire grate. I think one of Buchanan's people came back after he was killed and burned all of them, except the one that Inspector Whyte found. I don't think they were all love letters. Something in them must have provided a link between Thompson and the gang, and so they destroyed them."

The room fell silent as everyone considered Edward's theory. Then Alison spoke.

"Actually, that was Judy," she said quietly but precisely, the voice of someone imparting information she'd kept secret for a good reason but which she now felt able to tell. "Judy burned all the love letters she wrote to Nate Thompson and that he kept in a box behind his dressing table. She did it just after she fainted on stage that day, when the police told us he'd been killed. I saw her do it."

Edward stared at her, his mouth hanging open like something from a *Tom and Jerry* cartoon. He wouldn't have been surprised if his eyes jumped out of his head either, such was the shock he felt. He remembered Judy Faith saying she needed to go to her room, complaining that she'd had such a shock that she needed to rest. He shook his head and concentrated his attention on Alison. "You knew this all along, and yet you said nothing?" he asked, his voice rapidly rising in pitch, but it was a rhetorical question, and everyone knew it. "You never thought it might be something we'd be interested in?"

Alison gave no sign of being cowed by Edward's attitude, or by his words. "How was I to know you were so desperate to know that? If you remember, you never even admitted you knew the box existed until Whyte found it, and you never told anyone until now that you'd looked inside it long before then."

They were both on their feet now, the short, stout little actor, his round face bright-red and his eyes sparkling behind his glasses, and the petite, brown-skinned assistant stage manager, her face set in an expression of anger and hurt, her lips thin and tight, her eyes furious.

"We did try to return the key we found inside the box once we'd visited the house in the park," Edward pointed out, and John had the most inopportune desire to laugh as he realised how much what Edward had said sounded like a children's nursery rhyme or a foreign-language primer from his schooldays.

"The key in the box is in the house in the park," he murmured to himself, and everyone turned and looked at him. "Sorry," he said, and attempted to look more serious.

"What key?" Alison asked.

"The key to Thompson's house in the park."

"The one Judy stayed at?"

It was all too much for Edward. The redness drained from his face, and he lowered the finger he'd been about to point at Alison. He took a step backwards and fell into his chair, breathing heavily. "Judy stayed at the house in the park?" he asked once he'd got his breath back. "Not Sally?"

"Not that I know of, but Judy definitely did, quite often too. She told me all about it. I'd followed her out that day, thinking she might need a glass of water, or an aspirin, but when I got to her dressing room door, she'd already pulled out the make-up table and was holding a load of letters, all tied together with a bit of string. Before I could say anything, she dumped the whole lot into the fireplace. I must have made a noise or something, because she looked up as she set it alight, then burst into tears." Alison also seemed to have calmed down. She lifted herself back on the windowsill and continued her story. "She was so upset that she blurted out the whole story. I think she was just happy to have someone to talk to. She told me she'd met Thompson at ATV's studio in Kingsway when she was filming *Ready Steady Go!* and he was being interviewed for some show in the studio next door. She was overawed at the great theatrical knight taking an interest in her, I think. In any case, she ended up in his bed that night, and later on he got her a place at the Playhouse in Bolton."

"And then he set her up in the house in the park?" John asked, repeating Edward's earlier question in a far more insistent tone.

"He already had the place, Judy said. Apparently, he owned houses all over. But, yes, he gave her a key, told her to make herself at home."

"But why didn't they just live together in his actual house?"

"She said he had another woman who stayed at his place a lot. Sally, presumably, from what you just asked. She seemed OK with that, to be honest. I don't suppose she wanted to be known as someone who slept her way into jobs." Alison frowned and pinched the bridge of her nose tiredly. "But she *was* in love with him, at first at least. Partly awe too, like I said, but who can tell the difference at that age? She wrote him pretty passionate love letters when he was in Bolton and she was still in London – she knew where he kept them and, when he was killed, she decided it'd be better if nobody else saw them. If there was anything else in there, I'd be surprised. Like I said, they were all tied together."

Edward had to admit he was impressed by the quick way Judy had recovered from the shock of Thompson's death and immediately taken steps to ensure there was no link between them. He wouldn't have thought she was possessed of the necessary degree of cold calculation.

"Did she clean the house?" he asked as a new thought occurred to him. "The place in the park was scrubbed clean by the time we got there. All we could smell was bleach, and the only thing in the whole house which was out of place was that pile of library books."

Alison nodded. "I think so. She said she was going to 'cover her tracks'. And she wouldn't have known about any library books, or what to do with them, even if she'd come across them." She paused, apparently trying to remember some detail. "One of the things Judy burned, the only thing that wasn't one of her letters, it looked like it came from a library book – some kind of glossy coffee table book anyway. It was a page from a book on art, I think. A picture of a young guy in a floppy black hat."

"The Raphael painting," Edward sighed under his breath so that only John could hear.

"You didn't think any of this was the kind of thing you should be telling the authorities?" he asked again, but more calmly this time.

"Have you told them everything you've discovered?" she replied with a touch of her earlier sharpness. "No, never mind that. I'm sorry, I'm just a bit shocked by all of this. But, no, I didn't think to tell anyone. Judy was a friend, she asked me not to say anything, and I couldn't see it had any bearing on the police investigation. After all, Judy didn't kill Nate."

"No, she didn't," Edward agreed wearily. He took off his glasses and rubbed his eyes. "We still don't know who did, but it certainly wasn't Miss Faith."

He looked at each of the others, willing them to add something useful. Between John and Alison, he'd already had a significant amount of pertinent information kept from him – for what they each thought were the best of reasons, admittedly – but he'd be happy enough if they were to add some more.

Nobody said a word. Alison was still a little flushed in the face, and John was pulling at his ear, lost in thought. Jimmy yawned and blinked heavily. Edward realised they were keeping the younger man from the rest he obviously needed.

"Time to let you get back to sleep, Jimmy," he said, rising from his chair and smoothing down his dirt-stained trousers. "I need to go back to the hotel to change, and so I imagine does John. If you'd like to share a cab with us, Alison?"

"Thanks anyway, but I think I'll stay on for a bit."

Jimmy had already closed his eyes, but had he seen the look Alison gave him, Edward thought it might have had a positive effect on his recovery.

* * *

Out in the corridor, John pulled Edward to one side as doctors and nurses hurried past. "It's been a bugger of a couple of days," he said. "I've had two different guns waved at me, had a bag shoved over my head, been knocked out and been threatened with all sorts if I don't help smuggle two paintings pinched by the Nazis through customs. Frankly, I couldn't care less that my trousers are a bit grubby or that I could do with changing my shirt. What do you say to taking a walk until we find a picturesque little café somewhere and then having a beer and a bite to eat? Just take an hour to ourselves before we get stuck back into whatever hell on Earth this is likely to be?"

It was an attractive proposition. They did need to eat, and now that the Amsterdam run of *Hamlet* had been cancelled, they only had a couple of days before the company packed up and returned to Britain – with the addition of two illicit paintings, if they did as they'd been told. If they were to come up with a plan, they'd need to do so very soon, but an hour wouldn't make much difference.

Edward nodded and pointed towards the exit. "We passed a nice little place in the taxi here. Some tables and chairs right up beside the canal; it can't be more than a five-minute walk."

63

The little café sat on the edge of a cobbled square, sandwiched between a medieval church and a dark canal. John, carried away by being back in Amsterdam, asked the waiter to bring "two beers – and whatever the local delicacy is to eat," while Edward settled himself in his seat and fished a packet of Craven A from his jacket pocket.

To his surprise, it was only a few minutes later when the waiter returned with a platter that contained small chunks of cheese and matching squares of raw beef. Edward stared at him in astonishment. "Have you lost your mind?" he said. He poked one of the pieces of meat with the small silver fork which came with the dish, then shouted the waiter over before he disappeared back inside the café.

"Do you have such a thing as a frying pan in there?" he asked with exaggerated slowness, miming the act of holding a pan and wiggling the imaginary object from side to side. "Even a grill would do," he went on in the face of the young waiter's incomprehension. "You understand? A. Grill. For. Cooking."

The waiter's puzzlement only increased Edward's annoyance. He turned to John, exasperation plain on his face. "We can't eat this, it's not cooked," he complained, but the waiter had evidently decided this loud, wildly gesticulating foreigner was not worth any more time of his time and walked away.

"Absolutely disgusting," Edward said, drinking his beer and glaring balefully at the plate in front of him. "I'll wait and make myself some cheese on toast back at the hotel."

John said nothing. He smiled and used his little fork to harpoon first meat then cheese, which he popped into his mouth and chewed with an intense look of satisfaction on his face. After a moment, Edward speared a cheese cube in as put-upon a fashion as he could manage.

The weather was mild enough for eating outside to be popular, and the other tables around them quickly filled up. Edward took to eating two pieces of cheese for every one of John's and the plate was soon emptied.

"I'd hardly call that a filling lunch," Edward grumbled, sweeping a crumb of cheese into his palm and transferring it to his mouth. He looked around. "Can you see that useless waiter? Perhaps we can get something a bit more substantial – and a bit less raw."

Happy as ever to help, John craned his neck and glanced across the busy tables in search of the missing waiter. Seeing nobody, he twisted back towards Edward, only to freeze in place as a familiar figure stepped into his eyeline and from there into a spare seat at his table.

"I'm sorry, young lady," Edward began to say, but John was already speaking.

"How lovely to see you, Sally," he murmured, half-rising to his feet and giving a tiny bow. "I'd been wondering where you'd got to."

* * *

John thought that Sally looked just as tired as she had the day before. Her make-up had been applied as exquisitely as usual, but no amount of concealer could hide the bags under her eyes or the new wrinkles on her forehead.

Edward, still concentrating on the possibility of a cooked lunch, failed for a second to process exactly what had just been said but, when he did, the effect was highly comical, in John's opinion. Like a cartoon teddy bear, his head whipped back from its quest for a waiter and his eyes bulged out of their sockets like a pair of boiled eggs.

"Sally?" he spluttered. "As in your former wife Sally?"

"Of course, you've never met, have you? Do forgive me. Edward Lowe, meet Sally... actually, my darling, what surname are you using just now?"

"Munro, I suppose," Sally replied, after a momentary hesitation. "I haven't given it much thought, but it's probably time to go back to my maiden name, wouldn't you say?"

"Eminently sensible, in the circumstances," John agreed. Turning back to Edward, who was looking between them with all the confusion of a man witness to an unexpectedly mundane miracle, he repeated, "Edward Lowe, meet Sally Munro, my ex-wife."

"How do you do, Miss Munro." The words were out of Edward's mouth before he knew it, the polite platitude so ingrained in him that he instinctively uttered it, even to a woman he suspected of involvement in at least one murder.

"Charmed to meet you, Mr Lowe. But please, call me Sally. Miss Munro sounds like such an old biddy."

"With eight cats and a subscription to *The Listener*," John said and they both laughed at the old joke he'd dredged up from the depths of his memory.

"Never mind the damn cats!" Edward threw himself forward in his seat so aggressively that the table wobbled; John had to reach out quickly and save their glasses from falling to the cobbles. "The police in two different countries are looking for you, *Miss Munro*." He emphasised the name with an angry bark. "Not to mention the fact that you gave John your word you would stay in Cheadle Hulme, then absconded in the night without so much as a by-your-leave."

Sally flushed at Edward's words and put a hand to her mouth. It was terribly sweet to see she felt so bad for breaking her word to him, John thought. Even so, he wasn't sure Edward was being entirely fair and would have said so, had Sally not spoken first.

"I do feel awful for lying to you like that," she apologised, the skin crinkling at the sides of her eyes in a manner he remembered fondly from some of their more passionate marital reconciliations. "But when you hear the whole story, you'll understand that I really had no choice."

"I'm sure we shall," John said at the exact same time that Edward grunted "I very much doubt that." And John fixed him with a stare which he hoped communicated his disapproval of the other man's tone.

If it did, Edward took no notice.

"Perhaps you can begin by explaining why you arranged to meet John yesterday at the Rijksmuseum and then failed to turn up? You might also be able to shed some light on the thugs who held John up at gunpoint when you didn't arrive, and put one of our friends in the hospital."

Until that moment, John hadn't been aware of quite how much he needed Sally not to have been the bait in the previous day's trap. Only when he saw her eyes widen and her mouth form a perfect O of shock, did he feel a release from the tension which had been gripping his chest.

"Are you alright, John?" There was no mistaking the sincerity in the question, nor the confusion in her eyes. "I know nothing about that," she said. "I was a few minutes late getting to the museum. When I arrived, there was no sign of John, so I assumed I'd either missed him or he hadn't been able to come. Hence my appearance here today."

Edward grunted a reluctant concession. "Very well, we'll take your word for that. And since John is obviously willing to let you speak, I suppose I have no choice but to listen." He tapped a finger on the tabletop. "But, rest assured, if I find your explanation unsatisfactory – and I strongly suspect that I shall – we will be taking you along to the nearest police station, where I will expect you to give yourself up to the authorities."

John considered intervening, but, again, Sally appeared in little need of defence.

"That's fair," she said, nodding firmly. She lifted her handbag onto the table and removed her cigarette purse. Once she had a cigarette lit, she pulled her seat in closer to the table, making no attempt to lift it from the ground, and causing it to scrape noisily along the stones.

Several people sitting nearby looked across, seeking the source of this unpleasant sound, then turned back to their food and conversations without further interest. The occupant of one table, however – a broad-shouldered man who'd been sitting with his back to them – rose to his feet as though hearing a signal and walked towards them.

For one last time that afternoon, John began to say something, only for someone else to speak first.

"It's totally fair, Mr Lowe, but I think it would be a better idea for someone other than me to tell you the story."

She pointed the tip of her cigarette at the big man who took the final seat at their table, just as John finally found his voice enough to choke out, "Nate Thompson! My God, man, we all thought you were dead."

64

In the unexpectedly solid flesh, Sir Nathaniel Thompson was exactly as Edward remembered him from his film days: tall and imposing, with a long face almost overloaded with character. A pair of bushy eyebrows touched the fringes of his mop of curly reddish-brown hair, and his matching beard was thick and unkempt, giving him the appearance of a Russian Orthodox priest or a notable Victorian scientist. Nothing in his face was of any significance, however, when compared to his eyes. They were on the small side and sloped down on either side beneath folds of skin, but they were the palest blue Edward had ever seen, piercing and glacial, like the pools of water he had once marvelled at on a trip to the mountains of Canada. It was almost impossible not to stare into them.

His voice, too, demanded attention; it was warm and full-blooded like Richard Burton's and as commanding as Larry Olivier's in *Henry V.*

"Johnny, my boy! What a genuine delight to see you," he boomed then, more quietly, "And to quote the great Mark

Twain, rumours of my death have been greatly exaggerated. As you can see!"

He spread his arms out wide as he spoke, until Sally pulled the one nearest to her down to his side and he – sheepishly, Edward thought – mirrored the action on the other side.

"I am sorry to break this to you in so melodramatic a fashion," he went on at a more conversational volume. "I've had a hell of a strange few months and it's probably best all round that nobody finds out I'm still alive and kicking!" He turned to Sally with a grin. "Isn't that right, my love?"

Was that a muttered curse Edward heard coming from John's direction? He pulled his attention away from Thompson for a second, but, if John had said anything, he'd had time to rearrange his face back into a blank expression.

He saw Sally nod out of the corner of his eye. "Nobody can know. It really is a matter of life and death."

John said nothing. Edward had the sense that the sudden appearance of his ex-wife, followed by that of his allegedly dead ex-friend, had broken something inside him – hopefully only temporarily. For himself, his blood felt like it was surging through him far more vigorously than it had at any time since he'd left Bolton, convinced they'd messed up any chance they had to uncover Thompson and Judy's killers.

He couldn't deny he was dying (not the best choice of words, he chided himself) to hear what Thompson had to say. He cast another quick glance towards John, but he was still staring at Thompson, unblinking. Clearly he would be no help in questioning the pair of... well, runaways, he supposed you would call them, though exactly how Thompson came to be running rather than decomposing remained to be seen.

"Very well," he said to Thompson, taking charge of the situation. "For now, let's proceed on the same understanding I suggested to Miss Munro. If we think what you have to say has merit, we won't tell anyone you're still alive. I make no promises, mind. You may be alive, but there are two people dead and, from where I'm sitting, it seems you're linked to both of them."

"That's fair," Thompson said, echoing Sally's words of just a few minutes before. "But could we perhaps go somewhere a little more private? As you rightly noted, I am alive at the moment, but there are people who would love to change my alleged demise into a more permanently terminal one."

Edward noticed Sally lay a hand on top of Thompson's and give it a squeeze as he spoke. An almost inaudible sigh from John indicated he'd seen the gesture, too.

"Our hotel is a ten-minute walk from here and there's a little bar just around the corner from it," he said, wondering even as he said it whether it was the right thing to do. If Thompson was alive, who was the dead man who'd been found with Nate's wallet lying beside him?

* * *

The bar felt like an English country pub, with polished wooden tables and a long wooden bar behind which were displayed a huge array of different bottled beers. Thompson, who described himself as something of an expert, ordered drinks for everyone and brought them across to the corner table Sally had chosen.

"Cheers!" he said as soon as everyone had a glass. Edward found himself wondering if the man had perhaps suffered an injury to the head. He seemed incapable of keeping a low profile. God alone knew how he'd managed to avoid being spotted by someone since his "death".

Again, Sally pulled him into a seat and told him to be less conspicuous. He grinned, unabashed, and drank half his beer in one long gulp.

Edward waited until he'd placed his glass back on the table before asking the question which had been eating away at him for the past twenty minutes. "Tell us, then – if you're still alive, who was the dead man the police found with your wallet beside him?"

Thompson took a deep breath then puffed out his cheeks and blew out a stream of air. "That was a most unfortunate occurrence, it really was. Well, I say unfortunate. And so it was, in one sense. But for me it was a real stroke of bloody luck." There was something about the way he spoke that didn't ring true for Edward; a smoothness which suggested he'd rehearsed what he was saying. It didn't mean it wasn't true – perhaps, knowing one day he'd need to explain himself, he'd planned out the best way to do so – but the note of artificiality wasn't a good start in Edward's opinion.

"Unfortunate, how?" he asked.

"Unfortunate for poor Waldie, of course."

As soon as he said Waldie's name, John sat up straight and, for the first time since Thompson had appeared at their table in the café, showed an interest in what was going on around him. Edward raised an enquiring eyebrow in his direction, but John only shook his head quickly, then lowered it into his hands. Edward could hear him muttering to himself under his breath.

Thompson had noticed John too. For a long moment, he stared at him. Only when he was sure John wasn't about to say anything did he turn back to Edward.

"I found his body, you see. Lying there all bashed in. He must have been jumped. There are some right animals running about Bolton just now: they'd kill a man for the change in his pocket."

"You knew it was Waldie?"

"Oh, yes. I recognised the clothes he was wearing."

"Because you'd seen him earlier on, in the Spinning Wheel pub?"

"That's right."

"Which is all very well and good, but it doesn't answer the obvious question." Edward pushed his glasses more firmly on his nose and tilted his head to one side to relieve a sudden cramp in his neck. "Having found this unfortunate man, why didn't you just telephone the police?"

Suddenly, Thompson looked shifty. It was the only word for it. "Well, that's the crux of the matter, as it were. It's a long story, and... well, it doesn't paint me in the best light, I'll admit that up front." He lowered his voice and shuffled his chair closer to the table.

Edward leaned in so as not to miss anything, but John stayed where he was, no longer muttering but, it seemed, paying no attention to the others. Sally gave Thompson a hard look but said nothing.

"If you're willing to indulge me, this all began a long time ago, when I was a young man, before I met Johnny." Thompson's voice was rich and sonorous, an actor automatically dropping into storyteller mode, and Edward was reminded of Joe Riley reciting *Tam O'Shanter* on the set of *Floggit*. "You may be aware that I was something of a youthful prodigy and, by the time I was eighteen, I was already picking up small roles in films, as well as appearing on stage at Stratford at the new Memorial Theatre. It was barely a decade after the end of the Great War and, like many young men at that time, I decided that life needed to be savoured to the full, because it could be snatched away in an instant.

"Before long I was running with quite a fast crowd – mainly other young actors and actresses, but with a sprinkling of jazz musicians and even one or two people who… earned their livings on the edges of society, shall we say?" He laughed, but there was real bitterness in the sound. "Criminals, in other words. It was the same then as it is now, of course. You remember the Krays from a few years back? Well, I was friends with the late twenties version of them – the Buchanans, they were called. Charles, Harry and Georgie were their names, and as nasty a threesome as you were ever likely to meet. But they knew all the best places to go, and they had more money than they knew what to do with – plus they were happy to spend it so that they might be seen out and about with we bright young things." He smiled thinly. "And that was the set-up when I met Glynis."

Edward had the distinct impression that Thompson had told this story recently. His delivery was too slick and each name rolled across his tongue like fine wine rather than being dredged unwillingly from the darkest recesses of his memory. He wondered if this was news to Sally or if Thompson had told her already.

But "Glynis?" was all he said.

"Glynis McGovern her name was. I met her at the Silver Slipper, one of Kate Meyrick's places, a nightclub in Regent Street. Teddy Brown's band was playing, and Glynis was one of the dance hostesses." He paused and raised an eyebrow at Edward. "That might have been before your time, actually. They were young women who would dance with you so long as you kept buying bottles of over-priced champagne, and some of them would go home with you at the end of the night for a few quid more. Anyway, Glynis was one of those, and a pretty successful one too. I was there with the Buchanans and a couple of lads from whatever show I was doing at the time, and Georgie called Glynis over. 'She's just your type,' he said.

"You know, I can still picture it even today: the cigar smoke so thick it formed a cloud that billowed and swayed above our heads, the band playing 'Blue Danube', which was Teddy's big hit around then, Georgie snapping his fingers to get Glynis's attention and her hips swinging as she walked towards us with a scowl on her face. That was what attracted me to her really, the scowl. All the other dance hostesses would giggle and jump about as though you were the best thing that had ever happened to them, but it was three in the morning, Glynis was tired and the only reason she came over at all is because Georgie would have messed things up for her if she hadn't. So, she came over and sat beside me, and we hit it off. Straight away, we just hit it off." He waved a finger in front of Edward's face, as if warning him not to interrupt. "Now, I know what you're thinking – *of course* we hit it off. She was paid to hit it off with the punters. It was her job. But you have to believe me, it wasn't like that – we immediately liked one another's company. I danced with her a couple of times, bought her a few drinks, and then I would have taken her home, but I was staying in digs and the landlady was pretty strict about lady callers in the rooms. 'Never you worry about that,' says Georgie. 'Old Ma Meyrick's got rooms upstairs for special customers.' And off he went to speak to her."

Thompson stopped and took a swig of his beer, draining the glass. He smacked his lips in appreciation and wiped his hand across his mouth. "Sure enough, five minutes later, Georgie's back with a key and directions to a room upstairs. Me and Glynis head off and... well, you can imagine the next ten minutes or so." He glanced across as Sally, who sat glassy-eyed, staring straight ahead. "One minute after that, though, there's an almighty thud at the door. It flies open, nearly comes off its hinges, in fact, and standing there are two policemen in uniform and with their truncheons already out. I jump up, no idea what's going on really, and try to make a run for it, bollock naked. The first policeman lets me get about six feet from the bed, then thumps me across the back of my legs with his truncheon and down

I go. Glynis is screaming something, I'm rolling about on the floor trying to force some life back into my leg, and it's only when the second policeman uses his massive big boot to turn me over onto my front so he can handcuff me that I realise what it is she's screaming. 'I'm only fourteen,' she's shouting. 'I'm only a kid, you can't arrest me.'"

"My God," Edward said involuntarily, and the table fell silent. The barman, seeing Thompson's empty glass, brought a full replacement over and checked that nobody else wanted a refill. When he left, Thompson continued his story.

"As God is my witness, I didn't know. I'll swear to that on a heap of Bibles. She looked the same age as me, she acted the same age as me – for Christ's sake, she was a hostess in one of the most notorious clubs in London. But she said she was only fourteen, and the police believed her. A couple of them came into my cell that night and demonstrated in no uncertain terms what they thought of actors who corrupted underage girls. And after they'd booted me all over the shop, one of them leaned down to my ear and told me exactly what other criminals would do when they found out. 'Decent criminals don't take to ponces,' he said. 'This'll seem like a little kiss and cuddle compared to what they'll do to you.' I make no bones about it, I've never been so terrified in my life.

"At this point, I hadn't even asked for a solicitor – I didn't even know the name of a solicitor – but I'd heard one of the policeman who arrested me say something about the Buchanans. I thought he'd said 'We'll have to charge this one now, now she's said that. Mr Buchanan isn't going to like it.' I wasn't sure, but it sounded as though he was a bit scared of them. So, I asked if I could speak to the policeman in question, and promised the constable who's just kicked me repeatedly in the kidneys that I'd give him a fiver if he could arrange it. Long story short, he brought the copper to see me and, from there, I was able to get in touch with Georgie. And Georgie got me out."

"Arrested for a public morals offence," Edward said out loud as Frank Primrose's phrase popped into his head.

"What's that? Actually, yes, that's exactly what it said on my arrest report. Georgie showed me it, you see, after I'd been released. Showed me it then tucked it away in his pocket, alongside some other bits of paperwork from my arrest, including Glynis's statement saying I'd taken advantage of her, a poor innocent schoolgirl. 'It's all been taken care of,' he said. 'I've got the only copy of your arrest sheet, safe and sound. You don't need to worry about it ever again.' I was so grateful, you wouldn't believe. Just goes to show what an innocent schoolboy I was myself, babbling at him in the street, promising to do something to pay him back someday, telling him all he needed to do was say the word. And he just smiled and patted his jacket pocket."

Realisation dawned on Edward in a single, blinding flash. "The Buchanans contacted you recently, and told you it was time to repay your debt, didn't they? They wanted you to smuggle some paintings into the UK."

Thompson nodded. "Last summer I got a letter at the theatre. There'd been an announcement that the company was planning to take a show on tour in Europe, and somehow

Georgie had seen it in the newspaper. He's getting on now, and both of his brothers are long dead, but he's still got his fingers in all sorts of dubious pies. The letter didn't give much away, it just said 'Long time no see. Why don't we meet for a drink some time? Glynis sends her love,' plus a telephone number.

"Even after forty years I knew those bits of paper could destroy me, so I telephoned the number – what choice did I have? – and there was Georgie Buchanan on the other end of the line, sounding older but still recognisable. He said they needed me to bring two paintings through customs, that was all. Do that, he said, and we'll consider your debt partially repaid. *Partially* repaid, he said. And I knew then I had to disappear."

As Thompson stopped to wet his lips with his beer, Edward looked around the bar, feeling horribly exposed all of a sudden. He couldn't decide whether it was a good or a bad thing that the few other customers who'd been inside when they'd arrived had left, and the bar was now empty save for themselves and the barman. Edward quickly flicked his eyes towards John, but he remained in a world of his own, stranded there since Nate Thompson had returned from the grave.

"So, you stumbled over the body of this Waldie character and decided to fake your own death? Is that your story?"

Thompson held out his hands in supplication. "It's God's honest truth," he said. "I saw him lying there, and I thought 'this is my chance'. I could leave my wallet next to the corpse and get out of the country before anyone realised.

I'd changed my will to leave Sally everything and she was going to wait until the money was released then meet up with me and we'd live happily ever after somewhere nice and hot." He laughed again, but the bitterness was still there. "My career was going nowhere anyway. I might as well have been dead so far as the critics were concerned."

For the first time since they'd sat down, Sally spoke up. "It's all true. I was living with Nate more or less full-time by this point, and he'd told me he was being blackmailed. Then we had a row and he'd stormed off to get drunk for a few days, as he tends to do. I'd seen it all before, though, so I stayed put and waited for him to come home." She gave a shiver of distaste. "I wasn't expecting the state of him when he did, though. He had blood all down his shirt where he'd tried to pick up this man Waldie, and he was shaking and crying like a child. He told me what had happened and how he'd got a plan to get us away from these criminals who were after him. Everything that's happened since then has been us trying to make that plan work."

It made a kind of sense, Edward had to admit. Or at least it wasn't completely impossible. It failed to address one vital matter, however.

"What about Judy Faith? Did you have anything to do with her death?"

The look Thompson shot him was venomous. "How dare you suggest such a thing!" His voice rang out across the empty bar, prompting the barman to look up from polishing glasses. Satisfied there was no immediate threat of trouble, he picked up a new pint pot and thrust his cloth inside it.

"I adored that young lady," Thompson went on, less loudly but still at a volume that suggested his outrage had not completely abated. "Indeed, I only discovered she was dead some time after the fact, or I would have come back for her funeral, and damn the consequences!" Unconsciously, he smoothed down the front of his shirt and straightened his tie, as though checking his clothing for church. "No," he concluded in a sadder tone. "I did not harm dear Judy. All I did was stumble over a dead tramp and make use of his corpse to facilitate my escape from an intolerable situation. That may be a crime or it may not – I confess I have no idea – but I have killed nobody."

In the silence which followed this little speech, John – who'd been sitting so quietly, Edward had almost forgotten he was there – coughed loudly, and then did so again. Three sets of eyes turned towards him.

"That's not true though, is it?" he said in a voice quite unlike his own; a cold, hard voice, devoid of emotion. "I've remembered the thing I'd missed before, you see. I know that you killed at least one person."

65

"It's been on the tip of my tongue all this time," John continued in the same neutral tone. "You remember, Edward, I thought someone had said something important but I couldn't quite put my finger on it? It was that barman in the Spinning Wheel, back in Bolton. He said that Waldie was a perfect match for Nate. And we assumed he meant he could look after himself if it came to a fight. Remember, we were talking about him spilling his beer on Nate at the time and the fact there was a bit of pushing and shoving. But that's not what he meant at all." He shook his head and a determined look settled on his long face. "I should have realised when we spoke to Primrose. He said Waldie had Parkinson's disease – there's no way he could have gone toe to toe with Nate, not if he was shaking enough to be spilling his pint."

He turned from Edward to Sally, pleading with her to understand. "Don't you see? He didn't mean Waldie was a match for Nate in a fight, he meant Waldie resembled Nate.

He was a match physically. He even called Waldie a big guy, just like Nate."

Edward still didn't understand the point John was making. He frowned and half-shrugged. "So they resembled one another. What of it?" He turned to Thompson. "Do you know what he's talking about?"

"I've no bloody idea!" Thompson's voice was louder again, but Edward thought he saw a flicker in his eyes. He was worried about whatever it was John was trying to say. "Look, I don't know what you're trying to suggest, Johnny," he began.

"I'm not suggesting anything," said John, talking over him and raising his own voice to drown out Thompson's. "I'm saying it's a fact. You killed Cleland Waldie and smashed up his face enough that the police would think it was you."

Edward heard a stifled cry from Sally, but, if she intended to say anything, she had no chance. Nate Thompson looked stunned for a second, then laughed. "Kill Cleland Waldie? You think, just because we were the same build, I killed Cleland Waldie?"

"It seems more likely than the idea that you just stumbled across his dead body."

"Really?" Thompson twisted round in his chair and appealed to Edward. "I know Johnny doesn't care for me – I'd be the same in his shoes, I imagine – but surely you don't believe this foolishness?"

"It does seem quite a coincidence that you argued with Waldie in the pub and then, only a few hours later, came upon his dead body lying in the street."

"Yes!" John stood up suddenly, pushing his chair back so hard that it clattered to the floor. The barman looked up and put down his towel, but Edward waved to him to stay where he was. Seeing that the noise had been made by an elderly man in a suit and tie, he shrugged and went back to his drying, though he kept a weather eye on the group. Edward looked up at his friend and wondered if he was still feeling the after-effects of the bump on his head the previous day. There were beads of sweat on his forehead and his hand, as he pointed it at Nate Thompson, trembled slightly.

"That's the clincher," he said (and if it hadn't been John, Edward would have said he snarled it). "You found Waldie's body in the street. But what street was that?"

Thompson watched John closely, but made no response. For a second, Edward also wasn't sure what to make of John's statement, then the realisation hit him and he understood exactly what he meant.

"My God, of course. Waldie's body was found in a stairwell in Melbourne Street."

"And?" Thompson's voice held no indication that he'd understood, but Edward noticed that his knuckles had gone white where he was clenching the tabletop.

"And if you were on your way from the Spinning Wheel in Bell Street, why on Earth would you be walking quite a distance from your house and in the opposite direction?"

"Exactly!" John was no longer even looking at Thompson. His eyes were focused on Sally as he took three beermats and laid them out on the table. "This beermat is the theatre and this one is the Spinning Wheel pub." He placed one mat nearest the edge of the table and the next a little inwards. "And then this third one is the spot where the body was found." He placed the final beermat on the other side of the second, so the three of them formed a rough line. "We wondered about it at the time. You remember, Edward, I asked you what Nate had been doing way out there?"

Edward nodded, feeling the familiar exhilaration as questions began to be answered. "There's something else too. That woman mopping the stairs told us that tramps sleep in the park at the end of Melbourne Street. Could that be where Waldie slept every night?" He turned to Thompson. "Did you follow him back towards the park and, when he stopped in that stair, you attacked him and killed him?"

"Did you see him from your love nest?" John asked angrily. "Did you see him lying on a bench and realise he was the same build as you, the same height, the same size? Did you decide then to murder him, to use his body to get yourself out of a jam?"

"A jam! A bloody jam you call it!" Now Thompson was also on his feet, slamming his hands hard down on the table and bellowing as though he were declaiming a speech to the back stalls at the Lyceum. A thick vein in his head throbbed alarmingly. The barman moved forward again, but Thompson screamed at him to stay where he was. He did as instructed, but Edward watched him pick up a telephone and make a call.

"I wasn't in a *jam*, you smug bastard. I was trapped, and everywhere I looked I faced ruin." He glared balefully across the table. "On the one hand, I could tell Buchanan and his boys to jump off a cliff – then those police records would end up in front of some tame chief inspector or some squalid Fleet Street hack, and my life would be over. Even if there was no prosecution, the scandal would be enough to drive me out of the country. I'd end my days making terrible Italian horror movies and guest-starring on Greek soap operas. On the other hand, I could do as they asked: smuggle those paintings into England for them. But do you think they'd leave it at that? I thought they'd forgotten about me after all these years, but they'd always had me in mind and they always would. I'd never be free of them, and eventually I'd get caught."

He seemed to have calmed down a bit, Edward thought, and he tugged at John's arm to get him to sit. He did so, but without taking his eyes off Thompson, who followed suit, sinking back into his own chair.

Edward looked over at the bar, where the barman still stood with the phone in his hand. He said something into the receiver and replaced it in its cradle. "I speak to the police," he said in heavily accented English, "but I tell them not to come just now. I tell them that you leave after you finish your drinks." He held up five fingers. "Five minutes and you leave, yes?"

Edward nodded in agreement. "Five minutes and we'll be out of your hair," he called across. He turned his attention back to Thompson. The big man was breathing heavily, staring at John and refusing to meet Sally's eye, even as she pulled at his jacket to gain his attention.

"You killed that man?" she said quietly. Edward couldn't tell if she was asking a question or stating a fact, but Thompson chose to treat it as the former.

"I had to!" His fury had turned to anguish, the veins in his head smoothing out as tears welled in his eyes.

He seemed unbalanced, Edward thought, and speculated to himself about the best way to get out of his way if he snapped completely.

"I did it for us! Waldie was a waster, a drunken fool who slept in the park and spent every penny he managed to beg or steal on booze. You should have seen him, Sally – staggering about in the rain, snarling and muttering like an animal, *being sick on himself*, for God's sake. He fell into that stairwell, I saw him do it. I was walking behind him, not intending to do anything, not really. I just saw him and thought I'd follow him, remembering the row we'd had in the pub. I thought I might give him a slap, remind him that I was a knight of the realm and he was a man who slept wrapped in newspapers. And then he fell into the stairwell, and I was right behind him. He'd banged his head, you see. He was already dead, I think, stretched out on the ground. And then it came to me. If his face was gone and he was dressed like me, why, he could *be* me. So I took off his disgusting vomit-covered coat and put my jacket on him instead, then put my empty wallet beside him, like he'd been robbed."

He trailed off, tears forming in his eyes, but John was unimpressed. "Weren't you worried the police wouldn't believe it was you?" he asked. "Waldie had been in trouble with the police before. What if they'd checked his fingerprints?"

Thompson's laugh was a sharp bark. "Why would they? They'd got a body they had every reason to think was me, and I'd disappeared. Two and two made four so far as they were concerned." He shook his head. "You're giving the local bobbies too much credit if you think they were going to look too carefully at that bloody corpse." He fell silent for a moment and looked over their heads out of the window.

Edward wondered if he was considering the double meaning in his words.

It seemed he was. "It was horrible, Sally, but it needed to be done. I took that pipe and I hit him again and again, until all I could see was blood and bones. Until nobody could tell who he was. I did that to save us, Sally. All to save us."

He settled back in his seat, his story done. He sat motionless, bolt upright, ostensibly speaking to Sally, but with eyes only for John.

"What pipe?" John said quietly.

"It was… I had… I…" Having spent so much of his life speaking other men's words, it seemed that, when he needed them most, Sir Nathaniel Thompson had none of his own. "There was a length of metal pipe lying in the stair," he said finally, but the look in his eyes told its own story and the tears had stopped. He knew nobody believed him, not even Sally.

She stood up. "I need to get out of here. John, can you get me a room at your hotel?"

John stood too, and held out his hand. "Of course, my dear," he said, with a half-smile. "It'll be my pleasure."

Edward followed them out of the door. He stopped at the last moment and looked back into the empty bar. Thompson was still sitting at the table, self-pitying tears openly flowing down his cheeks. He reached over and pulled the other's glasses towards himself, then tipped the contents of each one into his own. As Edward turned away, he was gulping down the murky liquid as though his life depended on it.

66

The next day, the day they were due to catch the overnight ferry back to England, looted paintings and all, was cold and wet from the start. Edward sat in the lounge of the hotel and tried to read a book, but his attention was all over the place and he found himself unable to concentrate.

First, there was the question of Sally. They had taken her from the bar to the lodgings she shared with Thompson and quickly emptied it of her belongings. Then John had arranged for her to share a room with Alison: so far neither hide nor hair had been seen of either woman. He had tried to broach the matter of Sally returning to England to face the police, but John had waved him away. "She's been through a terrible trauma, Edward," he'd said. "She's discovered she ran off with a murderer, and all her plans for the future have come to nothing. Let her rest for now, and I'll talk to her later and let you know what she wants to do."

Then, there was Thompson. A self-confessed killer, no less, though Edward currently had no idea how to bring him to justice, given that the police thought he was already dead.

And there was the matter of Judy Faith. Thompson had said he had nothing to do with her death, and he sounded sincere, but he was one of the great actors of his generation. He had been having an affair with her, of course, which complicated matters, but surely that made him less likely to have harmed her?

Finally, there was Buchanan, who was blackmailing them into smuggling priceless works of art into Britain. He was fairly confident that the plan he'd supplied for doing so was a good one and they wouldn't get caught, but Thompson's words still rang in his ears. What was to stop them using him and John again for other jobs, once the criminals had them in their clutches?

He glanced at his watch. More time had passed than he'd thought. Buchanan's plan required him to go to an address near the Rijksmuseum to collect the rolled-up paintings at noon, and it was eleven already. He'd checked with the hotel manager how to get there – it was no more than a fifteen-minute walk, he'd said.

Perhaps a brisk walk would help clear his head and give him a better idea of how to proceed. He collected his coat and hat, and stood uncertainly at the bottom of the hotel stairs. He should really go and get John, but he'd had had a nasty bump on the head, and it'd do him good to have a lie-in. Besides, all he was doing was picking some things up.

He opened the hotel door and stepped out into the rain.

* * *

Five minutes later, Edward was cursing the impulse that had made him go out in a downpour without an umbrella. He'd never have done such a foolish thing back home, he chided himself. The water had soaked him almost immediately, and it dripped from the brim of his hat and the collar of his coat, finding ways of infiltrating everything he was wearing so that the layers which should be protected from the worst of it were, in fact, equally wet and uncomfortable. The rain was so heavy that he could barely see six feet in front of him. He was reminded of the figure stalking him through the rain at Thompson's funeral, and he shivered with more than the cold.

Fortunately, the street he was looking for really wasn't far, though it was tucked away in a minor labyrinth of avenues and alleyways, lined with garages and lock-ups. He'd just walked past one particularly rundown example when a voice from behind a rusty pile of car parts said his name, and Nate Thompson stepped into his path.

Edward felt panic flare in his chest. For a moment, he felt an ache in his right arm and a dull throb in his jaw and wondered if he was about to have a heart attack, but, as Thompson held out a hand in greeting, the feeling quickly abated and he berated himself for giving in to fear so easily.

"I just want to talk." Thompson's voice was quiet, subdued even. "You're soaking wet," he pointed out – rather redundantly, in Edward's opinion.

"Indeed. Perhaps we could make this quick, then. I have places to be, and I'm not getting any drier standing here talking to you."

Thompson nodded, as though Edward had said something which required his agreement. "This won't take long," he said. "But I needed to tell you that you've ruined my life. More than Georgie Buchanan and his boys, even. They're criminals, it's in their blood to take advantage of weakness. But you... you and Johnny are just actors. You're just like me – not as talented or as well-known, obviously, but just actors. Why did you have to get involved in any of this? What're you getting out of it?"

"Nothing. We're getting nothing out of this. That's the real difference between you and us – not acting ability or fame, but the fact that you think everyone is out for themselves, whereas we know that's not true. Some people are just good and some people – like me and John – can't bear to see injustice."

Thompson laughed, a sudden cruel sound, filled with malice. "My God, to think people said I was self-absorbed! You standing there, soaked to the skin like a fat wet toad, telling yourself that you're some sort of agent of justice, when what you really are is a nosy old busybody, poking about in things that don't concern you because the alternative is going home to your empty house and thinking about how pointless your life's turned out to be."

Edward had had enough of this. He had no intention of standing in the rain to be insulted by a man who'd beaten a homeless drunk to death to avoid being exposed as the seducer of young girls. "Out of my way, Thompson," he said coldly, and began to walk away.

With surprising speed for a big man, Thompson reached out and grabbed Edward's arm, crushing it in his fingers.

"You're going nowhere, Lowe," he snarled, all pretence of civility gone. "You think you can walk away from me? After what you've done? After everything *I've* done? I had to do so many terrible things, you see." His voice faded to a whisper as he stared at a point somewhere over Edward's shoulder. "So many terrible, terrible things…" he murmured.

While Thompson seemed lost in his memories, Edward tried to pull his arm away, but the movement merely brought the big man back to himself. He snarled and tightened his grip. "But there's a bright side, I suppose. Nothing I do now can be any worse than the things I've already done."

Until that moment, Edward would have said that the phrase "the blood turned to ice in his veins" was merely a metaphor, but as Thompson pulled him back, and he cast around frantically for someone to help him and found nobody, it felt as though his entire body was suddenly chilled. The implication was clear.

Stupidly, his first thought was that he didn't want to die in an alleyway, then he wondered if his death would make the *Ten O'Clock News*. He stared blankly at Thompson as these thoughts – and others equally asinine – flowed through his panic-stricken mind.

"Don't be ridiculous," Edward managed to croak. "Very well, you killed Waldie, but that was when you feared your world was about to collapse about your ears. You were panicked and terrified, and you didn't know what you were doing." As he spoke, he began to feel more confident, as though he were giving a speech in a film. "You're no more capable of killing in cold blood than I am!" He tugged his arm free, sending drops of water flying in an arc through the air. "Now, get out of my way and let me be on my way."

Instead, Thompson shifted himself directly in front of Edward and twisted his mouth into a comically exaggerated pout. "Can't kill in cold blood? Is that what you think? I wonder if poor little Judy thought that too."

Edward froze. The rain ran down his face, smearing his glasses until he could barely see. The curtain of unending rain, and the way the grey sky leached all colour from the buildings, combined with Thompson's words to create a world seemingly devoid of life. There was no sound save for the steady thud of rain hitting the paving and Thompson's voice.

"You know I had her shacked up at my place in Lovell Park, don't you? But what you don't know is that it was her I wanted to leave with me, not Sally. When I killed that drunk Waldie – oh yes, Johnny was right about that, I did take a chunk of steel pipe along to kill him with; what would be the point of killing him if the police could look at his face and see he wasn't me? – anyway, when I killed Waldie, I was pretty drunk myself, but I knew I couldn't go back to the park house, not in the state I was in. Judy thought of me as a glamorous star of stage and screen, not a drunken killer. Besides, she had many wonderful qualities, but common sense wasn't one of them. She'd have been no use when it came to the rest of my plan.

"So I went home to Sally, even though I'd already decided it was Judy I wanted to keep. I told Sally almost everything – about Buchanan, how I'd left her all my money in my will, and how I needed to get out the country and she could meet me later, once she'd collected it. The only lie I told her was that Waldie was already dead when I stumbled over him."

A window opened in one of the nearby buildings and Edward turned towards it hopefully. Before he could cry out, he felt a pain in his side which made him pause and look down at himself. The tip of a long knife had pierced his jacket and shirt and, from the agonising feel of it, had slid into his flesh just about his hip.

"Say a word and I'll shove this all the way in," Thompson warned him, shifting his grip on the knife handle so the tip moved inside Edward and made him gasp in pain. The window slid shut again, and the chance to shout was gone.

"Now where had I got to? Oh, yes, Sally lapped up the whole plan. She's a romantic at heart, is Sally; she loved the idea of giving everything up for love and going on the run with the man of her dreams. It helped that she'd got nothing to give up, with the kids off at boarding school, and that we wouldn't really be on the run, of course – but in her head, we were Romeo and Juliet, I'm sure of it. You can see the problem, though. No?" He frowned and shook his head in mock sorrow. "Well, I wanted Judy, but I had to leave everything to Sally – she and I had been living together for nearly a year, so it was natural enough for me to change my will in her favour. I couldn't have done that for Judy without awkward questions being asked. And since I had to give all my money to Sally, I needed her at least until we met up and she gave it all back to me."

Edward felt himself tremble with cold and fear as he realised what Thompson was saying. "You intended to kill Sally once she'd returned the money from your will!"

Thompson cocked his head to one side, apparently giving the question serious consideration. "I don't know about *kill*, necessarily. *Abandon* would be closer to the mark. It's not as though she could go to the police and claim she'd been defrauded of all her money by her dead ex-lover! She can be great company and she keeps herself nice, but, for God's sake, Sally's got thirty years on Judy. Given a choice, what man would take mutton over lamb? All I needed to do was let Judy know what was going on and arrange a rendezvous point with her, somewhere on the continent. I'd actually intended to suggest she tell that arsehole Fagan she'd decided to stay on in Holland at the end of the run."

"She rejected you." Edward's view of Thompson was obscured by his rain-smeared glasses, but he could hear it in the man's voice. The sound of someone about to get to the sad part of his story.

Abruptly, Thompson's voice was anguished. "It was the look on her face. Terror, which I expected – she thought I was dead, after all – but there was loathing too. I could see it in her eyes, repugnance and dread and, yes, hatred. All of sudden, I could see what she thought of me – someone to help her up the career ladder, someone to be used then discarded, a disgusting old man she'd been glad to see gone. I couldn't bear it."

"So you killed her?" Edward tried to keep his voice as level as possible, even while every one of the knife's tiny movements in his side made pain flare up sickeningly. He thought Thompson was crying now.

"I don't remember doing it, I really don't, but I must have, mustn't I? She bit my hand and I cracked her in the jaw, then I grabbed her... and the next thing I knew she was lying dead on the dressing room floor and I was standing over her." The groan he let out was filled with emotion, though Edward suspected it was mainly pity for himself. "She could have had everything, but she ended up with nothing!"

"And you went back to Sally." White spots of light were flashing in front of Edward's eyes and he could feel his legs wobbling. "She was your safety net."

"Until Johnny spoiled everything yesterday by telling her I killed Waldie. Cold-blooded murder doesn't fit into her romantic ideal."

From somewhere behind him, Edward heard a siren wailing, the sound fading away as quickly as it had come.

"I considered going to see John first," Thompson went on, "but I saw you leave the hotel on your own and realised you'd do as well as him. He'll pay the price too, though, in due course."

Edward's right leg suddenly buckled and he sagged to one side. Luckily, the direction in which he fell forced the knife to slide out of his side rather than further in, but, with his head spinning, it was impossible to keep his balance. He dropped onto one knee and braced himself with his hands on the rough pavement. The puddle of water in which he now crouched turned bloody red. "Why are you telling me all this?" he asked, though he already knew the answer.

"My life's ruined, but I had to tell someone how close it came to working out. For my own satisfaction, you know what I mean? And even if you wanted to tell someone, what would you say? You're in an even worse pickle than Sally – you can't turn me in without implicating John in covering up what Sally's done. And even if you decided it was worth the risk, who'd believe you?"

Edward could feel his sight beginning to blur. He wondered with a kind of detached curiosity if Thompson intended to stab him to death or let him go, but, really, all he wanted to do was sleep, so it hardly mattered either way. He peered upwards through his rain-smeared glasses as what had been one Thompson became two. Idly, he wondered if double vision was a sign the end was near. In a moment, he would close his eyes for good, he decided.

One of the Thompsons looked down at him. "I did wonder whether to kill you both, but, you know, I think this is even better. This way, you've got no choice but to go through with Buchanan's plan and, after that, you'll both be his creatures for the rest of your days. Even if he never speaks to you again, you and Johnny will both be looking over your shoulders, wondering when you'll feel a hand there." His laughter was cruel. "And who knows – that hand might not be Buchanan's, it might be that of a police officer. I wonder which one you'd prefer?"

One Thompson stepped back and raised a boot into the air, ready to stamp down on Edward. He was past caring and made no attempt to defend himself, though he wondered listlessly why the second Thompson, strangely bigger than the first, hadn't moved. Then, to his utter bewilderment, the second Thompson grabbed the wrist of the first one, twisting the knife in its hand around in one smooth movement and sliding it to its hilt into the first Thompson's chest.

For an instant, the two figures stood in an unmoving tableau, then the first one slumped forward and fell onto the rain-soaked pavement.

67

To his surprise, Edward didn't faint. Instead, he stayed kneeling on the ground until two rough hands helped him to his feet and guided him across to a bench at the side of the road and lowered him down. "Press this on it," a voice said, tearing off a section of Edward's shirt and holding the torn material against the disconcertingly wide incision in his side.

Thompson's body still lay on the ground in an expanding pool of bloody rainwater. Edward's rescuer, a big, broad-shouldered man with a strangely square head – Edward felt he should recognise him, but his own head was still spinning and the answer he sought remained tantalisingly out of reach – grabbed the corpse under the arms and heaved it across the road to a collection of mismatched car parts and rusty metal oil canisters.

With a grunt of effort, tyres were pushed down on top of Thompson's body and it disappeared from view. Edward felt sure this was something to celebrate, but any pleasure he felt came in a wrapper of numbness and dislocation. The urge to close his eyes and have a quick nap was overpowering. He let the ripped piece of shirt fall away from his side and laid his head back on the pavement. Forty winks, then he'd get up and see what needed to be done.

"No, don't!" The voice was annoying, poking at him like a stick in the side, ruining his nap and forcing him to open his eyes. The square-headed man squatted beside him and applied firm pressure to his wound. *His wound.* He'd forgotten he was wounded. He closed his fingers over the other man's hand, taking the fragment of shirt from him and pressing down hard. He felt a stab of pain sharp enough to wake him up fully. He looked up at the man who had saved his life; his glasses were still wet, but a name attached itself to the silhouette beside him.

Craig Mackay.

He tried to say the name, but his throat was dry as dust and only a croaking sound emerged. It struck him as terribly funny that he was so thirsty and, at the same time, also soaking wet. Rainwater fell into his open mouth as he laughed, lubricating his tongue and throat enough that, a moment later, he was able to speak.

"You're Craig Mackay. You spied on Judy Faith in Bolton."

"I heard what he said," Mackay replied. "I heard him say he killed Judy."

"He did," Edward agreed.

"So I killed him."

"You did."

"I've been waiting for him to say that, see."

For the first time, Edward noted the flat tones in which Mackay spoke. There was something mechanical about his voice, an absence of emotion which he found unsettling. Was the man a little *dim*? Not that he felt exactly on top of his game either. A question which should have occurred to him earlier bobbed to the surface of his mind and he asked it before the darkness which he felt smothering him overwhelmed him completely.

"What are you doing here, though? In Amsterdam. What are you doing in Amsterdam?"

"I was following him." Mackay's voice retained its monotone, but there was a flicker of anger in his eyes. "The police thought I'd killed him, but I knew he wasn't dead."

"You knew?" Desperately, Edward clung on to consciousness as the big man scratched at his beard and stared at him.

"I saw him outside the theatre. After they said he was dead."

"You saw Nate?"

Mackay nodded. "I visit the theatre at night sometimes. There's a bit across the square out of the wind where you can sit and keep an eye on the doors. I've seen Judy leaving sometimes and said hello." He smiled at the memory, but only for a moment, before a frown creased his forehead "But one night, it was him I saw coming out, not Judy. I didn't know he was supposed to be dead then, and he locked the door behind him, so I thought Judy wasn't there. I was going to leave, but I must have nodded off, all cosy, tucked away out of the rain. Next thing I knew, I heard voices and saw you go inside. You and your friend. Later on, I saw the police come and take a body away, and I knew what he'd done. And I knew what I had to do."

Mackay was crying again, just as he had at Judy's funeral, tears rolling down his face and mingling with the driving rain. He wiped a hand fiercely across his eyes and rose from his haunches to his feet.

"You had to kill him?" Edward asked with what felt like the last of his strength.

The big man nodded. "I'd warned him before. Back in Bolton, I told him I'd kill him if he touched Judy again. I've been following him for ages. I've been waiting to get him by himself. He's always with the other woman, though. Until now." He smoothed his wet hair back with his hands. "Will you be alright?" he asked. "Do you want me to telephone someone?"

Edward had wondered if Mackay intended to walk away and leave him to bleed to death in the street. Elation washed through him, bringing a welcome flush of pain-killing endorphins. "There's a telephone number in my top pocket," he said. "If you could telephone that number and ask for Mr Buchanan, ask him to send someone, I'd be obliged."

He felt fingers in his pocket and hot breath on his neck. Then Mackay walked off into the rain and Edward sat back and watched blood seeping through his fingers with a strangely detached lack of interest.

* * *

Less than five minutes had passed, Edward estimated, before two men pulled up in a car, stepped out into the unceasing downpour and walked towards him.

One crouched down and removed Edward's glasses with a curious gentleness. He polished them on a rag then slipped them back on his nose. Instantly, though briefly, Edward's vision was restored to its usual clarity. It was a thoughtful act. When he recognised the two men John had referred to as the Italian and the Swede, he rather wished they hadn't bothered, though.

The other man – the Italian – walked across to the disturbed pile of tyres and leaned down, pushing oil cans out of his way as his did so. Edward heard him tut in disapproval. He beckoned the Swede over and for perhaps a minute they talked in a quiet undertone, occasionally looking down and shaking their heads. Then the Italian walked back to Edward and, with another gentle movement, moved Edward's hand away from his side.

Over his shoulder he could see the Swede going to their car and pulling out a green tarpaulin. He laid it down by the tyre pile, then heaved Thompson's body on it. Edward marvelled at the confident manner in which he worked, apparently unconcerned that anyone might see him manhandling a corpse. Once the entirety of Thompson was on top of the tarpaulin, he wrapped it tightly around him and dragged it across to the car. He had just popped the boot when the Italian said something to him which more than caught his attention.

"I will stitch the wound," he said, angling a curved needle in front of Edward's face. "Going to a hospital would mean the police, and Mr Buchanan would not like the police to be involved." He grinned, exposing a mouthful of yellow teeth. "This will hurt a little."

Edward felt a sharp stinging sensation in his side. He looked down, thinking that stitches without anaesthetic weren't as painful as he'd expected, only to see the Italian pocket the bottle of spirits he'd just poured on the cut in Edward's side.

A moment later, the Italian did push the needle through Edward's skin and bent it around and out through the other side.

This time, Edward fainted.

68

"And when I came to, I was sitting where you found me, on the doorstep of the hotel, with these two beside me."

Edward winced as he twisted in his chair and pointed at the two wooden crates on the other side of his hotel bedroom. Approximately three feet by two feet, they were slim but sturdily built and contained wooden frames for the transport of paintings. Inside each frame was a priceless work of art, stolen by the Nazis a quarter of a century before and ready for transport across the North Sea. That was Buchanan's simple but effective plan – parcel the two masterpieces up in exactly the same way as the other prop paintings used by the theatre company and bring them through customs in plain sight.

True, there was no reason for there to be such paintings in a production of *Hamlet*, but the criminals were willing – rightly, Edward suspected – to gamble on the fact that a bored and low-paid customs official was unlikely to know that.

"You gave us rather a shock, my dear fellow," John smiled, handing Edward his cigarettes and lighter. He seemed entirely restored to his usual self since Sally had stormed off with him, and for the moment at least the two were inseparable. Edward had told them only part of the story of his morning, omitting the fact of Thompson's death, and claiming that Mackay's intervention had consisted solely of chasing him off.

Sally had not reacted well to the news her erstwhile lover had intended to betray her and then had murdered Judy Faith when she wouldn't agree to run away with him. *Well, why should she?* Edward pondered as he pulled in a welcome lungful of cigarette smoke. *It wasn't exactly good news, was it?*

On a more positive note, however, she hadn't reacted in grief or horror, but with an impressive display of rage, describing Thompson in terms Edward had never heard a woman use before and calling down curses on his head. John, Edward noticed, had appreciated every well-turned insult and foul-mouthed obscenity.

"Do you want me to tell Fagan that you won't be able to travel tonight? I know you said you didn't want to go to a doctor, and it does look as though that Italian chap did a good job with your stitches, but even so..." John's voice trailed off. Edward saw his eyes flick towards the two packing crates and knew he was only being polite. For a second, he considered agreeing that he should let the others take the paintings through customs while he stayed behind and recuperated, but John was in such a happy mood that it would be churlish to ruin it for him, even temporarily.

"No, I'll be absolutely fine," he insisted gruffly, though,

in actual fact, the wound ached and in normal circumstances he would have welcomed a couple of days in bed. "We should telephone for a taxi and shift the paintings to the theatre, mix them in with the rest of the props." He turned to Sally. "I wonder if you could be a dear and arrange that? There's a telephone at reception, if I remember right." He paused and held up a finger, as though a new thought had just occurred to him. "Actually, if you could ring the hospital and find out when Jimmy Rae is being released, that would be awfully helpful too. Alison is down there already, I think John said, but it'd be handy to get a definite time so we can all meet up before we head to the ferry."

After what felt to Edward like an eternity of billing and cooing from John and Sally – including what he was revolted to discover were their pet names for one another – Sally gave John a final kiss and headed downstairs.

As soon as the door closed behind her, Edward gestured to John to pull his chair closer. "I've had a thought," he said quietly. "I think I know how we can sort this whole mess out. I need to phone my cousin and then go to the post office."

69

It was wet enough to make Noah nervous, John thought as he peered through the porthole of his cabin. Rain lashed down on the exposed decking of the ferry and ran in sheets of water to its edge then over the side, back into the sea. Edward stood beside him, holding a yellow sou'wester and frowning at the deluge.

"I do hope this weather clears by the time we get home." He'd just arrived from his own cabin, one of the few "special" ones with its own shower and toilet. Most of the younger members of the company had settled down in the TV lounge for the twelve-hour trip, and napped on the reclining chairs there, but Edward had insisted on his own facilities. John had booked himself and Sally a cabin of their own, too, though one without a shower. Consequently, he felt grimy and unclean, which added to the nerves that were causing his stomach to turn somersaults, and left him considerably less relaxed than he liked. Sally was currently looking through the duty-free section along the corridor, and – as they'd discussed in Edward's hotel room before they left Amsterdam – Jimmy Rae, still battered and bruised but now at least ambulatory, had joined them for a final chat before the ferry reached Hull.

"So, do we all know what we need to do, and where we need to be?" Edward counted off on his fingers as he pointed to each man in turn. "You, Jimmy, will be driving the lorry. Mickey was fine with that; when I told him you'd been a long-distance lorry driver before you became an actor, he was delighted. The cancellation of *Hamlet* has cost the company quite a large amount, and saving the cost of employing a driver quite made his day. I'll be in the cab beside Jimmy and you, John, will be in the back of the lorry, keeping an eye on our special cargo."

John nodded at Edward. He wasn't one hundred per cent looking forward to sitting in the back of a dirty old lorry, but it was only for a short while and he knew someone had to do it. "Yes sir, boss," he said with a smile which just stayed the right side of a comical grimace. "I absolutely can't wait." He exchanged a look with Jimmy and raised his eyebrows in Edward's direction.

Edward checked his watch, blind to any misgivings the others might have. "One hour exactly until we dock. Time we headed down to the loading area."

John shifted his suitcase from the floor to the bed, then hefted it in his arms. "I've told Sally I'm helping with the lorry, but I can't expect her to carry two heavy suitcases off by herself," he explained. "I'll throw it in the back of the lorry and use it as a seat."

Edward spread his hands. "Whatever you think best, John. Just so long as you're there to keep an eye on the paintings, should things go wrong."

"Keep an eye on them even if things go right, Johnny," Jimmy chipped in. "The last we want is for the bloody things to go walkabout, leaving us standing with our hands down our pants."

Edward gave him a dirty look. Everyone was on edge, that much was to be expected, but was there any need for that kind of lavatorial talk? "I'm sure the paintings will be fine," he said testily. "All John has to do is sit still until someone opens the lorry doors and then hand the paintings over to them. As soon as that's done, we're done."

He was aware as he spoke that what he'd said could be interpreted in two ways. Luckily, he wasn't a superstitious man and he didn't believe there was such a thing as tempting fate. Jimmy, however, was clearly less enlightened, because he leaned across and laid his hand on the tabletop. "Touch wood," he muttered to himself.

"That's Formica, actually," John offered, then smiled weakly and added, "But it's the thought that counts, I imagine."

Edward hoisted his own suitcase up and pushed open the cabin door with his knee. His wound still ached, but he ignored the nagging pain and the swollen redness around the stitches.

If things didn't go to plan, a sore side would be the least of his worries.

70

Jimmy gently eased the lorry down the gangway and onto the road, then on through the ferry terminal into the customs lane. Apparently this new EEC thing would make it much easier to go in and out of Europe, but that was still some months off, and the current process, so far as Edward could see, was a bit hit and miss.

A layer of nervous sweat had formed on his forehead, but his mouth was dry as dust. He wished he'd gone to the loo on the ferry too. As Jimmy pulled the lorry into the line of vehicles, he leaned back and slid across the panel which connected the cab of the lorry to the rear section.

"Are you OK back there, John?" he called quietly into the darkness. "Paintings still in one piece?"

Edward wouldn't admit it, but he was hugely relieved that John had drawn the short straw and been assigned the role of Man in the Back of the Van, his designated task to ensure that if customs decided to check, he would use his considerable charm to guide them away from the hidden paintings. It was bound to be more uncomfortable.

"They are. I'm not so sure about myself, though." Even though John was standing well back from the hatch, Edward could hear the pained note in his voice. He really was a man who couldn't bear the slightest amount of inconvenience, Edward thought, shifting on his seat with a wince as the lorry hit a bump in the road and bounced in the air. From the darkness, he heard John curse and mutter something about never being the same again.

"Chin up," he said encouragingly, and slid the hatch closed.

"Everything alright back there?" Jimmy asked.

Edward nodded, and instantly felt dizzy. Too long on that damn ferry, he thought, crashing up and down on the waves. The lorry pulled forward a little more and he could see they were next but one to pass through the customs gate and into the customs hall.

"If this goes badly, we're looking at a few years in the slammer." Jimmy took a deep breath. "Pretty boy like me, doesn't bear thinking about," he went on with a broad grin.

"That'll do, Jimmy." Edward polished his glasses and put them back on as the lorry moved forward again, rocking from side to side as it rolled over a raised section in the road. He watched two uniformed customs officers walk around the car in front of them, examining it in the most cursory manner, then lean in and say a few words to the driver. Whatever he said in reply, it obviously satisfied the officers. They stood back and waved him through then beckoned Jimmy to pull the lorry forward.

Edward clutched at his stomach as a wave of nausea hit him. Jimmy had been his usual flippant self, but the point he made was a good one. Should this day go wrong, they would be disgraced at the very least, and possibly imprisoned. He rolled down the window as one of the customs officials held out a hand for their documents.

As the man inspected their papers, Edward watched the other official in the wing mirror. He walked the length of the lorry and knelt down by the rear wheel. From inside his jacket pocket, he pulled out a bulky black object which Edward recognised as a walkie-talkie. He spoke into it briefly, glancing back at the first official who continued to work his way through the documentation, his head down, paying his colleague no mind. The second man finished speaking, then rose to his feet and walked back towards the front of the lorry.

What's going on, Edward thought as a clammy wetness drenched him under his shirt. *What's that man up to?*

It was far too hot in the cab and he felt his breath catch in his throat as he tried to breathe in the petrol-heavy air of the ferry port. The official looked up as he handed back the documents and indicated they could be on their way. With a sick feeling, Edward recognised the Swede from Buchanan's gang.

Jimmy started up the engine; its loud growl filled the cab with sound, and its shuddering movement caused Edward's stomach to flip over again. Helplessly, he leaned forward and pressed his hands on the dashboard for support, his dizziness increasing in time with his nausea. In the wing mirror, he saw the Swede watching them and, for the first time, he felt real despair. Their plan had failed utterly.

The crash of a double door slamming open and rebounding off a concrete wall was loud enough to be heard over the roar of the lorry engine, and unexpected enough that, even as Edward reached down and felt blood soaking through his shirt from the wound in his side, he whipped his head around to see what was happening. Black-uniformed transport police rushed through the door and spread out across the customs hall.

Three men headed directly towards the Swede, pulling out their truncheons and shouting at him to lie on the ground. Beside him, the other customs official – the one who'd used the walkie-talkie – reached out to place a hand on his shoulder and advised him to put his arms in the air and surrender.

Instead, he thumped an elbow back into the customs officer's face, crashing the back of the man's head into the side of the lorry. Without a sound, he crumpled at the knees and slumped onto the concrete. With barely a pause, he pulled a gun from inside his jacket and fired behind himself as he raced for cover. One of the approaching policemen fell with a cry behind a parked car, while the other two took shelter in the shadow of a concrete pillar. From behind them, more police officers appeared, these ones armed with what looked like handguns. They, too, secreted themselves and shouted for the Swede to throw down his weapon. His only response was to fire towards the police, the bullet ricocheting off a wall and pinging across the hall. Through the open cab window, Edward heard screaming and wondered if it was the wounded policeman or a terrified passenger.

While this was going on, more officers had arrived at the lorry. They pulled open the doors on either side and gestured for Jimmy and Edward to get out. "We got word you were coming in," said one policeman, two pips on his shoulder identifying him as an inspector. "We need to get you both out of here and to a place of safety—" He stopped suddenly, pointing to Edward's side. "My God, have you been hit?"

Edward actually felt better than he had all day. Adrenaline, presumably, and he decided to make the most of the burst of energy. "Just a scratch from earlier, Inspector," he said, easing himself around to the front of the lorry, out of the line of fire of the Swedish gangster. From his new vantage point, he could see the passengers in the cars behind them – thankfully, not many – being shepherded out of the customs hall. He turned to remark that surely the cornered man would be forced to surrender soon, when what could only be a bullet thudded into the side of the lorry, leaving a large, round hole. He threw himself to the ground, gasping at the pain as the stitches in his wound opened even further, and rolled underneath the front bumper.

Jimmy was already there. "Blimey, this is a bit hot," he grunted. "I thought you said the police would just impound the bloody lorry and we'd be on our way?"

"That was the plan, yes," Edward replied testily. "Clearly, however, there have been developments." He peered along the ground, through the legs of police officers crouched in the lee of the lorry. Another shot rang out and Edward caught sight of a muzzle flash high on a gantry running along the side of the hall. *The Italian*, he thought with a shudder. It had to be. Another shot hit the lorry, making it rock on its axle. He hoped John had had the sense to lie flat in the back, preferably with a hefty sofa on top of him.

He scuttled forward on his stomach, the better to see what was going on, and was rewarded by the sight of a policeman armed with a rifle poking his head around the corner of the gantry. As he watched, he heard a single shot ring out and the Italian throw up his arms for a moment before tumbling like a prop dummy to the concrete floor below.

The death of his companion seemed to tip the Swedish gangster over the edge. In the silence which followed the Italian's death, he shouted something Edward couldn't make out and then presumably emerged from his hiding position with all guns blazing. Edward couldn't see that side of the lorry, but there was a flurry of shots, and then complete silence, except for the echo of gunfire. Policemen suddenly leapt from their sheltered positions and rushed forward, and Edward heard someone shout, "He's dead. Straight through the heart."

The head of the inspector who'd first spoken to him appeared in his line of sight. "Are you OK down there?" he asked, in the same tone one might use after a friend had slipped on the grass. "I think we better get a doctor to look at your side, Mr Lowe."

Carefully, Edward followed Jimmy out from under the lorry. He was delighted to see the policeman who'd been hit in the first exchange of fire clamber to his feet, clutching at his arm. Policemen moved here and there around the hall, crouching by the body of the dead Italian and picking up spent shells from the ground, but otherwise they talked in hushed tones or slumped against walls, the adrenaline of violent action quickly wearing off.

From the back of the lorry, he saw a metal door swinging back and a voice call "Mr Le Breton, are you alright in there?" followed by an answering "Quite tickety-boo, actually" from John. The tall man emerged from behind the open door and sauntered towards Edward as though he were taking a stroll in Hyde Park.

"My goodness, you are a bit of a state, Edward," he said as he bent down to brush some dust from the knees of his trousers. "I thought I had the mucky job, stuck back there, but you look as though you've been in the wars."

Edward considered how best to reply, but suddenly he felt enormously tired and it hardly seemed worth the bother. He stood and watched the injured policeman being helped out of the hall and then, with a heavy sigh, sat down on the step plate of the lorry. "I think perhaps you might be right about that doctor, Inspector," he said.

71

"I'm not sure that I deserve all this praise," Edward protested, though weakly and with a contented smile. "Had any one of you been held at knifepoint by Nate Thompson, I'm sure you'd have done the exact same thing."

A chorus of voices assured him that "No, that wasn't the case"; "Yes, what you've done was quite remarkable"; and "Perhaps you could be persuaded to tell the whole story, laddie?"

He sighed heroically, arranging his expression into that of a suitably reluctant storyteller, and studied the people around him. They were seated in the lounge bar of the George Hotel in Ironbridge, newly arrived for the first day of shooting for the new series of *Floggit and Leggit*.

Alison Jago had come down as the guest of Jimmy Rae, and Sally was sitting beside John, but otherwise everyone there was an old friend. A roaring fire was burning, and it was dark and cold outside. It was the perfect night for storytelling.

"The idea came into my head, I suppose, when Thompson

told me that John would be next to pay the price for ruining his life." He'd told this story many times now, but always he shuddered at this point, as though he felt someone walking over his grave. "He'd already made it clear he wasn't interested in killing either of us, and I had the distinct impression that he had something more in mind than simply leaving our fate to chance – or even having us beholden to Buchanan. After all, there are only so many criminal exploits a pair of decrepit actors can conceivably get up to.

"You have to remember, I'd just been stabbed and had lost a significant amount of blood, so I wasn't thinking as clearly as usual. But even after I'd been rescued by that chap Mackay, then delivered back to the hotel by Buchanan's men, I still had the impression that Thompson would have taken steps to ensure we came a real cropper."

John chuckled. "I do think that being murdered would have counted as quite a cropper," he protested mildly, prompting everyone to laugh.

Edward waited until the hilarity had died down, shot John a look which he hoped said *please don't interrupt* and resumed his story.

"That got me wondering what Thompson was in a position to do to harm John and myself. He was presumed dead, after all, and in Holland, using a dead man's passport. Add to that the fact that Sally had walked out on him and he had no money to speak of, and I couldn't for the life of me come up with a way Thompson could revenge himself on anyone – except, of course, for stabbing them to death in the street."

This time he was happy to wait for the clamour to die down. Joe Riley passed him a glass of whisky with a clap on the back, Donald Roberts roused himself enough to murmur "Jolly well done, Edward" and Clive Briggs mimed a man being stabbed and then dying in a prolonged – and in Edward's opinion, not terribly amusing – fit of twitches and blood-curdling cries.

"Then it struck me, the one thing that Thompson knew about John and me was that we'd replaced him in the plan to smuggle the Nazi paintings into the country. What better way for him to get his revenge than to put us in jail?" He looked across at his friend and smiled fondly. "I think I can safely say that, of all the men I have ever known, John Le Breton is the least well-suited to a life behind bars."

Again, laughter broke out, but this time Edward kept speaking. The wound in his side was almost healed, but he still felt some pain when he moved in certain ways, and he was keen to get to bed.

"Anyway, having identified that as the most obvious thing for him to do, I asked John to accompany me to where Thompson had been living."

"I wasn't keen, I don't mind admitting," John added, frowning at the memory. "I kept thinking, what if the mad bugger was sitting waiting for us like Norman Bates dressed up as his mother in *Psycho*? Edward didn't even consider letting that stop him though. 'He won't be there,' he said. 'And, if he is, I'll deal with him.' I was actually a bit worried that he'd got some kind of infection in his wound and it had sent him doolally, he was that confident."

"Be that as it may," Edward said, resuming the role of narrator with another piercing look in John's direction, "I knew we weren't going to the flat at all. We just needed to find the nearest post office and, luckily, there was one literally in the same street. I'd already telephoned my cousin, who lives in Amsterdam, to come and meet us there and, with him in tow, we went inside."

"And what a palaver that was!" John looked over at Clive. "You remember that turn old Harry Whatsit used to do where he would speak one language and another chap would translate into English but only by waving his arms in the air? It was just like that, with Edward telling his cousin he was interested in a telegraph sent by his good friend Nathaniel Thompson to England the previous day, and the cousin – whose command of Dutch appeared to consist of about four words and none of them *please* or *thank you* – doing all kinds of peculiar hand gestures and pointing at things while slowly losing his temper."

Edward glared across the room. "It worked, didn't it?" he snapped, then regretted it. "Sorry, I'm just a bit tired," he went on in a more level tone. "But it did work, in the end. I had expected there to be a great argument about whether we could see a copy of the telegraph Thompson had sent, but you'll never guess what the Dutch girl said after my cousin managed to communicate what we were after."

This was his favourite bit of the story. "'Groat Street Market,' she said." He grinned triumphantly at everyone in the room. "'Mr Wetherby and Archie Russell!' It would appear that *Floggit and Leggit* has made it to the continent!"

It had been a strange situation all round, in retrospect. The plump little Dutch girl beaming with delight at meeting the stars of what she assured them was her favourite British comedy, John – as ever – basking in the adoration of a young woman, and Edward's cousin thoroughly bemused by the whole affair. The girl had fumbled under the counter and pulled out a single telegraph sheet and handed it over to them, along with a blank sheet which she asked them to autograph. Briefly, Edward had wondered whether it was wise to leave evidence they'd been asking after Thompson, then he remembered that Buchanan's gang had taken the man's body away, and he suspected they had plenty of experience in making unwanted corpses disappear.

One round of autographs and a peck on the cheek from John later, and they were back in the street with the telegraph in hand and Edward's cousin grumpily heading for his car, none the wiser about what had just happened.

"The telegraph confirmed my worst fears. It was addressed to HM Customs and Excise and alerted the authorities to a gang of international smugglers, led by TV personality John Le Breton no less, who were intent on bringing looted Nazi treasures into the UK, hidden in a lorry on the Rotterdam to Hull ferry."

Although this was the second time he'd told the story that night, there was a collective intake of breath at this point, exactly as there had been during the first telling.

"Well, of course, we knew exactly what we had to do then. We did have a secret weapon after all!"

Frank Primrose blushed a shade of red so deep it was

crimson. "Golly, Mr Lowe, all I did was make a telephone call."

"A telephone call that let the powers that be know we were innocent of all wrongdoing! Why, without you, the police wouldn't have arrived in so timely a fashion!"

In reality, they'd cut it a bit fine, in Edward's opinion. He'd spoken to the inspector while waiting for the ambulance to take him to hospital, and he'd explained that his own boss had been a bit reluctant to take the word of a village bobby that a man he'd watched on television the night before was undercover in a Europe-wide criminal enterprise.

"Luckily for you," he'd said, "someone remembered a telegram that'd arrived a couple of days before, saying basically the same thing, but suggesting that you and Mr Le Breton were the brains behind the operation, not working to stop it. That was enough to convince my guv'nor there was something in it one way or the other, and we should take a look."

That was the great irony, of course. Had Thompson not sent his telegram, the police would most probably have ignored Primrose entirely and Buchanan's plan would have succeeded. Instead, so far as Buchanan was concerned, Thompson had ratted them out and Edward and John had only just escaped with their reputations intact, while the paintings had been confiscated by the authorities.

Though, as Edward had been at pains to ensure, behind the scenes the transport police were telling everyone that they would be keeping an eye on both men in future. "This way there's no chance Buchanan will think he can use us again," Edward had explained to John. He'd also told him that Thompson was dead, though they'd agreed that, for now, they'd keep that fact from Sally.

John had wondered what they should do about Craig Mackay, but with Thompson believed dead long before Mackay actually killed him, they'd decided to say nothing. It was a shame they couldn't tell Inspector Whyte who'd killed Judy Faith, but he'd concluded both she and Thompson had been killed by Buchanan's gang, so perhaps it was best to let sleeping dogs lie, rather than stir things up anew.

And as John had pointed out, revealing the truth would open up a rather unpleasant can of worms for Sally. She may not have killed anyone, but it was difficult – *impossible*, in Edward's opinion – to view her as completely innocent. The police would take a dim view of fraud, for a start.

He'd have to keep an eye on John for a while, though he'd been reassured when Sally had asked him to move back in with her, and he'd refused. "Too much water under the bridge, Edward," he'd explained. "And now the authorities have cleared her of any involvement in Nate's death, she's in line to inherit a pretty penny, so she doesn't need anything from me. No," he'd said, "best if we go back to how we were, before all this happened, with her in Cheadle Hulme, and me in London and Ironbridge."

Edward hoped he meant what he said.

He felt his eyes grow heavy as he looked around the room. Several people were chattering about the gunfight, with Donald Roberts of all people describing his spell in the Commandos during the War, and the best way to kill a man with your bare hands, and Joe Riley calling him an old blether and launching into a story about his time on the Atlantic convoys. Alison had just announced she'd accepted a job on *Floggit and Leggit* and would be staying for the upcoming rehearsals, and Jimmy Rae was either doing his best to look delighted or was genuinely pleased. It was so hard to tell with that boy at times.

He settled back in his chair and let the voices wash over him as he nodded off to sleep.

ACKNOWLEDGEMENTS

Thanks, once again, to my editor Rufus Purdy for his patience and expertise, and for knowing far more about the north of England in the 1970s than I do.

Thanks to Scott for listening to me badly describing plots over beer and curry, and to the friend of my daughter Alex who – when I picked Alex up from her book club – complained she hadn't known there was going to be the opportunity for an author signing or she'd have brought her copy along with her. And of course, a massive thank you to my family and especially my wife Julie, for putting up with me disappearing into my office night after night because "I've just had an idea and I need to write it down before I forget it".

ABOUT THE AUTHOR

Stuart Douglas, the creator of the Lowe and Le Breton mysteries, is an author, editor and publisher, who has written five Sherlock Holmes novels for Titan Books, and contributed stories to the anthologies *Encounters of Sherlock Holmes*, *Further Associates of Sherlock Holmes*, and *The MX Book of New Sherlock Holmes Stories*. He runs Obverse Books and lives in Edinburgh with his wife, three children and a dog named after Dusty Springfield. Follow him on Twitter/X: @stuartamdouglas; on Bluesky: @stuartdouglas. bsky.social; and on Instagram: @stuartamdouglas

For more fantastic fiction, author events,
exclusive excerpts, competitions, limited editions and more

VISIT OUR WEBSITE
titanbooks.com

LIKE US ON FACEBOOK
facebook.com/titanbooks

FOLLOW US ON TWITTER AND INSTAGRAM
@TitanBooks

EMAIL US
readerfeedback@titanemail.com